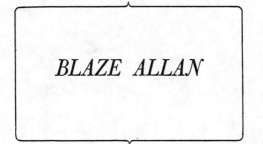

BLAZE ALLAN

In 1923 Lillian Bos Ross and her husband Harry Dick Ross hiked from the Hearst Castle, where he had worked as a tile setter, to Big Sur for the first time. They were enchanted by this magnificent and rugged land, extolled by Robinson Jeffers, and settled in for good. The photograph above shows Lillian Bos Ross at work in the kitchen of the Livermore Ledge homestead in 1924. She died in 1959, but Harry Dick still lives in the area. *(Photo by George Challis.)*

BLAZE ALLAN

Lillian Bos Ross

Author of

THE STRANGER IN BIG SUR

A Gary Koeppel Book

CAPRA PRESS

Santa Barbara / 1986

Cover painting by Francine Rudesill.
Printed and bound by Delta Lithograph Company.

LIBRARY OF CONGRESS CATALOGING IN PUBLICATION DATA
Ross, Lillian Bos, 1898-
BLAZE ALLAN.
Sequel to: The stranger in Big Sur.
"A Gary Koeppel book."
1. Big Sur (Calif.)—History—Fiction.
I. Title.
PS3535.074784B55   1986   813'.52   85-26916
ISBN 0-88496-241-5

A Gary Koeppel Book
CAPRA PRESS
Post Office Box 2068, Santa Barbara, Ca. 93120

I

As Blaze Allan carried the 1891 New Year cream cake out of the big cold pantry and across the split board floor of the warm kitchen, her eyes were as bright as the red currant jelly star she had just cut out and placed in the center of the swirls of whipped cream. She knew that her father was watching her and watching the cake.

There had never before been a jelly star on it in all the twenty years her mother had made it to mark the end of the old year, the beginning of the new, on the isolated Allan ranch perched high in the Santa Lucia mountains above the wild Monterey coast. As years piled up, the Allan New Year cream cake had become a tradition and Hannah Allan was famed for its airy richness in every fold of the Santa Lucias, all along the Big Sur coast. This year Zande Allan had suggested to his wife that Blaze be trusted with the New Year cake-making.

Although Blaze had been making cakes, good ones, since she was ten and would be twenty years old in February, she had never expected to make *the* Allan cake until she was in a home of her own, carrying her home tradition into a new life. She felt disturbed, uneasy. Her father must be up to something. But whatever that something might be, she had not failed in her task. She knew the cake was as good as it was beautiful.

As Blaze rounded the long table she saw that the defeated haunch of venison was already back in the Dutch oven in front of the fireplace, what was left of the crisply brown roast chicken was in the baking pan on the stove. Even the used plates were gathered up and stacked neatly on the worktable beside the big wood stove. In readiness for the cake's arrival were a stack of clean saucers and the wooden cake server that Avery had whittled out for his mother's Christmas.

With an air of ceremony Blaze lowered the cake slowly to the table, touched her mother's hand lightly as she said, "Happy New Year, Mother."

To a family chorus of "Happy New Year to us all, to everyone, everywhere!" Blaze climbed into her own place on the log bench beside her brother Avery.

Her mother lifted the cake knife as Blaze said happily, "I'm glad we do things nice, Mother."

Hannah nodded, intent upon getting pieces of the cake transferred safely to the saucers. Zande Allan reached out a long arm for the first piece cut, smiling at his wife as the thick cream oozed down the side of the cake. He winked at Hannah and turned a teasing face toward his daughter, drawling, "We do things fancy, I can see that, but the proof of the cake's in the eating."

He bent over his saucer and didn't look up until the last crumb was finished. Then he put down his spoon, leaned his elbow on the thick, hewn blank table. "Well, Daughter," he said slowly but with a warmth that Blaze found strangely moving, "looks to me like 1891 could easy be one of our best years. There's times I get to thinking you favor your mother, yes, I do, and no man could say more."

Blaze flushed with pleasure at this rare compliment and then tasted the cake as critically as her father had done. She put down her spoon and looked around mischievously, imitating her father's tone and manner as she said, "Well, it'll pass, I guess. Not bad at all."

Martin, her twin, looked up with his short bark of laughter and Avery doubled over with his smothered chuckle.

Smiling a bit wryly, Zande passed his dish back for more

cake. "Poking fun at your old father now, are you, my girl? Well, we'll have to see if we can't get you a younger man to try your teasing on. How will it be if I hold my tongue and only tell Joe Williams he'll marry a good cook if he gets you, Blaze?"

Avery stopped licking the cream off his spoon. "Aw, that old Williams. Ain't no one going to waste a good cook on that old mossback."

As his mother said firmly, "That's enough of that sort of talk, Avery," Blaze flashed her little brother an amused glance.

Then she looked directly at her father. "Joe is the last man I'd ever think of marrying. The truth is I'm like Avery; I don't even like him."

"You don't know what you like, Blaze. You've been getting notional lately, which goes to show you're ripe for marrying. I think Joe's a good man; everyone says so."

"I never heard anyone say so but you," Blaze protested. "I admit I never heard anyone say he was a bad man, but he"— she wrinkled her nose—"he's worse than that; he's dull; no fun to him."

Hannah said gently, "He's been very good to your grandma, Blaze, helping out like he's done ever since Gramp Allan got the stroke. I don't know how we'd of managed for your grandma and with that big ranch too, if Joe hadn't stepped in."

Blaze said slowly, "And it was soon after Joe took over that Gramma started talking about the ranch coming to me when I married. I don't suppose Joe had anything to do with that; just one of Gran's notions. But if he wants the ranch he can have it for all of me. I don't really want it a bit, or him either."

Uneasily Blaze noticed the patience in her father's tone as he answered, "Girls never do know what they want. Is the reason God gave 'em folks to look after them. You'd be safe, and you'd be well off with Joe. His place joining the home place and both of them built up, you'd be starting in as good as where your mother and me will leave off."

[3]

Blaze looked at him, her eyes wide with protest. "But you don't seem to understand, Father. I said I wouldn't think of marrying Joe. I couldn't, not ever."

Her father's voice held a warning note. "That don't sound like you, Blaze. You been brought up to honor your father and your mother and that means take your elders' council and not talk back. I think it's a good marriage and when Joe asked for you yesterday I passed my word to him that I thought it a good thing. Allans don't go back on their word."

Hannah looked rather puzzled at her daughter as she said, "You should of discouraged Joe at the start if you felt that way about him. Why didn't you, when he's been calling over here every month or so this past season?"

Blaze shrank back, embarrassed, bewildered. "But he never came to see me, hardly spoke to me. He came to ask Father about tools, or ask you things about Gramp." She blushed deeply as she asked, "You never thought he was courting me, did you?"

Her mother answered dryly, "Well, he never took his eyes off you, even if he was talking to your father about axes or whatever."

Zande snorted impatiently and Hannah turned to him saying, "I felt like you, that he was a good steady man. But if Blaze feels so strong against him, it's a better time to bring it out now than after a wedding."

Her husband answered, "A wedding is like a cake—you find out after you've tried it. You know that, wife. You didn't pick me out and I didn't know nothing about you till we was wed. Hasn't our marriage worked out good? You ever been sorry you took me?"

Blaze watched her mother, amazed to see how the years dropped away as her mother's face flushed faintly and her eyes brightened when she met her husband's searching glance. With a mischievous smile, she answered, "Sorry? No. Anyway, not very often." Then she turned serious. "But things are different

[4]

than when we were younger. The country is getting settled. Blaze has time to look around; she isn't twenty yet."

Zande pushed back from the table, spoke firmly to his family as well as to his daughter. "Blaze has no need to do any looking around. She's as good as promised. The Allan word has always been good as gold and our name is looked up to. It stays that way."

He stood up and Martin, the twin brother of Blaze, and the fourteen-year-old Avery both jumped to their feet waiting for their father to start back to work.

Hannah said fretfully, "I can't think what keeps Young Zande away so long. It isn't like him to not get back for the New Year dinner. He should of been back yesterday."

Blaze and Avery exchanged knowing glances but said nothing.

The older Zande answered impatiently, "I sent him out to get a good price for that stock, told him to drive 'em to Salinas if the price wasn't right in Monterey. He can look out for himself."

He made for the door calling, "Work won't do itself. Come on, you chaps."

The door closed. Blaze sat staring at the cake on her dish as though she were hypnotized. Her mother stepped quietly around the big kitchen, scraping plates, putting away food. At last she stopped beside the table. "Why don't you go out for a ride, Blaze? I can spare you easy, but get back before your father comes."

Blaze lifted her head. "If you'll sit down and make a square for your bedspread, Mother, while I do the dishes, then I'd like to ride up as far as the rock ridge."

Hannah protested that the prettiest part of the day was right now but Blaze got the crochet cotton, the hook, and put them into her mother's hands.

While she filled the dishpan with steaming water from the kettle, put another chunk of wood into the cookstove, poked up the fire in the fireplace to a brighter flame, her mother sat silently over her needlework. But when Blaze finished scalding the clean dishes and started drying them her mother put the fancy-work down on the table and asked, "Do you know, yourself, why you feel so strongly against Joe, Daughter?"

Blaze shook her head. "Not in words. I don't know—I guess if I heard Nella or Carmel, any of the Coast girls but me was going to marry him, I might even think they were doing well. But I can't bear thinking that he might be my husband." She shuddered as she set down the cup she had been drying.

Her mother seemed more to be talking to herself than to Blaze as she said softly, "I remember well how it is to be twenty. I was deep in love then. The preacher's son, he was, and way above me. I worked for his folks. We were both shy and both young; seems as if young folk were younger in my day than they are now. He hadn't ever said anything, really, but after he went to the war he wrote to me."

Blaze turned, breathless, her eyes asking what she felt she couldn't. Her mother shook her head. "He didn't ask me, not straight out. He only said he was coming back because I was there. His folks got the notice that he was dead. He was all they had. I couldn't bother them, didn't have the right to show my grief, so I didn't."

Blaze went over to the table, sat close beside her mother and whispered, "How could you bear it? How could you hide it and just go on living?"

Her mother picked up the crochet cotton, answered quietly, "Life is strong in people that's got any gumption to 'em. After a time I started eating again. Hope dies hard and years went slow while I kept looking for him to come back from the dead. At last I was able to give him up and I come out here and married your father, never having set eyes on him."

"How could you, Mother? Granny said you did; she mumbles a lot of stuff about old days, but I couldn't believe she knew

[6]

what she said. Did you—did you fall straight in love with Father when you saw him?"

Hannah smiled, shaking her head, "No. But I hadn't hoped for that. I was thirty by then and the few men that came drifting back to our little town married the young girls. I didn't have a chance there"—she picked up the crochet square and smoothed it out on her knee—"but the need for a full life, for a home and children of my own was strong in me, so I made a chance for myself the best I could."

Blaze got up, carried out the dishwater, rinsed the pan and was drying it with the dishcloth when she came back into the kitchen saying stoutly, "Well, anyway, I know Father fell straight in love with you. You're so brave and sweet and everything nice."

Hannah blushed, shook her head and laughed. "Well, we made out. It was hard at first; lone empty country, a rough dirt-floored shack. But by the time you and Martin was born and I made that cream cake for your christening party, things had straightened out and we've had a fine life, all of us together. I think you'd better give your father's idea about Joe some serious thinking over. Life isn't given to you ready-cut, Blaze. As you grow up you learn to take what you can get, shape it to fit the life you want."

Blaze protested, but gently, "I've never been anywhere, seen anything, anyone new. Joe would be just what I've always known. It must have been hard when you came here a stranger, but at least it was all new to you, something different from everyday."

Hannah only answered, "Better go for your ride; it gets late."

As Blaze reached the rocky narrows on the Santa Lucia ridge trail and reined in her sorrel mare, the sun felt hot on her back. It seemed more like early summer than like the first day of January.

[7]

The mare was restless, jerked her head, danced small hoofs impatiently. Blaze held her to the trail with no apparent effort and with no thought at all of the sheer drop so close on either side, or of the pinnacles of jagged marble rock, the pointed pines like toy daggers on the slopes far below. The mountain's stony backbone stood four thousand feet above the Pacific ocean and was no wider than four feet of storm-bleached rock here where the trail fell away dizzily to the sea on the west, and to nameless valleys and harsh granite mountains on the east where they guarded the broad Salinas valley. This spot was the best place on the trail for seeing all of the world that Blaze had ever seen. To her, Monterey and King City, the family trading centers, were as remote and mysterious as Rome.

The sun put bright life into her red-brown hair, brightened her few freckles into gold and softened the creamy gray of her old fringed chaps into the smoothness of fur.

Above the blue of her homespun shirt her eyes seemed more than ever the color of the red-brown madrone bark as she turned them slowly to take in Lucia Peak, Cone Peak, the wild and broken Ventanas and the floating blue range a hundred miles east and away across the Salinas plain.

She loosened the rein; Gipsy stepped off toward her barn, her pasture and the other stock as Blaze shook her head. The winter sun was as clear and luminous as moonglow, and as the trail dropped down to where pine, madrone and oak branched over it, Blaze gave herself up to the ecstatic sorrow of youth. It was a beautiful world, a world to be happy in, a world where wonderful things should happen. But nothing ever did. Just home and an ordered round of work, the occasional luxury of visitors. And they were almost always company for her father or her brothers. Her father was not one to encourage feckless young visitors.

He had as good as told Pete Garcia to stay away. Pete hadn't got his back up and stayed away. But he never lingered any more, or brought his guitar. Blaze sighed. The stern folk said Pete wasn't nice. But if she said a word Pete bent his curly black head and listened as though anything she said, or anything her mother said, for that matter, was wise, interesting, important. He was like that to all women, even grandmothers. He had dancing feet, hands lazy and loving on his old guitar, a big singing mouth and lying eyes. Pete was big and loose-jointed; he and his whole tribe were sea-otter poachers. Family men said he was no good, but their wives cut wide slices of the best Sunday cake for him even though he'd happened along on a Saturday noon.

Blaze shrugged her slim shoulders. Her father need not worry about Pete. She had no more urge to marry Pete than to marry Joe.

Gipsy danced sidewise down the rocky trail as Blaze held her in, reluctant to have her hour in the first sunshine of 1891 shortened by a moment. Here on the trail she could have moments of feeling that she was as wild and free as the gray squirrel who pattered his feet and scolded shrilly as she rode beneath his favorite oak. She lingered to watch a small calico-gray spider try, and try again, to float her web out wide enough to reach from the laurel tree to the cascara bush across the trail. Feeling triumphant when the spider won her struggle, Blaze pulled Gipsy off the trail, rode out into the tangle of scrub brush to avoid breaking the spider's hard-won anchor for her web.

Where the trail to the Allan ranch branched down from the more-traveled ridge trail, tne spirited mare and the laughing girl spun around and around until Blaze finally won, halted the half-broken filly on a round oak knoll just off the trail. From this vantage point Blaze could look down at her home, the fields, barns, fences—all the work of her father's lifetime. The whole place looked as precisely ordered as the cells in a comb of honey. Blaze looked at it warmly and yet with a sense of rebellion. Work, thrift, work and more work. It was beautiful; it was home; she loved it fiercely and yet—somewhere there must be life with time for laughter and dreams, for peace and love. She thought of her twin brother, Martin. There were times when Martin muttered about being twenty-one, being his own boss, striking out for himself. This never brought any encouragement from their father. Martin would slide out of the kitchen without an answer when his father said, "Strike out for yourself, hell! You'll never be man enough to do it or you'd of went when you was new-weaned. I was on my own and doing good at it when I was four years younger than you are right now. Looks like the Allan blood's already watering out."

Blaze drew a long breath. Martin wasn't the only Allan who would be twenty-one next year. Maybe—

She headed Gipsy back into the trail and heard a clatter behind her. She turned her head and saw the big gray horse coming at a good pace and heard the man riding him call out:

"Hi, young fellow, you going down by the Allan place?"

Blaze colored. The man was young. He was a stranger and he spoke with an air unlike the people Blaze knew. What would such a man think of her, riding a man's saddle, wearing chaps like a boy? If only she'd listened to her mother, not cut her hair so short it scarcely reached her shoulders.

She wheeled Gipsy around to face him as she said, "Yes, I'm on my way home. I'm Blaze Allan."

It seemed bold to name herself that way to a stranger, but he need not feel so big, shouting "Hi, young fellow" to someone he didn't know.

She was delighted to see him show some confusion as he lifted his hat and bowed, dropped his hat, saying apologetically, "I beg your pardon, Miss Allan; you see, I—I—"

Blaze could have forgiven a lot for those two words—"Miss Allan." That was her; she was Miss Allan. What a fine thing to hear on the first day of a new year. Everyone she knew had known her as a baby; she was "Blaze" to the whole Coast. It made her feel important to be called Miss Allan. But it made her more conscious of wearing chaps, riding astride like a boy.

"I'm on my way home," she said, suddenly shy and uneasy, even though he laughed as he swung off his horse, picked up his gray felt hat and dusted it off against the rough cloth of his coat sleeve. Her eyes looked down at his strong hand holding the bridle, but she was also seeing the unruly vigor of his thick light hair, that same aliveness in his amazingly blue eyes and ruddy skin. His voice, his clothes, even the way he got off his horse, were different from the Coast men.

He slipped the reins over his arm, still holding his hat in his hand and walked toward her, saying, "I'd planned to ride down soon and ask your family to a housewarming when our house is finished." He was close now, looking up at her as he said, "I'm Stephen Janson, Miss Allan. I've bought a place up the coast a few miles and my mother has come out from Norway to be with me. We intend making our home here and are eager to meet our neighbors."

Blaze said nervously, "Yes. I know. My brother Zande spoke of getting work from you packing out tan bark."

He pulled his thick blond brows together over puzzled blue eyes, thinking aloud. "Zande Allan? Your brother? I don't seem to remember—strange that I wouldn't."

Blaze felt a slight alarm. "He went down to take out cattle almost a week ago. He didn't come back home. He must be working."

Evidently he felt her unease, for he said, reassuringly, "Of course, he must be. My foreman hired a lot of new men lately; the *Constanza* is due in for a load of bark and we were not getting it out as fast as I'd hoped."

Blaze said the only thing she could think of: "My brother is a good packer."

As soon as the words were out, she wished them back. What

[11]

would the man think of her, boosting her brother like that? Of course, Zande was a good packer, but why did she have to say so? His work would show that he was. Feeling awkward, she said, "I'm late. I must be going."

He said easily, "I hope you'll forgive me for shouting at you."

Blaze muttered, "It's no matter," and blushed. She wanted this man to think well of her, but why should he? Those shabby old chaps she was wearing were terrible and then, when he spoke as though she should be treated as Miss Allan, she had to go tell him to think nothing of having hollered at her, taken her for a boy. Already his smile had taught her that being a lady had its own advantages. Her mother had told her that, over and over, but up until now Blaze had always thought all the advantages there were in this world went with being a boy! She never had been able to choose her words with wisdom and grace. Now the feeling that she had made a bad impression hurt like pain and she blurted out: "I have dresses; I wear them most of the time."

She saw his eyes for a second as he answered, "I admire your riding clothes, Miss Allan." He was laughing, looking right into her eyes, and she couldn't think of a word to say. But it gave her a feeling of satisfaction to note that her silence made him restless. She'd remember that.

After waiting a moment he said, "I was going to ask if any of the men of your family wanted to work in the bark for a few months during the dull season on the ranch."

Blaze sat quietly, and he hurried on, "I find it very good to get men in my crews who know this country. I got most of my men in San Francisco and these mountains have their own problems, when it comes to getting packs and animals out of the canyons."

Blaze answered briefly, "Yes, they do."

He seemed a trifle dashed but hurried on, "I'd hoped to send a message to your father, when I called after you. But right now the boat is being held for me. I decided to go to San Francisco on her for some things for the house."

Blaze said nothing and he pulled his horse around, got into the saddle.

Enjoying a feeling of advantage, she sat quietly as he said, regretfully, "I'd rather ride down the mountain with you." He moved his hat over to his other hand and said, "I hope you and your family come to our housewarming, Miss Allan."

Blaze gathered in the reins with her first feeling of the power of being young and a woman, as she said, "Thank you, but Father is no hand to go to doings. And if he doesn't go, none of the rest of us can."

She touched Gipsy lightly with her stirrup and the sorrel pranced. She wouldn't look back! Let Gipsy have her own way. And the sorrel showed her heels to the more stolid gray.

Blaze had to give her strength to the breakneck pace down the steep rough trail but her thoughts were racing far ahead of the wild colt's speed. Soon, maybe this very month, Stephen Janson would ride up to their gate on his big gray horse. He would come into the house—or at least into the yard. She would be wearing her green wool dress with the deep flounce on the skirt and the cream lace frill at the yoke. She would have had time to think about him, the words he had said, the light in his eyes and the tones of his voice.

As Blaze rode up to the home gate she decided to make a wish on the next new moon that her father would want to go to the housewarming, meet his new neighbors.

Gipsy nickered and Blaze came out of her rose-colored dreams to see Young Zande's horse tied outside the gate, and tied alongside his black and white pinto were the two palomino mares that belonged to Mrs. Gallo.

Mrs. Gallo and one of her girls must be at the house. But Blaze knew that was the most unlikely happening in all the world. She felt glad that her brother was home, but it gave her a start to see his horse tied outside. That was a strange thing, but it faded into nothing beside the presence of those two palominos.

Her father liked most people, disliked a few of them, but the very hottest strength of his dislikes centered on their close neighbor, Mrs. Tony Gallo, and her three girls, Dulcie, Carmel and Bonita. Blaze knew that the quarrel started even before she had been born, when Mrs. Gallo was still Maria Demas.

Gramma Allan liked to dwell on the old days and Blaze could sometimes get her started on talk of the time when Maria Demas thought herself the belle of the Coast, set her cap for Zande Allan and lost him to Hannah Martin, the stranger from Kansas. It seemed queer to Blaze to try to think of her mother as a stranger; Hannah Allan now seemed as much a part of the Coast as the granite old Ventana.

She found herself wondering if perhaps there was not more back of that old quarrel than homestead land.

Every time her father said Maria Gallo had stolen land that he had intended to file on, her mother always said, "I haven't any love for Maria, but it's not fair to say she stole that land. It was open government land and she had as much right to file on it as anyone had."

Her father always muttered, "You got no reason to stick up for that wench, and you know it."

Wondering uneasily about the old feud, Blaze unsaddled and turned Gipsy into the pasture and then walked slowly up the garden path toward the house. She felt reluctant to go inside and stood looking at the few wan January blooms on the strawberries.

She took a deep breath of the clear air of outdoors, stepped under the long pergola that sagged with the weight of the old grapevine, and opened the kitchen door.

Her mother, her father, Mrs. Gallo, stout but darkly handsome, Young Zande and Dulcie Gallo were all standing looking angrily at each other. Without taking notice of Blaze in any way Mrs. Gallo said, "I give you just once more the chance to buy the land. Take it or leave it."

Zande Allan said angrily, "Buy it? Buy it? At that price? Two hundred and fifty is high for that side hill and you got the nerve to ask twenty-five hundred?"

Blaze watched, wondered how any woman could make just a shrug of her shoulders so insulting. The brief lift of her shoulders held even more contempt than her voice as Mrs. Gallo said, "I'm not asking. I'm telling you what it's worth to me."

Zande Allan took one step forward, his chin jutting forward as he said, "Keep it."

He turned to leave the room, but Mrs. Gallo laughed, not a gay or amused laugh. "I'm not keeping it and I ain't selling it either now. I give it to my daughter and my son-in-law for wedding present."

Blaze saw her brother Zande shrink down into a new and too big town suit as though to get out of sight, saw Dulcie reach for his arm, hold onto it as Hannah Allan asked sharply, "Son-in-law? What son-in-law?"

Blaze thought no voice ever held such spiteful satisfaction as Mrs. Gallo's did when she said, "We forget to tell you—my Dulcie, she's Mrs. Zande Allan Second."

Blaze saw her mother's face go set, saw her long hand come up to cover her mouth. Her father's roar, "No, by God!" rattled pans on the shelf behind the stove.

His young face set and frightened, Zande Second took Dulcie's hand, pulled her forward a step toward his mother and said, "Yes, we are, Ma. Four days now. We was married in Monterey on the twenty-seventh, at the priest's house by the Carmel Mission."

His father's long arm shot out, grabbed the boy by the shoulder and swung him around to face him. "It ain't legal."

His voice shook with fury. "You ain't but just past eighteen and I can hold you to home till you're twenty-one."

Young Zande seemed to gain something of the stature and power of his father as he said quietly, "It's legal and it's the way I want it. I told the priest how old we both was and her mother was with us, was willing."

Zande Allan snatched his hand from his son's shoulder, slammed open the door and said, "Get out! Get out of my house and don't come back."

Tears spilled out of Dulcie's black eyes; her lips trembled but she spoke up clearly. "Suits me," she said. "I don't like you anyway. You're no good company."

Her mother looked triumphantly around. "That's how I wanted. I get me a son and my girl gets her a Zande Allan for husband. You be lucky if your girl does as good."

Blaze stepped quietly into the small hall that led to the bedrooms, as Mrs. Gallo, head high and step light, sailed out through the kitchen door, calling, "Come, children. We go home."

Dulcie followed her, but Young Zande stopped. He stepped toward his father and said, "I'll get my things, Pa, and I'll leave the suit till I got the ten dollars to pay you for it."

"Suit? What suit?"

Young Zande colored up painfully and stammered, "This here one"—gesturing vaguely toward himself. "Didn't seem right to get married in overalls, so I used fifteen dollars of the cattle money to pay for the suit and the hotel."

"And you didn't fee the preacher?"

Although Zande Allan's voice intimated that the girl wasn't worth a fee, his son answered simply, "Yessir, I did. I give him a dollar."

"Keep the goddamn suit and get out of here!"

Young Zande stood firmly beside the table, carefully felt inside his baggy black vest, unpinned a buckskin sack, set it on the table and pulled the drawstring, as he said, "I got the better price in Salinas like you said. Here's the cash." He stacked up the gold coins and used them to weight down a penciled bit of paper. "And here's the note for what I owe you."

His boots clumped loudly through the silent house, scraped on the ladder as he climbed to the loft. Blaze saw her mother's head turn to follow her son's broad back and a look of quiet pride momentarily erased the sadness from her face.

The boy was down in a few moments, wearing his old patched overalls, a half-filled packsack slung over one shoulder. He stopped by his mother's side to whisper, "Put some cedar shavings in so's the moths won't get it, will you, Ma? I got it big so I'd get good use from it."

Hannah Allan's hand tightened over her son's for an instant as he muttered, "Dulcie's right for me, Ma. She'll make me a good wife like you'd want."

He walked out of the door and then the kitchen was suddenly empty of everyone but Zande and Hannah Allan. Blaze walked softly down the hall, quietly shut the door of her own room behind her, and stood just inside it, her heart beating furiously.

What a thing to happen! That's what Zande had been up to when he told her and Avery that maybe he was going down to Janson's tan bark camp to ask for work. Martin would be furious, having Zande married before him. He always acted as though Zande were ten years younger than he, instead of only fourteen months.

From underneath the shelter of the big madrone tree a hundred feet down the mountain from her window that looked out to the ocean, Blaze suddenly heard the muted twang of Avery's jew's-harp. She smiled in spite of her troubled heart. In all Avery's fourteen years he had managed never to be around when there were ructions going on in the big old Allan kitchen. Avery could smell trouble, he always said. There must be something to that claim, Blaze thought, for he was always well clear of the house before any of the others sensed anything out of the way. "Dear life, be kind to my little brother," Blaze entreated silently. Their father always said there was no Allan to Avery. The slim youngster was everyone's friend, all music and laughter. He'd forget and let a branding iron go cold while he cocked his head and listened to a bird's song. And he was fearless. His father might look black as a thundercloud, but Avery never noticed it, would swing affectionately on an arm that was reaching to clout him, laugh and say, "You got a strong arm, Pa."

Blaze sat down on the mountain lion skin beside her bed, clasped her arms around her knees and bent her head over them, feeling the beat of a pulse in her arm almost as a sound, so quiet was the house.

Then she heard her mother stir up the fire, take the roasting coffee beans out of the oven, heard the comfortable whir as the beans ground through the square wooden mill. Soon there was a fragrant smell of boiling coffee and her mother's voice:

"Take a cup of coffee with me, Zande; it'll rest you."

"I ain't tired."

A small clatter of cups and then her mother's calm voice, "Here's your coffee."

There was a maddening sound of a spoon going round and round in a thick cup. It stopped at last and her father sounded tired as he said, "We never thought that first cup of coffee we had together in Monterey was going to bring us to this, Hannah."

Her mother said sturdily, "Good thing we didn't. No one would ever be able to face stuff if they knew for twenty years it was coming. But this could be worse, Zande. The girl is young. Zande's a good boy. She'll grow up into an Allan if we stand by them, help them get started."

Blaze heard the clatter of a dropped spoon, heard deep anger shake her father's voice as he said, "Help them? I told him to get out, stay out. I wasn't talking just to hear myself. I'm through with him."

There was a long silence. Blaze listened uneasily, trying to picture how her mother would take this. She'd have to take it. When Zande Allan spoke like that, his mind was set.

Hannah Allan said, "All right. You be through with Zande if you feel that way. I'm not through with him, no more than I'm through with you."

Blaze could hardly credit her ears. She was still sitting on the floor by her bed, but she turned to face her closed door, her eyes wide, as she waited to see what her father would say or do.

Her mother gave him no time to say anything, went on talking in a calm, even voice. "If there had to be a choice between you, Zande, I'd choose my husband. But it isn't that way. I have my two Zandes; aim to keep them both. I'm not giving my son over to that half-grown girl and her scheming mother."

Blaze got up, walked down the hall to the kitchen as her mother was urging, "That's just what Maria wants, Zande. She'd have them both, tell them what to do, get them in her debt."

Blaze walked in, sat down beside her mother as she said, "Dulcie's sweet. I think she'll try hard to help Zande."

Her father said grimly, "Keep away from them. None of them need to come whining to me. She's made her bed; let her lie in it."

Blaze saw her mother's eyebrows lift, watched her faded blue eyes darken as she said, "You didn't. Someone stood by you when you made your mistake—"

Her father's face grew tense; he half groaned, set down his coffee cup with unsteady fingers, muttered, "I didn't marry no fly-by-night like that girl of Maria's. They set a trap for Zande and he walked in. He can stay away from here; keep with the kind he's picked. You stay away from them, both of you."

His face looked haggard, uncertain. Blaze felt love and pity for him flood all through her; wished she knew the right thing to say, to do, to bring him comfort. He was always so quick and sure about what was the thing to do, no one ever questioned him. She felt half indignant at her mother when she said, "I'll go see them soon—take Blaze with me. You can lose a son if you want to, Mr. Allan. I love my boy and I'll not make a stranger of him."

Blaze looked for angry words from her father. None came. He stood up slowly, walked over and leaned against the door sill. His voice sounded old and tired as he said, "Don't let me catch you sneaking up there, that's all."

Without waiting for an answer he opened the door, shut it on his wife's firm, "You won't. I don't aim to do any sneaking. Me and Blaze will ride up after a spell, when I think the time is right."

Through the window behind the stove both women could see him pause for a moment and then walk into his tool shed, close the door behind him.

Blaze turned questioningly as her mother sighed, picked up the coffeepot and carried it over to the worktable beside the stove. "He'll be all right. Tool-grinding always smooths his feelings."

She sank down on the stout log bench beside the big table at which the family ate, brushed her hand up through her graying hair and sighed. "Even smart men act stupid, seems like, when a woman's mixed up in their problems."

Blaze said timidly, "You were pretty hard on Father, it seemed to me?" She made it a question and her mother considered a long time before she said anything.

At last she said thoughtfully, "You're no child any more, Blaze. Your brother married too young, but anyway he married. Your pa is so set on fixing you up with a husband of his pick that unless you watch out, you'll end an old maid like I was—have to take what you can get."

Blaze made a wry face, shook her head.

Her mother looked at her, shrugged her shoulders, half smiling as she said, "Well, I did, and I got a good man, stubborner than most, but he suits me. You know how I come out here. What I didn't know then, and for some time after, was that Maria Demas Gallo wanted him. When he come down the Coast, married to me, she felt jilted, for all the neighbors knew she planned on marrying him."

Blaze sat breathless, her eyes wide, waiting.

Her mother said, "Well, she took him away from me—"

Blaze stared, as her mother's face, her straight-held back, faced this fact with the same resoluteness with which she'd faced life in the wilderness as a bride. "If I'd done like she planned, she'd have kept him. I didn't let her."

Blaze said, her voice weak, "Oh, Mother, how dreadful it must have been! What did you do?"

Hannah's head came up, her shoulders, bent with work, straightened. "Don't act silly. I did what was right. I stood by my husband, bore his children, made a home."

The fire cracked in the big stove, the kettle chuffed out small clouds of steam, but Hannah Allan forgot housekeeping as she traced some invisible pattern on the worn boards of the old table with a work-roughened finger for a time, lost in thought. Then she looked directly at Blaze and told her, "Maria never got over her plan going wrong. She come back here, soon as her husband was cold, to get even, and I know right well she's planning to do it through Young Zande. Your father can act like an idiot—men mostly do—but I'm going to stand by both them children. We'll help Dulcie make a go of being Mrs. Zande Allan, and that's something her mother never got a chance at."

Blaze felt too shaken to say a word. Through her growing years, ever since she had felt the first uneasy stirring of a child's idea of love and romance, her feeling that it had completely passed by her parents made her resolve to find something beside the humdrum daily chores that seemed to her to be all the life her parents had ever had.

And now love, hate, revenge—all those emotions had touched her parents' lives, were still to be reckoned with after more than twenty years.

Blaze wanted badly to tell her mother about having met Stephen Janson on the Ridge trail, but somehow she couldn't bring herself to mention that meeting, not even to her mother.

She reached for the big sewing basket in the corner behind the table, pulled it over close to her and picked up the sock that was about half finished. The click and flash of the steel needles made a splendid chorus to her thoughts. "Miss Allan"— the odd way he spoke the words, not like a foreigner, but not like anyone else on the Coast.

Without thinking, Blaze spoke, "He's easy and natural as a horse in a pasture."

She heard her mother's "Who is?" before she realized she'd spoken out loud.

Blaze felt her cheeks redden, bent over her knitting and said, "Oh, I dropped a stitch in Avery's sock. Now I got to see if I can catch it up."

Her mother said patiently, "Give it to me, Daughter. I can set it right with no trouble. You start messing around in them stitches and you'll have to unravel a lot of it to get it even again."

Gratefully Blaze handed over the mass of springy wool that had grown, been sheared, combed, carded, spun, and dyed with pokeweed juice right on the ranch and would wear almost as well on Avery's active feet as it did on the sheep's back.

Before her mother could get her mind off the problem of the dropped stitch, ask again who she had been thinking of, Blaze asked, "When do you think we can go see Zande?"

"Tomorrow," her mother answered. "The longer your father has to brood over it, the more set he'll get. While he's upset as he is now, he'll scarce notice one more thing."

She handed the sock back to Blaze and stood watching as the needles started flashing again. "We'll carry that pair of white wool blankets I was planning for your hope chest. You sounded like you wouldn't be needing 'em."

Blaze bent attentively to the bouncing ball of wool and her mother sighed. Blaze looked up and smiled. "Zande won't need them much either. That fat little Dulcie ought to keep him warm, even in winter."

Her mother chuckled, but she said, "Now, Blaze, that sort of talk is not pretty from a young lady. Sometimes you sound as rough as the boys."

Blaze yawned, put down the knitting, and set the basket back in the corner. "I get it from Granma Allan," she teased. "Just the same, I wish Zande had found himself a pretty girl. Dulcie seems a strange girl, Mother. Of course, we don't really know her, seeing her only twice in the two years since her mother came back here. Carmel and Bonita are much prettier girls."

"Oh, well, beauty is as beauty does," Hannah Allan said wryly. "If she suits Zande, that's the main thing. But the poor child is terrible young to be a wife to anyone. Just a couple of babies, that's what they are."

Blaze put her hand on her mother's shoulder, gave it a little squeeze, and said, "Would it be all right if I packed a basket with the candied pumpkin and figs and some of the strawberry preserves for them?"

"Of course." Her mother's voice was worried as she went on, "Oh, dear, I hope Maria doesn't plan to live with them. They ought to have a place of their own. Zande wouldn't have a chance to be man of his house if he goes to live with all those women."

Blaze laughed but she shook her head. "It does sound crowded for a honeymoon, a two-room house with four women in it."

"Stop that, Blaze!" At the sharpness of her mother's voice Blaze put both arms around Hannah's spare waist, hugged her and said, "I guess you'll have trouble, Mother, if you start trying to pass me off for a lady. You shouldn't of let me run wild as a colt for almost twenty years and then think I'll come out all smooth and gentle straight off."

Walking across to the kitchen Blaze picked one of the two checked aprons off a peg beside the stove, tied it around her waist as she asked, "Mother, when can I have a silk dress?"

Her mother said shortly, "I suppose you'll get a black silk to be buried in. Work all our lives and scrimp and save, keep one good dress not for living, but for dying."

Blaze was so intent on her own problem she didn't even hear what her mother said.

"Dulcie is four years younger than I am and she had silk. Those little braid bows sewed flat on her jacket looked good. Did you notice how she rustled? It sounded nice. She wore sachet; some kind of scent too. Do you think she had a paper petticoat to make her rustle like that?"

Hannah sighed. "Oh, for mercy's sake, what's come over you, Blaze? Next thing you'll want a riding habit with a skirt, and then where's my tomboy gone? Of course, she didn't have a paper petticoat. What a notion! Buckram, that's what holds it out and makes it rustle."

"I wish I could rustle like that," said Blaze wistfully.

"Maybe you will," her mother said, her eyes lighting for a moment as she laughed. "Right now you rustle out to the spring house and skim those pans setting beside the door. We'll churn tomorrow and make cheese."

In the early winter twilight Blaze hurried out to the cool spring house. She never walked into the neat rock-walled room with its clean floor of baked tile, the little stream of mountain water running limpid through its tiled ditch, without feeling the spring house was one of the prettiest places on the ranch.

She and her mother had planted the maidenhair fern, the print fern, the wild iris and trilliums, all the cool, water-loving plants from their own wild canyons which made a play-pretty parlor out of what could have been just another work place.

The cream folded in pale gold wrinkles as Blaze ran the skimmer around the big pans and was so thick and firm that she could put the copper skimmer under the whole mass, lift it into the deep gray crock without losing a speck of it. The cream crock had a blue cover, a wide band of blue around its broad middle, and Blaze felt sure that no other sort of cream crock would ever yield up really good butter.

Robbed of its cream, the milk looked white and thin as she poured it into a pail to be carried to pigs and chickens. The skimmer and the three empty pans had to be carried into the house for washing. Thinking of silk, thinking of bright blue eyes with laughter and awareness of "Miss Allan" in them, Blaze washed the pans, scalded them with water from the big granite-ware kettle, humming the *Coast Waltz* softly to herself as she took the pans back to the milkhouse.

Potatoes to peel, table to set, bread to slice, put another stick of oak, two sticks of pine, into the shining clean stove; both women hurried silently; nothing must be missing from the table when the men came in.

Martin shoved the door open with his foot, dropped a big load of wood into the box beside the stove, sniffed the air hungrily and went out to the wash bench without saying a word.

Hannah Allan turned home-cured bacon in the big black spider, sliced headcheese, slid a dripping-pan of hot biscuit out of the oven as Blaze carried in preserves, pickles, honey, cole-slaw and a great pitcher of milk. Her mother gave a final check to the loaded table, nodded her head and said, "Blow for them, Blaze."

The girl reached up to where the wall beam made a ledge just under the rise of the shake roof and took down a horn made from a length of dried kelp. She stepped to the door, blew as softly as she could, and the kelp bellowed like a foghorn.

Outside there was a slosh and clatter of water and tin basins and then Avery bounced in, his pointed face beaming as he said, "Um, smells good! I'm hungry."

His father's hand closed over the boy's sharp shoulder, gave a derisive shake, as he said, "Lost your appetite, huh? You must of, thin as a rail, you are."

Avery took a poke at his father's chest, chuckling, "Eating don't make me fat; just makes me strong. I'm a Allan, I am."

Martin's feet clumped over the rough floor awkwardly, but he stood at his place at the table, waiting for his mother to take her place. She smiled at him as she hurried to her end of the table, managed to get settled before her husband slid into his place.

"Sit down, sit down," Zande Allan snapped at Avery, who was bending over the pan of biscuit with a rapt, angelic look. The youngster lifted his head, winked at his father, and flopped down on the bench, reaching for a biscuit as he said, "Where's Zande?"

Hannah looked at her plate and Blaze held her breath as her father said nothing for a moment. Martin seemed to feel something unusual in the air, for he stopped scraping slices of bacon onto his plate, looked up as his father said slowly, "With his wife's folks."

Martin set the platter of meat down, reached for the biscuit, and laughed heartily. "That's a good one. Wife! He ain't dry behind the ears yet."

Avery's chuckle shook him as he reached a searching finger, touched his big brother behind the ear and held out an accusing finger. "You ain't either, Martin. Lookit!" he called gaily. "Wet! Martin's wet behind his ear too." He butchered a biscuit roughly with his knife, shoved a great hunk of butter into it, folded it back together and filled his mouth as he asked thickly, "Where is that ol' Zande? Why ain't he come home?"

"He isn't coming home."

Hannah Allan put both her hands in her lap, clasped them tightly together. Both Martin and Avery looked bewildered for a moment and then Avery insisted, "Aw, come on, Pa! Don't tease. I wish he'd get home quick. Good abalone tide tomorrow and Zande's fun to go hunt abalone with."

His father chewed silently for a moment. It seemed an effort for him to speak, but when he did his voice was cold and even. "Zande won't be here any more. He married that Demas girl and I don't want him around here, or her either."

Avery's eyes were wide with amazement. "What Demas girl, Pa?"

It seemed to Blaze that for a moment there was a gleam of half-malicious amusement in her mother's face, but she bent her head over her plate as her husband barked, "The Gallo girl! Demas, her mother was a Demas—it's the same thing."

Martin asked, "Who you going to get to take his place? We're mighty short of hands for all this work as it is."

Martin got the full blast of his father's anger. "You let me worry about that. Work? You don't know what work means; none of you do. Never thought to see a bunch of Allan men scared of a little work. I've raised you up soft, that's what. But things is going to change."

Martin stood up. "You bet they are, or I'm not staying here. I want my share for what I put into this ranch and I'm not waiting for anyone to die before I get it either. I'm sick of working all day, every day, and never having a dollar of my own."

His father looked at him, kept on looking until Martin tried to avoid his look, but his father was not to be evaded. All his show of defiance gone, Martin pushed his end of the bench back, started to leave the table.

"Just keep on going." His father's voice had a quality as changeless as the mechanical tick of the clock. "And don't take anything away but yourself. You come here to this ranch naked and I've bought every last thing you've used these twenty years. You leave in what you got on; never mind any packing."

Blaze saw Martin's face change—look as young, as bewildered as Avery. He put his hand on the end of the table, trying to catch his mother's eye as he said, "Where you want me to go?"

His father drew a long breath, let it out as a snort of exasperation. "My God, a sucking calf!" He looked around at the frightened faces of his family and showed a tinge of satisfaction as he said mildly, "You're the one that mentioned going. I got no interest in where you go. Any place you can better yourself, go straight ahead. I did. I made a pretty good thing of it."

Suddenly anger swept over him again and he stood up, thrust his face within a few inches of his tall son's and ground out, "I don't want no back talk out of you. Just get going and right now. You need to learn something you ain't never learned here."

Martin turned to his mother. "Are you turning me out too, Ma?"

Blaze couldn't pretend to go on eating. She sat rigidly still, not breathing, as she waited for her mother to speak.

Hannah Allan looked at her son, considering her words, not looking at her husband. She broke a biscuit, put butter on it and fitted the two halves together very carefully, as though it were important. Then she said slowly, "You had the idea of leaving, Martin. You were the one who spoke of it, and this is not the first time. I think your father is right. You won't be satisfied until you have tried how things are someplace else. That's how I see it."

Blaze was certain she felt as bewildered as Martin looked. She took a quick glance at her father, saw that the grim, angry look had left him, that he'd picked up his fork, was eating as though food tasted good. He took time to spear out the widest slice of the new headcheese, tasted it with relish before he looked at his oldest son, said, "Well, you heard your mother, didn't you?"

"Yessir." Martin shifted uneasily, slowly sat down at the end of the bench, his face showing the uncertain state of his feelings. He looked down at the table as he muttered, "All I said was I wanted something—"

"Sure you did," agreed his father. "You wanted to leave. Well, no one's stopping you."

Hannah said mildly, "No need to rush off mad. Tomorrow morning's a better time to start any place. It's almost dark now."

Martin swallowed as though it hurt him. "Pa needs me here, needs Zande too. Avery ain't big enough for much."

"Well, well," Zande jeered. "Don't mind me. I left my pa when my time come and he got along. Maybe the crops'll go to hell and the stock get out of hand, but the ranch will be here. Land's one thing a man can count on. It takes no heed of the comings and goings of men. The ranch can spare you, Martin."

Mrs. Allan poured milk into mugs, reached across the table to set them carefully before each place as she said softly, "It's been a hard day. You eat your supper, Martin. You think about this tonight and you'll know better what to do tomorrow."

Martin still looked troubled, but a hint of defiance crept into his voice as he muttered, "I wouldn't want to go anywhere else if I had something of my own here I was working for."

His father struck the table angrily. "Something of your own! What's wrong with you? I said the land was here, and it is. I'm not going to take it along with me when I die. This here land's yours—Allan land. Every lick of work your mother and me's done here has been done for you, making a place that's good to live in, to bring children up in. We've a God-fearing family

[29]

and no drop of hard liquor or any kind of spirits has ever been here, nor will long as I live. It's a good place. The work you all do here is for yourselves, making something still better out of what will be all yours—when the time comes."

Martin and Avery lifted their heads, looked straight at their father. Martin spoke first. "I ain't spending my life waiting for my father to die. I want to do things for myself. I'm grown up, but you treat me like I was still a ten-year-old. If I ask for a dollar when we're in town, you make a mighty favor of it."

Blaze said indignantly, "But you get to town! That's something. I've never seen a town, never been more than twenty miles from this ranch in my whole life."

Avery put in, his voice reedy with excitement, "And I got plans of my own too. I'm not going to be any rancher."

"None of your lip, sir." His father's glance silenced any other information his youngest son might have offered. "Clear out of here, all of you. You too, Blaze. My God, what a day! One of 'em marries a hussy and the rest of 'em yelping like a pack of wolves." He frowned around the table, his gaze coming to rest on his wife's face. "A lot of this is your fault, Hannah. You put me up to be soft with this bunch of ingrates. But if they have to find it out, they'll find I'm still boss here."

Hannah met his gaze serenely, said nothing. He started to say something more to her, shook his head and looked instead at his children. "Go on, clear out and go to bed, all of you. There's been too much talk here already."

Blaze got up first, walked slowly over to the hall door and opened it. Martin and Avery followed and without saying a word to each other, the three young Allans parted in the hall. Blaze opened the door to her own room, hearing the scuff of the boys' feet as they climbed the ladder to the loft which they shared.

For the first time in her life, Blaze sat up wakeful in her bed, thinking with growing bewilderment of her own problem.

She wondered what more she could do than to say plainly, as she had already done, that she did not want to, did not intend to, marry Joe Williams.

Her father really acted as though what she wanted did not make one bit of difference. She felt fear, almost panic, at a horrible idea that suddenly occurred to her: suppose Joe should act the same way, not take no for an answer?

How much help could she get from her mother? Even her own mother seemed to think such a marriage might work out all right.

Her hands were cold and she was shivering long after she slid down under the warm covers thoroughly chilled by the thought that it was possible for her to find herself married to Joe.

II

ZANDE isn't up to Mrs. Gallo's place. Nobody's there at all."
As soon as he could get the words out, Avery dived for
his place at the breakfast table and reached for a stack of buttered buckwheat cakes.

His father echoed, "Nobody there? There must of been. Did
you knock at the door and holler?"

Avery nodded, swallowed, wiped the honey off his chin and
said, "Yessir. I made a lot of racket. Nobody was there at all."
He reached for the platter of ham, forked out a pink and brown
slice of the meat he'd helped smoke last October when the blue
haze of Indian summer filled the canyons.

He cut off a bite, chewed it thoughtfully, and looked up to
say, "Alder and oak is just right for smoking. Never tasted better
ham." No one said anything about ham, so Avery went back
to the subject of his brother. "The horses was gone too, but
there was this paper on the door." He reached down into his
pocket, felt about for a moment and brought out a folded paper.
His father frowned.

"Why didn't you say so?" He held out his hand for the note,
but Avery looked at him wide-eyed.

"This here is for Ma. It's got her name on."

His father answered, "It's all the same," and took the note
from Avery's fingers.

His wife held out her hand. "I'll take my letter, Zande."

Zande Allan turned the paper in his fingers, read the penciled
name, "Mrs. Z. Allan," and surrendered it reluctantly.

[32]

Hannah read aloud: "Dear Ma: I got a job so as to get money to start ranching here. I don't aim for Dulcie to have it hard as some has had. When I get money earned I'll be over to pay Pa my debt. We are both all right. We'll do good, Ma. Don't worry. Zande."

Hannah looked pleased as she handed the note to her husband. "I think they will do all right, just like Zande says. Pity he couldn't start right in on his ranch, a born rancher like he is. I wish he'd said where he got a job."

Avery looked up, bright-eyed, but before he could say anything, Blaze jumped up and said quickly, "Avery, don't you want some more buckwheats?" She was behind her father and as Avery looked up at her she put a finger across her lips. The boy looked startled, but he answered, "Sure, if they're hot." He said nothing about a job in the tan bark camp and looked down at his plate as his father sniffed, "I guess Maria'd give him a job if he's fool enough to take it."

"Over to Maria's place in the valley?" Hannah said. "That could be. She's had one of Tony's cousins looking after it since her husband died."

Avery's eyes widened. "That black stallion of his tramped Mr. Gallo right to death, didn't it?"

"You know it did." Hannah was short with the boy. Tales of this violent death had wakened a fascinated interest in death in her youngest son. It seemed to her too bad that the boy had heard of the tragedy. He slept badly, had bad dreams since Maria had brought the story of her husband's death, told it in horrifying detail to everyone she met.

Zande bent over his plate, chewing silently, now and again taking a quick glance at his family. Finally he shoved aside his plate, stood up and looked at tall Martin. "You getting the potato field ready, or you leaving the ranch today?"

Martin looked uncertain, tried to catch his mother's eye.

Hannah turned away, stood at the stove pulling the flatirons forward.

Blaze felt a pang as Martin, his head bent, muttered, "I'll get the team harnessed right off if Avery does my share of the milking."

Avery was busy wrapping a sliver of ham snugly inside a buckwheat cake as he said quickly, "Sure, you bet. I can milk three more cows easy as pie." He darted out the door ahead of his father and Blaze heard milk pails rattling out in the spring house before the door had shut behind the other two men.

She started gathering up the breakfast dishes, waiting until all the Allan men were deep into the work of the day before she said, "Mother, couldn't we pack the butter out next trip? I mean just you and me. I'd love to go the other side of all those blue mountains, see a town, walk inside a store."

Her mother was silent for such a long time that Blaze felt her heart sink. She must think it couldn't be done, that one of them would have to stay home to look after the house, the meals for the men.

But when her mother spoke there was a light of purpose in her eyes. "It's a plain scandal that you never been out of these hills. Martin's restless. The trip, without your father along to think for him, would do the boy good. There's butter and eggs enough to make it worth while." She drew her brows together, thought a moment, and then said, "You could get back in three days if you get an early start, both ways, and still have time to look you up a length of silk for your birthday."

Blaze felt bewildered. A trip to town and silk for a dress, both at once. It was too much. Her voice was faint, thinned with unbelief as she gasped, "Oh, Mother, you think we could go? Do you, really?"

Her mother answered, "You finish these dishes and then fly at the ironing. Once the ironing's out of the way you go put your things together for the trip. I think it would be best for you and Martin to go by yourselves."

"Father won't ever let us—"

Her mother sniffed. "You think so? Well, you get your stuff ready. It's just a shame, a grown woman like you are, and never been inside a store or saw a sidewalk."

"Sidewalk?" Blaze said. "You know I never even seen a road!"

Her mother came over close, put her arm around her daughter, patted her shoulder as though she were a little girl. "Try not to shy like a colt when you do, honey. Seems a queer thing maybe, but I know you'll feel more sure of yourself, of what you want out of life and why—once you've been to even such a pokey little town as King City."

Blaze spoke out firmly, "I know just what I want—a nice brown silk. And, Ma"—her voice dropped into a coaxing tone— "could I buy a printed pattern? Could my new dress have just a little bustle, so's to make my waist look small like Dulcie's looks?"

Her mother laughed. "Take more than a bustle to make Dulcie look small. But maybe you can find a pattern. Two years ago when I was over there Mr. Stakemiller at the Valley Store told me he was planning to get him a stock of printed patterns from the East. You'll maybe find bustles are all out of style. But get you a pattern if they have any. Get me one too. My blue silk is good as new, but it's nineteen years now since I made it up. I'd like to give it a new look before something comes up to wear it to."

At four o'clock in the morning the dawn wind moved briskly over the sparkle of frost which turned the dooryard, the grass-covered slopes, into silver. The wide mirror of the smooth sea reflected starlight so brightly that the mountains stood outlined almost as clearly as though the moon were shining.

From the Allan barn echoed sounds of brisk activity and in-

[35]

side the long kitchen the big stove glowed, two coal oil lamps made pools of warm light. The fireplace at the far end of the kitchen crackled briskly with blazing laurel and oak and beside it Blaze Allan crouched on a low stool, her hands shaking with excitement as she retied her moccasins.

"Here's the bite for your nooning," her mother said, setting the flour sack which held bread and meat, pie and apples, into a square rawhide case and fastening the straps. She looked out through the window at the sky, then took a glance toward the barnyard where the packed eggs were being lifted into the alforjases. "You'll make Careza Springs for lunch if you get started right soon."

"I can't believe I'm going to town."

Her mother spoke crisply. "You're not going any place unless you stop quivering like a quaking-asp and come eat your breakfast."

Blaze stood up, her mind busy with recounting what she had packed in the flour sack that held her good clothes. She had a feeling of panic. Suppose she had left out something she needed?

"You've got enough stuff in that sack to last you a month," her mother chided. "Quit worrying. Remember now, get the groceries, and them nails your father wants. Get all that stuff first. Then your mind will be free; you can have fun picking out the patterns, the silk."

Blaze's eyes were bright as the big stars that were dipping their golden beards into the dark sea. She clasped her hands around the bowl of hot milk her mother put down in front of her, but she couldn't taste it although she was vaguely aware that the bowl felt good against her cold hands.

"I got it all written down, Ma. The whalebone, the buckram, thread, buttons. I get them from the dressmaker, two doors off from the post office, and she's to put it on the store bill. I get the tablet and envelopes at the store, the stamps at the

[36]

post office. Oh, Mother, I wish I knew someone to send a letter to. I could put it right into the post office my own self!"

"Don't get so excited you forget to buy the stamps and to ask for mail for the Coast folks," her mother said patiently. "And if the store hasn't got the patterns from the East yet, you can get the dressmaker to cut you a pattern from the book of pictures she's got."

Blaze hastily set down the untouched bowl of milk, jumped up and ran over to hug her mother. "I wish you were coming too, Mother. I'd love it all twice as much."

"Well, I hope the weather holds for you." Her mother's practical words were warm. "Mind you get started back early, honey. I'll be watching the trail till I see you coming back."

"Like I watched for you that Christmas Eve when I was ten—" Blaze's head tipped to one side, remembering the way she and Martin had watched by the window while their father paced the floor and muttered. "Pa was in a terrible stew about you," she chuckled. "You know, that was the first time I ever noticed he cared anything about any of us."

"He keeps his feelings to himself," said Hannah, "but he's got plenty of them, don't worry about that." She leaned close to the window, looked out. "They're ready, Blaze. Here, you take the lunch; I'll bring your clothes. Wrap that cape around you good. You look all right, and you'd be wrinkled and creased if you tried to ride that far in your dress. And I'll be watching for you, day after tomorrow."

As Blaze and her mother walked down through the kitchen garden, the orchard and then into the barnyard, Blaze thought the bobbing of lanterns, the squeak of saddle leather, the bang and clatter of the packing as exciting as actually walking down the street of the far-off town.

Gipsy was saddled and waiting. So was Roany, the rangy horse that Martin always rode. The two black mules, Jill and Katy, were each having the last of their load lashed on. Jill had the cases of eggs, being the steadiest mule in the county. Katy was packing the butter, and now Martin was fastening the sack with his own things to Katy's packsaddle.

"Put this stuff for Blaze on somewhere," his mother said, handing him the flour sack she had carried. "Here, Blaze, you take the lunch on Gipsy and tie it on good. You'll both be plenty hungry by the time you get to the springs."

Blaze fussed with the saddle-strings, impatient to be moving east toward the first faint glow of sunrise. She swng up into the saddle lightly, feeling slightly silly to be riding her side saddle in buckskin chaps.

She started nervously when she felt her father's strong hand on her knee, but he gave her a casual pat and said, "Well, behave yourselves."

She looked down at him earnestly, as she murmured, "Yes, Father."

"Take this." He sounded bashful as he put something into her hand. "It's for your birthday. Get yourself something solid, girl."

Blaze couldn't say a word. She nodded her head, dropped the coins in her pocket and tightened the reins. Gipsy whirled around, started for the gate.

"So long, everybody." Blaze's voice was faint and shaken. She couldn't look back. Avery ran out ahead, had the gate opened and called up hopefully, "Why don't someone bring me a mouth organ, huh?"

"Yah, why don't they?" Martin mocked, but he half turned in his saddle to look back at the thin eager face of his little brother. He called back teasingly, "Maybe they will!"

Up the long grade from the Allan ranch to the top of the ridge the mules moved with great deliberation. Blaze held Gipsy in with a firm hand so that the two laden mules would not be trying to keep ahead and tire themselves out before they were well started on the long trip. The girl didn't mind the slow pace. Day came slowly, softly putting its touch on great white scars on the mountain's flanks where earth-slides had left the marble rock exposed. By the time they were up on the ridge the sun was warm on the tops of the pines and quail ran chattering along the trail in front of Gipsy, barely keeping ahead of the mare's small hoofs.

Blaze let her thoughts run far ahead of the quail. Already she felt she was riding right into town although she knew every rock, every tree and turn of the trail on this part of the trip. But when they reached the point where the trail to Jolon and King City branched off, Blaze stopped Gipsy. The two mules automatically slumped to a stop and Martin called back, "Come ahead, that's the turn."

Blaze knew the turn-off, had ridden past it many times. But she had never before had any reason to ride down it. Her life had seemed too busy for even a ten-mile dip into this unknown country.

She turned to smile at her twin, her look begging him to understand what she meant when she said, "I want to look a minute before I leave the trail I know. It's a big thing to me, Martin. I don't know—maybe things will never be quite the same again." She broke off, confused with her inability to tell him how she felt.

To her surprise he pulled out of the trail, rode back around the other stock and stopped his horse even with Gipsy, sat beside her looking at the tops of the rows of broken ridges they would cross before they came to the town. In the early light the far hills were softly blue and the deep canyons between them were filled with opalescent mist. Beyond the broad Salinas valley the distant mountains were touched with rose and gold and from the heights of the Santa Lucias the many-folded mountains looked deceptively small, easy to cross.

"I lost track now," Martin said. "Maybe I been over them hills ten, twelve times. But it always hits me when I get here, just like it did the spring Pa first said I could make the trip with him."

"Oh," Blaze said, "you know?"

"Sure." Then, as though he were afraid he had betrayed himself, Martin said, "We're going to stay at the hotel. I never done that yet." He looked a trifle uneasily at his sister, half turned his face and said, "Pa give me a twenty for my birthday; I'll pay for you."

Blaze gasped, ran her hand into her pocket, brought out the coins and looked at them. She had four gleaming golden pieces —twenty dollars, and she had thought it was four quarters!

"Oh, Martin—" She shook her head, her eyes misted. "I never care when Father's rough and short. That's how he is and he's Pa and he's ours and safe and all right. But this—" she shook tears out of her eyes, trying to laugh as she said—"I could cry."

She could see that Martin shared her feelings but he said briskly, "You're a sissy, that's what. But Pa—well, anyway, he's not so bad."

Blaze chuckled. "You sound just like him—'not so bad.' That's Father's idea of real praise. I want so much to be good, help him, make him feel happy about us." Her mood changed and turned serious. "But I want to live my own life, not have him live it for me."

Martin nodded. "Like marrying Joe Williams?"

Blaze wrinkled her nose. "Like *not* marrying Joe Williams," she said firmly. "I think Young Zande was foolish to marry so young and I'd never picked Dulcie Gallo for him. But that's what I mean, he did his own picking and I'm proud of him."

Martin shrugged his shoulders. "Maybe so. But I thought we were going to King City?"

Blaze nudged Gipsy and the animals dropped into line, their feet careful on the steep trail down to the floor of the first of the many canyons that lay between the ridge of the Santa Lucias and the Salinas valley.

The mountain ridges that Blaze had thought looked so small and easy to cross grew into high rocky barriers. Long stretches of steep trail led across loose shale where nothing grew and the footing was so bad that Gipsy picked her way as carefully as the sober Jill and Katy and long hours seemed to keep pace with the slow steady gait of the pack mules. The winter sun beat fiercely against the glaring shale and Blaze pulled Gipsy up to rest.

Patting at her face with her handkerchief she called to Martin, "I never thought any place could seem this hot in January."

Martin laughed. "It's no fun to cross here in July, I can tell you that. That's when I can't wait to get to Careza spring; such good cold water and big pines for shade."

"How long before we'll be there?"

"Hour, hour and a half, maybe."

Blaze straightened her back, tightened her reins and they plodded on. She knew from the sun that already it was past noon. But as each turn in the trail now brought her a closer vista of a great flat valley with high, treeless mountains beyond it, she forgot she was tired and hungry. Somewhere over in that great valley was the town, the sidewalks and stores. She rejoiced that the crumpled, rocky country she was riding through seemed to belong in a different world than the coast slope she knew. Growing among the rocks were so many sharp and thorny plants she had never seen. If the trail was so different, how strange the road would be, how exciting the town!

When at last the young Allans, the stock already cooled, watered, unsaddled and resting, dropped tiredly to a mossy bank beside Careza spring, Blaze shut her eyes for a moment. Martin opened the lunch case, saying, "We'll get to King City so late, might be better if we camped in the big cave tonight. What do you think?"

Blaze sat up, her eyes eager. "But you and Father often make it through in one day. Couldn't we?"

Martin chewed on his bread and meat, thinking well before he answered, "Well, we could. Only it'll be late, dark, nothing to see."

"But if we went on we'd be there for all the daylight."

Martin grinned. "All right, you're on your way to town."

Blaze stood up. "I'm ready. I'm not a bit tired now." She turned to Martin eagerly. "I'd a lot rather stay at the cave on the way back. This way I ride straight through in my buckskins and nobody from town will see me."

He jeered, "Nobody but Mrs. Ramirez at the Alta Vista hotel and she's got an eye like an owl. She'll look you over good when you get there past midnight, but don't mind that. Lots of the Salinas valley girls ride in from the ranches wearing leather."

It was dark long before they passed the cave where the first rough wagon road began. Blaze found it a marvel that the track was wide enough for them both to ride side by side, but as miles were wearily passed in the blackness she almost forgot the thrill of really riding along a road.

Then suddenly she dimly made out a great dark shape beside the road, another across from it, still another a bit farther along.

"Martin," she whispered loudly, "those buildings; what are they?"

"This is it," he answered. "King City. You're in town."

All she could say was, "Oh."

She remained silent until they stopped before the third dark building and Martin lifted her down. As her feet touched boards she felt of them with the toe of her moccasin.

"Sidewalk?" she asked. "Oh, Martin, I want to see it."

"You will, come daylight. Say, I'm beat out. Hope Mrs. Ramirez will let us in this late."

Blaze followed close as Martin opened a big door, felt his

way forward to a desk, felt for the bell and tapped it. Wide-eyed in the darkness, Blaze waited, hearing the sound of slow, heavy feet coming toward them. A door opened at the back of the room and a stout woman carrying a lamp came in, saying rather crossly, "Well, who is it? What you want?"

Martin stepped forward so that the light of the lamp fell on his face. The woman's voice warmed, "Oh, it's you, Martin Allan." Then her sharp eyes caught sight of Blaze sheltering timidly in back of her brother's broad shoulders and she asked sharply, "Who's this girl?"

Martin said quickly. "My sister Blaze, my twin; you know I got a twin sister."

The woman shook with some secret amusement, nodding as she answered, "I know Blaze, of course. I forgot about her, but what I never forget is that boys will be boys."

Martin seemed embarrassed and Mrs. Ramirez gave him a hearty poke in the ribs before she held out a knobby, work-worn hand to Blaze, took slim cold fingers warmly into her own. "Well, Blaze Allan, think of that. Last time I saw you was over to the Coast, must of been seventeen, eighteen years ago. Yes, 'twas. Don't listen to me, Blaze. I could go on talking Coast all night, but what you need is a room and some sleep, isn't it?"

Blaze said shyly, "Thank you. Yes, please."

Martin said, "Wait a minute. What's the charge for two rooms?"

Mrs. Ramirez opened her hand, shrugged her shoulder. "One dollar for one room. Two dollars for two rooms, and no rake-off even for old friends."

Mrs. Ramirez shook again with her secret mirth but Blaze felt quite embarrassed when Martin insisted, "Dollar-fifty is enough for both rooms this late. They ain't worth anything to you standing empty."

She laughed out loud this time. "Well, you certainly favor

[43]

your father, my boy. He wants his money's worth too, but he always pays on the spot."

Martin pulled out his wallet. "Ain't no Allan buys what he can't pay for," he answered.

Mrs. Ramirez nodded appreciatively. "That's right, Martin. Well, seeing it's you, and it's late like you say, you can have two rooms in back on this floor for the dollar-fifty."

Martin shook his head stubbornly. "No, Mrs. Ramirez. This is my sister's first trip to town. I'll take the back room, but she gets a upstairs one, at the front. Then if she gets tired she can rest up there and still not miss what's passing on the street."

Mrs. Ramirez looked very kindly in the dim yellow lamplight as she said, "Well, bring your sister's pack, Martin. She gets the best front room I got."

Martin ducked his head in gratitude for the compliment to his sister's worth, but before he started for the packs he said, "And a dollar-fifty for the both of them rooms?"

"Oh, for goodness' sakes, yes! And mind you bring the stuff in quiet, it's the middle of the night."

Blaze woke at the sound of a light knock on her door. She said sleepily, "Yes, I'm here. What is it?"

"You'd better step around if you want any breakfast," Martin whispered at the keyhole. "It's getting on for eight o'clock and your day's going fast."

"Oh, Martin, how dreadful! I'll be ready right away."

"Aw, you got time yet. Mrs. Ramirez said to tell you that you can have breakfast in the kitchen and she's got some irons on so's you can slick up your dress."

She heard his feet going down the stairs and then, in spite of her sense of haste, she got up slowly, crossed to the window feeling that the floor-length starched lace curtains she peered through added their own magic to the dimly seen street.

[44]

A wagon piled high with sacks of grain was moving down the street and Blaze thought she could have looked forever at the turning wheels with their mud-splotched yellow paint.

Then she saw the spotted dog that was with the wagon team rush forward to smell noses with a tidy white-vested shepherd dog. The shepherd dog was followed by a boy on a bicycle! That bicycle was more than she had hoped for in all her dreams of town.

Her delighted eyes roved down the short street taking in the two blocks of wooden sidewalk, the small wooden building marked "U. S. Post Office," a bakery with thin smoke curling from its tin stovepipe and a rich smell of warm bread and spice floating up from the open door. To the east of town was the railroad track, the depot, a cluster of warehouses, and for incredible miles to the north, south and east the unbelievable flatness of the Salinas valley.

What Blaze wanted most to look at she was saving for the last, savoring it. But the need for haste was pressing and she gave in, let her eyes come to rest on the painted sign that covered the whole second-story false front of the big adobe building half a block down on the opposite side of the street. The letters were very faded, but to Blaze they were utterly beautiful. She read:

STAKEMILLER'S GENERAL MERCHANDISE

DRY GOODS	HATS	BOOTS AND SHOES	
GROCERIES	PROVISIONS		CROCKERY
GLASSWARE	HARDWARE		PAINTS AND OILS
WINES	LIQUORS	&	CIGARS
WHEAT	BARLEY	HAY	

Her lips were soft as she whispered the magical words to herself. As she turned reluctantly from the window and started to dress, she was thinking: Funny thing that Mother never told me about that sign. Why, it·means a whole world. Everything anyone could ever want is right in that one place.

An hour later, in her nicely pressed green wool dress, she was hesitating at the door of the hotel. The big clock on the wall behind the desk said it was almost nine. Martin had told her to be ready to start home as soon as the noon dinner was over. He had the eggs and butter credited on their store bill and the promise of a dollar of his own for working until noon unloading grain from the wagons that were hauling it into town, helping stack it in the freight shed for rail shipment.

The last thing Blaze had felt she wanted was to have Martin at her elbow, sniggering as she tried out her first shopping. But now she felt very strange and lost without him. Trying to seem very much at ease, she gathered up the folds of her long skirt with one hand. Clutching her deer hide money pouch in the other hand, she pushed open the door and stepped firmly out onto the sidewalk.

She saw every knot, every nail and every crack in the walk as she stepped daintily, holding her dress from touching the boards. She had gathered quite a bit of confidence in herself by the time she crossed the street and was in front of the store. Here she had to go up two broad steps to reach the door level, and Blaze was much impressed that this porch was also the sidewalk. To go down the street people had to walk on Mr. Stakemiller's porch, pass right by his door. Braving the interested stares of two old men who were sitting on the far end of the long wooden bench where the sun could reach them, Blaze went up the steps.

Inside, she found the store dusky and rich with a combined scent of soap, spice, kerosene, calico and age. Before she could quite get her eyes accustomed to the change from the brightness of the street, she was aware of a tall slight man with very thin

[46]

hair, thin nose and a luxuriant mustache turned up at the ends. She had heard of that mustache.

"How do you do, Mr. Stakemiller," she said brightly.

"Very well, very well this fine morning, Miss Allan, and happy to see you in King City. And what can we do for you today?"

Startled, she looked wonderingly at him for a moment and then she asked, "Did my brother Martin tell you I was here?"

"That's right, he did," agreed Mr. Stakemiller, "but I'd have known you for an Allan, as well as for your mother's daughter. You got her walk and the tilt of her head and her friendly way to a T."

"Thank you. Do you mind if I tell Mother what you said?"

"Not at all, go right ahead," Mr. Stakemiller said heartily. "Never hurts to let people know you admire them, and your mother is a real lady." Then he bent down and whispered teasingly, "But don't tell your dad; he's pretty jealous of my mustache, you know." He straightened up, smiling as he twirled the end of the mustache, but he said seriously, "You're leaving at noon, so you'll want to get your trading done. What's it to be this morning?"

Forgetting that she had promised to do the grocery and nail buying first of all, Blaze answered, "Brown silk and a pattern."

"No patterns," the grocer answered. "I made up my mind I had too much stuff to look after already. I told Miss Dufore, the dressmaker down by the post office building, and she said she'd like to handle them. Better see her first and then come back here and get the stuff for your dress."

"Yes, thank you, that's a good idea, and I can stop at the post office while I'm there. She was smiling as she moved toward the door. Then she remembered the shopping list and came hurrying back, asking, "Would it be all right to leave the grocery list with you? You know what Mother buys, and the nails for my father are the eight-penny size." She held out the list she had drawn from the deerskin purse.

[47]

"Sure, sure," the grocer assured her. I'll get it all fixed up and packed in the alforjases so Martin will only have to swing them on when he's ready to leave. You look out for your ribbons and laces, enjoy your holiday."

Blaze felt so happy that her feet seemed to float her out of the store and down the street. What a lovely town, what a wonderful man, thoughtful as her own mother. What a day!

But there were no patterns at Miss Dufore's. The wizened and amiable little Miss Dufore, trimmed with a tiny black sateen apron and shiny scissors on a cord at her belt, bustled around opening tattered old fashion books. She made Blaze stand up so her waist could be measured, her skirt length noted and then started unrolling a bolt of tarleton to cut whatever pattern Blaze should choose.

To Blaze the fashion books were fairyland. Such beautiful ladies wearing dresses of such elegance that she felt humble before them. Trying to picture such dresses back in her own mountains Blaze grew more and more bewildered, jumped up startled when she heard, for the first time, the long mournful hoot of the train whistle.

She remembered about the train and sat down in quick confusion, glad that Miss Dufore had been looking downstreet, her back turned. Once more lost in the fashion book, she decided that her new dress had better be cut about like the green one she was wearing except—here was one with a triple fold of material, almost like a bow but still having some look of a bustle. She put her finger on this bit and turned to ask Miss Dufore her opinion about this just as the door swung open.

A little freckled boy stood there, shoving a large parcel tied with heavy cord up onto the counter. "Mr. Watkins at the station says you been waiting for this stuff. It just come in on the train and he said you'd maybe give me a nickel if I toted 'em straight up to you."

The dressmaker squeaked, "My patterns; they came at last!"

She took the package from the boy, pulled a cardboard box from the drawer of the cutting table and picked up two coins.

"Here is a nickel for you and another nickel and many thanks. Please tell Mr. Watkins my thanks. Oh, my patterns!"

As the boy ran from the store with his treasure, Miss Dufore picked up her scissors, cut the strings and opened the package.

"Now we can see something not already years out of date," she said. Eagerly Blaze joined her and the two women sat with the small table between them. Blaze saw every pattern twice and a few of them a lot of times before she decided on the just-right one for her mother and herself. Time passed unnoticed.

As she was handing Miss Dufore the first one of her gold pieces Blaze asked, "Do you know what time it is?"

"Eleven o'clock; still quite early."

Blaze made a little murmur of dismay and hurried for the door saying, "I've still got to get my brown silk, if I can find it. And I'll need buckram and bindings, buttons that go with brown.

Miss Dufore followed her to the door. "Stakemiller's have some twelve-yard patterns in silk, some brown ones, I remember. Ask to see those first. I'm sure you'll like them and I'll get the findings together."

Before Blaze remembered that she must ask for Coast mail she was past the post office. She turned so abruptly that she crashed against the man whose footsteps she had heard hurrying along behind her.

"So sorry."

She started at the sound of his voice and looked up into the bright blue eyes of Stephen Janson who said, "Well, this is the second time you've almost bowled me over, Miss Allan. It's delightful."

His hand, still on her arm to steady her, the teasing smile that curved his lips, the light in his eyes all added to her confusion. Feeling stiff and awkward, she said, "I'm sorry, that is, it's nice to—" No, that was not the right thing to say. She must

[49]

not tell him she was glad to see him, it would sound forward, and specially so right after she'd bumped him so stupidly. She tried again for the right words, "I'd forgotten that I must ask for the Coast mail and I'm in such a hurry; excuse me."

He answered, "Oh, the mail; I've already got that and there isn't any Coast mail except what goes down to my camp. So now, with the time I've saved you, why don't you do me a kindness and help me find the depot?"

Blaze raised her eyebrows. "Since you're not riding out of town you must have come here on the train. And since the depot is in plain sight you should be able to find it again."

Apparently he did not notice her short answer. He bent down and murmured, "But how could I see the depot when I could see you, and you looking so very pretty in that green dress?"

Blaze colored up, abashed by a compliment, and furious with herself for letting this bold stranger so upset her.

"If you will excuse me, please; I still have many things to do and must leave for home right after dinner."

He said, "And I'll have to run or else miss the train back to Salinas." Blaze thought he sounded really sad as he said this but he brightened up as he went on, "But we'll get acquainted yet. When you come to our housewarming, I'll have time to talk you into being good-natured."

Blaze felt her eyes widen, her mouth drop open. She never had heard such talk! He acted as though she were a child, and if she did not put him in his place quickly, he'd more than likely think she'd be pleased with a pat on her head.

"You've no right to think me bad-tempered," she said. "I scarcely know you. I wouldn't presume to think about your temper; besides, it does not interest me. Good day, Mr. Janson."

She turned to cross the street, but he turned also, keeping step with her and saying eagerly, but still in that light way to which Blaze was not accustomed, "I'm sorry if I sounded smart.

I didn't mean to offend you. It's just my way. I think you have a lovely temper, and plenty of it too."

He laughed so infectiously that Blaze couldn't resist laughing with him. He nodded, "There we are; we've laughed together and now we're friends. And you'll come to our party; promise you will?"

Blaze, being Allan, could not promise what she was not certain of, but she could not altogether hide the eagerness under her cautious, "I'd like to come but perhaps my father will think there is too much work to do. Springtime is our busy time."

"I'll send a note as soon as Mother fixes the date, and I'll count on your being with us."

Blaze found this new earnestness in his manner very exciting but she hid her feelings well with a grave, "Thank you, Mr. Janson, and now I must hurry, so good-by."

He raised his new black felt hat and bowed deeply. "Then good-by for now, and a good journey home."

Blaze hurried into Stakemiller's determined to find the makings of a dress that would be pretty enough to fill her with confidence, no matter where she wore it.

Dress material, patterns, sateen, all her purchases were together and in the leather packsacks at the back of Mr. Stakemiller's store. Glancing at the clock Blaze was elated to see that it still lacked one whole minute of noon. She was about to make one more flying trip down the street to the shop of an old Spanish cobbler. Miss Dufore had told her that he made all the pretty dancing shoes for the Valley girls, still made them in the bright-colored leathers of the old Spanish California.

But as she opened the door of the general store she met Martin, tired and dusty, just coming up the two steps to the long porch.

"I'm all finished," she called, "except for one errand."

Martin was still on the steps, blocking her way. He took off his battered old felt, let the valley wind blow through his damp hair and said grudgingly, "I bet you got more stuff than I can pack right now. Dinner's on over to the hotel already. Let's eat and get started."

For a moment, habit held her on the porch. But the thought of shoes, thin pretty shoes in a bright color and made for dancing, was stronger than her habit of deferring to what the men of the family wanted.

"You go ahead and start eating, Martin. I'll hurry, but I won't care a bit if I don't have dinner. I'll be ready to leave as soon as you are."

She was halfway across the street before Martin could answer and she kept straight ahead without listening for his voice. By the time he was coming out of the Alta Vista's dining room she was back and waiting for him with a parcel clasped tenderly in her arms.

"If that's your idea of a minute to run an errand," he started wrathfully, "I'd hate to have to wait five minutes for you. Dinner's over, Blaze Allan, and I didn't ask Mrs. Ramirez to hold back a thing for you either."

With rapturous unconcern Blaze answered, "Oh, Martin, I'm not hungry. I'm so happy I couldn't eat to save my life. I've got the prettiest pair of shoes you ever dreamed of."

"All right, all right. And you'll be wanting to eat your shoes, Miss, before we get five miles on our way, and I don't want to hear no complaining about how hungry you are."

Blaze tossed her head. "I'll give you a dollar for every word of complaint you hear out of me and don't expect to get rich, because you won't. Let's get started. I thought you were ready and waiting for me."

They were only about three miles from town and riding up the first of the long slow grades on the road to the caves when Martin turned in his saddle and grinned at her. "I got you a cheese sandwich and an apple turnover, Sis," he called back.

"Want it this minute or can you wait till we rest the stock at the top of the grade?"

Blaze was touched by such kindness and wanted Martin to know that she was. She laughed, saying, "I could eat Gipsy this minute, but the bargain I made was my choice. Won't hurt me a bit to wait until we get to the cave."

At the top of the grade Martin lifted the flap on his saddlebag and took out a paper bag, leaned over and handed it to her, saying, "Won't hurt you to eat a little snack now. I'd never collect any dollar from you for grumbling."

"Thank you, sir," she said, smiling at her twin, "and I think it's worth a lot of dollars to have you look out for me so well."

"Aw, forget all about that," he mumbled. "This was your trip; ought to have all of it as good as you can."

"It was all beautiful; more wonderful than I ever hoped." Blaze had a dreamy look in her eyes as she unwrapped the sandwich, which she didn't see, scarcely tasted as she ate. Her vision was a rainbow of silks and buttons, dancing shoes and the tall young man who spoke so lightly, bowed so deeply and was still her secret, the first real secret she had ever had. She did have a guilty feeling that it was almost evil of her to feel so pleased that Martin had not happened along and shared her few words with their new neighbor.

She rode happily toward home, thinking of her new slippers, the housewarming, dancing, but most of all she thought of the letter he said that he would send.

III

Above the jangle of cowbells as the milk herd was turned into pasture, the squawk and squabble of chickens quarreling over their supper, Blaze called, "I've been around the world, and home is the nicest place!"

Avery slammed the gate shut after the cows and came flying across the barnyard to open the trail gate for the travelers. Hannah Allan set two great baskets of eggs safe inside the shed door and hurried over to the saddle shed to greet her children as their father called out, "So there you are. I looked for you to be here in time to help with the chores, Martin."

He walked slowly forward and Blaze leaned over from her saddle to say, "Help me down, Father. I ache all over, I'm so tired."

"Teach you to stay home, not go gadding off to town," he growled, but he held up his arms for her as he did when she was little more than a baby.

Blaze dropped the reins, slid down into her father's arms, clinging to him tightly for an instant, her head against his shoulder as she said, "I spent all my birthday money for foofurah and frivols, Father, and I never had so much fun."

Zande Allan looked down at his pretty daughter, his brows drawn together in a frown, but his arm was warm about her as he said, "So that's your notion of something solid, is it? I counted on you bringing home anyway one plow to lay by for when you'd find it handy."

Avery came charging back from the gate, took a pigmy punch

at his father as he said, "Turn loose of her, Pa! I want to shake her and see if she brought me a mouth harp."

With a triumphant face Blaze announced, "I got something for everybody, but I don't know what! I'm silly, I've seen so many things and I'm so happy and so tired."

"And hungry, too, the both of you, is my guess." Hannah looked fondly at her children and urged, "Hurry along now and get ready for supper; it's ready for you."

Blaze and her mother walked side by side through the garden, silently, until Blaze said, "I saw a lot of people, Mother, and I learned something."

Hannah smiled, waiting.

Blaze stood with uplifted face, her eyes bright as she said, "Every time I come home, even if I've only been over to Granma's, I think this is the nicest place in the world. I couldn't wait to go to town. I loved being there, but—"

Her mother said a trifle grimly, "That's the Allan of us: no beef like our beef, no wheat could make as good bread as our wheat; we got the best strawberry patch."

She made a humorous mouth, her eyebrows lifted, but Blaze was serious. "That's how we are and I like it. Blaze Allan—"

She opened the door, put the few parcels she was carrying on the table and said, "I wouldn't be anybody if I was Blaze Williams. Not ever."

Hannah said cautiously, "He was over here yesterday asking where you was." Quickly she changed the subject, saying, "You wash your hands, honey, and help me dish up. Supper's late."

Obediently Blaze started for the outside wash bench. Her father, her two brothers, came up from the barn loaded with the packs and all asked the same thing, "Supper ready?"

Blaze flew about the room, setting out plates as her mother took the hot food from the oven. Her father said the very same grace he always said for meals, not even a word of thanks for the safe return of the travelers, and then, as he filled his plate, started asking Martin what he'd learned about the price of beef, of potatoes; what he got for the eggs and the butter.

"Home," thought Blaze sleepily, "this is our world. Fence the mountains, plow the fields, gather the eggs. King City thinks it's the world, but it's only the place that takes in what we raise, sends it to some other place that thinks *it's* the world." Her head was nodding, the kitchen was warm, cozy, she'd been in the saddle so long. She jerked her head up, straightened her back and felt abashed to find the family looking at her with amusement.

"I'll dry the dishes for you, Sis, if you just give me my mouth harp—" Avery looked at her, tense with longing.

Blaze stood up, intending to go and search the packsacks, but Martin drawled, "Go on to bed, sleepyhead. I'll hunt through that stuff, see if Av's got anything like a drum or a fife or a fiddle." He turned to his small brother asking, "A drum, was it, or a fiddle you wanted?"

Avery quivered like a spaniel but he refused to be baited.

Covering a yawn, Blaze murmured, "Well, good night, all."

Her mother and Avery answered but the two men were already talking field peas, cut green for feed, or pink beans for the plot that had produced table corn last season.

Blaze called back, "See that Avery gets his present, Martin," and knowing that her mother would see to it, shut the door and went down the hall to her own room.

The room was white with moonlight, the canyons were level full of fleecy white fog and over the place where the ocean should have picked up the moonlight was a new world of fog. It was piled up in great white mountain ridges, broad level mesas, mysterious and unsubstantial plains and canyons, all of it seeming to glow as though lit by some floating fog-moon. A cold wind from the northeast came swooping over the Ventanas shaking at the grapevine until Blaze felt she almost could hear a cold crying from the naked vine as it clawed for its old safe grasp of the pergola.

As the girl pulled off her warm buckskin chaps the cold breath of the room struck her sharply awake for a moment. She slid gingerly into the icy sheets, murmuring to herself, "It can't be very wicked to get warm before I say my prayers."

The feather tick billowed around her as softly as the fog moved up from the canyons, but warm, comforting, not like the icy embrace of fog. Blaze cuddled down closer into the feathers, pulled the log-cabin comforter up around her shoulders and hoped there were no angels flying around in that wilderness of fog—nothing to keep them warm but very small wings and a very thin shift.

Her new brown silk was so beautiful any angel would want it. "Oh, God, please make me as good as I am happy. Little angels have blue eyes, yellow hair. Blaze! That means you can find your way home; just follow the blaze. Goodness must be the same thing as happiness. God bless Ma and Pa, my brothers and Granny Allan and—"

Her long slender hands were loosely clasped across her young breast, the drift of hair on the pillow glowed with the red of madrone bark, and in her sleep young Blaze Allan rode Gipsy across dream ranges of fog mountains toward a shining city that had two main streets, but there was a post office on either end of both the streets and the letter might be anywhere or nowhere. The mare wouldn't go into any of the post offices but wanted to go sit on the steeple of the only church in town.

"I shouldn't have prayed on the feathers," she dreamed, "but who would write me a letter?"

The wind was rising; the fog froze and fell as frost on the Allan acres. The magnificent city with two main streets faded, curled up into a drift of cold fog and the horse floundered and slid across endless mountains—fog mountains that piled higher and higher and never held their shape long enough for the rider to know if she were traveling in the right direction. She tried not to feel frightened. Blaze. That meant you could find your way home. But there were no pines, no laurels, no blazed oaks in this strange cold world. She suddenly knew what was wrong. She'd come down the wrong side of the steeple. The main street she followed when she left the strange town was the one that went to Tomorrow. The blazed trail she was hunting for was the one that went back to Yesterday.

Avery went past her door, down the hall and up the steep ladder to the attic playing *Juanita* very softly on his new mouth organ. Blaze heard it as part of her dream. The dream horse seemed to hear the music also. She turned and took the road toward Tomorrow and Blaze was suddenly warm and happy. She felt sure of herself, certain that if she never said his name to anyone, not even to her mother, when she got to Tomorrow he would be there.

Breakfast was over and the house quiet, when Blaze and her mother opened the packages. Hannah Allan sat fingering the spools of blue silk, brown silk, the skirt braid, the bindings. There were hooks and eyes, buttons, braid, buckram. Hannah's roughened fingers touched each one tenderly, and she kept repeating, "I remember when I never expected to see the like of this is my day—not on this ranch."

She was enchanted with the pattern for making over her good dress, the blue silk Zande had brought for her from San Francisco almost twenty years before.

Her face radiant, Blaze told her mother, "Miss Dufore said this was the very newest thing, right from New York. Look at the sleeves!"

Hannah looked. The fitted bodice seemed very like the dresses she had worn for years, but the sleeves were amazing. Enough material went into each sleeve to cover a good-sized barrel, and the sleeves stood out from the shoulders so bravely that waist and hips looked too delicate to belong to anything as earthy as a real woman.

"You should use this pattern, Blaze. Just look at that skirt. It certainly looks nicer than any hoops or bustle. Eight gores, and its sets so smooth and flares out so pretty."

"Just right for you, Mother. Isn't another mother on the Coast as slim and straight as you are. This will set you off so good that even Father will notice how pretty you are."

Blaze was surprised at the soft look in her mother's eyes, the deepened color in her cheeks. She dropped a light kiss on the tip of her mother's ear and said, "Look, this is your town present."

Hannah unfastened the long roll of paper and peeked. She jumped up, her voice shaken, "Oh, Daughter, you shouldn't have done it—blue sateen for a petticoat! I needed it; I love it. But did you have enough money to get what you needed?"

"I got everything," Blaze said triumphantly. "What do you think of that, and I never bought anything before in my life! I didn't have to put one of our things on the store bill. That sateen's measured so's to have enough for three full ruffles, and look—this dark blue is for binding them. Won't you be proud when your petticoat shows?"

Her mother laughed but urged, "I want to see the goods you got, your pattern too."

Blaze tenderly undid the package holding her dream.

"There," she said, a catch in her breath.

A changeable silk taffeta, brown with a rose-colored thread woven through it, flowed in splendor across the worn kitchen table, filling the winter-dark room with the glory of a grove of madrone trees wearing their new soft color of spring. Hannah gasped, "It's the very same as your hair. Hold it up to you."

Blaze lifted the shimmering stuff proudly, smiled at her mother as she stroked the fabric. "Wait," she said. "That's not all. Look here!"

Over her shoulder went a length of velveteen the color of new turned earth, blending perfectly with the brighter silk. "For the jacket. It's called a Russian sacque. Oh, Mother, it's all so heavenly I can hardly stand it!"

Hannah said gravely, "It's right for you. I'm glad, Blaze. A woman should know what she needs to set her off. I was saving those gold shell earrings of my mother's for your twenty-first birthday, but you must have them now, and the gold brooch too."

Hannah started to her bedroom to get the gold jewelry out of her round-topped trunk. Blaze was busy with her last package, had it untied but still not uncovered when her mother returned with the heavy gold sea-shells that Blaze had loved all her life.

As the girl took the trinkets in her hand her eyes misted. "If I was any happier you'd have to pick me up off the floor with the dustpan. I could just bust!"

Hannah looked serious. "It'd make extra work and we got our hands full as it is, finding time to sew up all this stuff. What's that you're hiding under your hand, honey?"

Blaze slowly drew the paper back and disclosed a pair of soft green slippers with little heels and a brown buckle. Her face set rebelliously "Father's not going to see them until I'm at the next party. I'll put them on after I get there."

Her mother shook her head doubtfully. "Your dress is long and full; maybe he'll not see them."

Blaze said, "Father doesn't miss much and if I thought I was going through a polka with no one seeing my green shoes I'd feel cheated."

"Cheer up." Her mother laughed. "They'll be the talk of the Coast."

Her hands flew to her mouth, her eyes were wide above the long fingers as Blaze said, "Oh, no, Mother! Nobody has ever said a light word about me. That's the thing Father is so proud of. I'd never risk making talk."

"Don't be foolish," her mother chided. "If a girl can't have a pair of pretty shoes *and* a good name on this Coast it's time someone shook 'em up. You wear your new shoes and put 'em on when you put on your dress. You've never been sneaking about anything."

Blaze hugged her. "You're so dear, Mother. I'll always act nice enough to deserve you or die trying."

"Tut," said Hannah. "Let's get the patterns spread out and figure how they go and what matches what."

The short January days sped away in a flurry of basting and pressing and fitting. Blaze ached with her joy as the new finery took shape. Each day now she hoped for Mr. Janson's letter or that he would stop by. The hip draperies were finally basted on and in the small kitchen mirror Blaze could see how gracefully the folds swept around her hips, how cleverly they turned and tucked under, became the swirls and puffs that made the bustle effect. She turned and twisted, trying to see it all in the far too small glass, showed a radiant face to her mother as she asked, "What do you think, Mother?"

Hannah laughed, nodded as she said, "It'll do. You go measure out the starter and mix up the bread and I'll work on the lining of your jacket. Then if you can find time to sew on all these buttons before tomorrow, your new dress will be done for your birthday."

Blaze looked startled. "My birthday? Is tomorrow the tenth of February?"

"That's right," her mother answered. She gathered up the jacket and her scissors, went off to her bedroom.

Blaze measured butter and honey, salt and milk and stirred in the yeast starter, sifted in flour to make the dough. Her hands flashed over the big bread board, kneading the bread.

Her birthday tomorrow. The days had gone so quickly and yet each day had seemed so long. If only she had heard some word from Stephen Janson about the housewarming. Well, there had been a lot of bitter weather and plenty of rain. Maybe they were holding off until the weather was more settled.

She looked around at the kitchen, wondering what his house would be like, hoping there would be one room big enough for dancing. Their own kitchen was plenty big enough to give a dance in if people waited their turn, but they never had given a party. Maybe when Martin was twenty-one their father would let them have a dance in the house. A year was forever. A year went pretty quick.

She put her finger on the dough, lightly, and started to count slowly. When she came to "thirty" she lifted her finger. Yes, the bread was worked enough; it didn't stick to her finger. She lifted the great round of dough and settled it carefully into the buttered iron pot. A clean dampened towel went on first, and over that, the heavy iron lid. Blaze bent sideways with the weight of it as she carried it over to a warm shelf above the stove.

As she washed the dough from her hands and stood beside the wash bench drying them she suddenly turned her head to listen. That sound was no stray horse grazing along the trail behind the big cascaras outside the gate. That steady gait meant a rider.

Lightly she stepped back into the kitchen, looked in the little mirror. A pat at her hair, a bit of smoothing of her dress and she was outside again, casually strolling past the strawberry patch and toward the gate. She was glad her black and white calico looked so crisp, her apron so white and fresh. Feeling sure this rider must be Stephen bringing the letter bidding them all to the party, she bent down over the strawberry bed hoping she looked more interested in gardening than she felt.

Disappointment showed plainly on her face as she heard the gate latch move and looked up to see Joe Williams.

"Blaze," he called. "Walk on down to the pond with me, will you? I'll tie out here and save time."

Her first impulse was to say she was busy but she knew she

hadn't looked very busy, and, like it or not, she'd have to listen to him some time. Better have it done with.

She walked forward. Against her will she gave the mountain greeting, "Could you stay for a bite with us, Joe?"

His eyes glistened but he shook his head. "I'd like nothing better than a sample of your cooking again, Blaze. But there's such a power of work waiting. Can't let it pile up or it would get the best of me."

Annoyed because she knew his words were well calculated to please her father, if repeated, she was still enough relieved by his refusal to be able to smile as she said, "That's how it is here too. I've got plenty of undone work waiting on me."

He stepped closer to her, his eyes eager. Blaze knew he'd trimmed his hair and beard for this call, put on his best coat and his gold chain with the crystal ball locket. His eyes were so intent on her that she felt she could not bear another second's silence, but she would not break it either. She waited.

He gave in. "I know your pa told you he'd give me leave to ask you, Blaze. I been wanting to get the day set but you was in town when I come over. I always hear that girls think May is the prettiest month. How would May Day suit you?"

Bluntly she said, "I told my father it wouldn't work out, Joe. We're not suited; anyhow I'm not, and my mind's made up not to marry."

He nodded patiently. "Yes, I know. He told me you was feeling notional. I don't mind you feeling shy about marrying; I like you for it."

Blaze said steadily, "But I'm not going to marry you, Joe. Not any day; not ever."

His eyes closed reflectively, his voice still patient as he answered, "Remember your father gave his word. It's his right to do, and you won't go back on his promise. You're an Allan."

She looked at him steadily. "I didn't make any promise and

[63]

I'm tired of being bullied because I was born an Allan. I think you'd feel shame to try to hold me against my will."

Blaze drew back as she felt the edge of a threat in his careful, "I'm not the man to jilt, Blaze. The last thing I want is to threaten. I'm just warning you."

"Warning me? About what?" She made no effort to cover the contempt in her voice.

She couldn't ruffle him. He still spoke softly. "I saw a thing you did that I'd never tell a soul. I'd never think about it, even, long as you was mine to protect. You got nothing to worry about as long as you keep your father's bargain with me. But I could tell a tale that would bring shame to you and make all you Allans the laughingstock of the county."

Blaze was too startled to speak. She just looked at him.

He said softly, "Remember that I got your interests to heart. But think over what I just said."

His softness frightened Blaze more than the strange threat in his words, but she answered, "You take a strange way to prove that you care anything about me, Joe. But go right ahead and tell anything you want to about me. I couldn't possibly think less of you than I do right this minute."

She started toward the house, but he hurried after calling, "Forgive me, Blaze. If you could only know how I feel. I think about you, I dream about you all my time. That's what gets wrong with me. You drive me crazy."

She looked at his drawn face and an angry pity made her say, "I'm sorry, Joe. But there's nothing I can do about it. Can't we forget this whole thing?"

He looked confused, ashamed, as he shifted his hat from one hand to the other, shoved it awkwardly onto his head, took it off again and stood looking down at his hands.

When she started to walk away again he said, "If you're asking me to forget I love you, Blaze, you're wasting breath. I'm sorry I forgot myself, talked mean to you. Give me the chance to talk nice to you tomorrow; show me you don't hold it against me."

She was going to tell him she did not want to see him for months, much less tomorrow, but he broke in before she got started. "You folks are all going over to the doings at the Janson place tomorrow, ain't you?"

Blaze felt that she'd suddenly stepped into an open well.

She managed to turn her sharply caught breath into a little shriek, brushing at an imaginary bug on the back of her neck and shuddering. Joe smiled indulgently on such feminine folly. She managed a shaky laugh, protesting, "Well, I don't like bugs crawling on me. I can't stand them." She looked back at him, steadied her voice as she answered his question. "We may not go. Father is very busy right now." She had to pause for a moment before she could finish lightly, "If we do go, I'll see you there."

She hurried on without looking back and by the time she was at the kitchen door she already heard the sound of hoofs plodding up the steep trail.

Blaze went into the house slowly, picked up the bodice of her dress, her needle and a button, went over and lifted the iron cover and looked at the dough before she sat down. The bread would rise tonight, be baked tomorrow. The dress would get all its buttons sewed on, be done tomorrow. And then what? No one new and exciting to share the fragrant bread with, no one strange and disturbing to wear the dress for. Her chest seemed to hurt and she couldn't stop asking herself, "Why? Why?"

Why should Mr. Janson snub the Allans? If he did not mean to ask them to his party, why had he said anything about the housewarming?

She picked up another button, remembering how happily she had chosen them, small brown velvet balls ornamented by two crossed gold threads. They had seemed more beautiful than the smallest, most perfect wild button mushroom. Now her needle flashed through them and they seemed only another task added to a day that had become flat as a dead fox.

She bent over her sewing more closely as she heard her mother come into the kitchen from the hall. Her cheeks burned, thinking how silly she had been to think it was fun to have a secret about having met the new neighbor. She had her secret and now she could not ask her mother what she thought of the Jansons' reason for leaving them all out, asking Joe, who lived so much farther away.

Hannah built up the fire, pulled her chair close to the work-table and sat down, saying, "Well, your Russian Sacque is finished, Daughter."

Blaze dropped a button on the floor so she could lean over and hunt it, hide her trembling lips. Her mother went on gaily, "It certainly is a pretty thing; neat as a grasshopper's coat." She took a quick look at her daughter's bent head, asking, "Blaze, what's wrong? I saw you with Joe down by the gate. Are you upset because he asked you at last?"

Blaze shook her head, relieved that her mother thought Joe the cause, instead of the smallest part, of her trouble. She said, half under her breath, "No. He did ask me and I told him I wouldn't marry him." In spite of herself she shuddered as she blurted out, "He threatened me."

Her mother's mouth straightened. "He can't do that. I'll speak to your father."

Blaze jumped to her feet, scattering buttons in all directions. "No, no. Please! You mustn't, ever." She stooped and began to gather up buttons, keeping her face hidden as she said nervously, "He—oh, dear—he says he knows something." She straightened up but her voice trembled with shame as she said quickly, to get it over, "He says he knows something nasty about me and he'll tell everyone, make a scandal of me all over the Big Sur, unless I'll marry him."

Hannah spoke angrily. "Why didn't you tell him he must be pretty nasty himself to want someone he thinks he knows nasty stuff about? I'll give him a piece of my mind. You just wait—"

Blaze fumbled with her thread and scissors, flushing as she said, "I don't know a thing he could tell, honest I don't."

Her mother jumped up, tried to put more wood in the already full grate, dropped the stick back in the wood box and gave the lid a sharp bang. She straightened up and looked searchingly at her daughter. "It isn't like you to let someone scare you with a lie. Why are you afraid, when you know there's nothing wrong?"

Blaze faltered. "I'm not sure what he might think was a wrong thing." Her face burned but she made herself say, "I know plenty about animals but I don't know a thing about myself, seems like."

Her mother looked embarrassed as she said, "You know enough to be the nice girl that you are. Women got instincts that tell 'em plain when anything's wrong. I'll have a word with Joe Williams," she went on. "I'll ride over to his place tomorrow and you come with me."

Blaze shook her head. "I don't want to, Mother. I feel ashamed. All I want is to know that you'll stand back of me if Father keeps on trying to push me into marrying Joe."

The clock struck four times, reminding the mother of her Allan men already riding down the mountains from the back country where they had been rounding up young stock. Hannah helped Blaze fold up the sewing, saying, "We'll finish these things easy tomorrow morning. The men will be riding into Indian valley and we'll have the whole day to ourselves. Mine's done too. All but a few bastings to take out and the pressing. All we need now is a place to wear our fine feathers."

Knowing she was not able to answer her mother's lighthearted mood, Blaze hurried off to her own room with her dress. The days had passed slowly enough while she still had all her faith that the letter would come. Now that was over. There was no handsome rider on a big gray horse coming to name the day of the party. There was no letter—nothing to look forward to.

IV

IT seemed that it must still be the middle of the night when
Blaze heard a great clatter of wood falling into the kitchen
wood box, the scrape of ashes being raked out of the grate
and her father shouting cheerfully, "You wenches fixing to lay
abed all day?"

Blaze sat up, blinked her eyes, trying to see daylight through
her window. There was a dim light but it was moon on fog, not
daylight. The fog shapes hurrying past the window between herself and the sea had a cold breath and she shivered.

"It's still yesterday, Father," she yawned. "Anyway, it's the
middle of the night and it's cold."

The fog was so close-folded over the house that Blaze could
smell the trail of sulphur when her father lit a match, held it
to the pine shavings. She swung her feet reluctantly out from
under the warm covers. Even the lion-skin rug felt damp and
cold as her bare feet touched it.

"It won't be cold by the time you're out here tossing up some
flapjacks." Her father's voice came booming down the hall with
unusual good-nature, but he sounded less confident when he
said, "And anyway, you'll get warm dancing this afternoon if
you get up and get your work done in time to get to the
doings."

Blaze's heart gave a leap; she pulled her feet back into bed,
tucked the cover about her and shivered with delight and terror.
She mustn't let herself hope too much. Maybe it was all a joke.

Then she heard the door of the big bedroom jerk open and

her mother demand sharply, "Doings? Where? What are you talking about?"

"Them new folks up Torre canyon. Jansons."

"First I heard about it, and a fine time, I must say. It's the middle of the night."

Zande Allan's voice was mild. "Well, I thought you'd want to know about it soon's you could. If you don't want to go, fine. Me and the boys would a lot liefer spend the day picking up some more strays."

Blaze felt as though the fog had crept right under her covers. Nothing could be easier than Pa talking himself out of going to a doings. She didn't dare say a word, and her hands clutched both sides of her straw tick as she heard her mother click rapidly down the hall, open the kitchen door and close it after herself. The split-redwood partitions were thin and Blaze could hear the raised voices easily. "Blaze and me won't be going any place today. I got bread set and we both got our dresses to finish. You could of said a word sooner, if you'd of wanted our company."

Blaze was thrilled to hear the spunk in her mother's voice. Wasn't often she stood up so sassy. But she was filled with a terrible urge to call out, "I want to go, please, I do." She clapped her hands over her mouth, her eyes big above them as she shivered nervously and waited to hear what would happen.

There was silence and Blaze held her breath, waiting to hear her father storm.

Far off on the slope of Bald mountain the faint bawling of cattle drifted down on the wind and the fog was already lifting. From the kitchen there was only a crackle of dry wild-lilac twigs. Then a firewood stick banged against the side of the wood box and her father called loudly, "You, Martin, Blaze, Avery! Tumble out, the lot of you. We got a day's work to do ere noontime."

[70]

In spite of its starting to break, Avery's voice came as gay as the song-thrush, "Party, today's a party! I'm awake, Pa."

Hannah Allan didn't sound quite so set, though still firm as she said, "Allan men's all that's going to any doings on such short notice. Blaze and me are not going anywhere till our dresses are done. That's what we got them for."

Zande snorted but he explained, "That's why I called you a little early. I only just found out about this damn housewarming."

Hannah sounded skeptical. "You just now found out? How? Did you pick it out of the air?"

Zande answered, "Ain't we going to get any breakfast around here? Yup, I picked it out of the air, or just about."

Blaze heard the flick of fork against bowl as her mother started beating eggs for the flapjacks, heard curiosity conquer annoyance as she said grudgingly, "Well, stop teasing, Zande. Tell me what you're up to anyway."

"All right, all right—man can't have any privacy around a prying woman. Let's see. Well, about a month gone, I met Pete Garcia on the trail. He was coming up from the tan bark camp. He's been working for Janson, packing bark. I was on the trail and the boys was driving the stuff up out of the bottom of the canyon. Pete, he give me this message, and he was starting in to tell one of his tales of his goings-on but right then Martin hollered up that Avery's horse was down and they needed help to hold the cattle."

"What's all that got to do with you telling us in the middle of the night that them new folks are having a party?"

"I'm telling you, Hannah. Give me a chance, will you?"

The fork made very brisk clicks against the bowl, but Hannah made no answer.

Her father's voice sounded very put-upon but not angry. "The cattle was stampeding, Avery's horse was down, a fool calf was thrashing around with a broke leg." He waited, but nothing in

[71]

the way of encouragement came from his wife. Blaze could hear her now, pulling the big griddle over the firebox. She ought to get up but she couldn't dress and go into the kitchen, as though it were any morning instead of this exciting, very special one.

Over the clatter of stove lids, the scrape of the griddle being settled in place, Zande Allan went on, "By the time I got all that ruckus straightened out, I clean forgot the party doings."

His wife said, "And I suppose a bee stung you in the dead of winter and the middle of the night and that made you think of it."

Up in the attic Avery's boot laces stopped slapping on the floor boards and his high young laughter echoed through the house. There was a loud thump, as though he'd rolled from his low bench to the floor and through whoops of laughter he gasped, "Sounds so funny, a bee—in the middle of the night!"

"You get down here, young fella, or nothing's going to seem so funny to you. Get a move on."

"Coming, Pa." The answer was prompt and respectful, but it ended in a smothered giggle.

Now her father turned short. "Well," he said, "you can go or stay, suit yourself. I was trying to tell you—"

"Blaze, where are you?" Her mother didn't wait tor Blaze to answer, but told her husband, "Go ahead. I'm listening."

Blaze started to dress as quietly as she could, listening breathlessly.

"This morning I was going out back and it was cold and I remembered how cold it was that day on the trail and then I remembered Pete said about a party on the tenth of February."

Hannah said, "I remember 'twas the second week in January when you brought in that veal. And I think you should have remembered a party, on the twins' birthday too. But we can't go now. There's the bread, for one thing. I can't leave that."

Blaze heard Avery flip down the ladder, run along the hall and into the kitchen, still gay with his joke as he said, "Well.

take the bread dough along, Ma. That would fix it and it'd be something new, I bet, taking dough to a doings."

His father growled, "That's enough out of you. Skin out and get them calves out of the corral and into the pasture and start feeding. You'll hear the breakfast call."

"Yessir."

The door shut and Avery was gone as Blaze came into the kitchen so quietly that she surprised a tender amused smile on her mother's face, saw her father put his big hand on his wife's slender waist, draw her close as he said softly, "We must a both been laughing when we made that one."

Blaze shrank back into the dim shelter of the hall. It seemed almost shocking, thinking of her parents as people who were united in a love that went on growing under the round of work and years. She felt young, realizing that she had never thought of her parents as people—they were parents. Her mother was good, patient. Her father was good, but crusty and quick-tempered. She felt a rising eagerness for life and a deepened faith in its magic. Work and disappointment, some things done; maybe not all you hoped for—but life shared. Sharp words but soft glances, a secret sharing that made it all good.

Blaze walked into the kitchen, went to her father and smiled at him as she asked, "Can't you talk Mother into stopping work for even one day? I'd like to take my new birthday-present dress out larking around."

She picked up a stack of plates, put them on the warming oven and urged, "Why not go, Mother? Seems like it would be a fine thing to get some music into February before we get so much rain we'll all be house-bound and fidgety."

Her mother laughed. "Oh, well, I peeked at the bread. It's coming up good and you can set it over a kettle of hot water to hurry it some." She poured batter from a big gourd, thin buckwheat batter hissing onto the hot griddle, rising and browning so quickly that the first one wanted turning by the time the last one was poured. "What time is this gathering, Zande? Did Pete say any special time?"

Zande shrugged. "Said dinner at one o'clock. I like my meal at right noon. Thought everybody did. I suppose it's some foreign notion—them Jansons is Swedes."

"Norwegian, I think," Hannah ventured.

" 'Squarehead' was what Pete called 'em," Zande said indifferently. "Not that it makes any difference; they're all alike, foreigners. Take them Grigsbys up to Vine canyon. English, they are. All of 'em but the young ones straight from England, and by God, they talk as funny a lingo as any Portygee or Swede. I talk English. Don't see why they don't, since they claim they come from there."

Hannah said, "Blow for the boy, will you? Martin must of stayed up, I never heard him come down. Be a good thing to lay off work for a day. They work hard."

Zande blew the kelp horn, put it back in its place on the timber behind the stove, and growled, "Martin got up when I did. He's at work. Don't be soft with them, wife. Work never hurt anyone."

Wrapped in a dream of all the things that *might* happen, Blaze made bread, swept floors, sewed on buttons, pressed her dress and thought the day was only started when her mother called, "Almost ten o'clock! Go make yourself pretty, honey."

Blaze held her hand above the row of brown loaves, asking, "You think they're too hot to pack in the basket for Mrs. Janson, Mother?"

"Yes, they'd sweat and go soft-crusted if we cover 'em too soon. You done enough, Daughter. Take time to fuss over yourself a bit. That's half the fun of a new dress anyway."

Smiling at her mother, Blaze gathered up her finery, went to her room and put it down on her bed.

But she couldn't start to dress. With the door to the hall shut behind her and her window facing the sea swung open, Blaze felt that this was her special world, that this was a day different from all the other days in her life. She wanted to hold it back, keep it ten o'clock for hours. If only her father had remembered to tell them. She could have had a whole month to fill with dreams and fancies about who she would see, how the house would be, who would be there. It seemed as though half the joy was in all that came before the few barbecues that she had been to.

She would take a few minutes to be happy in thinking before she started to dress. Without a backward look at all her finery she walked over to her window and stood looking at the zigzag lines of Allan fence that went from the mountaintop clear down to the sea. There was no beach. The Santa Lucias dropped steep to the sea and the surf beat against their stony shoulders. She could look twenty miles to the south and as many miles to the north from her window. Blaze turned her eyes, looking at all she could see, thinking again how strange it seemed that her mother sometimes said it was an empty, lone land. Canyon after canyon marched in orderly row down to the sea, and in each canyon lay a stream, a thick growth of redwood. The redwood canyons were lush with ferns, singing with waterfalls and sparkling with trout. On every green or golden slope cattle or, at any rate, deer were feeding. How could anyone think such a land was lone, empty? There was even a party to go to, a new house and new people to see. Lone? Empty? She shook her head, turned slowly away from the window and began to unlace her buckskin blouse. She kicked off her moccasins, stepped out of her leather skirt.

Blaze poured water into her basin and when her bath was finished she slowly drew on her new long stockings of fine white cotton. They were her first store-stockings and after a lifetime of wearing her own, or her mother's hand-knit ones, they seemed very fine and delicate. She made a ritual of fastening her new stays, stepped proudly into new white muslin drawers and three flounced petticoats. With a growing excitement she fastened the last tiny button on the basque, thrilled because she had to hold her breath to get it fastened. She patted at it approvingly; the basque really fit. She never before had whalebone hidden in firmly stitched seams. She was a lady; the whalebone and the bustle proved it to her.

But her hair! "Just baby hair, that's all, and I can't fault anyone but my own self. Mother said I'd be sorry if I cut it off again."

She peered into the mirror, trying to gather up the short ends of the thick red-brown crop, but it slid out of her fingers like quicksilver.

"Top and bottom of me's both all wrong." She pulled up the wide skirt, glanced at the moccasins she had meant to wear. Quickly she went over to her redwood chest, lifted the lid and took out the green slippers. She started to put them back, changed her mind, and slipped her feet into the pretty things. She would wear them, even though her father spied them, made her take them off or made her stay home. Her dress deserved those green slippers. She stepped out timidly, the heels clicking on the floor boards. In moccasins she could walk easy as a mountain lion. But in the green slippers she could walk proud, like a lady. Smoothing the thick red hair that hung straight and almost touched her shouders, she knew she was ready.

She started for the door but went back to stand again by her window looking out at the sea. She wanted to hold onto this breathless feeling of new and different things just about to happen, but keep inside this time, the way that things were right now.

At this moment she loved everything, everybody. She listened tenderly to the shouting and clatter of the Allan men storming the kitchen.

"Martin's got the mutton tallow and I want to grease my boots too. He's just hanging onto it to be mean."

"You come here, Son. I'll give you a lick of my grease for your boots. It's special, lots better stuff than that measly ol' can of grease."

Pa's voice could be as warm and kind as anyone's.

There was a crisp warning from her mother. "Both of you, wash them faces good and lather up your necks."

A respectful chorus, "Yes'm." Pa must have his eye on the boys. Quiet again. Then a step, a word.

"Hannah!"

Was that her father's voice? Blaze felt her head go dizzy. It was warm and tender as the song-thrush telling of a new home built in the madrone tree. There was a little soft sound and then her mother's voice, breathless, "I'm glad you still like me in blue, Zande."

Then everyday was back, and maybe a note of warning in her mother's quiet "Blaze is in her room getting her new dress on too."

Blaze felt her eyes mist. They were still in love with each other. Thinking of them that way made the sheen on the sea seem brighter, the new green on the hills softer. Long ago they had shared together the dreams of spring, lived them together into the full summer. Love was something more than the song that poured from the hills in the time of wild lilac. It was life, plain as daily bread and sweet as new butter.

She didn't want to leave her open window. It seemed there could be no place so lovely to be thinking these new thoughts as here on her own mountain inside the fences of home, behind the shut gate of her own heart.

"Everyone's ready, Blaze. You've had plenty of time for your primping."

Blaze came slowly into the kitchen, half expecting to see a radiant glow over the worn redwood walls. Her father looked slightly impatient, watching her mother pack four loaves of the new bread, some currant and strawberry jam into a rawhide

[77]

packbag. Then he turned away, finished drying off his razor. Blaze looked at him carefully: wind-burned and weathered, a man of bone and muscle without a speck of fat. His clean overalls fit as though they had been painted on him, his black sateen shirt, the blue bandanna tied around his neck, were just like any Monday when he started the week all clean. Then Blaze turned to look at her mother. For all Hannah's hands so quick and deft over the packing of her gift, she had a look of holding a secret, something that didn't come just from a blue silk dress.

"Mother, you look just like those lace valentines I saw in the store in King City. You lift up a heart and underneath it says 'I love you.' " Startled by the quick flush on her mother's face, abashed at her own boldness, Blaze turned quickly to her father and asked shyly, "Is the birthday-present dress you bought me all right, Father?"

Her father squinched down his eyelids, teetered back on his heels and hung his thumbs from his overall pockets as he looked her over carefully. "Nothing much wrong with it, I guess. But I call that dress-top a pinch on the tight side. Didn't you have goods enough?"

Blaze looked harried, but her mother put in briskly, "Don't pick at the girl, Zande. I made that dress just like the pattern and it looks good; sets her off nice."

Her father snorted. "Too nice, I'd say. Shows damn near everything she's got."

Blaze felt furious. She walked over close to him, pulled up her skirt and thrust her foot forward. "Not quite everything," she said; "you missed these."

Her father's eyes brightened. "Green shoes! I never saw the like before."

Blaze stared at him, her quick anger dissolved in amazement, but he took no notice of her. He went over to the table, put his hand on his wife's shoulder for an instant before he picked up the rawhide bag. "I'll take this out now." He shifted the straps

[78]

in his big hands, half smiling as he said, "Your mother come to this country with the first pretty shoes I ever saw. You do favor your mother in lots of ways, my girl."

He walked out quickly and Blaze gasped. She looked helplessly at her mother and found her smiling, dabbing at her eyes. "That man," she murmured; "twenty years of him and he's still full of surprises." She chuckled at her puzzled daughter, saying, "I should of remembered that a liking for good leather is a weakness of your father's."

Suddenly, as the two women looked at each other, the kitchen bubbled with their suppressed laughter. Blaze finally said, "And I was cold-scared he'd see them, make me take them off!"

She jumped to her feet, hummed a scrap of a dance tune and gravely waltzed the length of the kitchen. "I know this is going to be the very best day I ever had in my life."

Amid the good-natured jeering of her brothers Blaze held up her skirts and daintily picked her way to the saddling shed. Neither of the boys said a word about the green shoes. Blaze watched her father give his hand for a step to her mother, watched her sail up into the saddle. Blaze was used to giving a run at Gipsy, getting mounted as easily as she vaulted a fence in her buckskins. For a moment she wondered if all the ruffles in the world were worth having your feet tied to the ground, but just then her father came over to her, his hand ready.

Her eyes danced at this acknowledgment that she was grown up. She stepped lightly on her father's big calloused hand, settled to her saddle like a bird on a twig, and spread her skirt as carefully as she saw her mother doing.

Zande swung into his saddle and Dandy, the big-boned black, swept off with his long swinging step that covered trail at amazing speed. Hannah fell in behind the black, and Blaze pulled Gipsy out ahead of Martin's roan. Last in line but perfectly happy about it, Avery ambled along on his runty pinto, his mouth organ breathing the tune to the *Ballad of the Big Sur Hills*. This was really an Allan song, for it had been made by Uncle Mel and the Mr. Avery that Avery was named for. Blaze often thought of Mr. Avery. He was a strange man who haunted the Coast the first summer her parents were married. Like Gran said about Uncle Mel, this Mr. Avery was a great cherisher of a music tune and the ballad had been made right on their own ranch. Uncle Mel had followed off after Mr. Avery and his music, and gone looking for a warm island off somewhere in the tropics. They never came back to the Coast again.

Blaze often thought life must have been romantic and wonderful back in those far-off days when there wasn't a stove or a proper cooking pot in all the Big Sur country.

Blaze turned all this over in her mind as Gipsy followed the trail, but she forgot it when the trail dropped into a big canyon and she saw the first wild iris of the year nodding its dark blue head to the talk of the stream.

It was called four miles from the Allan ranch to where the Jansons had built their new house on the old Ramirez place, but that was crow-fly trail. Bird miles took no heed of deep canyons. There were four canyons to cross with all the dips and swoops, the twists and turns a mountain trail had to take to get a horse, or even a foot traveler, safe across the steep and stony Santa Lucias.

Blaze came out of her dreaming to chuckle as Gipsy stopped suddenly to avoid running into the Ginger mare. Her father had sung out, "Anyone got any stock needs watering, here's your last chance. Around that redwood hill and we're in sight of the house."

Her mother protested indignantly, "Might as well squat right in their dooryard as to have you yelling about it at the top of your lungs."

The boys were laughing, holding in their horses but touching them up slyly at the same time, making them fidget. Their mother turned to look back at them and called out, "Ride on ahead if you're so anxious to get there, but you better wait for us around that turn."

Blaze and her mother pulled over as close as they could safely get to the trail's edge above the canyon and the boys rode carefully by the narrow spot.

The two women caught up with the men and as they rounded the redwood hill at its first turn the new house came in sight.

Hannah whispered, "What a house!"

Blaze couldn't answer. She had thought her father's house was pretty fine. Four rooms just for the family and a hall and storeroom beside had made it the best house on the Coast. But this wasn't a house she was riding up to. It was a log castle. It looked to Blaze like a king's house all mixed up with an Indian hogan. It seemed to have miles of roof, but all the roof lines had a strange fringe of long boards sticking up two feet in the air. Not only were there queer designs like wooden pictures hewn right into the oversized doors, there were big upright logs, all carved, too, and fitted into each of the house corners. On the west side, where the hill dropped sharply toward the sea, the house was three stories high. All the rest of it was two stories. There were wings running out and porches here and there, even on the second story. The Allan second story, the boys' attic that Blaze had been so proud of, shrank to a small thing.

As she rode closer to the big house Blaze began to lose confidence in her new finery, wished that she owned a hat. No wonder her mother looked so much at ease; her hair wasn't all blown around by the wind. It was neat and ordered beneath the black scoop bonnet tied firmly under her chin.

Blaze's head was down as she ran her hand quickly over her red crop, trying to smooth it into order before she had to dismount. But she lifted her head quickly as she heard her father mutter, "Be damned, the fellow's got his night rail stuffed into his pants."

His white teeth lighting up his bronzed face Stephen Janson was running gaily down the broad front steps. The shirt he wore was like nothing Blaze had ever seen. It was white homespun stuff, the sleeves fuller than any she'd ever seen. It had a collar but no buttons, just pulled over the head and the collar not even fastened. She thought her father was right; it did look like the top of a man's nightshirt and yet, somehow, it seemed nicer than any shirt she had ever seen.

"Welcome, neighbors," he called out cheerfully as he came closer. "Tie your horses to any of those rails and come in. Food and drink is all ready and we've found a guitar player too."

Blaze was terrified that he'd speak of meeting her. Her father was still staring at the stranger's queer shirt, but Hannah Allan said, "We are glad to have a close neighbor. We're the Allans, just four miles south. My husband"—Mr. Janson held out his hand and Zande touched it briefly. "Our sons, Martin and Avery." The boys both grinned but said nothing, looking a trifle uneasy.

"And I am Stephen Janson." Blaze felt her breath let go as he bowed politely to her mother, said nothing to her until her mother said, "Nice to meet you, Mr. Janson," and in the same breath said, "Blaze, our new neighbor, Mr. Janson. This is our daughter, Miss Allan."

Blaze held her breath again but he glanced at her, said "Miss Allan" very gravely, then turned back to her mother. "May I help you, please?"

He helped Hannah down, turned to Blaze and as he set her on the ground said, very softly, "I'm delighted to see you."

"What's that?"

Her father looked suspicious but Stephen Janson only said, "If you will excuse us, ladies, will you go right up to the house? I'll help with the horses then."

As though he had decided that everything was all right, Zande Allan got off his horse, stepped between his two women and the strange man, dismissed them with a wave of his hand, and motioned to the boys to ride over to the tie poles. He walked off beside Stephen Janson, drawling, "Queer business you're in, Mr. Janson, peeling the bark off trees. Any money in it?"

Blaze saw the look of annoyance cross her mother's face, but she gathered up her skirt and started picking her way toward the house through the litter of chopped logs, split shakes, crooked and rejected roofing poles and redwood chips that were left from building. "Martin will bring in the packbag," she said.

"Yes."

Blaze looked back and found her father absorbed in talk of the tan bark industry which was new on this part of the Coast. "Couldn't we wait for Father and the boys?" Blaze whispered. "I feel shy about going up there alone. Maybe his mother doesn't speak English."

"I guess if we smile and she smiles back, she'll know we're friendly. A smile talks every language."

Blaze smiled at her mother, but as she walked forward the big house made her feel that all her ways were as mountain-made as moccasins. She made up her mind to turn back, wait for her father, who was never scared of anything, man or mountain lion. But as she plucked at her mother's sleeve the wide door opened and the sound of a guitar playing a lively tune made Blaze lift her face eagerly. It was dance music!

Standing in the doorway was a tiny woman in a black dress, a crisp white apron tied around her waist, a frilled white cap on her head. No one could be frightened at such a doll-sized woman, even if she had been frowning. She was smiling, holding out both hands in a friendly way and saying, with a singing lilt to her voice, "Make yourselfs velcome, please."

Blaze felt that her mother was holding back a bit as she only bowed and said gravely, "Thank you."

Under the crisp white cap Mrs. Janson's hair was white, but she had the same deep-set blue eyes, smile-crinkled, and the same upturned mouth that had made Blaze think so often, this last month, of Stephen Janson. She wanted to make herself welcome and liked, though her mother seemed more sparing of words than usual.

"You must be Mrs. Janson?" Blaze smiled down at the neat little woman. "I'm Blaze Allan and this is Mother—Mrs. Allan," she corrected herself, feeling clumsy.

"Come in, come in," Mrs. Janson urged. "There is music, and smörgåsbord all set for everyones."

She turned and trotted briskly ahead of them down a hall that was as wide as the Allan kitchen. They passed three doors opening into this hall before Mrs. Janson stopped, opened a door and gestured them into a big room with windows on two sides.

There was a great oversized bed of some dark carved wood polished until it reflected the light from the windows. It was set on a platform of its own, one step above the floor and hung about with pleated white draperies. There was an elaborate white cover on the bed, but the thing that made Blaze gasp was a bolster covered like the bed and tied at the ends with great blue satin bows.

Her mother whispered down the back of her neck, "Don't gawk like you never saw anything before."

Blaze flushed but her mother turned to Mrs. Janson and said easily, "Hardanger work, isn't it? I never saw it done so nice before."

Blaze looked curiously from her mother to Mrs. Janson and saw that her mother had known the very word. Hardanger, whatever that was, brought a smile of happiness to the face of the new neighbor.

Her blue eyes were bright-misted and there seemed a sound of home-hunger in the way Stephen's tiny mother breathed, "Hardanger, yes. You know my country?"

"I worked for some Norwegian folks back East a long time ago."

Mrs. Janson sighed. "Foolish I am to be thinking back vhen this coast is like the fjords of home." She asked anxiously, "But do you know the feeling to be far from old friends, old vays?"

Hannah nodded. "I come here, a stranger, from the prairies. I liked the country fine but my heart held back for a time."

Smiling, eager, Mrs. Janson chimed in, "The green hills here in February, the flowers underfoot, so lovely! Dark vinter holds my homeland now, and foolish it is, but this wrong time for spring makes me feel too far, too new." She left the subject of her own country with a resigned little shrug of her plump shoulders. "Come now with, please." She was brisk and smiling as she opened the door and led her visitors down the hall. "Ve take the young miss to the music and the other young folks, yess? And you, Mrs. Allan, could you like with me to look at all the rooms and the cellar too? Such a nice little house and all so new, I enjoy to show it."

While Hannah was answering that she would like to see the house, Mrs. Janson opened a door close to the front entrance and ushered them into a room so large, so full of tables, books, pictures and people, that Blaze felt an impulse to shelter behind her mother. But as she got inside the room the confusion left when she saw that all the people sitting around stiffly were the folk she had known all her life. The one group who seemed to be making themselves very much at home were Pete Garcia, his tipsy mother and his slant-eyed sister Nella, intently staring across the room.

Blaze traced the glance and made a nose to herself as she saw the Portuguese girl was staring at Joe Williams. He seemed restive, his hands clutching his hard hat nervously, his eyes meeting Nella's glance for an instant and then looking quickly around to see if anyone was watching.

Blaze felt that she had never really looked at him before. Last year she would have thought his get-up was quite impressive. Now his soft-toed boots, his round-legged trousers, the tail coat with the split in the back draped either side of the chair, seemed slightly ridiculous—even the gold chain and crystal ball charm that looped across his crackling front.

She thought of the light touch of Stephen's big hand, the easy way he had helped her down off Gipsy. What a nice manner he had. How finished he looked, not dressed up. That wasn't what made his difference. He was brown, but he wasn't weathered. Big, but not clumsy.

Martin and Avery came clumping into the room and Blaze looked at them as she would at a stranger. Their feet and hands were big, like Stephen's, but they didn't know what to do with them. They didn't stand straight and they walked with a lope, like they were crossing a plowed field. Their hair stuck out.

Blaze looked around the room quickly. Every man there had rough-looking hair but Stephen. His fit his head. So it was partly his hair, partly that his hands never seemed to get in his way. And when he bowed, he took his time about it, made it seem a real greeting. She wished she knew some town-raised girl she could measure her own ways against. Maybe Mr. Janson and his mother noticed how awkward she was too.

Blaze almost wished the party was over, that she was back home in her own room looking down the canyon at the stars dipping into the sea's far edge. She needed time to study about all these new things and Stephen Janson.

She wished that he would come into the room, but when she heard her father's voice out by the front door, heard Stephen laugh as he answered, she couldn't stay in that big, strange room. He might walk right over to her, say something she wouldn't understand, couldn't answer. She didn't yet know what hardanger meant.

Her worried eyes caught Joe Williams looking at her and she hurried out of the room. There was a narrow door right across the room from the big entrance, and she stepped through, closed it after her. She would have liked to stay, watch the eager way Stephen's gay head lifted, see his square white teeth flash when he laughed.

But she closed the door against the cheerful voices and looked around. She was in a long kitchen and her mother and Mrs. Janson were smiling together over the brown loaves, the gift of preserves.

Mrs. Janson held the great brown loaf in her small hands, looked bright over it as she called, "But how good for you to come help with the smörgåsbord. Your mother helps too, and Tena, my niece, so is easy for all, yess."

Wondering where Tena was, Blaze answered shyly, "Glad to help, whatever I can do."

She felt furious to be so tongue-tied. Why couldn't she sound gay and easy, as these people did? But something to keep her hands busy was comforting. She felt so mixed up. One moment she wanted to run out the door and keep running until she was safe in her own room and didn't feel clumsy. The next moment she thought of carrying one of the great platters her mother was now busy filling with queer dishes, offering it to the blond giant who lived in this enchanted castle.

"Isn't this floor fine, Blaze?"

Her mother's voice had the wish hunger in it and Blaze looked at the floor, then looked all around at the kitchen, which was as big as any whole house on the Coast.

The floor was made of great crosscuts of redwood logs fitted together so that they all matched and made a solid flooring without any cracks to catch litter. The floor looked as solid, as lasting, as the stone part of the wall. It was laid up high enough

[87]

so that the windows were set half into the stone and then the rest of the wall was made of thick redwood planks. The planks were dressed down with something that made them smoother than a plane could get timber—maybe sandpaper, the girl thought. There was something fantastic to Blaze about all the work that must have gone into the building of this house. As she knew life, no matter how well menfolk used their time they never got enough time to take care of the fields and the cattle, the fencing and branding, the hay and the barns. All ranch work had to be done before any mending or fixing could be done to a house.

Whatever Blaze and her mother could mend around the house got done, but if it took a skill they didn't have, then no matter how bad it needed doing it might be days or weeks or forever before the men could spare time.

Whenever Hannah Allan spoke about a leak in the roof or a rotted floor board that needed fixing she always got the same answer, "You got the best house on the Coast and I got no time for fooling around with it now." Now he could never say again that they had the best house on the Coast, not after he'd looked at this one.

The gleaming new stove was twice as big as the famous Allan stove. It had all sorts of fixings to make it even handier than the one Blaze and her mother were so proud to have. Most of the other women along the Coast were still doing their cooking at a smoky fireplace, baking bread in a Dutch oven.

Hannah pointed out the copper-lined tank at the end of the stove which held water. "Gallons and gallons of it," she said, and it gets steaming hot, ready for dishes or the clothes wash just from the cooking fire." Blaze nodded. "And it doesn't take up all the top of the stove like a wash boiler set over the lids."

Built around the stove, like a little stone house with a half roof that jutted out over it was a smooth stone wall finished up with a bright copper hood. On each end there were benches set inside the stone wall so a body could sit out of the draught and dry himself on wet and windy days.

Blaze looked at her mother. "This house was all thought out ere ever a stone was laid," she said, her voice reflecting the wonder on her face.

Hannah laughed. "Must of been," she said, but her voice held almost a touch of envy as she went on, "Maybe they built the table first and then had to build a room big enough to hold the table."

Blaze looked at the great redwood table and started counting; it held plates for twenty people without much crowding. There was no tablecloth, but the top of the table had been smoothed and polished until dishes and silver were reflected in it almost like in a mirror.

But even more amazing to Blaze than a table big enough for twenty plates was the fact that the plates were all alike: twenty gleaming white plates with a narrow band of blue around their edge, and not a cracked plate in the lot!

Mrs. Janson bustled over from the stove, fussing, "That Tena. She has vent vhere? Well, we look once more the table at and if all is there, we call peoples for the eating."

Blaze stood by the table and put her finger lightly on one of the fringed squares of snowy cloth with a pattern of wild roses somehow woven into the goods. Her mother's voice came softly behind her, "Napkins. You wipe your fingers on them." Blaze took her finger hastily off the napkin, still wondering what sort of cloth it was. Instinct told her that the heavy cloth she had just touched was good, solid—like ripe wheat or cold spring water is a good, solid thing. She felt bewildered. Her father was the most prosperous rancher on the Coast, but in the Allan house there were no fringed napkins, no gleaming stack of blue-rimmed plates.

There were not even enough store dishes for the family, and what they had must be eked out with gourd bowls, bark platters.

[89]

Blaze felt sad to think that the money she had spent for her new dress and shoes might have been enough to buy her mother the set of dishes she wanted. Every year when the steers were driven to market Hannah Allan always asked if there wouldn't be money this year to spare for a set of china. Her father always said there was too much truck in the house already.

Mrs. Janson picked up a tiny bell and opened the door to the big room. Under cover of the bell's silvery chime Blaze whispered to her mother, "There's so much I don't know anything about that I feel like a big gawk. If I could work in this sort of place for a while—"

Her mother whispered, "It would be a good thing for you, child, but your father would never hear to it; you know that."

Blaze drew a long sigh, but there was rebellion in her whispered, "I'm going on twenty-one now. He can't run my whole life, can he?"

Her mother didn't answer and Blaze thought of how rough and careless the Allan men were in the house in spite of her mother's gentle ways. They ran their greasy fingers along their buckskins when they were eating. Their mother was always reminding the boys to wash before they came in for meals. People like the Jansons must think that Coast people were just trash.

If she could only get rid of the strange feeling that the light in Stephen's eye, the touch of his hand, had put on her. Ever since she got long dresses most of the Coast men and boys had looked at her with that strange glow in their eyes, but it never meant a thing to her. She looked right back at them and laughed. They were all alike to her; men or girls seemed much alike. She tried to wish that she had stayed home, never had this strange unsettling feeling, and yet she knew she'd rather have it, be miserable with it than never to have seen him at all. It seemed queer that an unhappy ache could be something too precious to put away.

Blaze could hear Stephen talking to his guests in the hall between the kitchen and the big room. How warm his voice sounded and he had an easy word for everyone that passed. Now he was talking to Joe Williams. She could hear Joe's nervous voice trying to meet the ease of the stranger.

"No, no, Mr. Williams, there is room for everyone inside. You'll find a place saved for you. First eat and drink, then we will dance and be gay."

Joe came through the door and Blaze saw him tapping his head. He was signaling to the others that their host was touched. Martin grinned, raised his eyebrows, but to his sister's amazement he walked right through the kitchen out the back door.

As each guest came timidly in, Mrs. Janson stood waiting with warm smiles and still more words that seemed too hearty to the cautious, self-contained Coasters.

"Here vill you sit and right down, please," she sang out, shooing each one to a place not of their choosing, but of hers. Blaze saw that she was breaking up families, putting husbands, not alongside their proper mates, but even on the other side of the table and possibly next some woman his own wife had been jealous of at the last barbecue.

"This will be Coast talk for the next twenty years," Blaze told herself as she turned to the stove to lift one of the great coffeepots. She stood holding it, forgetful of how hot the handle seemed even through the thick pot-lifter, when she saw Nella Garcia stop in the doorway, lean toward Stephen and try her dimples on him as she challenged, "You been saving me a place by you, Mr. Janson?"

"You are a mind reader," he flashed back at her. Blaze felt her heart suddenly as hot and black as the coffee she was getting ready to pour. "How was it you figured, Mamma? Miss Garcia here on my left, isn't it?"

"So that is, yess! And for me on my right comes our neighbor Mr. Allan. At the left—who vas it?" She ran over to a sort of chest with shelves and a mirror above it, peered at a paper lying on top of the chest. "To my left goes Mr. Tom Logan from the tan bark camp."

It seemed to Blaze that Tom Logan sent a regretful glance over to Nella as the hulking tan bark foreman with his hammer hands and hammerhead, small for the great body, came around the table slowly. He walked as though trying to tread on air and still his shoe-calks left scars on the floor.

"You can the coffee start now, Miss Allan," Mrs. Janson called out; "more peoples to come but we keep hot for them. Where is that Tena?"

There was a squeal of laughter just outside the kitchen, the door flew open and in bounced a girl that looked like a live doll. Flaxen hair in thick braids hung over her shoulders and down to her waist, her eyes were china-doll blue and her face as rosy-pink as morning. Martin let go of the strings of her striped apron just as she came into the room. He was blushing but he followed her into the room in spite of all the curious eyes turned on him.

"But he was holding onto me, Aunt Kari!"

Martin ducked his head and looked helpless as Mrs. Janson hurried forward. "This big fellow, vas it, Tena?" she teased. "And for that he must then sit by—let me look—yess, here." She pointed to a chair two places away from Tom Logan, and Martin dropped into it as though glad to be settled.

"Tena," called the little lady, "you sit over here by this Mr. Allan we vait yet for."

Blaze saw her mother clutch the other coffeepot and she felt nervous herself. Another Mr. Allan? Could that be Zande coming with Dulcie, maybe with her mother too? Her knees felt weak at the thought. How would their father act?

But she soon had no time to worry about that. Mrs. Garcia wavered into the kitchen, her feet uncertain, her smile a trifle vacant and refused to sit down. "Wha's a matter? Who wants to eat? Pete, get the guitar and le's all dance. Come on! Come on!"

Zande Allan stood up and Blaze almost let go the coffeepot. It would be just like him to start quoting strong words out of the Book, all about whoring and drinking and hellfire. Blaze had heard him on the subject of Mrs. Garcia and her drinking and he didn't mince words. She clutched her coffeepot, and prayed in her heart, oh, please sit down and shut up; sit down and shut up.

Stephen was talking to Nella who acted as though she wasn't at all put out at the show her mother was making of herself. But as Stephen caught sight of Zande Allan towering up at the other end of the table, he slapped his hands together and said, "That's a good idea! Mamma, couldn't we hold the coffee back while Mr. Garcia played just one tune?"

Blaze closed her eyes, expecting an outburst from her father, thinking, I'll just die. I'd rather be dead than hear him go on like he can when he gets started.

Stephen ran into the other room, came back almost at once with the guitar. Nella was laughing, her dimples twinkling as the guitar was put into her brother's hand.

Nella flashed a knowing look at the two men and then made her way down the length of the table, slipped her arm through the rigidly held arm of Zande Allan. Blaze thought she sounded sticky as damp cake frosting when she almost laid her dimpled cheek against Zande's leathery face and whispered, "Thank you so much, Mr. Allan. If you'll just dance her around the table once then she'll sit down if you say so. To handle Ma takes a strong man like you." Nella's fingers tightened over Zande's and she whispered, her mouth close to his ear, "Thanks, Mr. Allan."

Looking slightly puzzled and not a bit righteous Zande went over to Mrs. Garcia, bowed a bit stiffly, but as Pete Garcia struck into a lively schottische, the two dancers galloped off.

Blaze turned a worried face toward her mother and found her struggling with laughter. As she caught her daughter's anxious glance she gave a chuckle. "That girl's a smooth piece, all right. She's got the right idea for handling the stubborn critters."

Blaze knew she must have looked as bewildered as she felt, for her mother said sharply, "You've got a lot to learn about men, my girl. Better put the coffeepot back on the stove before it gets cold. Your pa will dance now till the tune's done; you'll see."

Blaze watched Pete Garcia, his heaa thrown back and his black eyes shining, as he speeded up the time and the couple fairly flew around the room, their clicking and stomping helped out by a hup hap of palms slapped together in time with the catchy tune. Clear around the room, passing the big hot stove, around the big table once more, and then Pete laughed.

"I'm starved." He balanced the guitar against the wall behind him and picked up his spoon, clapped it against the rim of his cup and called out, "You ladies saving that coffee for your own selves?"

Blaze turned to the stove, picked up the coffeepot again and following her mother's example, filled each cup as she came to it. At home they always filled the men's cups first, but by now she was sure her mother knew how things were done in a fine place like this. She turned this thought in her mind as she went quietly about pouring the strong black coffee into the thin cups. Her mother knew how to do with things, but at doing without, making something else do, she still had it all over everyone. Her mother was wonderful.

Trotting briskly around, Mrs. Janson was looking out for her guests, urging them to try this, try that, and offering strange-smelling cheese, queer dark fish to men and women who tried to keep a look of panic off their faces. Faced with a coyote or a mountain lion none of them would have any doubt whatever about what to do. But an unhealthy-looking cheese with queer seeds or green streaks of mold in it—even the stoutest-hearted shrank from taking hold of such a thing. Not Mrs. Garcia, though. She heaped her plate with anything passed to her and started right in to eat without even turning it over with her fork or acting suspicious.

Hannah filled her husband's cup with coffee and moved on to Jauro Garcia's chair as Mrs. Janson hastened forward from the stove carrying a great platter. "Take lots from the fiskaballa, Mr. Allan," she urged. "Is best in the vorld." She set the platter down, took up the big spoon and said firmly, "I'll help."

Zande Allan looked at the platter. "If that there's fish, I don't want none."

Mrs. Janson laughed. "You never taste fishes till you taste my fiskaballa; nothing is better."

"I don't want none of it."

Blaze felt her eyes smart at her father's gruff refusal. And to make sure he was safe from fiskaballa, he'd picked up his still empty plate, turned it over. Mrs. Janson colored slightly, but she passed it off. "You be sorry after vhen you taste vonce." She laughed and carried the dish over to place before her son.

The lids were down over his deep-set eyes and Blaze thought he was taking care that no one should see the anger that must be in them. If a man came to the Allan house and turned up his nose that way at food his wife had fixed, her father would toss him right out the door and never bother to dust off his hands.

As though he were thinking of nothing else, Stephen speared out three of the roundest, brownest fishballs, smiled up at his mother and then suddenly turned his head and looked at Blaze. He didn't look angry. His eyes were as deeply blue and merry as usual and yet, in spite of herself, Blaze felt timid.

He patted the bench on his right hand, indicating the empty place, and said, "I'm still waiting for you to sit here."

The coffee cups were all filled, the coffeepot was light now to handle. Mrs. Janson was already settling herself alongside Zande Allan, her mother had returned her coffeepot to the stove and was sitting talking to Bud Masters.

Blaze knew she must go sit down, but it seemed that she had never done anything harder than to walk the distance of halfway around the big table. Her feet felt big, heavy, she'd forgotten all about her pretty green shoes. She knew her hands hung awkwardly and she could hear the loud clump of her unaccustomed heels on the hard floor. But the long journey was over at last and she sat down as quietly as she could, clasped her hands in her lap and dreaded to look up from her plate.

Stephen picked up the plate, put onto it some of everything that was within his reach, and handed it to her.

She hoped he didn't see that her hands were shaking when she took the plate from him.

"Thanks."

That was all she could say and she didn't look at him. Trying to pretend she felt at ease she leaned over the table and said, "Pass that cold beef, will you, Martin?"

Martin jumped. He reached for the plate too quickly, tipped over the holder with the extra spoons.

As the spoons clattered across the bare table top the tension inside her let go. Her confusion over her own lack of grace vanished when she felt Martin's horror at having called attention to himself. It suddenly didn't matter one bit to her what these elegant Jansons thought of their mountain ways. But it was important that Martin should not feel so abashed.

"Good shot, Martin!"

Blaze reached boldly for the platter that Martin was holding onto as though it were slippery, said, "Save me one of the spoons, Martin, before you start them around. If the Jansons are like the rest of us Coasters, they're short of spoons."

Martin gathered up the spoons, passed one over to Blaze and handed the holder to Mrs. Masters.

Blaze turned the spoon in her fingers, unable to resist the charm of a spoon that not only had some gold-colored metal laid onto the bowl, but had the picture of a castle and some strange-looking words printed right into the silver handle.

Stephen was leaning toward her but she took no notice until he said, "We must be short of lots of things, I suppose. We won't care as long as we're not short of good neighbors."

Blaze looked around the big room and then back at her host. "I don't notice any lack," she said. "Here in the hills we go pretty plain and count ourselves lucky to have enough to last from one harvest to the next."

She wondered why she had to sound exactly like her father.

Stephen Janson looked at her admiringly. "That is what I think is so wonderful here. You make your own life. Out in the old cities people struggle to make an art of living. Here it seems to me life is itself art."

If anyone had asked Blaze just what those words meant she could not have told. But they gave her the same feeling that she had when she looked out of her window this very morning and felt that there was more in life than just being alive. Then she felt that she was the only one in the world who looked out of a window, down a dark canyon and across a bright sea and thought that life was more than three dozen eggs gathered, a better price for beef—life was something that should turn and spin like the sun, be warm and wonderful. Now she was sitting beside a man who said words about life as though it was something you could take into your own hands, shape to your own needs.

She didn't try to answer, just sat still, filled with a happiness that seemed almost too bright and shining. She hoped it didn't show, and was glad when Pete Garcia finished chewing up the coffee grounds he'd spooned up out of his cup and said, "Any-

one that's aiming to dance better be at it. I'm not going to be
playing tunes all afternoon."

"You got anything better to do?"

Tom Logan winked at Pete, ran his eye over Nella, who
looked back at him for an instant and then lowered her eyes.

Pete looked at Tom and his sister and then drawled, "I bet
you wish you did—" and his lazy fingers stroked the guitar
strings as softly as though they were a woman's hair.

There was a sound of running feet and Dulcie Gallo Allan
came breathlessly through the door, calling, "It's my fault that
we're late. Don't anyone go blame my husband. I got him dancing and we both forget it was late."

Stephen jumped up, went to meet her and swung both her
hands in his as though she were a little girl. "How's the bride?"
he asked.

Dulcie blew out her cheeks, batted her eyes and gave a good
imitation of her mother's shrug. "It's awful," she pouted, "that
man of mine, eating in the cookhouse like he is, still he asks
me will I make apple pie?"

"Perhaps we ought to put some pressure on the cook," Stephen
laughed. "I thought he made lots of pie."

Dulcie nodded. "Sure. He makes 'em. But Zande wants apple
pie in the house too. So I worked like anything all this morning
on that pie."

Back of her Young Zande stood smiling proudly as though to
say, "Isn't she wonderful?"

Dulcie saw that she had an audience so she went on rapidly,
"I thought first what is it makes apple pie? Apples, I tell myself. So I boiled up a lot of apples. Pie goes into a crust, so I
made the best corn massa, I patted it thin as thin and that
wasn't easy because I put lots of grease in—then"—she shrugged
her shoulders, looked up at Stephen earnestly—"I fried that tor-
tilla just so crisp you could kiss it and I dumped in them apples.
That's all."

[98]

She turned as though that really was all, but Stephen caught her plump shoulder, held her back and said, "That's not half of it. How did your husband like the pie?"

She turned both her tiny plump hands palm upward, pursed out her lips and sighed, "Santa Maria, that one. He took one look, not even taste, mind you—and then he says, 'This is not pie.' And I worked on it all morning!"

Young Zande looked self-conscious but he put his arm around Dulcie and coaxed, "Never mind the old pie, Mrs. Allan. Let's eat; I'm starved." He smiled at his host, "We're sorry to be late."

Mrs. Janson hurried over with two hot plates full of fiskaballa, ham, cheese, herrings and thin slices of dark bread full of caraway seeds. "Plenty more, no one comes late, any time you come is food and music. Sit now." She led Dulcie over to sit by Martin Allan, Young Zande went next to Tena and Nella Garcia, who immediately started whispering to him.

Apparently quite unconcerned over the effect the wiles of Nella might have on her husband, Dulcie bent over her plate and started eating like a hungry child.

Hannah got up from her place, came over and said, "I'm glad to see you here, Dulcie. Blaze and I were going up to see you but Avery said there was no one living on your mother's ranch."

Dulcie popped half of one of the crisp fish balls into her mouth, chewed, and when she'd swallowed it, said, "Well, thanks, Mrs. Allan; it's our ranch now. Ma give it to us, but I can't cook, only a little Spanish stuff, and so it's better we live down to the camp, eat in the cookhouse. I don't like housekeeping anyway."

Hannah looked amused as she said, "Well, there's plenty of time; you'll learn when you need to."

Dulcie shrugged. "I guess he don't care so much for a cook anyway. This way, we got time for fun. Zande only works ten hours now—then he's all done; none of them chores, and so we laugh, we dance, we fool around and have fun. Is best way."

"Yes," Hannah said softly, "it's nice to be young and happy. And if you need any help, with sewing or anything, you ride up to the house and Blaze and I will help you."

Dulcie looked at her curiously for a moment, then she said, "You talk nice, Mrs. Allan, but my mother, she give me plenty stuff. We don't need nothing."

She jumped, startled when her father-in-law said harshly, "That's a good thing. Stay that way."

Blaze held her breath as the two Zandes measured looks for a moment, but Pete Garcia picked up his guitar, started playing the old *Coast Waltz* and called out, "Here's your music; don't waste it!"

Blaze sat rigidly, between the strained relations of her family and the fear that if Stephen asked her to dance she wouldn't be able to follow any strange foreign steps.

He didn't ask her. Instead he shoved back from the table, went down to her mother, bowed and held out his arm. A lifetime of hard work had done nothing to Hannah Allan's slender grace and Blaze felt proud of her mother as she saw her moving smoothly and evenly as though the two dancers were a bolt of ribbon being unwound on a level table.

Bud Masters, a young fellow from Santa Cruz, who had married Alice Ramirez, was the first to ask Blaze for the waltz. She started dancing, thinking that Alice was out either nursing the youngest baby or changing a diaper on the next to the youngest. It seemed to her a pity that Alice, who used to be the dancingest girl on the Coast, had babies so fast she never had time for dancing. Bud danced smooth too, and as though he really enjoyed it a lot. But she couldn't spend her time worrying about other people's babies. Maybe Dulcie had the right idea—let someone else cook and housekeep, find time to laugh and dance, be a friend to your husband.

Blaze found a new interest in watching Stephen dancing, watching her mother smiling, talking easily to the young Norwegian. Her mother had something of the same ease and smoothness in her voice, her gestures, that set Stephen Janson out from the rest of the men.

Alice, a baby draped over each hip, put her head into the room and called, "Bud!" She sounded impatient and Bud hurriedly led Blaze back to the table, seated her and left to join his wife.

For a time Blaze enjoyed looking about at the dancers, thinking that her father looked nice. He always did look fine in his work clothes, buckskins or overalls, a bright scarf over his black sateen shirt. Zande Allan wore those things as easily as he wore his own hide. But put him in his black cloth store-suit and a tie and he didn't look right at all.

Joe Williams got up from where he had been sitting near Pete and edged through the dancers until he was standing behind Blaze. He bent over and said softly, "You been thinking this is a good time to tell the neighbors we're getting married in May?"

She looked at him steadily. "Why should I think anything like that? I told you what I thought and nothing will change my mind."

He sat down beside her, leaned toward her with a show of devoted interest that set her nerves on edge and said calmly, "You don't know how your mind can change. You don't know how crazy for you I am, Blaze. Might be I'd have to hurt you some to get you, but I'll make it up to you."

Blaze looked up and saw that Stephen Janson was looking at her over her mother's shoulder. She made herself smile at Joe as she said, "Would you like me to tell my brothers what you were telling me yesterday?"

"You won't need to do that. I'll tell them myself if I have to. I only want you to remember I love you, Blaze. You're like my breath to me. I got to have you."

Blaze shrank away as far as she could and whispered, "Please let me alone, Joe. I'm sorry, but that's how it is."

He stood up slowly, bowed politely, his voice still soft as he said, "I've been watching you." Startled, she looked up at him and felt chilled at the strange look in his eyes. There was something inhuman about that glow deep under his steady staring. Blaze caught her breath as he moved away, felt her arms roughen as she shivered. For the first time she wondered if he was completely sane. She felt a sense of shame at having such a thought about Joe, but she could not get rid of the idea.

She looked around to see if she could catch Martin's eye, but he wasn't in sight. Neither was Tena. Avery was eating at the young folks' table in the out-kitchen. Then she saw that Joe Williams was whispering something behind his hand to Pete and that they were both looking at her. Pete's face seemed sly and amused and as he caught her glance he winked at her, started the same tune all over.

Feeling she couldn't sit still any longer, Blaze began to gather up the dishes within reach, but Mrs. Janson saw her. "Not at all, Miss Allan. The table makes nothing. They finish this dance and then in the parlor ve go for dancing and a little tastè aquavite."

Pete looked interested. Over the sound of his guitar he called, "What we do with the arkvite? Do we smell it, rub it on or drink it?"

"You do not aquavite know? Make finish the valtzing and ve show you something."

Pete's limber fingers swept out one more chorus and then he turned the instrument over, began drumming a quick march step on the back of his guitar.

The dancers halted but Stephen fell into step with the march time and brought Hannah Allan back to her place at the table. Then with his head back, laughing, he marched over to Blaze, bowed, holding out his arm. "Would you dance this?"

Hesitantly Blaze put her fingers on his arm but as she fell into step with the music she was smiling, her head lifted as she and Stephen led the march into the big room with the fireplace.

Pete strolled in last playing very softly one of the old Swiss airs that had been played so long on the Coast that they were called Coast tunes. Without waiting for anyone else to begin, Stephen swung into a smooth, yet fast and whirling waltz.

It was like no step the girl had ever danced before but it suited the music, it suited her mood. She forgot that anyone else was in the room. The music turned the world and the whole world swung with the music and their flying feet.

No one else started dancing. Everyone was watching, but Blaze was scarcely conscious of her neighbors' eyes.

If life could only be always like this. Not corn to hoe, beds to make, meat to smoke—none of that—only the blue light of early afternoon and feet floating soundlessly forever.

She came from her dream with a start as she felt Stephen's lips close to her ear, heard his whisper, "In Norwegian I could tell you what I'm thinking."

She flushed but she looked up into his eyes as she answered, "Music talks Norwegian too."

"Wonderful!" He was looking at her curiously. "You are not like any girl I've ever seen. I've been thinking of you ever since New Year's Day."

Her eyes traced the pattern of the smoothly laid floor. It was better than trying to talk when she didn't know exactly what he meant. Confusedly she thought that she didn't even know what she meant when she said music talks Norwegian.

Worry that perhaps she should not have said it kept her silent and she was almost glad when his mother called from the kitchen door, "A little help I vould like here from Miss Allan vhen this show-off valtz is done."

Pete hit a discord, stopped playing. "It's all stopped, right now. Maybe we'll find out what this arkvite is and I don't mind saying I'm dry."

Stephen was still holding onto her fingers, urging, "I want another dance. Save me the next one, will you? Please?"

Her heart was singing his word "wonderful" but she answered, "Maybe I won't dance any more today." Before he could protest, she broke from his hold and went to the kitchen.

Everything *was* wonderful. And not the least part of it was the satisfying swish of the flounces around her feet, the flash of the green slippers.

How good Mother was, to make her this dress. It must be the dress that made this man who had been all over the world look at her so warmly, say "wonderful." How good Father was too. He hated to spend money, but he gave her the gold to buy bolts of stuff so she and Mother could have their petticoats and ruffles, ride out in shining silk, good as anyone. Never in all her life had a day seemed so perfect. Even Father was behaving. He might have rounded on Mrs. Garcia. But he hadn't. She had feared he would have hard words with Zande and Dulcie. But it all passed off so easily. This was her day.

Pushing open the door to the kitchen, Blaze found Mrs. Janson filling two trays of small stemmed glasses with something that was colorless as water. The plump little lady took great care to get each glass filled exactly alike, each one so nearly brimful that Blaze thought it was going to be hard to carry the tray and not spill anything.

The glasses filled, Mrs. Janson opened a cupboard door, put what was left of the watery-looking stuff in the cupboard along with a lot of other bottles of various sizes, shapes and colors.

She explained, "All from home." She shook her head and sighed, "So many miles of vater back avay, who knows vhenever?" Her round elbows lifted slightly. "So it is —Vell, ve go now."

She lifted one tray and motioned Blaze to take the other.

Blaze followed slowly, holding back until she could see how Mrs. Janson was serving her guests. Noting that all the women were being served first she followed her hostess's example, feeling gay as she passed right by the waiting men. It seemed a fine thing that for once they should have to wait.

Blaze wondered if the liquid in the glasses was sweet, but mostly she wondered if it would fall to her lot to carry Stephen his glass. Taking a quick count she judged it would work out that way. Mrs. Janson would reach her father just as she got to Stephen.

But at that moment Blaze felt nervous. The courage that grew out of her new ruffles, the happiness that was bright as creek water left her when she found Stephen and her father so busy arguing about tan bark that neither man noticed she was there.

Stephen was saying, "I was at school in England when I first heard about the California tan oak. You know the English are great leather workers, getting leather and dyes from all over the world."

Her father said, "It's best to learn to use stuff that's close to hand; that's how we do."

Stephen laughed. "You can do that. California seems to have almost everything anyone would need, but other places are not so fortunate. The English market will take all the bark I can get out. I'm opening another camp next fall, farther down the Coast."

Blaze stood uneasily, wondering if she should interrupt or should put the tray on the small table near them, take her glass and go sit down beside her mother.

Mrs. Janson sailed up to the two men but she didn't wait. "Here is, Mr. Allan," she chirped; "take now or avay it goes."

Zande looked around, frowned and said, "Eh?" Then he saw the tray and rather doubtfully took one of the few glasses left on it. Stephen, too, reached absently toward the tray that Blaze held out to him, murmured, "Thank you" without looking at her and went on with his talking.

Blaze put the tray down, took the last glass and walked toward her mother. Pete Garcia crossed the floor, stopped Blaze before she reached her mother, and bent over her to whisper coaxingly, "Tomorrow I'll be waiting on the trail by Lime Creek. Going down to the beach for abalone. I'll show you a cave no one knows about, if you happen along."

Blaze laughed, shook her head. "The boys have to cut wood tomorrow. Father wouldn't let me go with you unless one of them was along; you know that."

He leaned closer to her. "Do you have to tell him? You're no baby to have to ask if you can go. I'll be waiting for you." For an instant he looked at her, his bold eyes holding a look that Blaze found provoking. She didn't want to go to the beach with Pete, not a bit. But she did want to be able to go if she felt like it. She covered her feeling with a smile and said mockingly, "Don't wait too long, Pete. You'll get cold."

He said, "I won't get cold, not when I'm waiting for you," and turned away.

Blaze slipped over to join her mother and Alice Masters who had the baby on her lap and three other children crowding against her.

Stephen put his glass down on the table beside him, clapped his hands together for attention. All the noses bent over the glasses for a cautious smell before tasting something strange, now raised and carefully blank eyes were leveled at the young man.

He lifted his glass. "This is the drink of my homeland," he said gravely. "A word of welcome and a toast to us all, new friends in a new land. I would like to share this with you in the ancient way of my land."

He waited a moment but no one spoke. No one wanted to chance answering. This was new; nothing to rush into.

Since no one raised a voice against whatever might be the old custom in Norway, Stephen smiled and said, "So—I taste the drink first so that you all know it is not poison—"

As fright, suspicion and anger flew about the room in exchanged glances, it seemed to Blaze that Stephen was almost on the edge of laughing. His next gesture did nothing to quiet the unease of his new neighbors. Stephen tipped his glass slightly so that a few drops fell on the polished floor, bent his head and watched the slow drip of the liquid. Then he looked around, his eyes bright with comradeship as he murmured, "To the old gods underground that this house may have a foundation of peace."

He set the glass down for a moment, then picked it up, turned the stem in his fingers. "And now the toast." He drew himself up, tall, golden and smiling as he looked around and called out, "Good luck, good health, good friends together always!"

There was a muffled response of "Kindness!" Glasses were raised, motioned outward as though to salute the house and its owners, and then everyone took a careful taste.

Most of the men seemed pleased with the fiery taste, but the women shuddered, made wry faces and looked shocked.

Alice put her glass down with finality. "You'll have to excuse me," she said stiffly. "That's liquor and I'm nursing the baby."

Stephen protested, "But this is the water of life; it wouldn't harm even a baby. And you see how I gave a taste to the old gods; they will protect you."

Zande Allan frowned, but he sounded more curious than quarrelsome as he asked, "What gods you talking about? Ain't but the one God, less'n you're a heathen."

He was raising his glass slowly to his lips as Stephen answered, "But the gods are as many as the blessings of men. The gods are as old as memory, and as strange."

Zande's eyes watched his joyous neighbor coldly as he took

[107]

his first taste of the liquid in his glass. He pulled the glass from his lips, set it down on the table angrily.

Blaze, who hadn't tasted the drink, felt her hand tighten around the stem, her back go cold as she saw her father's gesture. Trouble, there was trouble coming.

"What sort of business is this?"

Instantly there was tension in the room. Zande Allan didn't speak that way unless he meant to follow up his words. Blaze saw her mother's hands tighten over each other, the blue veins stand out and her head tilt warily as her husband took a step toward his host.

"What is it? What's the matter?" Stephen sounded bewildered.

"This here stuff *is* hard liquor, like Alice said."

Zande's voice sounded deadly. Stephen seemed confused as he answered, "But, of course, it's liquor—what else would it be?"

Zande's roar shook him and everyone listening. "You stand right there and tell me you let my girl carry that stuff around? Let her give it to the women—to my wife? What do you think you're doing, putting that devil's brew into a young girl's hands?"

"But I don't understand, Mr. Allan. What would you drink a toast in if not in good liquor?"

"Understand? You bet your life you understand. Just like you did when I told you what I thought of bringing your tan bark business into a ranching country, stealing the boys right off their own places with your dollar a day. You tolled off one of my boys with your Judas silver and now you're starting the ruin of my girl. We're through with you, and don't forget it."

Hannah Allan went over to her husband, her face worried as she begged, "Zande, don't be foolish!"

He looked down at her. "Get whatever stuff we got laying around here," he ordered, "and be quick about it. We're leaving right now."

Blaze found she was still clutching the delicate glass. She set it down. This was how it was. This was how it always would be. It was useless to hope for even a little happiness.

Mrs. Janson came over to Hannah, holding out her hand and as Hannah took it, said, "I vill come see you. You are very velcome."

Hannah's smile, her daughter noticed, was an effort but she managed one of a sort as she said, "You are very kind. Thank you."

Blaze found herself praying that they could get away quietly. She wanted to get started before her father made things worse. But she had little hope that they would leave quietly.

At the door Zande stopped, turned, his angry eyes hunting Stephen Janson. "You," he said, "with your old gods. I thought poor of you from the minute I saw this place, but I was willing to give a stranger a chance. You're a foreigner and I made allowance for that, even held back when you started that wild talk about your old gods. Pour out hard liquor for your gods if that's your way in your country. But in this country you don't give strong drink to women and girls."

Blaze tried to swallow the pain she thought would choke her. Her head was bowed and she felt that her feet were frozen to the floor.

"Blaze!"

The harsh file of her father's tone rasped her hurts. In spite of herself she shivered. Pete had edged over behind her and he whispered, "Don't forget I'll be waiting by Lime Creek."

She didn't answer. Pete didn't exist for her. She tried to take one last glance at Stephen Janson, but she was afraid. As quietly as she could she followed her parents, aware of the silence in the room she was leaving. Stephen said nothing. Not one of their neighbors said good-by. She caught a glimpse of her mother's white face and felt she'd never be able to hold up her head on the Coast again.

Zande strode off toward their horses, calling angrily, "Martin! Avery! Get along here and look smart about it."

Silently the two women walked toward the mounting block and Blaze wished that she were dead. Dully she wondered how long anyone could live, feeling every instant that they were smothering.

Avery came running from around behind the house, still laughing. He ran up protesting, "Aw, we're not going home, are we? It's my next turn at the horseshoes!"

"Where's Martin?"

At that tone the laughter left Avery's eyes and his thin face became a peaked triangle. He turned to his mother and she nodded. "Tell your father if you know," she said.

Avery's eyes darted around as though seeking something and he said, reluctantly, "He's gone someplace. Some of them walked off and he went along."

"Well, don't stand there then, go find him and then the both of you come along."

In spite of her feeling that she'd never breathe again, Blaze felt some warmth return to her as Avery walked soberly across a corner of the dooryard, making for the little canyon with the redwoods. How good Avery was, how dear and how smart! She felt sure that Tena, as well as Martin, were with the ones that had gone for a walk. But Avery would never tell any more than he had to; he was always loyal and loving.

Zande looked after his youngest for a moment and then started tightening cinches, led the horses over to the mounting block. Headed homeward the horses stepped out as though sure they'd soon be shed of their saddles and rolling in the pasture.

To Blaze the journey seemed endless. Her dream of kneeling by her own window, of watching dusk come slowly over the sea, of waiting for the wishing-star low on the west—those dreams were gone. The heart that had pushed quicksilver through her veins such a short time ago now beat slowly.

Her father had killed her dream as completely as though it were dead of a gun shot. She knew how it would be now. Once inside the Allan gate he would give his orders and there was nothing to do but take them. Her father wouldn't have to order Stephen Janson to stay off the place. Even if Stephen seemed to like her a little no man would overlook such an insult given in his own house. She had seen the last of the first man she'd ever taken notice of. There was nothing left now but work.

V

BY noon of the day after the Janson party, Zande Allan had stopped pointing out morals and lecturing on the evils of drink. Twelve o'clock dinner was even enlivened by talk between the father and his boys of firing up the forge, starting shoeing the saddle horses.

Blaze asked, "Could you leave Gipsy until later? I'd like to go for a ride as soon as I finish the dishes."

Her father answered, "Well, all right. But mind you don't go far, and get back early. There's a big windstorm making up."

Blaze looked out of the window. Not a leaf was stirring on the trees; even the tall grass was still. "I'll be back before the wind gets here," she said.

As she rode away slowly, taking in the bright, still day through her eyes, her nose, the last thing she heard was her father reminding Martin and Avery to see that anything which could blow away was safe under cover, to fasten down coops and bar all doors before nightfall. Blaze looked at the clear sky and shook her head, half smiling.

Under the redwoods, in a sheltered place a thousand feet closer down to the Coast, Blaze smelled mushrooms. She knew her mother prized these redwood glade mushrooms as much for their beauty as for their tremendous size. But when she found them, instead of stout white stems, pale fawn top and jewel-pink underside, they were old, tattered and tipsy black derelicts. She got back on Gipsy thinking that it was strange that their fragrance was still as savory as when they were new and bright.

Riding down the canyon she turned in her mind the fact that dying mushrooms were sweet, dying roses sweeter than new ones, and dying pine-tips were sweetest of all. She tried to laugh, think it was funny, when it suddenly occurred to her that woods things were better off than humans. Dying people were not sweet. But the laugh wouldn't ome. She wished she hadn't thought of death coming in such an ugly way.

As she dropped down another thousand feet, the canyon widened out, the stream grew less turbulent and she rode slowly, looking at the pools. It would be fun if she could see a big salmon come up the stream to spawn like they did in February, chase one into the shallows and get it with a rock. The boys hadn't been out for salmon yet. Would be a nice thing to bring home the first salmon of the year.

She got off Gipsy again and slipped her arm through the bridle, walking close to the stream and keeping alert for the big shadowy fish. She was getting close to the Coast before she saw a big one, still, in a landlocked pool. The water from the last rain had sent the stream out over its banks and the last ten days of clear weather had shrunk the stream so quickly that this big fish was left in his little lake. He would be easy to get. But when Blaze got set, rock poised, she turned away quickly, a little shiver rippling down her back. The big fish was dead, half his underside was eaten away. He didn't smell good.

She rode down through the last of the big redwoods that fringed the stream, trying to shake off a sense of uneasiness. It seemed a queer thing that both gifts she had thought to take home should be spoiled.

Her depression lifted when she came to the end of the level canyon and drew rein for a moment just above the spot where the stream plunged almost to the ocean. The water gathered a tremendous smooth and strong force in the last ten feet before it shot out between the narrow granite walls and then plunged noisily down a drop of almost two hundred feet. At the bottom was a deep granite pool and then the mountain gentled out into one of the steep meadows that Blaze thought of as the flat land above the cliffs of the Coast.

The trail veered sharply north, following the top of the granite cliff for a few yards and then became a switchback moseying leisurely among lilac, madrone and laurel with an undergrowth of sage, wild briar, thimbleberry and horse nettle.

Blaze smelled all this riot of new growth with delight. The flowers she called wild-bells hung in thick bunches under the shelter of the budding lilac trees, the dark blue of the early wild iris made the yellowish white of the wild-bells seem almost pure white. The bells were not fragrant; they were not flowers to gather. Blaze had always felt a little guilty because she thought they were not really pretty. But she loved them dearly, for like the long-billed thrush that sang his wild mocking-bird notes on the high peaks, they were the bringers of real spring. There might be a sudden flurry of snow and hail up on the ridge but if the song thrush called his song brightly through the cold wind, Blaze knew that as soon as the storm broke she could ride down the mountain a thousand feet and find her first wild-bells.

Where the trail was dug out beside a bank she leaned over and broke off a leaf of print-fern from under the granite ledge where it sheltered. Riding along she placed the underside of the fern against the back of her hand and let the reins go slack so that she could hold the warm palm of her other hand over the fern. She was almost to the place where the mountain trail joined the trail that followed the headlands above the ocean before she raised the fern and looked to see how good a print she had. Across the back of her hand the pattern of the fern was perfectly printed and she felt just as thrilled with this wild decoration as she had when Iowana, the Indian boy who had worked for her father when she was little, had first shown her the magic of the print-fern.

This was a good day. The gods loved her or the fern would

not print. Iowana's god was nice. The ferns always printed and made a child feel safe and loved.

Thinking of Iowana made her feel sad. He was so gay, so kind. Her mother and father had both been just as fond of Iowana as she was, but one day Zande Allan got furious because the pasture gate was left open. He said Iowana did it. Then he said that Iowana lied because he claimed he'd not been near the gate and so he was ordered off the place. Seven years later Martin got up courage to own that it was he who forgot to latch the pasture gate. Zande Allan said Iowana was too long gone then to go after and her mother said it was just as well. Blaze always felt that her mother thought maybe Iowana was more gay, had life easier, over in the Jolon valley.

Turning Gipsy south when she came to the fork of the trail Blaze reined in and stopped and looked in the three redwood boxes nailed to three posts and set out hopefully at this cross-road of trails in the silent empty land. There was nothing in any of the boxes, not even a last year's bird nest. There never had been anything in their box, but maybe some spring of some year before she was really old, she might ride down here, look in the box and there would be a note, a letter or a package!

She glanced again at the fern print on the back of her hand and tightened her knees on Gipsy. The mare dropped into an easy lope and Blaze felt better. She knew she had been dawdling, not really wanting to get to Lime Creek and see Pete —if he was there. She felt sure he wouldn't be. Maybe she should turn around, ride back home.

But she set her chin and looked ahead on the trail. She rode along swiftly, crossing Thorn Creek, then May Creek and as she rode up the steep pitch out of May Creek and pulled Gipsy to a halt she could look across the half mile of narrow grassy benchland and make out a horse standing, as if tied, on the near bank of Lime Creek.

She sat undecided, annoyed because she was tense and nervous. She wanted to go back, but—if it was Pete, he would have been watching for her, seen her coming. If she turned around he'd think she was afraid. "Well, I am," she told herself. It was a bold sort of thing to do; cruel too. Pete could easily get the idea she was taken with him.

The ground was fairly level and Gipsy went along at a good gait. Soon Blaze could see that it was Pete's black horse tied by the canyon rim. Then she saw Pete, his back cushioned against small brush and dead grass on the bank where he was leaning.

As she rode closer he got to his feet, took off his cap and stood waiting for her, an eager look on his dark face. Blaze had no idea that she looked lovely. She knew she rode well; but everyone rode well. The sun shone on her red hair and it blew in the fresh breeze like the banner of spring. She looked small and slender to be handling such a spirited horse and her kelp-brown eyes were bright as the sparkle of the sea.

"I didn't think you'd be here," she called teasingly. "But I wanted to go for a ride and this seemed as good as any place."

He said slowly, "I didn't think you'd be here either."

Blaze said, "Oh!" For a moment she couldn't think of another thing to say. She didn't want Pete to get an idea that she thought this ride down the Coast was anything unusual. Suddenly she remembered the mushrooms and the salmon and she started to tell Pete about them.

This seemed to put him more at ease and he urged, "Blaze, we go down to the mouth of the creek and get some abalone. There's lots there, big red fellows, nice. Your mother'll like, and anyway I want to show you a cave I found under the Lime Hill where the sea beats it."

Blaze looked doubtful. "It's a hard climb down. Be nice to get the abalone, but we'd save time if we went over to Abalone Gulch. It's not far and it's so easy to get down to the beach there."

"Yah, but this cave! I want to show someone my cave, and

[116]

I picked you. I'll help you get down, Blaze. Come on, or the tide will come in so we can't get around the point to the cave." He held up his arms to lift her down with such confidence that Blaze found her feet on the ground, Gipsy tied beside the black horse, and herself following Pete down the steep cliff.

She found it fun. Even though she was surefooted as a lynx it was dangerous enough to be thrilling. She shook her head and laughed every time Pete tried to give her a hand over a bad place. "This is fun," she called down to him as he waited the other side of a perfectly smooth rock face that looked impossible to cross. Pete had crossed, but he was tall, his legs were longer than hers. Below her was a straight drop of fifty feet to a broken rock ledge topped with big boulders, but she scarcely gave it a glance as she flattened herself against the smooth serpentine rock and tried to catch a toe-hold on the other side of the rock. She couldn't get footing. It was too far.

"No," she called, "don't help me. I want to see if I can make it." She shifted her hand forward from the solid rock she was holding, tried a stunted lupin whose roots dug into fissures in the rock. If the lupin would take part of her weight just for a second she'd be across and proud of herself. She gave a tug at the lupin and it seemed to be holding. Bracing herself by the slender plant and with her eye on a rock hand-hold just beyond her fingertips Blaze shifted her weight, let herself slide along the face of the cliff with her back to the ocean and the rocks below her. For an instant she felt a surge of triumph and then the lupin gave way before her fingers had grasped the rock on the other side.

Pete caught her shoulder, pulled her forward, slid his long arm around her waist and she was safe on the other side of the dangerous rock, her heart pounding against his stout chest. She hadn't had time to feel frightened, to think she'd be killed on the rocks below.

[117]

"I should of took you piggy-back," he laughed. "Never thought you was such a little thing."

There was only room on the ledge for one person; he had to hold her tightly to keep her balanced for a moment before he could move on to the next safe footing. He was so casual about having his arm around her, didn't try to hug her or act as though he was any different than Martin hauling a clumsy sister to safety. Blaze felt a rush of warm affection for Pete. Why, he was nice! She felt ashamed. Telling herself that she was as mean and lowdown in her mind as Joe Williams, she lifted her head, smiled and said, "Let's get after those abalone. I'm going to be a hard load to haul out of this place. If we weren't almost down there I'd say we ought to start back right now, but it's such fun to do something people say can't be done. All my life I've been hearing people say no one could get down this cliff."

Pete laughed. "So have I. That's why I come, the first time. It's risky, that's sure, but it can be done."

"We haven't done it yet," Blaze taunted. "Let's go."

The rest of the way seemed easy and she was as proud and pleased as though she were any small boy when her feet touched the beach. "I bet I'm the first female that ever got herself down that cliff," she called above the roar of the surf.

"I bet you'd lose," he grinned; "maybe five hundred years ago some Indian miss slid down here to meet her big chief and maybe they even set up housekeeping in the cave. Just wait till you see that cave."

Blaze looked doubtfully at the sweep of the breakers. "I don't know," she called. "The tide's coming in fast. Let's get the abalone first. The water is almost to the edge of that point, and didn't you say the cave was around it?"

Pete was down in the edge of the breakers, standing in the lee of some big boulders and as the waves drew noisily back, churning pebbles, he had reached forward, balanced himself and brought the heel of his boot down smartly on a huge pink abalone, tore it loose from the rock. No eagle could be quicker, Blaze thought, as she watched him bend, snatch up the heavy shell from the wave that came rolling toward it, toss the abalone back and out of reach of the tide. Twice more his heel flashed. Each time he had an abalone off the rock and safe above high water. He gathered his catch, slid them into a flour sack he took out of his pocket and then tied the abalone sack to a stout root well above high water.

He came striding back, grabbed Blaze by the hand and called, "Let's go! Take just a minute and maybe you never get the chance again."

Laughing, she tightened her fingers in his grip and to the ring of laughter and the surge of spray they ran past the rocky point that stood out boldly from the rest of the cliff. Pebbles churned and foam spattered them, but they made it dry-shod.

Blaze was so enchanted with the waterfall that flowed down sheer granite into the little harbor, the jagged pillars of mussel-crusted rock that guarded its entrance, the stone walls that almost closed the smooth cup of the bay and kept off the wind, which was rising, that Pete had to pull her up the sand and clear of the surging breakers.

Her mouth was soft, her eyes sparkling, as she breathed "Long as I live I'll never forget this, Pete! Isn't another spot like it on the whole Coast. No wonder you called it a cave!"

"You're talking too soon. This is just the front yard to my hideout. Come on and see the rest."

She laughed like a pleased child and urged, "Show me, quick! We've got to get back around that cliff quick or we'll have to swim out."

"Have to be a seal to swim out of this," he answered. "Come on, hurry up."

"I hate to have to hurry. I'd like to stay forever in such a place. Oh, Pete, I love it so!"

He didn't answer, but hurried ahead of her up the slope of

the beach and she followed, picking her way among the tangles of seaweed and kelp, longing to stop and dream over the round sea pools in which tiny crabs scuttled, sea anemones blossomed like pink and green lilies.

But she forgot the pools, the harbor, when she climbed up the cliff and bent her head to get inside the cave. It was a high-ceilinged granite and limestone room with an opening in the rock high up near the curved ceiling. The floor of the cave was sandy and dry and close beside a tiny trickle of sweet water the wall of the cave was darkened with smoke of ancient fires. Big abalone shells, polished from long washing among the pebbles of the tide, gleamed here and there and at the far end was piled up a mat of dry seaweed with a clean but worn canvas covering part of it.

"It's a whole house!"

She turned her head to share her pleasure with Pete and found him looking down at her as though he was embarrassed. He looked at her, looked away and then down at the few sticks of dry wood by the place where fires had been built.

"It's my house. I found it for you, Blaze." He swallowed and then he said quickly, "I want you to stay with me here."

"I'd love to," Blaze said regretfully. "Just think, we could gather mussels and abalone and catch a big fish and play house for a whole afternoon if that old tide was right. Let's get a crowd, early in summer, and have a picnic here, Pete?"

She started to walk toward the mouth of the cave, but he stepped in front of her. "No, you don't," he said harshly. "I been fixing this for you, and you don't walk out on me like that."

Startled, she looked up at him and drew back. "Don't be so crazy, Pete! You sound like you meant it."

She walked on, but he took two long steps, stood in front of her. "I said no. You knew what I wanted when you come down here with me."

She said, "What's got into you, Pete? You're not being very nice to me."

"I'll be nice to you. What do you think I am? A clumsy fool that don't know nothing about women? I'll be a damn sight nicer to you than your *nice* Joe Williams."

Blaze forgot to be frightened. She was trembling, but it was fury that shook her as she asked, "And what do you think you mean by that?"

His voice was nasty. "Oh, don't play innocent. I'm a better man to be seeing the brown beauty spot on your back than that old fossil."

Her face burning, Blaze put her hand behind her, covered the brown mark with her hand and gasped, "Who told you that?"

"Oh, stop it! You know who told me. I was watching them brown eyes of yours when he was telling it up at the Janson place."

Blaze tried to pull away from him, her voice thin as the bark of a trapped fox as she threatened, "My father and my brothers'll tear you apart if you touch me." She caught her breath, stammered, "Oh, Pete, I'm sorry! I know you won't. You like me. Let's forget this. Come on, quick, or we'll be caught here."

He softened too. "We'll never forget it, Blaze, but maybe we'll think it's funny when we're old married folks. I don't care what you've been to Joe. The hell with him. We'll ride on into town and be married tomorrow. I meant to marry you anyway."

She pulled her arm back, threatening him. "You hateful—hateful—" She shook angry tears from her eyes and started to run toward the entrance of the cave. He was right behind her and Blaze ran faster than she had ever been able to run before. It was no use. Pete kept right behind her, not trying to stop her.

The waves stopped her. The tide had already turned and solid walls of water were smashing against the rock point they had run around so easily not fifteen minutes earlier.

Blaze looked at the breakers, then her eyes followed up the rock point trying to find some foothold on that smooth perpendicular wall. It was hopeless. She swung around to look at the south end of the closed-in bay. Deep water there too. Wildly she searched the face of the cliff that was behind the cave. No tree, no shrub, scarcely a knob of rock broke the concave cliff. It towered above the cave like a great shell. No one could climb out of this place.

Blaze forgot the terror she had just run from. Now she turned and ran back to Pete, catching his arm, shaking at it with the feeling of a child waking from a nightmare. She couldn't keep her voice steady as she urged, "Pete, we're caught in here. What will we do?"

He shrugged off her shaking hand, said roughly, "Take it easy. We can get out tomorrow just as easy as we got in."

She stepped back from him, her eyes wide. "But I can't stay here! My mother will be so worried. My father will look for me. Everyone will think—" She couldn't say it.

"What do you take me for? They'll think just what I think. Any girl that'll come off the trail into this sort of a place alone with a man will go further than that."

Blaze walked over to a stone ledge below the entrance of the cave and above the reach of the waves. She sank down on the cold stone, shivering, but not conscious of the wind that tumbled her hair, shook the fringes of her buckskins. She couldn't think, she couldn't plan. She felt she couldn't breathe. What had she ever done to give Pete such ideas about her? The mole on her back. How could he know about it? Nobody did except her mother and herself. Blaze thought it ugly, a round brown patch the size and color of a penny and just below her waist on her back. Hannah Allan said it was a Martin beauty spot, that she had a smaller one up on her shoulder.

Blaze forced herself to stand up, go back to Pete and say, "How could you know about—?" Her face reddened and it seemed she couldn't say it. But she had to. She stammered, "If Joe Williams said it, how did he know a thing that no one in my own family, except my mother, knows?"

Pete looked at her coldly. "Stuff like that goes from one to another. Made Joe feel big to tell it. You want to prove you ain't got the brown spot, all right. Then Joe's a liar and he's going to get hurt."

Blaze had to say, "It's true I got such a spot on me. But how could he know it?"

Pete folded his arms, gave her a look that made her shrink as he said, "Joe's out of this; he don't count. But you came down here with me on your own feet. I didn't drag you. I didn't have to beg you none either. What do you expect when you do that?"

Blaze stammered out, "I didn't think anything. Why should I? It's just the beach. What's the difference in coming down here or riding along the trail?"

She saw he didn't believe her. His laugh was angry.

"I'm no mind reader," he said. "How was I to know you'd rather just go off the trail? You been playing hard-to-get so well you had me fooled till Joe said you went walking naked in the woods so he could see you."

Her mouth dropped open, her breath came in gulps and her mouth felt dry as salt jerky. She made an effort to defend herself, but no sound would come out of her mouth. Blaze turned and ran back to the ledge, stumbled and fell against it and lay there.

After a time Pete came down to her and asked uneasily, "You hurt?"

She heard the words, but they seemed to have no more meaning than the boom of the surf hitting the big rocks. Hurt? What was hurt? A bruise, a broken arm? That wasn't what hurt meant.

[123]

It was being dead and going on breathing and feeling and thinking.

Suddenly the phrase "walking naked in the woods" came back to her. She sat up, lifted her head and looked at Pete.

"It was over at Gram Allan's." Then she shook her head. "No, that couldn't be it. It couldn't be. I put my clothes on a log and walked all of ten feet down to a big hole in the creek. Wasn't a soul on the ranch but Granma, and she was up to the house."

There seemed a bit of doubt on Pete's face. Blaze wanted terribly to blow on that doubt, fan it into some belief in her, but she had to be honest.

She said sorrowfully, "Joe wasn't around there. He'd gone to help corral some young stock, and brand."

She slumped back against the cold rock ledge, thinking. Suddenly she jumped to her feet. "It must have been! It was that very summer he started staring at me, trying to make me take notice of him." She bit her lip, rubbed blood off it onto the back of her hand without being aware of it and said fiercely, "My father said I'd marry him. I never did. And then he started threatening to tell something about me if I wouldn't promise to marry him. The low-down sneak!"

The white face she raised to Pete was drawn and streaked with tears and she was shivering. He pulled off his coat and put it over her shoulders gently, sat down on the ground in front of her. "Don't you now, Blaze! I can't stand it to see you crying and wore out. You stop your shaking and I'll figure a way to get you out of here."

She clasped her hands together, held them firmly against her knees to stop their shaking and asked in a small voice, "Maybe you can't believe me, Pete, since I played the fool coming down here. I did know better, but I was mad at my father for acting up yesterday."

Pete sounded a trifle sour in spite of his half grin. "You

shouldn't take your spite agin your pa out on me. Will you marry me, Blaze?"

She shook her head. "I like you, Pete, mostly. I didn't like you any today, but maybe— Oh, I don't know much about how men think, I guess. But I aim to love the man I marry, if I ever do get married."

"That's how I wanted it, I guess." He stood up, stretched and said casually, "I'll get you out of here and safe home. Let's see." He walked to the ledge between the little bay and the cliff that led up to the trail at Lime Creek and looked at it carefully. Then he tried the other side.

Blaze stood up hopefully, amazed to find that already she felt glad she was alive. No matter what happened now, nothing could ever compel her to marry Joe Williams. Always, before, even though she said she would not marry Joe, she knew that deep down she had a fear that her father could force her to do it. Now she knew that no threats, nothing would make her give in.

Pete came back slowly, a worried look on his face. "I don't see any way to get you out of here, Blaze."

She swallowed, thinking her father would be wild, her mother sad, to think she'd get herself into such a mess. But she smiled at Pete, said cheerfully, "Well, we've just got to make the best of it then." She tried to laugh, but it sounded put-on to her own ears as she said, "Now we'll really have a reason to get some mussels and try to catch a fish."

He looked at her. "Don't, Blaze. I've got to get you out of here somehow."

She sat down on the rock ledge, tucked her feet under her and wrapped her arms around her knees to keep the wind from plucking at her. "Well," she drawled, "maybe you can fly, Pete. I know I can't—so—we make ourselves as warm and comfortable as we can and wait for the tide to turn."

"No, we don't." He sounded as stubborn as Zande Allan. "I don't want to talk rough to you, Blaze, but I got to."

She lifted her face, her puzzled eyes looking frankly into his worried ones. "I don't want you to talk rough to me," she said, "and you don't want to, so why do you? Let's let it go. I'd rather hunt wood for a fire—it's getting cold."

He sounded impatient as he answered, "Cold or not, right now, doesn't matter. You got to get out of here before you're missed and people start hunting you."

She shrugged. "I'll catch a good tongue-lashing, maybe worse. But what's that? If they start looking they'll find us—Gipsy and Solito standing up there by the trail." She looked hopeful as she asked, "Couldn't they get us out with a rope? Give me any sort of hand-hold and I know I could shin out of here."

"Oh, my God, Blaze, stop talking like a ten-year-old! Don't you know that if anyone on the Coast finds you down here you're worse off than if you'd drowned? Do you think Joe Williams, or any other man for that matter, would believe on anyone's oath that you came down here with me to get some abalone and look at the beach?"

Her face reddened, but she said, "He doesn't count. I don't care what Joe thinks of me, the worse the better, far as I'm concerned." She looked up at the cliff, trying to cover her embarrassment. "People aren't so low-down as you think they are, Pete. Why should they believe—" Her voice trailed off in confusion.

"That you was down here to lay with me in that cave," he finished grimly. "You're damn tootin' that's what they'll think. You got to get it right square between the eyes, I guess. All right. That's what I wanted when I asked you to meet me."

She shrank back, suddenly cold all over. He drove brutally ahead. "I knowed you would—when I saw you come riding down the Coast to meet me."

She hid her face in her cold hands. Pete came over to stand

[126]

close by her, his hands hovering close enough to her red hair so that she could feel them, but he didn't touch her. "I'm sorry, Blaze. But you got to know. I want you bad. I always will. But I wouldn't touch you for a hundred otter hides if you didn't want it that way."

She moaned, steadied herself and told him, "You're good, Pete. You *are*—better than I ever thought you were. I'd think myself lucky if I loved you. Only I don't. No one but dirty men, like Joe, will think anything wrong about us being here. I know they won't."

He walked away without looking at her and Blaze felt that was harsher than if he'd said any more.

Pete backed off from the wall about ten feet, then ran at it, leaped as high as he could, trying to catch a small knob of rock that was far above his reach. He tried it three times before she stood up, called sharply, "Stop that, Pete! You're acting crazy. Your hands are cut now. You'll have a black eye or break your leg if you go on that way. I come down here by myself just like you said. I'll stay here and take whatever happens, long as it's my fault."

Pete picked himself out of the jumble of boulders he had dropped among, felt his arms and legs for a moment and then limped over close to her, laughing. She stepped back and he followed her, reached out and took her hand in his, put his other big dark hand softly over both their hands. "You'd make a man a fine wife, Blaze. You got some fun to you and you're no coward either."

He let go her hands so hastily that it had the effect of being dropped and Blaze felt bewildered, uneasy. She was deeply conscious of her ignorance about men. And she had a sense of anger that it should be so. Why should men make all the rules, expect women to keep them when they were never told anything about how men thought?

She was scarcely conscious that Pete was picking up wood,

carrying it into the cave, she was so intent on thinking of how much help, what sort of help her own menfolks had ever been to her. Whenever they had gone to a barbecue when she was first thinking of herself as a young woman, her father had said harshly, just before they got to the doings, "Mind you behave yourself now."

Always she answered dutifully, "Yes, Father." Then she went off to find whatever fun she could. And if ever she did get mixed into a game or play that seemed fun, along would come Martin to say, "What you doing in this? Go on back and stay around Ma."

There was never any explanation of what "behave yourself" meant. Never any reason from Martin as to why she should leave Nella and Alice and the boys alone. And now here was Pete, who was nice, telling her he'd asked her to come down here when everyone would think bad of it. None of it made sense. Wrathfully she told herself that what she was going to do was be an old maid, have a lot of children and let them have fun all the time. She tried to imagine how it would be to have a little house all her own, packed jam-full of children singing and dancing and laughing and not one cranky man-creature to shout at them to behave.

The smell of new smoke brought her back to knowing that she was cold, rather hungry, and completely terrified at the thought that as soon as she got home she would have to try to explain this trip to the beach to her father.

She made her way slowly into the cave and then hurried up to the fire that Pete was still piling with driftwood. He looked up at her, his face smiling but rather serious.

"I got in enough wood so you can keep warm until I get out and let down a rope for you."

"Get out?" Blaze asked. "How?"

He didn't look at her as he said, "I can swim around the north point of rocks. Then I can get the rope off my saddle and have you out of here quick."

"No!"

"Oh, sure I can."

She tightened her hand on his sleeve, pleading, "You mustn't try it, Pete. If the undertow don't drag you down, then the waves will grind you to pieces on the rocks. You'll be killed."

"Not me," Pete said lightly. "I can swim like a sea otter."

Blaze stepped between him and the entrance to the cave. "I don't doubt it, if you're swimming out where the otters swim. They got too much sense to try to fight current and waves and rocks all at once. Don't try it, Pete!"

"It won't be anything."

She knew what that meant. That was what her father said when he was going to fall a dangerous tree, ride an outlaw horse.

She spread her arms out as wide as she could reach, trying to block his way, pleading, "That means there's a good chance you'll be killed. Pete, you wouldn't put your death on me, would you? How could I go on living if I always had to remember that it was my fault that it happened?"

"Stop making fun of me," Pete growled. "Now I got to prove to you I can swim. So get out of my way, woman, and stay in this cave looking at the fire."

He took her by the shoulders, swung her around close to the warmth of the fire, and growled, "Now stay there for a while."

She made a start after him and he turned back, drawling, "Unless you're set on seeing a man pulling off his britches you better stay back here till I whistle for you to catch the rope."

He left the cave before she could say another word, stopped by the ledge of rock she had been sitting on and began to unfasten his shirt.

Blaze ran out of the cave, down the rocks toward him, calling, "No, Pete! No! You can't do it; you'll be drowned!"

His face betrayed no sign of having heard. He pulled his shirt over his head and tossed it toward the high point of the ledge. His skin was a clear smooth brown, his muscles long and supple as a mountain lion as he bent down to unfasten his shoes. Blaze felt no impulse to turn away, not look at a half-naked man. Even the shining black mat of hair on his thick chest seemed part of his aliveness. He was so quick, so warm, so living. The water, the rocks, the undertow, so close and cold, so menacing.

Blaze stepped closer to him. "Please, Pete! Think of all the life you've got ahead of you, all the fun. Don't throw it away. I'd a thousand times rather the whole world turned against me."

"It will." He sounded grim, but he was smiling at her, his voice gentle as he warned, "The pants come off next; you better act like a lady, Miss Allan."

Her shoulders slumped; she turned her back wondering why she couldn't feel any love for Pete Garcia. He was the sort of man she had wanted her father to be like, a man who could relish living, laugh when things went wrong. If only she had never seen Stephen she could have thought this warm affection she felt for Pete was what was meant by love. She said, "Stay out of that water and I'll marry you if you still want me to."

He moved toward her swiftly, spun her around to face him and for an instant she saw a look of wild glory in his dark face. Then his hand dropped and he said roughly, "Oh, for Christ's sake, Blaze, shut up! Go on back and keep up the fire."

He kicked off his shoes, stepped out of his trousers and strode up the beach, plunged into the icy water just before he reached the rock point.

Blaze felt that she, too, had stepped into that fearful water. As she watched his black head disappear beneath a huge comber, saw his body shoot up halfway out of the water and his strong arm reach out, push himself clear of the mussel-covered rock, she could only stand, cold and numb as though she were frozen in a block of ice.

She had an instant's glimpse of his hand covered with blood from the knife-edge of the mussels before he thrust it strongly into the onrushing wave and gained a few feet in his fight to come clear of the rock point.

The sight of his bleeding hand unlocked her from her numb horror. She ran to the water's edge, screaming, "Come back! You've got to come back!"

She leaned forward, her hands stretched toward the rocky point he was straining to round. The surf surged over her moccasins, splashed her skirt, but she didn't know it. She watched one of the big green combers lift Pete up as though he were a match, spin him backward and roll him in toward a huge black rock.

"His head's going to hit it!" She was screaming, but she didn't hear her own voice as she pressed forward into the water.

The rocks under her feet were sucked into the churning mass of sand, pebbles and boulders that the undertow was dragging seaward. She lost her footing, staggered and righted herself. Her leather skirt was wet and draggled clear above her knees and she felt the hampering drag of it as part of the evil force of the churning surf.

The tide swept out and the water was only above her ankles as she caught her balance, stared into the churning crosscurrents for a sight of Pete.

He shot to the surface, his arms above his head, and Blaze felt weak with relief as she watched his arms flail the water. He was coming back. He was swimming toward shore.

She stepped back out of the reach of the tumbling green crest that was sweeping Pete toward shore and safety. He was less than forty feet out. In only a breath of time he would be safe again.

She could see him clearly now, watch his cut hand redden as

it came momentarily out of the water. As the big wave, gathering for its final moment before it roared shoreward in a tumbling green wall, swept Pete on and up, she saw his face clearly. His eyes were closed. He was swimming, but without direction or purpose.

Certain that he had been flung against the big black rock, hurt badly, Blaze got ready to help him. Her fingers were numb, thick from the cold spray that drenched her as the whistling wind tore the tops off the combers, sent them flying shoreward like needles of ice.

She got her skirt unfastened, stepped out of the soggy mass of wet leather and flung it behind her out of reach of the breakers.

As though in answer to her prayer the sea drove Pete straight toward her. In a moment she would be able to reach him, grab his arm and hold him until the rolling backwash had passed.

She knew that if she was to be any help to Pete she must not only keep her head, she must be sure of her footing. She waded deeper into the treacherous flood, feeling how strongly the cross-tides swirled around her legs, how the shore she stood on fell away beneath her feet as the undertow churned and sucked like a savage mouth.

"Here I am, Pete!" Her voice rang shrill as the cry of a wind-beaten gull and with all the force she could put into it. "Swim, Pete!" He *had* to hear. He must. One strong stroke would hold him on top of the green wall that was already starting to tip toward Blaze.

Her eyes were blind with terror as she watched the thick green wall of water move toward her with the cold strength of death. But she couldn't run from it. Somewhere in that terrible green force Pete was fighting for life. With all her faith she prayed that the breaker would fling him clear. The rocks on the beach were ugly, could bruise him, cut him, tear his flesh if the water flung him far enough. That was nothing. He was strong, he would heal of that sort of hurt.

"Oh, God, don't let the sea have him!"

Now at the north end of the little cove the mighty wave was falling like a great waterfall. Blaze took a deep breath, and got ready.

"There he is, there—he's right here. *Pete!*" Even as she screamed to him she saw it was no use. He could not hear. Pete was not swimming. She saw his set, locked face for an instant and then she saw the crest of the wave fold over him, saw him spin in it helplessly.

Moved by the tide of her own terror she rushed forward to battle the green monster that was beating Pete to death.

There was no time for Blaze to think. She somehow kept her feet and touched Pete's outflung arm. It was wet and slick, too thick for her hand to close around but her other hand grabbed his hair and hung on as the tons of icy water swept her from her feet, pulled her down among the churning pebbles.

She had one instant of thinking that whatever happened she must hold her breath, not let the water strangle her. She felt herself spinning dizzily, lost all sense of where the shore might be. Her last conscious thought was an unbearable urgency to know that she was still holding onto Pete's hair. Then she felt herself strike the rock.

VI

IT seemed to Blaze that she must still be in the sea. Icy water beat on her and she could feel herself striking against the rock with the regularity of a clock ticking. She fought the water, but she couldn't make any headway. Dimly it came to her that in spite of the great dashes of water that struck her face, she could breathe. The feeling of being struck every second was the labored beating of her own heart.

She tried to lift her head, see where she was, but the effort was too much. Her body lay limp against the rough boulders of the beach.

The next time she tried to rouse herself she heard the screaming of the wind and felt the icy downpour of rain. This time she tried to drag herself a few feet farther from the waves that still sent foam flying over her. It was useless. She was too numb from shock and cold to be able to move, too dazed to remember where she was, what had happened.

When she was tormented into making another effort to escape the cold agony of the wind and rain she realized that it was growing dark, that she was on the beach instead of still swimming in the water. She was puzzled for a moment by seeing what looked like stars moving slowly down the cliff, but it was impossible for her to keep her head clear for more than an instant.

When she heard a voice above her she tried to say, "Get Pete. . . . I couldn't hold onto him. Find him!"

No voice answered her. She tried to point to the ocean, ask for help, but her hand did not move.

Presently, above her head, she was aware of voices, but the words ran together, meant nothing. But when someone lifted her, the pain of it shocked her into flaming awareness.

She tried to shout "Where's Pete?" but she couldn't hear herself make a sound and she was too exhausted to try again. Dimly she knew she was being lifted, carried. But from the beach, during the long struggle up the cliff until the moment she knew she was being lifted onto a horse, it all seemed a nightmare into which she woke, something she was grateful to forget in stupor.

When Zande Allan said to some unseen neighbor or neighbors, "You see the Garcias, tell them. I can get her home all right," Blaze heard the words, but lost their meaning. She whispered, "The wind came, like you said."

When she woke again it was daylight. She was in her own bed and her mother was sitting beside her.

"Did they get Pete? Is he safe?"

Her mother said, "Don't worry, Blaze. Try to rest. Go back to sleep for a while."

Silently Blaze gathered her strength, then she insisted, "Did they find him? Is he all right?"

Her mother's voice seemed stiff and wooden as she said, "I don't know. There's a lot out looking for him now."

Blaze groaned, tried to sit up, and fell back. She shut her eyes and the memory of those last few seconds when she had reached for Pete, caught him, been swept away by the wave, came back to her. She felt that she was dying.

She had to know that Pete was warm and alive, that he could laugh and play his guitar.

"I've got to get up, go help look for him."

Hannah Allan stood up, lifted the white homespun cover down near the foot of the narrow bed, felt of the hot river rocks wrapped in a worn piece of woolen shawl. After six hours out of the oven the rocks were still hot. She shifted them carefully so they would reach the bottoms of her girl's icy feet and then pulled the cover smooth and tucked it in well about Blaze's shoulders.

"You're staying right where you are," she said and sat stiffly erect on the rawhide-covered stool beside the bed.

Between spasms of shivering Blaze was aware of her mother close by and yet seeming far away. Her back seemed unnaturally straight, her mouth grim, her eyes haunted.

The day failed toward evening with long patches of blankness broken by spells of shivering so violent that Blaze groaned as she tried to turn over in her bed.

Every time she groaned or moved her mother bent over her with some healing dose brewed from the wild herbs of the mountains. Obediently Blaze swallowed an elixir of yerba romano, certain to ward off a fever. When she heard her mother telling her to take this yerba santa syrup for the hoarseness and sore throat she was sure to have if she didn't take it, she tried to raise her head, help her mother. Yerba santa was the favorite medicine of every Coast child. Decanted from the stiff and shining leaves of the fragrant santa, it was mixed with honey and had a pleasant flavor, like mixed horehound and sassafras.

Swallowing the yerba santa, Blaze tried to smile as she gasped hoarsely, "Tastes good."

Her mother lowered her gently back to her pillow and fled the room, was gone only a moment and marched in with a tablespoon in her hand.

Blaze smelled, rather than saw, what was in the spoon, wrinkled her nose and tried feebly to shake her head.

Her mother was firm. "Nothing like bear-berry bark to run the fever and ague out of you. I brought water to wash it down."

Blaze looked piteously unwilling, her face crumpled as she started to open her mouth.

"Well, I must say you're a big girl to act the baby," Hannah said crossly, but she went out, came back with the bitter cascara bark wrapped tightly in the thin dry skin of an onion. Helped along with a sip of water the onion-skin capsule slid down easily, tastelessly.

Blaze blinked her gratitude for this, but her mother was fretful. "Medicine ain't meant to take for the good taste of it," she grumbled. "You swallow it bitter and you know it's good, does you good. Wrapped up tight in that onion peel there's a chance you never get the good of it at all. You need the healing purge of that bear-berry—all flushed up and your skin dry and hot like it is."

Blaze turned her head toward the wall so her mother would not see her tears. She felt that she could swallow anything if only it would help unlock the hasps of hurt that held her mother like an iron band. Blaze knew so well that right now her mother's only release was to feel that she was doing something to heal her physical hurts. Until Zande Allan returned, this small room was a sheltered place in which both women could pretend that everything was as usual. Hannah could stay apprehension by working to heal her child's hurt body. Blaze could keep from thinking of her spirit's pain by swallowing dark doses, giving her mother the comfort of her ministering.

Blaze was not yet steady enough to face anything beyond her growing fear that Pete was lost. Her mind would not admit that except at moments. As the twilight deepened, bits of the shattering things Pete had thought, had said, came plucking at her mind, but she shuddered away from them.

When it would seem that she could not possibly lie quietly in her bed, that the ceiling was pressing down on her, when every nerve was taut beyond endurance, she stayed quiet, she endured. She would picture Pete, above the reach of the waves, coming back to himself through his pain, just as she had. Then her mind would follow his inch-by-inch painful crawl to safety, his collapse on the fringe of sand above the rock beach of whatever point he had reached.

At that picture her heart would stop beating at her ears with its maddening boom, she could draw a breath deep enough to keep away the feeling of smothering.

Pete would come. Her father would bring him. Her father would be furious, shouting, impossible. And the burden of his complaint would be that Pete must marry her.

That sort of thinking wouldn't do. At her picture of what Zande Allan's state would be when he was shouting himself out of a son-in-law who owned six hundred and forty good acres, in favor of a ne'er-do-well who never owned more than a guitar, never intended to—Blaze shuddered. Another time it would be uproariously funny, but she had left her Allan sense of humor back on the black rocks of the little cove.

It was getting dark in the room. She struggled to sit up, had herself propped up on one elbow when her mother came in with a bowl of warm milk.

"Don't worry, Blaze. Everything will come right, you'll see. Now you just drink this milk, then I'll sponge you off and give your back a rub."

Blaze put up a hand to keep the cup away, gasped, "Where's Father?"

"He'll be along. You drink your milk now. I'll call you as soon as he comes."

Blaze took the bowl, raised it to her lips, but she couldn't drink. Her eyes had the alarmed look of unbranded colts' eyes, and she whispered, "I can't." She was gasping for breath as though there were no air anywhere. "I'm choking! I can't drink!"

"Don't fret, honey. You don't have to if you don't want it. Here, give it to me."

Blaze let go of the bowl as though it held all she would have to swallow when her father returned. Her hands free of the bowl she struggled to a sitting position, started to get out of the bed.

Her mother was right there, substituting patient words for the bowl of milk, offering patient hands in the slow soothing stroking of her bruised back.

Under her mother's gentle insistence Blaze sank back on her pillow, let herself be turned, gave herself up to the comfort of her mother's nearness. Hannah's hand, work-worn but warm, alive, stroked with the rhythm of a lullaby, and bit by bit Blaze sank deeper against the pillows into a dreamless sleep.

It was a new day before Blaze woke. She heard Avery's light step on the ladder from the loft and then her door was pushed open, his head came slowly around the door. He told her, "Say, you nearly got drowned!"

Blaze nodded, then asked, "Where's Martin?"

"Out hunting for Pete with the rest of 'em." He looked downcast as he muttered, "I got to stay here and milk the cows."

Blaze sank back against the bed. "Out hunting for Pete," Avery had said. That meant . . . but it couldn't be! Pete was laughing and gay and warm; he was too young to die. But the memory of his drawn white face against the angry crest of the wave formed into a hard core of certainty that interfered with her breathing.

There must be some way she could get free. If only she didn't ache so dreadfully she would get right up, saddle Gipsy and ride away. Where to? There was nowhere she could go; no one who would want her. If Pete was gone, it was her fault.

It was late afternoon before her mother hurried in, straightened the cover on the bed, picked up the few things out of place, said nervously, "Your father's coming."

As her mother closed the door Blaze, her eyes dull, her hands restless, muttered, "Let him come."

She felt that nothing he could say or do would matter. She

was sure that Pete was dead. Beside that sorrow what happened to her seemed of no consequence.

After a time she heard guarded voices out in the kitchen and now and then her father's voice, bewildered and furious, "I can't make head nor tail out of it. I can't take it in."

Blaze felt a quick sympathy for him. She couldn't take it in either. Fifty times in her life she must have ridden down to the Coast with one of her brothers, ridden back, and that was all there was to it. If they stopped at the Garcias, she brought home a present of sea fish. From the old Demas place she carried home a lively dish of gossip, a pail of figs or an early melon —anything that Mrs. Demas had she wanted to share.

Blaze lifted her tired arm, pushed her hair back from her damp forehead. She felt she knew what made the difference. Always before she had ridden away, happy with her world, going out gaily to bring back small items of news: Mrs. Garcia had a new apron, Mrs. Demas had lost another of her few remaining teeth, Tao Ramirez was working the brown colt, the Chinese men were camped at the springs again, gathering seaweed. This time she had ridden away full of anger and she had brought home death.

Outside in the hall she heard her father's step. It stopped before her door, his hand seemed uncertain on the latch, but he lifted it and came into the room.

He looked terribly tired and he looked old. Her mother stood beside him, nervous and haggard, urging, "Let her rest, Zande. She's clear beat out."

"I'm all right," Blaze protested.

There was no anger, only weariness and an icy contempt in her father's tone: "Where's your leather skirt?"

Blaze felt anger quicken in her, but she answered quietly, "I lost it."

His clenched fist fell heavily on the peeled sapling bedpost as he said, "That's a hell of a thing to say."

[140]

"You asked me. I thought you wanted to know."

"No high and mighty airs, young woman. Keep a civil tongue in your head. Where's your skirt?"

Blaze had to fight down an urge to laugh, to beat at the bed with her fists. She held her breath until she had to take it in with a gasp, but the effort steadied her and she was able to say, "I'm not sure. I think the sea took it."

"So you think the sea took it." He began to tremble and Blaze shrank back into her pillow as she saw the queer yellow-white color above his upper lip, heard his voice shake as he stepped toward her, "What the hell do I care for your skirt? You've made a damned fool of yourself and blacked the decent name of Allan. Half-dressed in a hide-out on the beach—and your partner stark naked! Everyone knows what you were up to. You're done. You're finished."

Blaze looked at him as though what he said meant nothing. She whispered, "Is Pete all right?"

Her father stared at her for what seemed eternity to the waiting girl and then he said, "Yes, he is! He's dead and out of it. You got to face it alone."

For an instant Blaze felt her stomach rise and heave as though she were going to be sick. Then a great hum started in her head and she felt herself whirling into space as her mother's voice came to her in strange broken waves, "Raise up her feet; she's fainted."

The waves kept breaking over her face and the hum in her head was like the intolerable pound of icy waves. Feebly Blaze tried to shield her face with her hands and heard, "You'll be all right. Keep your head down and try to breathe deep. That's it, you're all right now."

It was her mother's voice. The waves hitting her face were no more than a wet cloth being rubbed over her mouth, her forehead. "Don't, Mother. I can't bear it."

"Yes, you can. A body can do anything they got to do, even put up with trouble. Breathe deep and lay quiet; you'll feel better in a minute."

"It's worse all the time," Blaze whispered. She tried to stay quiet, but her nerves seemed to snap and vibrate like an electrical storm. "It gets more horrible. I don't care what happens to me, I got it coming. But Pete tried to help me. He lost his life for nothing." A shudder went through her. "It's my fault. There's nothing I can do."

"Yes, there is. You can face trouble. You can set your mind to getting strong enough to go to Mrs. Garcia, tell her how things was, give her all you remember of Pete's last minutes on earth. You can tell her you loved Pete—that's something."

The haunted look in Blaze's eyes deepened; she shook her head and whispered, "I can't tell her I loved him. I didn't."

A sound, half sigh, half groan, broke through Hannah's tight lips. She picked up the damp cloth, the basin, and walked out of the room, closed the door without a glance at the bed.

For a minute Blaze watched, hoping the closed door would open. It didn't. Her mother's feet went firmly down the hall and then the door to the kitchen closed.

With a mouth so dry it would scarcely form the words, Blaze whispered, "Mother's turned on me. She acts like she believes what Pete said they'd all think."

She didn't feel anger, only a great sense of sadness and loss. Her own had deserted her, took the shadowy appearance of evil for evil's self.

Pete had lost his life for nothing.

It seemed to Blaze that she couldn't bear to draw another breath until she was on her feet, telling her parents how good Pete was, how foolish, how noble.

Blaze struggled to her feet, crossed the room and gathered her clothes together. She had to lean against the wall to keep

[142]

from falling, but at last she had her work dress on, her hair smooth.

Dizzily she made her way down the hall, opened the door to the kitchen. She saw her father and mother sitting stiff and silent beside the table as though they were rigid with death

A sudden wild anger braced her and she made her way to the stool beside the stove and sank down, leaning her head back against the dish towel spread to dry beside the stove.

"You have no right to think wrong of Pete Garcia."

Her father said, "I'm not thinking of Pete. You're the one to blame."

Blaze straightened her back, leaned forward. "What do you know about what happened? Did Pete tell you? Did I tell you?"

"You didn't, and you needn't. Save your breath. Joe found you down there with your clothes half off. You can't talk that away."

Blaze looked at her mother. Her mother's face was creased with lines that had never been there before this day, her eyes looked as dark and bleak as the rock against which Pete had been flung.

"You go back to bed, Blaze. You'll catch your death out here in the draught."

"What would that matter?"

Blaze stood up, walked to the table, put both hands on it to brace her sagging body and drew a long breath. "You're both acting like Pete said other people would. I hope it never seemed to him that you'd be like this."

The two faces she saw wavering before her were set as the cliffs of marble rock at the top of that ridge.

Blaze shook her head wonderingly, suddenly felt the tension in herself lessen. "It's like you were strangers," she said; "like I don't know you at all. I can't seem to care for myself. Think anything you want to about me. But not about Pete. I got to make you know why Pete drowned."

[143]

"Do what your mother said. Go on back to bed. Pete drowned trying to cover up for the both of you. No one will blame him. Women set the tune men dance to."

Blaze opened her mouth to try to protest, but her father broke in, "There's no more to say except to tell you you're damned lucky that Joe is standing by you. He saved your life and if he wants it, it's his. You owe it to him."

Blaze swayed toward the table and her mother stood up, put her arm around her and helped her back to her own room. Loosening the dark dress, she steadied Blaze while she slipped a nightgown over the bright, bowed head and half lifted the girl into bed.

Blaze lay unmoving, unprotesting, as the sheet was pulled smooth, turned back neatly over the covers. Her mother's hands were deft as always, but her voice sounded dead. "We just got to make the best of things. Once a thing's done, it's done. Try to rest and get strong, Blaze. Then you will feel braver."

Blaze lay quiet, unmoving. All her life she had felt that she and her mother were almost one person. They were so close. They laughed at the same things, grew angry at the same injustices. A look between them had been as good as a word. Now a cold smooth wall seemed to have grown between herself and her mother.

Trying to puzzle out why a good woman should be so quick to see evil in her own child, Blaze felt her heart hammering, her breath seeming to strangle her, and again her one idea was to run from the hateful weight that seemed to press her down, down, down, in a sea of misery.

There was no place for her to run. She knew the pain, the weight, would run with her. It was no use to rush down the hall, fling herself into her father's arms and say, "Give me your love. Prove it by believing me. Pete is dead because I knew nothing about life, about men. I am sick with shame, aching because I am ignorant. That sin isn't all my fault. You should have told me how men think."

Half out of her mind with grief and worry, it seemed to Blaze that the scene was real, that she had spoken to her father, felt his rough hand as he pushed her away, saying, "I told you what not to do." She cried out in a loud voice, "But you never told me why!"

The door to her room opened and her father stood in the doorway, his stern face softened with a look of tenderness and pity.

"Hang onto yourself, Blaze. Your ma and me, we'll stand by you. You tell us the whole truth of what you been up to and we'll figure what's best to do. Joe will stand by you too."

Blaze turned from him shuddering, hid her face in her arms and felt the terrible trembling start over her whole body once more.

She gasped, "I dreamed you. You're not real. Go away, go away!"

Zande Allan stepped inside the room, stood uneasily beside the bed. "What's come over you?" he asked. "You light-headed? Don't you know your own father?"

The concern in his voice touched Blaze. She sensed that he was as troubled for her as for himself. She lifted her head and though the room seemed to turn, her father to waver in the fading light of evening, she tried to smile at him as she said, "It's all right, Father. I was dreaming, I guess. I'm so tired I don't know anything."

He stood above her a moment and then his hand reached out, smoothed back her hair as he used to do when she was a small girl. "Get some sleep," he said. "Your mother'll be needing you. She's plumb wore out."

Blaze whispered, "Yes, Father," and turned away lest he see the sudden tears that blurred her sight. She heard the sound of his swallowing and in it all the things he couldn't say. The door closed behind him and Blaze heard the tired drag of his boots as he went down the hall to the other bedroom.

For a few minutes she could hear the muffled sound of talk between her parents and then it stopped.

Night, softly dark as a cupped hand over a tired eyelid, covered the Santa Lucias and on the unfenced mountains the stillness was as deep as the darkness. But Blaze knew that on a dozen ranches the fireplaces burned late and much talk must be breaking the quietness of night.

VII

Moving through the usual breakfast chores Blaze felt as though she had become invisible. Martin looked at her curiously for an instant and then hurried out to the barn without speaking. Avery ate his breakfast as quickly as possible and went off to the upper field with a sack of seed potatoes balanced over Old Black's pack saddle.

After they had finished eating and were outside Zande Allan spoke briefly to Martin about sharpening the plow. From the milkhouse window Blaze saw them lead the work horses out of the barn and make their way across the canyon to the plot that was to grow field corn.

Hannah Allan seemed twice as busy as usual, although her days never held a moment's idleness. But now she checked over all the winter supplies, inspected strings of dried apples as if a speck of dust or mold were ever to be found on the fruit she had cut and dried.

Blaze went silently around the house, busy with dishes, sweeping, bed-making and her dairy work. When the butter was churned and the last pan scalded and set out to sun she untied her apron, sat down limply on the bench by the table, her arms stretched across the clean table boards.

Instantly Hannah came out of the storeroom, half of a flour sack of dried beans in her hand, and put them on the table in front of Blaze.

"Sort these, will you, Blaze? You can do it while you rest and it will save us time when we're really rushed."

She put a dishpan in front of the girl to hold the cleaned beans, a small saucepan to catch the stones and bits of leaves and stems which were left after the rough threshing.

Blaze had run many handfuls of the richly red dried beans through careful hands and the pile of small granite and marble rocks was mounting in the stewpan before she looked up from the task and met her mother's eye.

"We ought to go down to the Garcias' place, some of us, offer to do what we can, shouldn't we, Mother?"

"Martin rode down yesterday."

Her mother's short comment seemed to indicate she considered the subject closed. Blaze found herself placed outside the family council. She forced herself to ask, "When will Pete's burying be?"

"Tomorrow."

Blaze took up another handful of the beans, bent her head over them, but though she felt hurt by her mother's shortness she asked, "Does Father mean for us to go?"

"Not you. He don't think you're well enough to make the trip."

Blaze lifted her head. "I'm all right. If I'm well enough to sweep and churn I'm certainly well enough to ride to an old friend's funeral."

Her mother looked at her curiously. "You want to go?" she asked.

Blaze shook her head. "No, I never want to go to funerals. Everyone suffers and feels heavy-hearted. But I'd never be such a coward as to hide from hurt. It's what you do to show the family you share their trouble. I wouldn't slight Mrs. Garcia for anything."

Blaze saw a strange look on her mother's face and felt a coldness creep up her spine as Hannah Allan put out a hand as though to soften her words. "Don't go, Blaze. You won't be welcome."

Blaze gasped and the handful of cleaned beans she was ready to put into the dishpan fell from her hand, bounced along the table, scattered on the kitchen floor. Her head was bent, her voice low but steady as she answered, "I thought of that, but I don't see why I should spare myself."

The mariana blue eyes of Hannah Allan clouded and she turned away and walked quickly into the storeroom. Her voice was harsh as she said, "I don't think anyone was planning to spare you. You'll have to start learning to take and to hold your own troubles. You're old enough to think of other people. You might think about sparing your own family."

Blaze stood up, said slowly, "I guess I don't know what you mean by that."

Her mother came out of the storeroom, her step quick, her whole bearing overwrought. "Of course, you know what I mean! You, a girl that the whole Coast looked up to, found half naked on a lone beach with a stark-naked man. I'd think you would at least want to stay out of people's sight right now."

"Mother," Blaze whispered, "us Allans stick together. Why do you turn on me that way?"

Her mother shook her head hopelessly. "People will remember this as long as you live."

Blaze walked over to the window at the far end of the room and stood facing it, not seeing the madrone tree, the garden. She was searching for strength, for quietness. She shut her eyes and took a deep breath and when she turned around to meet her mother's unhappy glance she seemed to have passed girl-hood, gained dignity.

"Yes, they'll remember," she said, "but not like you're thinking now. They remember the dry year of seventy; they talk about the summer the whole Coast burned and folks lost everything they had worked so hard to get. They remember that Ana Bation hung herself twenty years before I was born. But fires and floods and hangings don't make them stop living. They fret about things, but they go right on living. I will too."

"My poor baby." Hannah's voice hurt Blaze and when her mother's arms folded her and the graying head drooped down against the young bright one Blaze felt that she knew the feeling that ached in her mother.

"I wish I'd never gone down there, Mother, but I did. I wish I could take the shame of all the talk there'll be for all of us. But I can't. All I can do is hold my head up. People get tired of talking if no one answers them."

"I suppose so." Her mother's voice sounded taut. "Only keep out of your father's sight much as you can. And stay home from that funeral."

Blaze looked squarely at her mother. "Don't you think that if I don't go, everyone will be sure I'm afraid to, that I really did do what they're saying I did?"

"They'll say it anyway," her mother cried. "You could at least stay out of sight for a while till they all get tired of chewing it over. You could consider your own folks and spare your father and brothers the shame of being there with you, knowing what everyone was saying and not able to say a thing back."

"You mean," Blaze asked slowly, "that neither Father or the boys would say a word for me?"

Her mother answered flatly. "What could they say?"

Blaze drew back. After the first shock passed, anger deepened her eyes until they looked almost black.

"All right," she said. "If that's how you feel, I've nothing to say either."

Her mother turned, ran out of the room, down the hall and her bedroom door slammed shut. In a moment Blaze heard the first sound of sobbing she had ever heard from her mother.

The knowledge that it was because of her that her mother suffered plucked at the hard anger that possessed Blaze. She wanted to rush to her, make her listen to what had really happened, but a sense of outrage wouldn't let her.

She went outside the house, down the trail to the lower gate and eased herself through the rail fence instead of opening the gate. The open ridge was still silvered with the dried grass and weeds of last year. In the early sunshine they looked like a silver mist floating above the sturdy green under-carpet of new grass. Blaze bent her head, searching for the first short-stemmed baby-blue-eyes and the tiny magenta flower that was not much bigger than the head of a pin and yet made so brave a show.

"I wish I'd known. I wish I'd taken Pete. He'd be alive now. I'd be Mrs. Garcia and I'd hate him, but I'd have his children and I'd love them and after a while I'd be old and fat and I'd think of Pete as one of the children. Scold him when he came back drunk, praise him for little things a body should never take note of. It would be life."

She sank down on the grassy carpet, picked one of the bright-eyed magenta flowers and looked at it curiously. "You just come up with the first warm day, bloom for a day, make your seed and die and never worry about anything. Only a few days ago I thought life was as simple as that. Now I don't know what to do."

It was no use to talk to her parents. They hadn't even asked her anything. Her father had asked one thing: Where is your skirt? He hadn't listened when she told him why she had taken it off. Now it seemed that her mother condemned her without even one question. Martin must have brought the Coast talk when he came back from the Garcia house and they must have listened to that talk.

She tried to make herself picture what her parents must believe had taken place between herself and Pete. Feeling her face burn, her mouth get dry and tears gather behind her eyelids, she had a glimpse of the horror it would be to walk among the neighbors

[151]

she had known all her life, feeling their curious eyes follow her wherever she went.

How could she go down to the Garcia house when everyone along the Coast would be there, all of them filled with contempt for her? But how could she stay away? She found her head turning from side to side like a trapped animal. She shuddered, her hands cradling her bowed head.

She tried to say, "Now I lay me," or "Our Father Who art in heaven," words that Hannah Allan had taught all her children and which Blaze had always felt opened a window on eternity. She thought of it as a place higher than Mount Lucia, deeper than Big Creek canyon, and with a pattern of its own stars that spelled out in the heavenly sky the names of good children. Now her thoughts were so scattered, so confused, she could not say the simple, beautiful words.

Gradually she relaxed against the softness of the thick dry grass and let her thoughts spin and whirl in her weary head as they would. After a time she got to her feet. The sun was warm, the day was beautiful and she was young. Courage began seeping back into her. She lifted her eyes to the hills and as she walked back to the house a spring came into her step.

That night the first real sleep she had had since her father packed her home held Blaze deep and long. The clatter of dishes, the scuff of feet in the hall and the kitchen failed to wake her and when she finally struggled awake, she saw that it must be late. The room was fully light; it could be midmorning. She hurried to dress and join the family, but when she got to the kitchen, the room was empty.

The stove was still warm, but the fire was down to a handful of coals. She put in a couple of sticks of wood, opened the drafts and saw that there was a place set for her at the table. The boiled wheat was keeping warm over another kettle of water pulled to the back of the stove.

She ran outside and called, "Martin, Avery!"

Even as she called she knew there would be no answer. Breakfast was over, the dishes had been washed. The family had gone down to the funeral at the Garcias' place. For a moment she felt half frightened, half affronted. That was a strange way to treat her. But the strength she had gathered through the night served her now.

She hurried back to the kitchen, looked at the clock and found that it was a few minutes after eleven. No wonder the ranch felt deserted. The family had been gone for an hour by this time.

It was much better so. Now she would have no argument with her father about whether she should go or stay home.

She sat down and nibbled at a small dish of the beautiful golden wheat, but she had no appetite. She carried what was left in her dish and in the cooking pot out to the chicken yard and came back to wash up the few dishes, put everything neatly in place.

As she walked out to the pasture she felt heartened that it was such a bright spring day. It had always seemed to her the final touch of sorrow and loneliness when any of the Coast people were buried on a day that was cold and gray with rain as well as gray with sorrow.

Whistling for Gipsy she went along the field which was blue with marianas and gold with little yellow violets. This was one of the mornings when the mare was easy to catch and Blaze led her, holding a handful of the thick bright mane until she turned her into the saddling shed.

Gipsy saddled, Blaze went back to the house and dressed in a black calico with white pin dots and white collar and cuffs. All the older women on the Coast owned one plain black dress of some sort which was kept for funerals, but the girls wore any plain dress they happened to have.

There were flowers in the yard and flowers in the field, but Blaze knew her mother would bring flowers for the Allan family.

After she was in the saddle she rode Gipsy under the shelter of a beautiful laurel tree and took off one small sprig. Pete loved the laurel trees best of all. She would drop that small, fragrant offering close by his hand when the crowd formed to file by the coffin and take their farewell of Pete before the box was lowered into the earth.

Blaze didn't hurry. Funerals were held at two o'clock and before that the people who had come from far would be eating, doing some whispered visiting with friends and relatives they had not seen for a year or more. If she was to avoid her father she'd better time her arrival for the moment when the ceremony would begin.

When she was still far back from the Coast the trail crossed one of the great open ridges where the yellow bush lupin framed the new green of the wild pasture. Blaze pulled Gipsy up and sat looking down into the cove where she could see the bark boat. It was so small, so faraway and unreal that she let herself dream how things might have been if only her father had not quarreled with the Jansons. It was too bitter, thinking that she might have, someday, been riding down with Mrs. Janson and Tena to see the bark boat come into the cove, might even have had a chance to go onto the boat, see what it was like. She shook her head, moved the reins and Gipsy stepped out eagerly. Blaze wanted to hold her back, but knew it was no use.

When Blaze arrived the table was still set up for late-comers, though there was no one sitting at it. A girl whom Blaze had never seen before but who looked astonishingly like Pete walked forward to meet her and said, "Have you et? Most of them are done, but there's still plenty."

"Thank you, but I've only come a short way. I had food before I left."

"You alone?" the girl asked, her eyes curious but friendly.

"Yes. My folks came earlier. I'll help you clear the table if I may?" Blaze felt ashamed at her own interest in this strange girl's clothes. The black silk skirt rustled and had a flounce of box pleating around it. Her black blouse was boned and she wore a white stock wrapped high around her throat and a short black cloth coat with white buttons. Blaze was sure she must be a town girl, perhaps one of Pete's cousins from Monterey. And for the first time in her life Blaze found herself thinking about another girl, thinking that the white face, red lips and black hair and eyes of this girl were something that the young men of the Big Sur would remember as they rode the trails of the back country.

"My aunt's just near dead, she's so broke up over Pete," the girl said as she bent over to lift a great platter of fried abalone from the table. She looked at it a moment doubtfully and went on, "I guess we can clear off. Shouldn't be any more coming this late."

Blaze stacked a lot of plates together and followed the girl into a shed kitchen where the tables, shelves, even the stove, were covered with untidy piles of used dishes. None of them had been scraped and Blaze felt a housewifely horror. "You carry in and I'll straighten these up, get them ready to wash."

The girl looked at her blankly, then shrugged her shoulders said, "Suit yourself," and went tripping out to bring in more.

Blaze looked around for a moment and saw a big bucket standing on the floor beside the stove. It would hold the scraps. She hurried to clean off the plates, the platters, the bowls, and make neat stacks of everything. All the dishes were in order on one table, the kettles filled with water and a dishpan found before the strange girl got back.

As she drifted in, her hands absently holding a few used forks and spoons, there was a warm light in her eyes, a half smile about her mouth. "I got talking," she said, half apologetically, and then her eyes widened. "Well," she said, "you're pretty handy." She glanced at the kettles on the stove and shuddered.

"Say, we're not going to wash all these dishes! It's almost time for the funeral to start."

Blaze felt as though a cold hand had touched her. The idea of walking out and facing all the curious eyes on the Coast suddenly seemed more than she could endure. Wouldn't it be more of a service to Pete's mother to stay right where she was, get all this disorder clean and straight?

Pete had not shrunk from the cold ocean when he was trying to help her.

"We can get the big table cleared if we hurry," she told the girl who looked like Pete. Without waiting for an answer she hurried into the other room, started deftly clearing up the big littered table and the other girl carried things into the kitchen as Blaze piled them up.

When the last dish was cleared off and the table wiped up the girl sighed. "Well, Aunt Amalia ought to be glad you come along. You're a good worker." She patted her skirt, felt of her white stock, touched her hair and said, "Let's go see if there's a place left to sit down. Pete was my cousin. He was awful full of fun, poor fellow."

Blaze didn't try to answer. She followed the other girl, who said, "They're having the funeral out in the grove because the house is too small for the crowd. The boys fixed a lot of extra benches, but there ain't enough."

Gipsy was tied by the front gate, but as Blaze followed her guide down a narrow little-used trail toward the beach she saw that horses were tied all along the zigzag fence that meandered toward the cliff, horses were tied around the outside of the branding corral, under the trees, everywhere.

The trail turned sharply, dipped down into a small sheltered depression where sea pinks and beach daisies almost covered the sand. Rows of benches had been roughly arranged in a half circle and people were seated with their backs to the mountains, their faces to the cliff and the sea beyond.

The top bench was almost empty, all the children who had been told to sit there were crawling around on the sandy slope, busy digging the sand away from the leaves of the sand strawberries, searching for the sweet ones that ripened early under the warm sand.

Blaze started to sit down on the end of the bench, but her guide whispered, "Let's go down in front where we can hear and see what's going on. There's going to be speaking; come on."

Blaze shook her head, but the Garcia cousin continued to urge her until heads started turning and whispers began making a small sound like the wind over the sand.

The two girls walked down in front and sat down. The other girl took a rosary out of her pocket and bent her head, her lips moving with a rhythmic prayer. Blaze sat, cold and still, miserably conscious of eyes on the back of her neck. She didn't dare look up for fear of meeting her father's stern glance. She dreaded looking straight ahead, for there was Pete's coffin, and right behind it, facing her, were the whole Garcia family. She was conscious of them as she had followed her guide to the front of the row of benches, but the moment she sat down she bent her head, closed her eyes, trying to breathe a prayer for Pete's safe arrival in a warm, happy heaven where he could feel at home. She reproached herself that at a time like this she couldn't keep her mind on her prayer, but kept wondering if Pete would feel at ease in heaven, if it was his sort of place. It seemed strange to Blaze that she had very little idea of what heaven was like. Nobody ever really came straight out and said. They were all very vague about that mysterious but radiant land which was the hereafter. Then it suddenly seemed reasonable that the geography of heaven should be a mystery. After all, no one ever came back to tell the living what it was like. Perhaps it was not tellable, that it was something which would suit everyone, a place as widely varied as the people who hoped to live there when they were done with the mountains that they knew.

Blaze was conscious of a sound, of movement, and she saw a heavy-set man get up from beside the huddled heap that was Mrs. Garcia and walk forward to stand beside the coffin which had been made for Pete. The rough split boards had been completely covered with the beautiful iridescent abalone shells and Pete rested in what might well have been a great jewel box.

"They set it on saw-horses covered with a sheet so's to be able to build the flowers up around. Looks good, don't it, all them shells?"

Blaze nodded, whispered, "Who is the man that's going to speak?"

"My pa, and I bet he's scared. Aunt Amalia's his sister. She feels terrible. Cried herself sick, she has."

Blaze swallowed the cold lump in her throat, sat very straight and attentive as the big man turned purple, looked around as though hunting a place to hide, and then he spoke in a small, timid voice that carried surprisingly well.

"This is my sister's oldest, her first one, and a boy. He's just a young fellow and she's lost him. That comes hard, but it's done and we have to take it, learn to stand it."

He lifted his head and looked slowly over the benches filled with the Coast ranch families and spoke slowly.

"Maybe this is not the time and place to say this, you may think, but here and now, with my hand on my nephew's coffin"—he took a quick step over and reverently placed his hand on the corner of Pete's box—"I say that if Pete's life could of been saved, if there was anyone living who was to blame for the death of my sister's oldest son, the head of his family, if there is such a person, I got a word for her."

Blaze felt faint as she saw his eyes search the company as though seeking some special one.

"As long as there is a live Garcia we will pray that such a one is tormented like already in hell. We'll pray that Pete's drowned face comes always between her and the food on her plate, between her and the laugh on her lips—that the seaweed and the salt drip of the sea comes forever between her and any man she takes to. No Garcia will touch a hair of her head, but their prayers will hound her to hell."

He stood facing the people on the benches for an instant while everyone sat rigidly still.

A brown wren on a wild lilac tip broke the spell with his bubbling five-note trill and the people let out their held breaths with a sigh that was as audible as a groan.

Pete's uncle turned away, shaking, and felt his way back to the bench by his sister, who broke into a moan of such high intensity that it seemed more like the whine of a sawmill than anything that could come from a human throat.

Here and there among the neighbors women dropped their heads into their hands and began sobbing in sympathy until Nella Garcia spoke up loudly. "Stop it, Ma! That's no way to treat Pete."

Mrs. Garcia stopped instantly and hung her head dejectedly on the high shelf of her breast and wept quietly.

Blaze sat stiffly upright, her hands clenched in her lap, praying for strength to see her through whatever was still to come. Her eyes looked straight ahead, but she saw nothing.

A new voice made her forget for a moment the horror that held her.

Stephen Janson had walked forward and spoke softly. "Mrs. Garcia has asked me if I would say a few words. We are here today, together in sorrow. I know how deeply you must all feel the loss of Pete Garcia for I, who have only known him a short time, feel that his fun and music were the first things that made my mother and me happy in our new homeland.

"For us, his friends, and more especially for those who were his kin, the sudden loss of a son, a brother, a friend, is hard to

[159]

endure. But our faith in a life everlasting is our comfort. Through it we know that our grief is for *our* loss, not for Pete. We know he has gone home, gone while he was young and strong and gay, never touched by sickness or sorrow. Those of us who live long will grow gray and bent, our step up the mountain will be slow and uncertain, but always in our minds Pete will walk beside us in the bright strength of youth and all its promise.

"Let us pay respect to Pete today by loving and helping each other, trying to be as gay, as helpful to every neighbor as he was ever ready to be, and of our deepened kindness make a monument that will keep our friend's name living long in the memory of the Coast."

Stephen paused, folded his hands together and bent his head as though praying and Blaze, watching him, felt tears running unheeded down her face. Blessed tears, she thought them, dissolving and carrying away the cold stone of despair that gripped her heart.

As Stephen Janson spoke it seemed so easy to be good, to be kind, to be patient with the love that turned into fear and became blind to truth. She would tell her father and mother, word by word, exactly what had been said, what she had done, how good Pete was. Her heart beat faster, thinking of them listening, coming to understand, taking her back into their hearts. She could even feel sure that once her father knew and understood what had happened, he would ride down and talk to Mrs. Garcia. Remembering how well he had handled Mrs. Garcia when she was tipsy at the Jansons' party, Blaze was sure her father could persuade the Garcias not to curse her in their prayers.

Upheld by hope, Blaze felt secure enough to take a quick look around the company. She saw Mrs. Janson stretching up from the bench on which she sat beside Dulcie and wondered what she was motioning about, pushing her palm back toward the Garcia family and then tapping her mouth. She was looking at her son just starting back to his place beside his mother.

Blaze watched a puzzled look on his face and then his face cleared, he nodded to his mother. He turned back and stood at the foot of the casket and said, "My mother would like to ask if you would join in singing *Sweet Beulah Land*. Pete played it for my mother, taught her the English words and she would like to sing it for him, but is shy to sing alone."

There was no answer. Blaze knew the silence of the big crowd as politeness and interest, but she wondered if Mrs. Janson would understand. Any other time she would have said right out that she would help sing. Now she did not dare. It was not fear of her father's telling that it was a woman's place to speak when she was asked, but a bigger fear that the whole Coast blamed her for Pete's death and if they thought she wanted to hear a song would stay silent to show their disapproval of anything she did.

Before the silence could get too noticeable Stephen lifted his head and started the hymn, singing strange foreign words. His mother chimed right in, her voice a sweet thin soprano, but very clear and true.

> "Oh, Beulah Land, sweet Beulah Land,
> As on thy highest peaks I stand
> And look away across the sea
> Where mansions are prepared for me
> I see thy hills, thy shining shore,
> My heaven, my home forever more."

Blaze did not sing. For the first time since Pete's death she was completely carried away by her emotions. Mixed with anguish that Pete was not still there, stroking his guitar, half smiling, lazily singing along with the rest, was a fierce joyous uplift. She could see Pete so clearly going up the hills above that shining shore. Pete would be at home there; heaven was a land of shining shore and hills, canyons—everything he knew and loved.

Once more Mrs. Janson sang the chorus that she knew and this time Blaze sang and every voice that could carry a tune was lifted high. Those that couldn't sing spoke the words. When the song ended the silence was as warm as sunshine, sweet as the breeze from the east which sent the perfume of blue wild lilac down over the sparkling blue of the ocean.

The girl beside Blaze whispered, nudging Blaze with her elbow. "That Mr. Janson isn't married. He's a good catch for some girl. Got the money and knows how to spend, too. Say, you know he give my aunt all Pete's wages for the month and he hadn't worked but a couple of days of it. You don't find many like that."

Blaze felt there was no need to answer. She didn't want to talk of Stephen to anyone. All she wanted was that the rest of Pete's funeral would go off peacefully, in the feeling of kindness that had been in Stephen's talk, in his mother's few words about Pete teaching her a hymn.

Now, at a sign from Pete's uncle, the men who would carry the coffin to the family plot beneath the cypress trees, stood up and edged their way awkwardly past the people sitting on the benches.

Blaze looked to see who had been selected. Not Martin, and not Young Zande. She saw Arvis Demas and Timotaeo Ramirez, both of them much older than Pete and never close friends of his. Then Tom Logan; that was natural enough, he was Nella Garcia's beau. Juaro Garcia, the young brother of Pete, got up from beside Nella and stood beside the box and Bud Masters handed the baby he had been holding on his lap over to Alice, who took one child on each arm and tried to hold and keep quiet the squirming lapful.

Without too much confusion the men got the box, which had no handles, balanced on their shoulders, save for Juaro, who was not tall and he carried his share of the weight resting on the top of his head.

They walked forward a short distance and then waited for

the Garcia family to line up behind the casket. As soon as the coffin and the family were moving toward the cliff's edge and the cypress trees, the rest of the mourners came straggling along, some carrying flowers, some fruit jars with water to keep the flowers fresh, or babies who, tired and hungry, wailed as plaintively as the dipping gulls that drifted across the springy green meadow above the sea.

As soon as people began standing up, the cousin from Monterey hurried to take her place in the family group. Blaze felt relieved. She was sure that if the girl knew who she was she would not have been friendly. And with her gone Blaze could now take a place toward the end of the procession, avoid any word or look from her own people.

The trail to the burying ground wandered across the meadow in big curves so that by the time Blaze fell in behind the last of the adults and just ahead of the straggling group of children, the first of the mourners had already reached the site of the new grave.

Everyone was clearly in sight in the long line and Blaze felt a small shiver run over her as she watched how slowly, how patiently, the black-clad women moved forward. There was a burying yard on almost every ranch in the Big Sur and there were few of these women who had not stood on their own land and watched their own dear ones covered by earth.

Ahead of Blaze old Mrs. Ramirez was shuffling along, swinging her rosary, but saying sadly, "It falls so heavy, the grave earth does. It hangs on your heart for so long—too long."

Just ahead of her mother, Alice Ramirez Masters plodded tiredly, one baby in her arms, the promise of the next one already making a curve beneath her skimpy shawl. Her mother carried the youngest grandchild and a toddler clutched each of the women's black skirts.

Unheeded tears ran down Alice's face, and knowing that Alice must be thinking of her little boy and girl who were resting forever in the small fenced plot on the old Ramirez place, Blaze felt the sting of tears behind her eyes. Fear caught at her breath as she thought for the first time how the green of spring was already hurrying toward the death of autumn; how every firmly planted live foot that moved toward the broken earth of Pete's small plot was taking a step closer to its own end. Blaze shivered. It was a mournful idea. She could not grasp its truth. But she could sense a clamor for life rising in her. Days which had always seemed so long now suddenly seemed precious, part of her time alive.

And yet she could not keep from wishing time away. If only this day was done. If only a week, a month, even a year could be finished and done in the time of one breath, she would gladly give that time. Right now other people's lives seemed short, their deaths sudden and unexpected, but her own time alive insisted on stretching endlessly and none too brightly into the days ahead.

What would her father say, what would he do, when he faced her with disobeying his order to stay home, not come down to the Garcias' ranch? She shivered involuntarily, but there was no faltering in her step as she moved along with the rest of the procession.

As Blaze neared the open grave she could hear Mrs. Garcia crying softly, saying in a monotone over and over, "Not Pete . . . not Pete . . . not Pete."

Blaze set her teeth as her turn came to pause by the coffin. She saw that Pete was hidden by a white sheet, except for a small part of his face and one hand. She tried not to think how the big savage fish must have been tearing at Pete's rock-battered body.

She fought a feeling of faintness and quickly put her small sprig of crushed laurel leaves down beside his hand and moved on with the rest of the mourners.

As his neighbors took their last look at Pete and passed on, they formed in small groups about the open grave and stood quietly waiting. Quickly Blaze found her own people. Martin stood beside his father and mother, Avery was on the outer edge of the crowd with some of the younger boys. Young Zande stood beside Dulcie, his shoulder touching her, his hand holding hers. Tena stood right in back of them next to Mrs. Janson. Blaze wondered miserably if she had better go over and stand with her father and mother, but a quick look at her father's face, brown and hard as a pine knot, decided her to stay where she was.

When Mrs. Garcia's brother stepped forward and read the funeral service from a small black book, Blaze was glad she had not joined her parents. No wonder her father looked grim. This would be the first funeral in her memory when her father had not said the words for the dead. He said them from memory and his voice, clear and rich, could fill a whole field, rise above the beat of the waves and bring the message of hope and comfort to every listener.

As the town man stumbled through the service in a faltering voice, heads turned and many curious looks were sent toward Zande Allan. Blaze knew he must be aware that his neighbors were looking to see how he took this public rebuke from the Garcia family. His face betrayed nothing. Except for the small twitch of a muscle on his jaw line, he showed nothing but reverent attention to the stumbling words that were being read over Pete.

At last the dreary voice stopped.

Tom Logan and Arvis Demas lowered themselves into the open grave and steadied the coffin as the other bearers got it worked over the edge, tipped toward their waiting hands.

Mrs. Garcia screamed as the big box tilted, then slid over the edge and was lowered out of sight. Tom and Arvis scrambled awkwardly out of the grave, brushing the fresh earth from their knees before they stood with bowed heads as Pete's uncle flung a small handful of wild flowers on top of the sealed coffin, muttering, "Ashes to ashes."

He stepped back and the pallbearers picked up the shovels that had been neatly stacked at the foot of the grave.

As the first heavy clumps of dirt and rock hit the coffin with a hollow sound, Mrs. Garcia and Nella broke down completely and fell into each other's arms, sobbing and wailing until old Mrs. Ramirez and the uncle from Monterey united in trying to comfort them, patting soothingly at Mrs. Garcia and slapping savagely at the young Garcias who had become frightened at their mother's grief and were screaming with terror.

The shovelers bent and swayed rhythmically and the sound of falling earth soon became only an undertone to the quick metallic scrape of the shovels.

For all her grief Blaze found she still had room for anger and contempt as she watched Joe Williams edge forward, start patting at Nella and Mrs. Garcia, murmuring to them and turning, as they lifted their heads, to help them stare at Blaze. Whatever he had told the two women seemed to have taken their minds off their grief. As the grave was finally filled Mrs. Garcia left Joe comforting Nella and walked forward, saying with authority, "Smooth it over good and round it nice." Her face broke into strange folds for a second, but she said quietly and evenly, "Pete likes a smooth bed." She turned away, her shoulders shaking and her face hidden in her gnarled hands.

Nella put her arm about her mother, led her over to where the Garcia family was standing in a group ready to say a word to the neighbors, who were leaving now that the funeral was over. The folk who had ridden in from ranches as far away as the Little Sur or even Piedras Blancas, so far to the south, were in a hurry to be off, and made their farewells a brief and wordless clasp of the hand.

As people began moving about Blaze became aware of the buzz of talk. People gathered in small groups and she noticed

[166]

much shaking of heads. With a growing uneasiness she looked around for her father and saw him talking earnestly to Joe Williams. She looked away quickly as she saw Joe glance at her. She had turned and started toward Dulcie and Mrs. Janson when Joe's voice, raised and barbed, said, "I wouldn't touch her now with a ten-foot pole—not if you threw in two ranches."

He walked away and a small titter of laughter broke out among the buzzing women.

Without stopping to think, Blaze walked rapidly after Joe, headed him off, and said, "If you have anything to say against me, say it to me!"

He waited until he had everyone's attention and then said, very slowly, "I haven't got anything to say against you. I guess it's your business if you want to run naked in the woods and lay around in caves with men. I was only telling your father I don't want that sort of woman for my wife." He bent down, whispering savagely, "I told you I was not the man to jilt," and noisily kissed her square on the mouth.

For a stunned instant Blaze felt as though she had been dipped in fire. Then she slapped Joe across the face with all her strength.

He stood staring at her, his face bone-white except for the reddening welt. There had been a gasp from the crowd and then half-smothered laughter from some of the men.

Timotaeo Ramirez called out, "That's it, Blaze! Don't take nothing off him. Swing on him again!"

Joe pulled himself up, looked down his nose and sneered, "Another of your men friends, Miss Allan?"

Zande Allan stepped between them, growling, "I'll take care of this. You stay away from my girl, Williams. And keep your mouth shut or you'll get it shut."

Joe stepped back out of reach, but he said loudly, "I'm not the only man on the Coast that admires that pretty brown spot on her white back. Ask her about it."

The crowd pressed closer to hear more. Zande sagged back as though he had wilted and Blaze heard her mother's lonely little whisper, "Oh, Blaze, how could you?"

Blaze was not conscious of breathing, of feeling anything. She answered, but it was as though a dead girl said, "I told you it wasn't true. It's no use to keep on saying it."

She thought she had already touched the depths of pain and humiliation, but found she had not until her father bent over, her, put his arm protectingly about her shoulder and whispered pleadingly, "Tell me the truth, Blaze. That's all I ask. I know my own self what it is to make a mistake and try to lie out of it. Truth cleans and heals. Only tell the truth and I'll stand by you no matter what."

Blaze slid out from under the circle of his arm muttering, "What's the use? Everyone's gone crazy."

Stephen Janson was standing just behind her father, but she looked right through him. She didn't look at anyone, make any attempt to say good-by to Mrs. Garcia, but walked blindly up the trail to the house. Before Blaze was conscious that she had untied Gipsy she found herself riding along the Coast trail.

VIII

BLAZE had no will to fight. All she had left was an urge to keep moving. The reins hung slack on Gipsy's neck, but Blaze clutched the leather in her hand so hard that her hand became completely numb. She did not notice it.

She must keep moving, keep going, keep her lips closed tightly. The thought that her terrible ache was trying to get the best of her, turn itself into the sound of pain, terrified her. She would not give in to it, let herself give way. She tried to think what to do, where to go.

Suddenly aware of where she was, she gathered up the reins. The trail was only wide enough here for a horse and careful rider to pass along without scraping the wall of rock beside the trail on the mountain side. On the sea side of the trail the cliff dropped straight to a rocky beach three hundred feet below. This was no place to put all the burden on Gipsy.

Her ears pointing forward, her feet nervous on the trail, Gipsy tried backing away from a boulder that had come down the cliff, lodged in the trail and almost blocked it. The mare had never seen that crouching granite monster before and shied.

"Steady, girl! Come on, Gipsy."

Gipsy tried to approach the rock sideways. There was no room for any foolishness on this bit of trail.

Blaze leaned forward, spoke very softly, and Gipsy, her legs trembling, picked her way past the boulder. Blaze started thinking that her own problem was like an unfamiliar boulder in her path. She must not run at it or shy or try to turn back on her

[169]

narrow trail. Quietly, calmly, she must go forward—but where?

"Oh, God, our everpresent help in time of trouble, take my hand and lead me, let me find the right way."

The trail made a wide swing out onto a rocky point, and as Gipsy reached the tip and started to make the turn Blaze saw again the cove and the bark boat. It was less than a mile away and she could see that it was still being loaded.

Slowly the thought formed in her mind that the boat carried people as well as tan bark. Maybe she could go to Monterey, even to San Francisco, on the boat. But it was Stephen Janson's boat—besides, there was Gipsy. What could she do with Gipsy in a town?

She had no money. She had nothing but the black calico dress she was wearing, no knowledge of towns. But she could not turn back.

Behind her on the trail Blaze heard something and turned her head. Stephen, the last person on earth she wanted to see, was close behind her, riding as though he wanted to catch up with her.

Blaze felt she hated him. How could she go down to the wharf, ask for the captain, and try to bargain with him for a ride to Monterey with Stephen right there, hearing that she couldn't pay?

The Allans always paid for what they got. She could ask a strange captain if she might work her way, but not before a man that her father was neighbor to, and certainly not before a man her father had insulted. No matter what her father had done to her, she could not make him feel as small and cheap as that would.

She decided to ride past the landing as though she had no interest in it whatever. Maybe Stephen was only stopping for a moment to give some message to someone on the boat or to send out a letter. She could ride around the first turn in the trail, be out of sight and still be where she could watch and see if he went away before the boat sailed.

"Miss Allan?"

Blaze pulled Gipsy over on the trail, stopped so that he could ride by, only answering his greeting with a nod and a murmured "How do you do, Mr. Janson?"

He did not ride by. He stopped his horse close beside her and sat looking at her with an air of grave courtesy.

Blaze felt trapped. There was nothing she could say to him. There were too many things; the sorry way she had left his house, the dreadful scene she had just been through. She would not say any of those meaningless things that people said when they did not want to talk. How would it be possible for her to say, "Spring seems a bit early this year," or "How nice it seems to see the hills all blue with lilac again, doesn't it?"

A rising indignation that he should stop her, then sit and stare at her, put a sparkle of temper in her eyes, a touch of color in her pale cheeks.

In spite of not wishing to betray her feelings, she raised her eyebrows and said, "Well, Mr. Janson?"

That should put him in his place.

It seemed to make no difference in the steady way in which his eyes regarded her, though she suddenly felt that he was as upset and uncertain as she was.

"I stopped you to ask you if there was anything I could do to help you?"

Blaze felt her eyes fill up, but she held her head high as she looked at him, making no effort to apologize for the tears.

"You are being sorry for me," she said. "I'm sure you mean it kindly, but I will take care of my own troubles."

"Yes?"

She flushed at the question in his voice, but she answered simply, "Yes. I can't pretend I haven't got plenty of trouble;

[171]

everyone on the Coast knows that after this afternoon. But I got myself into it. It's mine to take care of the best I can."

There was a warmth in his voice that she hadn't heard at first. He pulled his horse close to hers, reached out and touched her hand. "You're a very brave little lady, Miss Allan, and I think you are a fine woman."

Blaze said gravely, "It was a help having you talk to me. Thank you for being kind."

She sat very straight in her saddle, giving Gipsy the signal to go on, but Stephen still blocked the trail.

He bent his head, his face thoughtful, and Blaze felt a catch in her breath. How good he was, how kind and dear! He must never suspect that while he was offering kindness, she was fighting an urge not to take him at his word. She had prayed so earnestly to see and know the right way. Was this the answer?

She looked at him quickly. His head was still bent, his eyebrows drawn together as though he were thinking deeply.

"Mr. Janson," she said timidly.

He raised his head, smiled at her.

"Yes?"

"I'd feel very proud to ask a favor of you."

"Anything," he answered. "Please ask and I will see that it is done."

"We Allans don't ask favors easily. Is there any way you could fix it for me to go to Monterey on the bark boat?"

His face lightened. "That's not a favor. That is a pleasure. I was going out on the boat. You are my guest on the trip. I'll have one of the boys take the mare up to the camp when he takes my horse."

He wheeled the big gray around, calling, "We better hurry; the loading must be about done."

Blaze held Gipsy back, blushing scarlet as she called after him, "I couldn't do that."

[172]

He pulled up, sounding a bit impatient as he asked, "Why not?"

Blaze blinked her eyes, swallowed, and then blurted out, "If I went away on the boat with you it would be a worse scandal."

He put his head back and laughed. "But my boat is very respectable. I put you in the captain's charge; he is the perfect chaperon anywhere in the world."

Blaze looked at him. "I don't know that word 'chaperon.' But whatever it means in your language, it's no good here. I'd be in a worse scandal than I am now if I left the Coast on a boat with a strange man."

"I'm not a strange man. I live here; my home, my work, it is here."

She put up a protesting hand. "But I—"

"Nonsense," he interrupted. "Of course you're going. I haven't any real reason for going, so I'll ride down to the landing with you, introduce you to the captain, and you'll be in Monterey tomorrow morning at daybreak."

Blaze swallowed. She tried to keep the eagerness out of her voice as she said, "If it's not really putting you out? I thought of riding in, but I wouldn't know what to do with Gipsy in Monterey. Besides"—she colored again, to her own annoyance— "my father could easily catch up with me on the trail. I feel I can't go home—not now."

"I understand that," he said; "but you'll come back. This is your place."

Blaze touched Gipsy and rode along silently. This was her place. She would be lost anywhere else. As she drew near to the turn-off to the landing, every rock, every tree, every rugged peak, seemed dearer than they had ever been. High above the gleaming red of madrones, up where the pines held candles of pale new growth aloft, she could see the wide wings of a pair of condors making for their perch on the Ventana. The high lift of the hills of home would call after her wherever she went.

She forced her head to turn from the hills, look at the wharf, the boat and the last of the mules and burros still standing like live haystacks, almost completely hidden by their loads of tan bark.

Stephen too glanced over the animals being unloaded and Blaze saw his jaw set, his laughing mouth firm into a straight line as he said, "I'll be with you in a moment, Miss Allan."

He stepped quickly in among the loaded burros, stopped beside a tall man who was unlashing the load from a tiny burro that stood trembling, its head hanging. Stephen didn't raise his voice, but Blaze felt shaken by the note of controlled fury under his quiet, "I told you not to pack this burro, Wilson. She's overloaded again and her back is raw from sloppy handling. Go up to the camp and get your time."

The man started to protest, but Stephen made no answer, stopped by a stocky, towheaded man a moment and said, "You take over Wilson's string, Begs; finish the unloading. And then turn them over to Zande Allan to doctor up. I want them kept in the corrals until those sores are healed."

Begs answered, "Yessir," and went on with his work.

In an instant Stephen was beside Blaze again, smiling as he told her, "The boat should have been loaded and cleared by noon, but everyone went to the funeral except the Santa Cruz men. Good timber men, those Santa Cruz fellows are."

The bark was being sent onto the boat in slings by a cable stretched from a rock back to the level land a short way up the Tan Bark canyon, and the boat had been worked in close enough so that it was anchored right by the big flat rock. A narrow walk-way of planks on pilings led out to the rock, and as Blaze started along the makeshift wharf, a big voice on the boat called out, "Lower the gangway; is coming Mr. Janson and a lady."

Blaze was startled to see a sort of chute with side rails come tilting down from the deck of the boat, and then a slim man in a white coat hurried down and stood, as though ready to help, right at the end of the chute.

Stephen didn't even glance at this polite young man, but put his arm under her elbow and guided her up the narrow incline. Blaze felt confused; it seemed shockingly bad manners to pay no attention to people who were eager to help you.

But at the top, when she stepped onto the boat deck, Stephen seemed gay and pleased as he said, "Captain Rudd, Miss Allan is a guest of my mother and myself. She is making the trip to Monterey and I know you'll see that she has a good trip."

The captain was splendid—his ruddy face, the gold braid on his sleeve and his cap, the way he swept off the cap and bowed from his waist were enchanting.

"To make Miss Allan comfortable, that is what our ship is for. You are sailing, Mr. Janson?"

"Not this trip," Stephen answered. "Is a cabin ready for Miss Allan?"

"It is always ready." The captain spoke with bluff confidence, but he called down to the white-coated lad still standing stiffly by the gangplank, "Olaf, the owner's cabin? Is it ready?"

"Yes, Captain."

"All right; so bring the lady's bags up and put in her cabin."

Blaze felt small. What would this gold-braided captain think of her? A traveling lady should have a leather bag with clothes in it. Even her father had a fine leather bag; her mother a small one, and a trunk.

Before he could say any more she hastened to say, "I have no bag with me."

The captain didn't look startled. Stephen laughed. "This is an unexpected journey. But Miss Allan will be with friends in Monterey." He turned to Blaze and said, "And now I'll wish you a good voyage though it is a short one. And I hope to see you soon. The boat is leaving at once."

The captain's eyebrows said, "That is news to me," but he

touched the resplendent cap, bowed. "I will give the orders. Will see you next trip, Mr. Janson."

He walked up the deck, turned into a small room full of maps and charts, closed the door. Bells started ringing somewhere down in the ship, were answered by shouts and orders in a strange language.

Stephen was looking at Blaze with a curious light in his eye as he murmured, "Must have surprised Captain Rudd to be hustled off this way, but your father could be out looking for you, you know. You'll get along fine, Miss Allan, and I'll see you very soon."

He touched her hand lightly, raised his hat, turned away and his long legs swung him easily down the swaying gangplank.

From the landing on the rock he called back, "I'll see to Gipsy. Don't worry about anything."

He waved his hand with a cheerful grin, touched his hat once more, and walked off without looking back.

Blaze clasped her long brown hands tightly over the smooth rail, fighting a queer lonely feeling.

The man she loved walked back to the land she loved and was soon lost to her sight among the great stacks of tan bark. The gangplank was shoved back onto the deck of the ship. A bell rang. The boat's hoarse hoot startled Blaze so that she jumped, and then the rock was suddenly moving away amid a great swirl and churn of green and white water.

Stephen was gone. The little wharf became a thin line, the tall pines on the high hills dwarfed to pigmy pines, and great faces of cliffs that Blaze had never seen before swung into view as the water widened between the little boat and the distant shore.

Suddenly the world seemed frighteningly big to Blaze. This close and breathing ocean seemed much wider than the flat shining sea she had all her life looked at two thousand feet down below her window.

[176]

Ahead of her what had always been the stubby finger of Pfeiffer's Point now loomed dark against the sky like a whole world in itself. And beyond it the ocean stretched endlessly. Somewhere along the shore of all this water was the town of Monterey.

She wondered if Stephen really thought she had friends in Monterey. Why should he tell such a thing when it wasn't so? She had no friends anywhere. She didn't have even a penny, much less an extra pair of stockings. What could she do when she got to a place so far away as Monterey? Suddenly she knew she was hungry, and that added to her confusion. How did anyone eat when they had no money and were away from their own pantry?

In times before, when she had thought of leaving home, of finding work in town, she had always thought of someone taking her to where the work was, saying to whoever it was that needed help, "This is Blaze Allan. She is a good girl and a good worker."

Who would say such a thing now? Not anyone she knew, unless it was Stephen Janson. She couldn't ask any more favors of him. And in her heart she felt ashamed that she didn't want him to know she was going to try to find work as a servant girl. She told herself that it was honest work, it was what she knew how to do; she could bake, wash, milk, churn—anything that was done in a house. But his house was so fine, his clothes so different, his manner so easy—she had a cold little feeling that he would not think much of that sort of work. He hadn't even bothered to name to her the men who were doing the rough work of loading the tan bark. Instinct told her that it was not because he intended to slight those men; he just did not see that they were there. Neither would he see the servant who brought in the glass of milk or ironed his shirts. His ways were not like anything she knew.

It was a good thing that he had walked away so carelessly.

Even if none of this stuff about her and Pete had ever happened, even if her father hadn't stopped any friendship with the Jansons by picking a quarrel with them in their own house, still she felt she should have hesitated to set her heart on Stephen Janson.

She looked at her worn dress, her brown hands, her shabby shoes, and shook her head. No. He belonged in a different world. Was he making fun of her when he said he wanted to help her? She turned away from the rail in disgust with herself. What had come over her to make her think such common, mean things? Never before had she thought that anyone meant anything but kindness when he said or did a kindly thing.

She must remember how her mother always said it was foolish to try to run ahead of time—you must wait and go along with it, let each day take care of itself.

She sighed, and behind her she heard Captain Rudd's cheerful voice, "You walk with me, Miss Allan, and I show you your cabin. Maybe you like to have a little rest before you come up for dinner? You a good sailor?"

Blaze felt confused. Dinner? It was long past noon. Maybe he meant she could eat supper on the ship? What was a good sailor?

"I would like to rest a little time, thank you. But not too long. I'm hungry already."

"The sea gives a good appetite." The captain chuckled. "We go find your cabin." He crooked his elbow and bowed as though suggesting that she take his arm. Surely he wasn't asking her to dance? In spite of herself her shoulders shook with a ripple of suppressed laughter.

"You got a joke to tell me?"

She shook her head. "Not really. It made me laugh to think I know so little about a boat. I've never been on one." She looked up at his broad and hearty face with growing confidence and said, "I was born back in those hills. I've only been in a

[178]

town once in my whole life, so there are many things I don't know about. What is a good sailor?"

"Oh, if you don't get sick from the motion of the boat. If you like the sea and are hungry your first hour out."

Blaze looked up at him. "I think maybe I'm a good sailor. I like walking on a floor that swings and tilts—it's like riding on a horse, isn't it?"

"I wouldn't know about that. I never been on a horse."

Blaze couldn't hide her amazement. "But how do you get places when you can't go to them on your boat? I thought every-one had a horse!"

The captain said chidingly, "You are walking on a *deck*, not on a floor, my good little sailor. You're a good sailor, I see that. You walk with the ship, not fight it. And when I'm not on my ship I walk, go on a train or ride in a cab."

Blaze, holding to his arm, smiled up at him. "That's all there is to riding—just swing with the horse." She wondered what a cab was, but wouldn't ask.

They went down a very narrow little staircase and the cap-tain called out, "Here you are. This is your stateroom, Miss Allan. Would you be rested in an hour? I'll send the boy down to call you then if you wish?"

He opened the door before which they were standing, bowed, saying, "Will be pleasure to see you at dinner," and then he walked away.

Blaze felt glad that he had gone away and let her be alone while she looked at the small cabin. There was a soft red carpet on the floor, a real bed, a cabinet for clothes and a washstand with bowl and pitcher, a kerosene lamp snugly anchored to a brass bracket and a round window through which she could see the Big Sur coast seemingly moving south as the boat churned along toward the north.

To Blaze this little room held everything of luxury that any-one would ever want. It was so clean, so white and pretty, so utterly peaceful. For tonight it was hers. She could slide the brass bolt across the door. She could lie on that smooth white bed and watch the waves and the shore and no one would call her to wash dishes, to churn or anything else.

She slid the door bolt forward quietly, took off her shoes and her dress. As she stood beside the bed, lifted off the white fringed spread and folded it neatly, she found that the floor had a queer way of coming up and tilting under her feet.

But with two pillows behind her back and her hands clasped over her breast, she took delight in the softness of the bed under her, the gleaming white of the painted walls, the soft glow of the polished brass fittings on the door, the chest, the curtain rod holding crisp white curtains.

Through the porthole Blaze saw that the boat was passing Pfeiffer's Point. That was as far as she could see from her own window at home. Now she was going into a new world, but she shut her eyes against it, panic-stricken with the sudden thought that this night, for the first time in her life, her mother would not know where she was, what she was doing.

She felt a tide of sorrow, cold and lonely, wash over her as she forgot her anger that her own had turned against her. She admitted now that her father had tried, in his own way, to stand by her. Her mother had spoken, not in anger, only in grief and pain.

Perhaps Stephen Janson would see that they got word she had gone away on the boat. But why should he? He had gotten no courtesy from Zande Allan, for one thing. Blaze swallowed, thinking that if Stephen had any scrap of what the Coast called common sense he would stay outside of her folks' troubles unless they called on him for advice.

She tried to shut out the vision of the look of evening at home: her mother's patient face, hands sure and quick above the pans on the big cookstove. Avery bringing in the milk, lighting the lamp. He still had a sense of marvel when he touched a

[180]

match to the wick of that kitchen lamp, although they had owned and used it for over three years. She could see her tired father drop heavily into his place at the head of the table. Martin was the only one who had looked at her with shame for her in his eyes. Was there a place set for her at the home table? Of course there was, and that empty plate would drag on her mother with the weight of a coffin.

Blaze felt as though she were smothering, and sprang to her feet, stood with her hands pressed across her mouth, wondering why such things had to happen to people who loved each other.

For a moment she had an impulse to ask God to reach out His hand, turn back time, let her be still leading Gipsy out of the pasture, be riding, but making up her mind not to meet Pete.

"But He gave me my chance then," she thought. "I had the choice. I was mad and mean when I took it; now I got to stand what I did."

She sat on the bed, put on her shoes, and then went over to the washstand. There was a towel on a little bar at the side of the stand, but the delight of discovery was all gone.

She washed, smoothed out her hair, and put on her dress and then went over to peer through the thick glass at the darkening Coast. There was no house, no light, to be seen, nothing but an empty and strange world, almost formless in the growing dusk. The eager blue and white dance of the ocean had changed to a black unease that whispered as it sped by the little boat and sometimes slapped so sharply that the boat shuddered and seemed to drop down into the black water for an instant.

The small room seemed to close in on her, and Blaze welcomed the sound of a knock on the door.

"Captain Rudd vaits in the saloon for you. Dinner in ten minutes, Fruken."

"Wait, please," Blaze called, opening the door in nervous

[181]

haste. "Will you take me to the captain, please? I don't know my way around this boat."

"Come, then"—the young fellow sounded very good-natured, and Blaze followed his starched white coat through the dusky white corridors, up the narrow stair and along the deck to the center of the boat. Here the guide opened quite a wide door with a flourish and said, "Thank you, please. The Captain Rudd."

Blaze smiled at him, said, "Thank you too," and thought what pretty manners he had, as he bowed again and softly closed the door, shutting out the sharp east wind.

The captain was sitting in an easy chair at one end of the dark paneled room, the light from a green-shaded hanging lamp throwing his ruddy cheeks and white teeth into bright relief as he jumped to his feet.

She could hear the relief in her voice as she said breathlessly, "Oh, here you are! The boy said you were in the saloon."

"And so I am, and so you are, and happy to have your company for dinner." Again the captain bowed, crooked his arm, and this time Blaze felt a thrill of triumph as she gravely put her fingers on the bent arm and walked with him to a small ell-shaped extension of the room. Here was a table covered with the same sort of white linen cloth that had been on the Janson table. A low bowl of green branches and four lighted candles throwing dancing light on the silver and glasses made a scene of such splendor that Blaze felt shy and conscious of her crumpled black calico dress.

But the captain pulled back one of the big chairs with striped red cloth seats, and when Blaze sat down, saw that her chair was moved slightly so that she would be more comfortable.

Blaze drew a long breath and it escaped as a sigh. What a world of elegance and manners this was that she had wandered into. Could she learn how to say and do what was proper in this world? Could she earn herself a place in it—did she want it if she could?

The captain was talking and she lifted her head, hoping for the effect of an easy smile as she listened.

"And so he said you would find me in the saloon and so you did, and here we are. But now I know—" he twinkled his sea-faded eyes and gave the effect of pouncing like a hawk as he said—"I know, yes, let me think. That's it. In America the saloon is only where you go to drink the grog, the rum. Isn't that it?"

Blaze nodded her head. "Up in our hills a saloon is the place your father tells the boys he'll skin them alive if they ever go in one." She laughed. "I never saw one and my father never thought to tell me not to go into one." She turned her head sidewise, twinkling back at the captain. "I thought it would be all right. You wouldn't ask me to go someplace my father would forbid."

The captain's voice sounded a bit husky as he smiled. "Well, you are a nice child, like my own Helga. Only Helga is a bit of a devil like her father. I have to tell her not to do things that I do."

"Oh!"

Blaze felt her eyes go round with surprise. This was strange talk from a father. The captain talked as though girls could have a will of their own; even do things that they had been told not to do.

The captain seemed to be amused as he looked at her for a moment and said carelessly, "Sometimes she feels it is better to try things for herself than to listen to me."

There was shock in the second "Oh" that escaped Blaze, and a note of sympathy. She said, "My father is very wise about almost everything. You see, he is more than fifty years old."

The captain raised one eyebrow with humorous effect. "We are about the same in age."

"Well," ventured Blaze doubtfully, "my father looks older."

"So?" The captain pursed his lips, picked up a small bell at his side of the table and gave it a shake as he said, "And what wise age are you? Seventeen?"

"Why, I'm twenty. Seventeen is very young. Don't you think I seem much older than that?"

"Well, yes—and no."

"That doesn't sound like a very honest answer."

"Indeed? I must admit, my dear Miss Allan, that it seems a novelty to be asked to be honest by a pretty young woman."

Blaze said gravely, "I thought that if anyone were honest they would be honest with everyone."

The captain nodded his head. "And a moralist too," he said, sounding to Blaze as though he were sad. She felt more at ease when he turned to her and said briskly, "But now we will discuss dinner and forget morals. My cook is no moralist; he is a genius."

It sounded both witty and wise to Blaze, but she had very little idea of what the captain meant. She saw the young man bringing in a tray and forgot to worry about meanings as she smelled the steaming soup and remembered how very hungry and tired she felt.

Blaze had to restrain herself to be as leisurely about her soup-eating as the captain was, but she managed to come to the bottom of her soup bowl only two spoonfuls before the captain was finished.

When the same boy who had brought her to the saloon removed the bowls and cleared the table, Blaze had a slight pang, thinking that the dinner must be over. Almost wistfully she said, "I never knew that men could cook. But I never tasted such good soup. Do all boats have men cooks?"

"Maybe not." The captain leaned back in his chair. "But you will learn that cooks who are artists are unmoral, are brigands, with rapine and thievery, that snatch from all the earth for one blend of perfection. Do you know that in that small bowl went part of a turtle who once swam about Galápagos? That the cool limestone caves of Spain were rifled of a spoonful of sherry with the white light of the Spanish hill country sparkling in it? That brown men climbed a slender tree in the faraway Spice Islands so that my lovely drunken cook could bring you just that soup, with just that flavor?"

Blaze had the rapt look of a child listening to a fairy tale. "I never knew anything but what happens up where I live. We just cook what we raise"—her eyes begged him to understand, but her voice was firm as she finished—"and it tastes good too."

She thought carefully over what she could remember of what he had said and then asked timidly, "But when does the cook get time to go catch turtles? Where do they live? What is a galapagos?"

The captain started to chuckle, went into laughter that ended by his dabbing at his eyes with the biggest, whitest kerchief that Blaze had ever seen. "Forgive me, please do!" he begged. "But you are such a lovely child. I envy my friend Stephen."

Blaze looked at him in startled inquiry, but he hurried on, "That was all a lot of talk to impress you with the idea that it is not always the moralist who tastes the real flavors of life. My cook, he cooks. The turtle from the Galápagos Islands, which are off Central America, are sent to markets in tin cans, just like the spices."

"I don't much like to be teased, not when I don't understand any of it," Blaze protested, laughing, "but I see part of what you mean. Like when we have coffee. We don't have to go where it grows and pick it, we just roast it and grind it after we get it from the store in King City."

"You understand perfectly," he agreed gravely. "And now here is something from close to your home."

He picked up a wide silver server and deftly slid it under a slice of the broiled salmon which the mess boy had just put down in front of him. "Maybe this fellow started life in one of your own creeks."

"Perhaps he did." Blaze agreed, thinking of the salmon she had hoped to bring home to her mother. She shook off the depression of that thought and managed a smile as she tried her hand at the captain's sort of talk.

"Do you think he was born and grew up so he could come on this boat and meet your cook?"

The captain seemed pleased as he asked, "Do you?"

Blaze laughed. "I'm sure of it."

In spite of the stimulation of strange talk and strange surroundings, the soothing quality of good food, the flicker of the candles and the warmth of the cheerful room made Blaze feel more and more sleepy and she was grateful that as soon as the last dish was cleared away the captain said gently, "You hide it very well, Miss Allan, but I have eyes. I know young folks from my own Helga. You are very tired. I can see that."

She smiled up at him as he rose to his feet and nodded. "I've loved all this, so new, so nice. But I'm ashamed to say how tired I am, and how sleepy."

"Then off you go." He sounded as cheerful as Blaze remembered her own mother sounded when she was very small and got sleepy over supper. The captain walked with her down to the small stateroom and told her, "Your door locks; you are safe as in your home. Sleep well and you will wake up in Monterey."

"Thank you! Good night, Captain Rudd. You are very kind." Blaze felt her voice dying away to a sleepy mumble as she shot home the door bolt, hung up her dress and made her way in the dark to the bed.

But once her head touched the pillow her sleepiness left her and the strangeness of everything made her feel wide awake.

There were queer new sounds the boat made as it pitched and swung with the moving ocean. Strange footsteps echoed on the deck over her head, and tomorrow in Monterey everything, everyone, would be strange. No kindly Captain Rudd would be waiting there to tell her jokes, be kind and look after her.

Uneasily she thought of how these last few hours on the boat had taught her that the world outside of the mountains was very different from the life she knew. There were so many things she knew nothing about, and yet somehow she must find food and shelter, make friends of strangers.

Stephen Janson had been a stranger. It seemed honest enough now to think of him as a friend. She must try to feel grateful for that. It was not enough. She could not in any sort of honesty call what she felt for him friendship. The curse of Pete's uncle haunted her: "That the seaweed and the salt drip of the sea comes forever between her and any man she takes to."

Was it already coming true? The seaweed and the salt drip of the sea was making wide miles between them already. It was not fair or right for her even to think of Stephen with love and longing. Right this instant the Garcias could be on their knees asking payment for their loss of Pete, praying her into deeper trouble.

She hid her face in the white pillow, and her shoulders shook as she whispered, "Stephen. Stephen."

Outside in the darkness the sea answered: Hush, hush.

IX

BLAZE turned over in bed sleepily, thinking she heard the far-off sound of thunder, but as she settled the pillow more comfortably under her head she opened her eyes for an instant. It was bright daylight.

Startled, she sat up and as the sound came again she realized it was someone knocking on the door.

She jumped from bed, held the calico dress over the shift she had slept in, and asked timidly, "What is it, please?"

"Your coffee, Miss Allan. I leave the tray here by the door for you. The ship's in, tied up already."

That news shocked her sharply awake, more frightened than pleased that her journey by boat was over.

She tiptoed over to the door in her stocking feet, unbolted it and opened it a cautious crack. The boy was gone, but on the floor beside the door was a covered tray. She took it into the room, put it on the small table beside the bed and lifted the hot metal cover.

Pleased as a child, she surveyed the cup and saucer, the squat little brown pot holding coffee and a piece of warm coffeecake smelling of cinnamon. Everything thrilled her: the tiny glass pitcher with cream, the amazing sugar in neat squares.

But there was no one to share the pleasure in all these things. How her mother would love these pretty dishes, the crisp white napkin folded beside the cup, the white cloth that covered the tray.

She hurried through her solitary breakfast, thinking of the

[188]

porridge, the ham and eggs, the hot bread and potatoes that made up the ranch breakfast, trying not to think of her empty place at the Allan table.

She finished the coffee and then went to look anxiously at the dress she had hung up so carefully last night. She shook it out, turned it around. It was not so wrinkled as she had feared and by smoothing the collar with her hands and shaking the flounce out carefully, she made it look quite fresh and neat.

There was a small mirror above the washstand, and Blaze looked doubtfully at her hair. She certainly needed a comb; some soap would be a help, she thought. But there was water and a towel. She filled the basin and then she noticed the little knob beside the mirror and rather doubtfully she tugged at it. The mirror swung forward. It was a door and behind it were three narrow shelves holding a wrapped bar of soap, a small comb in a paper cover. Feeling slightly guilty, Blaze picked them up, one by one, and looked at them. They were marked "guest" and she put them down regretfully. She would like to have the use of that soap and the comb, but they were being saved for a guest. That was not her. She hadn't been invited, but had asked if she might ride on this boat.

For a while she stood looking at the tray, troubled as to what she should do about that. Should she carry it to wherever the kitchen was? At last she decided that in this queer upside-down world where men brought food to women and carried off the used dishes, the best thing to do was to leave the tray. It seemed an untidy sort of trick, but after all, the boy had carried everything out of the saloon last night.

So she went over to the bed, stripped off the covers, neatly folded the sheets and the pillow slip she had used, put them on the chair beside the bed and then smoothed up the covers and the spread.

Looking out of the porthole she could see the worn piles of the wharf the boat was tied up to, see the great bundles of tan bark going over the side and onto the deck. A wagon with two horses came clattering smartly over the loose boards of the old wharf and a whistling boy stopped the team, jumped down and began to unload wrapped-up packages from the back of the wagon. The boy in the white coat who had brought her breakfast came in sight and began sorting the packages, putting some of them into a big basket.

All the world seemed busy, but now she had the bed made and there was nothing for her to do but leave. She took one last anxious look at herself in the little mirror, wishing she had a hat and a wrap of some sort. She knew she would look strange in a town without a hat or coat.

She shrugged her shoulders. Well, she was here; she would have to get along with what she had.

Her feet, practiced now, went lightly up the narrow stairway, along the empty deck and to the gangplank. She stood uncertainly looking around. She had hoped to see the captain, to thank him for his kindness, but the ship seemed completely deserted.

Slowly she walked down the gangplank and when she reached the dock stood looking back at the boat. If the mess boy came in sight again she could leave a message for the captain with him.

The grocer's wagon had driven off; the mess boy had vanished. She knew that she was dawdling because she was confused about what to do next. Having admitted that, she brightened up, gave her head an independent Allan tilt, and walked up on the wharf.

Captain Rudd, with a sheaf of papers in his hand, came charging around a great pile of tan bark and almost ran her down.

"Oh, I was afraid I'd missed seeing you. I did want to tell you how much I liked my first trip on a boat."

The captain chuckled. "You must believe me when I tell you

I was thinking about you so deeply that I didn't see you until I almost ran over you." He took her empty hand, patted it and said teasingly, "That is all right for an old man like me to tell you, my dear, but when the young men of Monterey tell you they think of you, don't let it turn your pretty head."

Blaze looked at him earnestly. "Turn my head? I think you are teasing again, but I'll be careful to look straight ahead." In spite of herself laughter bubbled up and she told him, "I don't know any young Monterey men."

"Well, you will."

But suddenly he became serious. "You are not going uptown alone, are you? You could wait on the boat for your friends; that would be better."

Blaze colored, stuttered, "Thank you. But no one was sure just when I was coming to Monterey."

"So? Well, the town is small; you'll have no trouble. Will you be coming back on the *Vesta*, Miss Allan?"

Blaze shook her head. "I'm planning to stay for some time; I'm not sure of my plans."

Feeling that there was still a look of anxiety for her on the captain's kindly face, she hastily murmured, "Thank you again, Captain Rudd. It was a lovely trip."

Head high and trying to appear at ease, she walked straight ahead as though she knew just where she was going. At the end of the dock she turned, waved gaily to the watching captain, and then walked up a twisted narrow street that was lined with old adobe houses.

By noon Blaze was hungry, weary and forlorn. It seemed to her that she had been in every house in Monterey. Few of the women she had asked for work would even talk to her; all of them seemed to look at her suspiciously.

The day was bright but the wind from the bay felt cold through her calico dress. Her feet were so tired that she stumbled on the grass-grown cobbled street and sharp voices seemed to follow her saying, "Where do you live? Where are your references? I couldn't bother with a green country girl. I don't hire any help. Why did you leave your last place?"

She found herself again walking down the narrow twisted street that she had walked up with such eagerness only a few hours before. Now, as she came in close sight of the wharf, she saw that the *Vesta* was gone. Her last link with anyone she knew had vanished and for a moment she felt hopelessly alone and lost.

But as she looked toward the south on the cross street she realized that the shops and stores of the town were on this street. Courage returned, and she set off briskly thinking it might be a lot easier to find work to do in one of the stores.

The street seemed strangely empty even when she reached the place where the few stores were. Then she noticed a card in the barber shop window that said: "Closed for lunch. Back at one o'clock."

The law office had the same sign; the hardware shop sign just said: "Back soon."

She looked at the sky and by the sun she thought it must certainly be one o'clock or more. She stood undecided, shivering in front of the closed hardware store, thinking a bit wistfully of the Monterey people who had work to do, lunch to eat.

Then one elderly man came walking slowly down the street toward her, his hands in his pockets. He was almost up to her when he stopped, drew a key out of his pocket, and unlocked the door of a shop.

Blaze looked in through the dusty window, saw that it was a grocer's shop, and followed the man inside. He was tying on a big white apron, a rather wrinkled and used-looking apron, Blaze noticed, as he walked forward and said, "What can I do for you?"

She gulped, "I'm looking for—" Courage failed her and she

backed up a couple of steps, stammering, "For a friend that I thought might be here."

The grocer said crossly, "The store won't be open"—he turned and looked at the big clock behind the counter—"for ten minutes yet. Come in when the store is open for business."

He turned his back on her and walked toward the rear of the dark adobe shop.

For a moment Blaze felt discouraged. She was worse scared than a mouse cornered in a kitchen and a plain liar as well. She was licked before she'd even started.

She had walked out of the door before she turned, went back and followed the man to the back of the store.

"I was scared," she told him. "I'm not looking for anyone; I'm looking for work."

He growled, "I thought you was up to something. Well, there's no work here for anyone. Ain't got enough for myself to do."

Blaze stood her ground. "I could wash the windows. They need it."

He sniffed. "So could I wash 'em, but I'm not going to. Nobody buying anything anyway."

Blaze urged, "But the windows are so dusty you can hardly tell what's for sale in here. I could make them shine and the whole place would look brighter."

"No. I said no. I've got no money to pay out for help."

Blaze felt her voice was small and uncertain, but she pleaded, "I'd wash them, and then if you didn't think it looked better and helped your store, you wouldn't need to pay me anything."

He took another hitch on the strings of his soiled apron and snapped, "Oh, for heaven's sake, go on and wash them. I don't intend to pay you a cent."

Blaze unbuttoned her sleeves and, taking care to see that her still white cuffs didn't get crumpled, she rolled the sleeves above her elbows, picked up an empty sugar bag that was lying on top of a heap of grain sacks, flour sacks and empty boxes, and tied it on to serve as an apron.

"Where is the well?"

"The well?"

"Yes, to get some water."

For the first time he looked at her as though he noticed her. "Country girl, huh?"

Blaze looked startled, but she didn't answer. The grocer unbent enough to say, "Here's a basin. This tap is my well." Above a smelly wooden sink a brass faucet jutted out of the wall, and Blaze was fascinated to see how the water poured out of it, filled the basin and then stopped as soon as he gave the top of it a turn. "There's some cleaning rags"—he gestured toward a couple of stained cloths hanging on rusty nails beneath the sink. "Now what else do you want?"

Blaze took the basin, turned to a can with a potato on its spout, and set the basin on the floor beside it. "Nothing but a spoonful of this coal oil," she said, pouring it out before he could move to stop her. Rather to her surprise he offered no objection, but picked up a lopsided broom from beside the sink and began to sweep great clouds of dust toward the front of the store.

Blaze picked up the cloths, lifted the basin, but she stood watching him for a moment before she said, "It's no use to wash the windows if you throw dirt around like that."

"I'm sweeping," he shouted angrily.

Blaze shook her head. "I wouldn't call it that. If you'd sprinkle that floor with just a little water with coal oil in it you wouldn't have a bit of dust flying around. The oil would keep the flies out too," she coaxed.

The grocer leaned on his broom, regarding her sourly. "Look here, young woman, this here's a grocery shop, not one of your fancy millinery parlors. It's my place and I run it to suit myself."

"I'll use this water to sprinkle the floor for you and then I'll get some more for the windows."

Half expecting him to raise the broom and chase her from the shop, Blaze stepped out ahead of him, sprinkling the water as she walked. She heard the angry swish of the broom behind her, but she didn't hurry. If she was going to sprinkle this floor, she was going to do it right. At any rate, the clouds of dust were no longer boiling up to the ceiling beams.

"I'll be darned!"

She was at the front of the store carefully spreading the last drops of water, but she stopped and looked back over her shoulder as he called, "Say, it works. I'm not even coughing!"

Blaze smiled at him but said nothing. She went back to the fascinating faucet, held her basin under it, and wanted to laugh with delight as the clear water poured out. She added more kerosene to the water, replaced the potato on the spout, and called cheerfully, "That's a handy way to get water."

The grocer laughed as though he were pleased and swung his broom vigorously as he answered, "This is a handy way to sweep."

Blaze had to go to the back of the shop again, find a box she could stand on to reach the top of the windows, and she had to wash the inside and outside twice before she was satisfied. But cleaning the windows made it too easy to see how dusty and neglected the two display shelves looked. She lifted out the few battered cardboard signs, made the shelves and the display space as clean as the windows.

Proud of her work, she carried the basin back to the sink, rinsed it and the cloths and hung them back on the nails. Full of confidence, she began to roll down her sleeves and fasten the buttons that held her cuffs as she walked over to the grocer.

"Well?" she asked. "Do they look any better?"

The elderly grocer seemed to have a queer look in his eyes

as he glanced at the clean windows and then let his eyes stray over her.

"Sure they do." He took a step toward her, said, "So do you. Give us a kiss and I'll pay you off."

Blaze backed away. She tried not to show her prickles of fear as she said, "Please pay me whatever money you think the work is worth. I'm in a hurry."

She thought the man must feel ashamed of himself, he looked at her so angrily and spoke in such a harsh, loud voice. "I told you I didn't intend to pay you. You heard me."

Blaze said quietly, "Yes, I heard you say that. I guess I didn't believe it."

She watched a change come into his eyes that reminded her unpleasantly of Joe Williams, and she backed away another step.

But he sounded really friendly to her ears as he urged, "Don't be scared to speak up for yourself, Miss. And don't be in such a hurry to go without your pay. You work good and I was meaning to pay you all the time. I was just fooling, you might say."

Blaze smiled at him, feeling thoroughly ashamed that she had been as full of suspicion as the women she had talked to up on Monterey Heights. She said, a bit sheepishly, "Well, you certainly fooled me all right. I'm sorry I was so snippy, but if you think the work is all right, I'll be very glad to have what you think it's worth."

"No hurry about that," he answered easily. "I think I'll have more work for you and I'll pay well. You're a stranger in town, aren't you?"

Reluctantly, Blaze answered, "Yes."

"Living with your parents, my dear?"

He sounded too fatherly to be looking at her so eagerly. Wanting only to get the money she had earned, be out of this dim shop, Blaze answered, "Not just now; they—they're not here."

His face brightened and he stepped toward her, holding out his hand. "You come along with me into the back room for a few minutes and I'll make it worth your while. I'll give you a dollar."

Ignorant as she was of the world outside the mountains, instinct, the thing her mother had said nice girls could depend on, sent shivers of fear prickling along her back. She tried to hide her fear, say calmly, "A dollar seems a lot for the work I did. I don't want to overcharge anyone."

He moistened his lips nervously and then seemed to throw aside any further effort at pretense. His face looked damp, his hand was shaking as he held it out coaxingly. "I'll give you two dollars if that's what you're holding out for. But for God's sake, quit this fooling around and come on. I'll lock the door before anyone gets a chance to come in." He stepped past her saying, "I got just the place for such a pretty piece as you; just go through the door behind you."

For an instant Blaze stood as still as though a rattlesnake had just buzzed by her foot. Then she sped around the counter, dashed out from behind it, and was at the door before he could reach it. He caught her arm as she brushed by him, but she managed to jerk her arm free, catch the open door frame with her other hand and push herself violently into the street. She felt she couldn't stand, her knees shook. He stood in the doorway calling in a threatening way, "You'll pay for this, damn you. I'll show you. A word to the sheriff from me is enough to throw you in the lock-up."

Terror lent wings to her feet, and she was soon out of sound of his threats, but the fear of them went right along with her. She saw two well-dressed, pleasant-looking men strolling down the street toward her, and she hid herself in the deep entrance of a still locked and shuttered shop. She dared not come out until they were well past. The grocer might be hunting the sheriff right now. She came from hiding as soon as their shadows had passed the doorway and went south on the street as quickly as she dared. She must not run, attract attention to herself. She turned off the main street at the first cross street and hurried along until the road became a path. She still looked about fearfully as she paused to take her bearings, and she noticed the path beside a sizable stream. She saw that it led slightly toward the east and she hurried along, stopping suddenly to catch up a few leaves of sorrel to nibble on as she walked.

The taste of the crisp sour leaves made her realize how hungry she was.

Presently the trail she was following crossed a rough road which led up a hill. Blaze looked at the road. It was long and steep, but it led into pine timber and it went south.

The road was steeper, the hill longer than she had guessed. She climbed for what seemed hours before she gave in to the temptation of a pine log lying beside the road and sat down. She was drooping with fatigue. Monterey bay still danced, blue and white, below her although the slow white curve of its eastern sand shore was far enough away now to be faint and unreal.

If she felt so tired after only an hour's walk, how would she get out into the country she knew? She drew a long breath and relaxed. She would know the answer to that when the time came.

Suddenly she straightened up and looked fearfully down the road. A horse and wagon were coming up the hill, going the same way she was. Perhaps it was only a rancher, not a sheriff hunting her. She looked again, more carefully, and sighed with relief. The man driving was one of the old Chinese who came down into the Sur gathering seaweed. Everyone loved and trusted the seaweed gatherers; she could feel safe with him. He might even offer her a lift!

But she couldn't sit there as though waiting for that to

happen. She jumped to her feet and marched straight ahead as though nothing was farther from her mind than the thought of getting a ride. She didn't look back, but after a time she knew the horse was gaining on her. Now she could hear the creak of wheels over rocks and ruts, now the sound of the horse's hoofs, the tug of leather.

She stepped politely to the side of the road to give the wagon room and allowed herself a glance at the cart and driver.

The driver stopped his horse, looked at her and said, "You want ride?"

"Yes, please, I'd like it very much."

She saw that the old wagon had no step, so she put one foot on the hub of the wheel and climbed nimbly over it, drawing herself up with the help of the curved iron arm at the end of the seat.

Blaze had been brought up with horses to ride, to use for plowing. They dragged wood home on sleds over bumpy trails, but she had never been in any sort of wagon before. She found riding in one almost as novel and exciting as the fact that she was sitting beside a Chinese man.

Many of them came down into the Big Sur on the Coast trail to gather seaweed or to get and dry abalone. Sometimes they stopped and helped make crop when it was haying time. Even the ranchers who most resented foreigners would say of the Chinese men that they were good workers, quiet and clean and honest.

Blaze got a quick look at her rescuer without seeming to stare. He was short, slight and old. A battered and sunburned old straw hat sat soberly over the braid which wrapped his head. His overall was thin and faded but beautifully patched and he wore a short blue coat that fastened with braid buttons and loops. She didn't know which fascinated her most, the stubby felt shoes, low-cut and trimmed with the same sort of braid which fastened his coat, or the strange yellow color of his face.

[199]

The wagon moved slowly up the hill, the driver very withdrawn and silent. That pleased Blaze. He had done her a favor and now he was politely waiting for her to speak, just as any Coast man would do.

Blaze puzzled over breaking this silence. She didn't want to tell him who she was, where she was going, and it would certainly be rude to ask him where he was bound.

Finally she had what she felt was a wonderful idea. She would prove her gratitude by asking another favor.

"I'm going to cook my dinner when the Big Sur trail gets to a fishing creek," she said, "but I haven't any matches. Would you happen to have one you could spare?"

"Plenty matches."

He slapped the lines on the back of the nodding old horse and said very loudly, "Whoa now!" Blaze hid her amusement. The horse stopped as though he was used to this sort of mixed-up order.

The Chinese man felt in the pocket of his blue coat, took out a block of matches and offered them to Blaze who protested, "Oh, I only need one match, or maybe two, if you can spare them."

"Take." He held out the whole block and when she still hesitated, he put his hand back in his pocket, brought out a still bigger square of the slim sulphur matches. "I got more. You light, wind blow—you got nothing. Needs plenty match on this Coast. You take."

Blaze gave him a grateful glance and silently took the matches, put them in the pocket which was set in the side seam of her skirt.

The wagon bumped along over the road which seemed to become narrower and rougher with each turn of the wheel. "How far does the road go?"

He looked surprised. "You never been?"

She hesitated. She was sure he meant to ask if she had never been down in the Big Sur country. She evaded, only saying, "I've never been over this road before."

"Bad road, rough. Don't go far, about one hour more."

She clung to the iron seat rail and looked ahead as far as she could see. On one side smooth green treeless mountains swooped up toward the sky. On the other side of the road green surges smashed against the piled-up rocks that spilled out into the water forming small bays.

Except for the road it was all wild and quiet and lovely. Red-tailed hawks quested above the steep grass slopes, white gulls drew lovely curves above the water mountains. Blaze felt fiercely glad that in less than an hour now the road would be gone. Her feet would skim the trail as silently as the bird-wings tracked the sky. In some deep canyon she would find a sweet-voiced stream, leave the trail and follow the stream up the mountain a short way.

She could easily find a good place to make camp. She shut her eyes, dreaming pleasantly of how it would all go.

First she must catch fish and have food. Then she would look for soapweed and wash all her clothes and herself. The wind and the sun and the fire she would build would soon dry her things. Before darkness came she would make a shelter of poles and limbs laced together with wild morning-glory vine. All she needed was just enough shelter to keep off the worst of the wind and she would gather enough wood so that she could keep her fire going through the night.

The need for fire and food and shelter would keep her from thinking, and the work of finding it would make her tired enough to sleep.

Tomorrow she would work her way far back into the hills and find a place that would become home. She would need a cow, some chickens. How would she get such things?

She started as she heard the slap of the lines on the back of the plodding old horse, was ready for the sound of "whoa." It came, and the horse stopped. The wagon didn't. It slid sideways off the edge of the road and, very tilted, came to rest against a big boulder.

"Good. He safe now."

The Chinese man climbed nimbly up and over the high tilt of the wagon. Blaze stepped out on the boulder and then stood looking down into the mouth of the narrow canyon with a clean sand beach, a small fire going, two men tending the kettles that were hung over the fire from green forked limbs.

"Mussels!" she called delightedly to the old man. "I can smell mussels cooking."

He nodded. "Come eat."

Blaze felt herself redden with confusion. She had just as good as asked for food. Very brightly she said, "Oh, no, thank you so much, but I've got a long way to go. I must be on my way."

"Eat first. You go better then. Big Sur trail very hard trail, plenty hungry country. Come eat."

He marched on down the zigzag trail that led into the canyon without tying the horse or looking back, but it was evident that he was sure Blaze would follow him.

As they neared the camp Blaze was trying to puzzle out what were the square black mats that were spread out on the sand. As they drew closer she saw that the mats were the dried seaweed. She was so curious to know what anyone would want with mats of old dried seaweed that she·forgot her manners and asked.

"Do with? We eat 'em. We send to China, make eat, make medicine, very good."

The wind was rough and cold until they got to the sheltered place where the two men were bending over the fire. Blaze walked close to it, held out her hands, shivering as she smiled at the unblinking men. Behind her her guide made a strange singing sort of speech and his friends came back with words so strange to the ear that Blaze felt it was kelp-horn talk.

[202]

The old Chinese man who evidently was the only one of the three who spoke any English picked a big abalone shell off the driftwood that was serving as a table and filled it from the two buckets hung over the fire.

He turned toward her and put the shell in her hands, saying only, "Eat now."

One half of the bowl was heaped with beautiful-looking rice, the other half held mussels which had been taken from their pointed blue shells, and the yellow-orange meat made an almost jewel color against the opalescent shine of the lovely abalone shell.

The dish was as good as it was beautiful. Hot and savory, it put vigor and courage into the plans Blaze went on making. Her camp must not be too far from the shore; mussels and abalone would be the easiest thing to get for food, seeing that she had no gun to shoot game. She suddenly realized that in the days of playing Indian none of them had ever snared a bird or a rabbit. They played that they had; they built a play fire and made believe that it was the best food they had ever tasted.

Already Blaze knew that hunger was not going to feed contentedly on make-believe quail or rabbit. But cress and sorrel, wild mustard and acorns, abalone and mussels were waiting for anyone who wanted to take them. She would not starve.

She looked at the sea-bleached log where the three Chinese were sitting and again she felt the charm of her chance friends. Smoothly yellow, swathed in their faded blue, they sat on the shining silver of the old sea-washed log, their faces bent over the bright color of the mussels, and Blaze thought of the colored pictures in the big Bible at home. It seemed to her that in another time and place these gatherers of the grass of the sea might well have been following the young carpenter of Nazareth.

"Surely goodness and mercy shall follow me all the days of my life."

Goodness and mercy. Those were beautiful things that were held to no time or place. They were like the rain and the sun, the seeding and the harvest, and as long as the earth lasted and the seasons changed, goodness and mercy would be in the hearts of people.

For a moment Blaze wondered. There seemed little goodness in the old grocer; not much mercy in the women who demanded references, spoke so rudely.

The girl stood up, went to the stream and rinsed out her empty abalone shell, scrubbed rice and mussels off her fingers with the help of a handful of sand, and came back to the fire.

As she set the empty shell back on the table, she smiled at the older man who had driven the cart, said, "I was very lucky when you asked me to share your food. It was so good, and I was hungry, too."

"Good luck with your sea fishing," she called cheerfully to the whole group, and gathering her skirt above the sand her feet sank into, she trudged up the steep trail to the road without looking back.

She stopped for a moment by the wagon and talked to the patient old horse, rubbing his ears, giving his neck a comradely pat, and then she turned to the south.

Twenty steps and the road was behind her. This was trail country now and although the level trail twisted in and out among big rocks that dotted the narrow benchland above the sea, ahead Blaze could see a harsh mountain that put its head right into the surf, and high on the mountain's flank she could trace a steep line of ancient trail that wound up and up to find a crossing where the creek would be small and the canyon narrow.

High in the canyon's fold and so dwarfed by distance that it seemed not much bigger than a stand of woodwardia fern, was a dark patch which she knew to be the tops of redwoods. Blaze felt content. Where there were redwoods there was living water.

It would take an hour and a half, or two hours, of brisk walking to reach that place and she would make camp there for the night.

But no matter how lovely it seemed when she got up among those redwoods she would not stay there long. It was too far from the sea, too close to the town.

She tried to keep a good pace, but she couldn't pass a clump of sea-pinks growing on the sheltered side of a towering granite rock and not stop to look at them carefully. Farther on, a blue bush-lupin and a yellow one blooming side by side led her feet from the trail. A bright orange butterfly claimed his share of her time, a big black beetle whose hind legs seemed longer than his front ones was using the trail for his highway when she got back to it, and Blaze loitered, giving him the right of way.

He turned off among some scattered wild strawberry plants, and Blaze forgot her fellow-traveler in the delight of discovering a few nearly ripe strawberries about the size of a green pea. She searched the little patch carefully, not for the brief pleasure of eating the tiny, almost tasteless berries, but for the lasting thrill of finding this token of springtime.

When the patch had yielded the seventh small green berry, Blaze stood up, looked at the mountain still too far ahead of her. Startled by the length of her shadow, she looked at the sun and knew that the afternoon was far gone.

Now she really swung out and for a time the rocks and bushes almost seemed to be running to meet her—but the mountain stayed right where it was.

She covered the weary miles to where the trail started up the steep grassy slope and became so steep that she had to slow down or else lose time by having to stop for rests.

"Slow and steady goes far in the day." The memory of her mother's saying brought a wave of sadness and with it a feeling of being homeless. There was not much fun in having no duties, no sharing, no one depending on her to carry her share of the day's work. The dishes to wash, the heel of the sock to be turned, all the hundred and one tasks of everyday at home were the things that had given such sharp savor to time snatched to follow a beetle, watch the butterfly in the garden. The supper fire, the lighted lamp, her father's head bowed for the blessing— all these things of yesterday seemed achingly dear and safe as this nameless mountain began to gather newer, deeper golden light with the sun going closer to the ocean's rim.

She drew a deep breath and hurried, trying to reach the shelter of the canyon before the sun was down. Redwood canyons were dusky even at high noon; darkness came to them almost as suddenly as blowing out a lamp. She walked faster, thinking she could do without supper, but she would have to gather up wood enough to last her through the night.

She stopped for breath beside a big flat rock, struggling with a desire to sit down and rest. She knew she should not, but her heart was pounding, her head felt dizzy, and as she reached for her handkerchief, dried her hot, dripping face, she admitted she had never felt so weary before. She sat down.

"No good for town and not much use in the mountains," she grumbled to herself.

The rock was warm; the sun beat against the rough golden shoulder of the mountain, and Blaze found it hard to remember how cold it would be without coat or bed once the sun was gone.

She struggled to her feet and plodded on, achingly aware of the bruises she still carried from her battle with the surf. Her head drooped. The dark bruises on her body would heal, but the soul-scars of the day Pete drowned she would carry as long as she lived.

Trying to put it from her, but in spite of herself living over again the pain and humiliation of the last week, her feet moved automatically, and when she again became aware of her labored breathing, her beating heart, she stopped and looked up to see how much farther she must go.

She judged the redwood tops were still a thousand feet higher than where she stood. But the thought of gaining the crest of the slope, starting downhill toward the timber, first smelling the water and then at last hearing the stream, urged her on. She could be within sight of the stream in half an hour if she could only keep going.

The sun was a strange lampshade shape, red as the pentstemon flower beside the trail, when she took her last short breathing spell and looked back over the limitless copper ocean. Below her on the slope the drifts of golden poppies were already folding their petals against night and the honey-fragrance from miles of sea-blue wild lilac drifted up, warm and sweet, on the first stir of the evening breeze. It seemed too lovely to leave, but she knew she must do it. Once the sun was down this warm fragrant spot would be pounced upon by icy winds that would seem to pick her bones. Tomorrow she would have her camp all set, could climb up out of her canyon and watch the golden cities, the towers and steeples that sometimes grew like magic out of the edge of the sunset.

Reluctantly she turned her back on the glory spread out far below her, ready for the last climb, but she didn't move. She heard something. She turned her head sideways, listening intently. Puzzled, it seemed to Blaze that she *felt* the noise more than heard it. But she knew there was something coming.

For an instant she was sure she heard it—a regular thud, thud.

No wild animal walked like that. Then sound faded out again and her feeling of panic heightened. Hoofs made that sort of sound: too heavy for a deer, too quick and light for a stray steer or cow; too steady for range horses, even if they were on their way to their water hole.

Now the sound was louder. It was coming up out of the canyon toward her.

Blaze looked around for a place to hide, but she knew it was useless. A rabbit couldn't hide on the barren slope she had just climbed.

It was no use to run. No matter how fast she ran she would still be in sight for an hour.

There were at least two horses; she was sure of that, and also that any moment would bring them in sight. Blaze stood trembling, hearing now the musical sound of saddle leather above the thud of shod hoofs. These late riders might be someone from down in the Big Sur. A story of her wandering, friendless, coatless, alone on a mountain with night coming on, that sort of tale being carried to her parents was the worst thing that could happen to them. It must not happen; it couldn't.

Blaze straightened up and walked forward. It was against all Allan principles to hide, but she would have gladly hidden if she could spare her parents more worry. Since she had no chance to betray her Allan upbringing and hide, she must walk forward calmly and face whoever was coming.

She took twenty or thirty steps, and still no horse's head lifted above the canyon rim. But not far away on the south side of the trail was a sizable rock and a small manzanita bush growing beside it. If she could reach that she could make herself small, sit perfectly still and it could be possible that whoever it was would ride right by, never notice her. If they did see her, then she would seem to be only resting, not hiding like a scared rabbit.

Blaze wavered for a moment, full of indecision. The horses should be in sight by now; they had sounded so close. Then she realized that she no longer heard the thud of hoofs. It must be that the riders had pulled up for a rest. She forgot caution and ran, cutting off the trail and around the shoulder of the mountain on a direct line for the rock and bush.

The foxtail grass was already ripe, and the barbed seeds clung to her stockings, caught on her skirt, worked down into the tops of her shoes and stabbed like pointed tacks. She stepped into a gopher hole and almost fell, caught her footing and struggled forward.

"All that lacks," she thought, "is for me to find a nice big rattlesnake sleeping alongside the rock."

A few more steps put her on the shady side of the bush and she gave it a hasty look before she sat down in what she knew was the most unlikely place for resting on the whole mountain. Foxtail and red thistles were thick on the ground and a swarm of midges hovered over the rock. Blaze felt her shoulders sag with despair when she saw that the midges were deer flies. No pest in the mountains had a quicker, sharper bite than this hungry swarm above her head. If she sat quietly through their attack she would have reason to be proud of herself.

She sat down, folded her hands in her lap and set her teeth.

The foxtails scratched, the thistles stung, the flies bit—and no riders appeared. She thought, "A few chains to tie me to this rock and a few vultures to come tear at my liver and I'd be right back in the Old Testament."

The temptation to swing her arms, chase off her tormentors for a few seconds, was almost more than she could resist, but her hands stayed stubbornly in her lap.

She was shivering under the strain before she again heard the sound of the horses and realized that they were on the trail right above her.

She held her breath. The last rays of the sun would pick up all the red in her hair. If either rider glanced her way they would be certain to see her. But she sat unmoving, waiting.

The horses plodded steadily down the trail and in a few moments Blaze cautiously turned her head.

There was only one rider. Topping the gray horse was Stephen Janson. On the lead rope, saddled, was Gipsy.

[209]

Blaze opened her mouth to call after him, but her stung hands clapped tightly over that impulse, smothering it into a stifled gasp.

Her head drooped. She could feel her upper lip and one eye swelling from the stings. She knew her tired and dusty face was as peppered with welts as her swollen hands. The hem of her dress was thick with burs.

She could see the gay tilt of his light felt hat, the shine of his riding boots with the clean light trousers neatly tucked into them. He looked as clean and fed and cared for as the shiny gray or the burnished Gipsy. Knowing how she looked, Blaze felt that she would rather face Mrs. Garcia's brother, who hated her, than to face Stephen, who, with such confidence, had helped her get to Monterey.

Stephen was nearing a switchback in the trail and when he turned onto that, the shoulder of the hill would cut him off from her sight.

Blaze shut her eyes. It was bad luck to watch anyone out of sight. Besides, she was afraid to look for fear she would give in and call his name.

He was riding down toward the shore and the sun. Her way led back into the dark of the canyon, and the thought left her cold.

Why was he leading Gipsy? Why did he have to come by at all? She had been getting along all right; not happily, but all right. And now the sight of him brought fresh depths of despair and self-pity.

Miserably, she stood up, stepping on the rock to catch the last sight of him before tears of angry frustration blinded her. She shivered as the first of the night winds down from the high mountains blew through her thin dress, and then she froze into the cold stillness of granite as Gipsy pulled back on her rope, turned her head and nickered.

Stephen swung half around in his saddle, looked straight at her.

Blaze slid down beside the rock, put her head on her arms and gasped, "I can't stand any more." It wasn't fair that Stephen, of all people, should see her in such a state of wretchedness.

To run would be ridiculous. It was unbearable to stay, face him with tangled hair, a skirt maddening with scratchy burs, her face swollen from bites and stings.

Unreasonable anger flooded her and she raised her head. He was off the trail already, walking toward her.

Blaze drew herself up to sit on the rock, back very stiff and head arrogant.

"What do you want?" she asked.

He stopped, looked startled.

"It *is* you, Miss Allan." As though bewildered he asked, "What are you doing here?"

"Resting."

That seemed to bring him up with a jerk. But he looked very concerned as he said, "But I thought you were going to Monterey?"

"I've been there."

His voice lost some of its warmth, but it still held a grave courtesy as he said slowly, "I hope you won't think I'm rude, but I'm puzzled as to how you got here."

"I walked," she stated flatly.

His face reddened at her tone, giving her a fierce satisfaction. How could he stand there looking so washed and pressed, while she looked worse than a last year's scarecrow?

Blaze couldn't understand, herself, why she suddenly felt that he was to blame for all her troubles. She only knew that if hard words would not drive him way, in a moment she'd go all to pieces, start to throw rocks at him.

She saw distress replace annoyance on his face as he looked at her closely, observed the stings and swellings.

"You're hurt, Miss Allan. What can I do to help you? What's happened?"

"Why, nothing, really," she said with icy brittleness. "I've just been fighting."

That did it.

"Indeed?" There was no more of the gallant knight to the lady-in-distress attitude. He was very remote as he bowed. "I'll bring up your horse if that's your pleasure, and then I'll be on my way."

Blaze gave an indifferent shrug. "Don't trouble. Just drop her reins and she'll stand. I'll pick her up when I'm ready to leave."

He lifted his hat and bowed, replaced the hat and walked stiffly away without another glance.

Blaze watched him untie Gipsy's lead rope, coil it and tie it securely to the saddle. Then he dropped the reins in front of the mare, swung into his own saddle and rode off, the ramrod set of his back eloquent of his feelings.

When he was out of sight, she stood up. When he was out of hearing, she thought her heart would stop beating. Why had she been so horrible to him when he had been so kind to her? Her throat ached as she tried to swallow, and her tired feet stumbled as she made her way back to the trail and down to Gipsy.

She stood a few feet in back of the mare, listening intently. He was not only out of sight, but so far down the mountain that the sound of the hoof beats didn't drift up. That was strange.

She felt herself start to tremble, thinking he must have stopped. Perhaps he was listening to see if she came for Gipsy, was waiting to see if she would ride after him.

She held her breath in order to listen better, feverishly picking the most annoying of the stickers from her skirt while she waited. Still there was no sound of Stephen's horse. She had gotten rid of the last friend she had on earth.

Struggling with an unreasonable disappointment, she gathered up her reins, turned Gipsy on the trail, and felt the cinch before she put her toe in the stirrup.

Gipsy stepped out before she was well settled in the saddle, and every step the mare took up the steep trail in the gathering darkness added to her sense of desolation.

There was a good spring at the base of a big redwood and Blaze drew rein, let the mare ease over and drink. She had lost all desire to spend the night in this canyon. It seemed that to move on, keep moving, was all that mattered. She would have to stop sometime, someplace, but she wouldn't think of that now.

She urged Gipsy on, and the mare set herself to the steep climb that started just beyond the spring. The narrow canyon was like a wedge driven into the mountain, the trail down to the spring so steep that Gipsy had slid part of the way. The trail up was just as steep and the flat that had held the spring very little wider than the length of a horse.

Suddenly, she flopped the reins on Gipsy's neck. The mare whirled on the trail, narrowly missing the side of the canyon, and set her nose toward Monterey.

X

STEPHEN was halfway down the long hill above the town of
Monterey when Blaze caught up with him. She rode silently
beside him for a few seconds, hoping that he might say something that would make it easier for her to say, "I'm sorry."

Stephen was no help. Beyond lifting his hat and bowing, he
ignored her.

Blaze set her teeth and plunged in. "You have been very kind
to me and I was as rude as I could be to you. I came to tell
you I was sorry."

For a moment his shoulders were stiff, his chin set, and Blaze
decided miserably that he was going to act as though she was
not there stammering out her apology.

Then he turned to look at her and he was smiling. "I'm glad
you're sorry, if you like it that way. But I'm not sorry I found
out what a sulky young woman you can be."

Blaze swallowed, said, "Oh." So he'd found her out, was
washing his hands of her. She couldn't find it in her heart to
blame him, but neither could she quite control the little prickle
of resentment that ran over her, warming her tired cold body.

Very gravely he said, "I'd be in a bad way if I married a red
head thinking she was an angel, wouldn't I?"

"Angels don't marry," Blaze said. "My father says there is no
marrying in the hereafter."

Stephen chuckled. "I wasn't planning to wear wings to my
wedding." He leaned over toward her, peering at her in the
thin moonlight. "I don't want a winged bride either. I was

thinking of marrying a girl with tumbled red hair, one swollen eye and a bee-stung lip."

Blaze blushed in confusion. "I'm draggled and dusty, tired, cold and hungry. Don't say things to tease me or I'll cry."

"Now for heaven's sake, don't do that or you'll scare the life out of me," he protested, sounding in earnest this time so that Blaze had to struggle not to give way to his kindness and really start crying.

Stephen, after a sharp look at her, said no more, and they rode along in silence.

She felt that she could no longer sit straight, her head kept dropping down on her chest, and she came out of a daze of fatigue when she heard Stephen say, "Turn here, please."

She looked around, blinking herself awake and saw that they were on the edge of town, already among the scattered adobe houses and the few timber ones that marked the town's southern end.

Stephen was wheeling his horse into a wide, better-traveled-looking street than the main street of town and Gipsy was turning to keep pace with her friend, the gray horse.

Blaze said, "I don't know where this road goes, but I don't see that it matters. I have no special place I'm going."

"Oh, yes, you have." Stephen was cheerfully casual. "My mother has a dressmaker friend who lives down this road, quite close to the Del Monte hotel. She has an extra room and you could stay there for the night if you'd like. Mrs. Swen is a Norwegian and Mother likes to stay with her when we're in town. They drink coffee and talk Old Country. I go to the hotel and let them have their talk without the bother of a man around."

Blaze protested, "But I couldn't stay there. I look so tacky, for one thing, that no stranger would let me in. Besides, I haven't any money."

Her voice, in spite of herself, rose on the last words.

Stephen said indulgently, "You're so tired you're silly, Blaze

[215]

Allan, or you wouldn't say a thing like that. I'll pay my wife's bills, you know. Or didn't you?"

Blaze! Even though he'd added the Allan, it still thrilled Blaze to hear her name from his lips. But she said flatly, "You haven't a wife—or have you?"

"Not quite," he said gently, "but I hope to have one tomorrow. Do you think I shall?"

Blaze stopped Gipsy, turned a worried face toward him. "I know I'm so tired I'm silly, like you said. But so are you." She said slowly, "You're feeling sorry for me and you've lost your good sense."

He reached over and took her hand in his, held it lightly for a moment and then he said, "There isn't any need for you to worry any more. Everything will be all right."

Something bigger than the sea seemed almost compelling her to clutch his hand, put her head on his shoulder and cry out, "Don't be sorry for me! Don't be kind. Only love me and tell me so and then nothing would matter."

Instead, she told him, "You keep acting as though you don't hear a word I say. I've given you no reason to think that I mean to marry you, have I?"

"Every reason in the world," he answered gaily.

"How can you say that? It isn't so."

"No?"

She turned on him, weariness, anger and confusion sharpening her voice. "Certainly not. How often do you have to hear me say 'no' before you believe it?"

He sounded so lazily sure of himself, so sure of her, that Blaze trembled as he drawled teasingly, "As long as you keep on getting mad when you say 'no,' I'm sure you mean 'yes.'"

She could feel her lips tremble as she said, "You talk as though this was fun. Well, it isn't; not to me. I'm sick and tired of having you be sorry for me. That's what you are; sorry for me. Do you think I'd marry anyone just to save myself?"

He took her hand and his voice was very serious as he said, "No. I never thought that for a minute." He edged the gray over, stopped, slid his arm around her shoulder, and drew her close to him. "Forget troubles," he said in a smothered voice that frightened her and yet made her blood race. "If you can stand it, so can I. I love you too much to lose you, Blaze."

She ached with her longing to believe that love, and only love, not pity, was what he was offering, but she could not so easily feel convinced. She drew away from him, protested, "Don't say that. You don't mean it. Why should you love me?"

He laughed, but under his lightness she could hear an undertone of deep emotion as he said, "God knows, maybe, I'm sure I don't. Does anyone ever know why? But I do love you. Horribly."

As the full significance of that wonderful word "horribly" came home to her, she felt her heart set up a furious tattoo under her ribs. He did mean it; he must. *Horribly.* No one who was playing at love could think up that word. It was a true word for love. She had grown up thinking it was a soft sweet dream-like thing—love. But in truth it was terrible and wonderful and horrible.

In spite of herself she blurted out, "You do love me. And I love you too, so I know how it hurts to love." She tried to look at him but she couldn't. She took refuge in murmuring, "But why didn't you tell me so, instead of going on so high-handed about marrying?"

His arm, which had been almost harsh about her, softened as she yielded toward him and his voice melted her utterly as he whispered, "My dear, my little dear one! I'll take good care of you. I'll help you to be happy."

Blaze said, "You've already made me happy. You made me clear forget everything I ought to say. But love must have some quiet happiness to it as well as this horrible ache. There'll come a time when we'll both be happy that we have love for each other."

He looked at her inquiringly, chuckled as he said, "You funny little mountain whippoorwill, what's the matter with being happy right now?"

Unshed tears blurred her voice as Blaze told him, "I'll take small pleasure in making you a figure of fun to the whole Coast. Oh, Stephen, how can I marry you and have them saying for all time that . . ." She found she couldn't say the words herself, and she took refuge in murmuring, "Saying all the things they say when they know a girl is in trouble."

He sat very still for a while, not looking at her. At last he said, "I've thought about all that, Blaze. I thought about it before I asked you to be my wife."

Blaze shut her eyes, and tides of warm happiness that she had never thought to feel swept over her. Stephen did love her. He loved her enough not to be worried that the neighbors would pick at her name like chickens picked at flung-out bones. In a mist that was fragrant as the breath from the sea-pinks she thought that she would love him, she would honor him, she would obey him. She would live and die for him, but she could never tell him so in words.

Stephen said gently, "I'm waiting to hear you say 'yes.' You can say it if you try."

Her voice shaken with laughter and shyness, Blaze whispered, "Yes, please." His arms seized her and for a long moment everything else seemed blotted out.

Then Stephen leaned over, gave Gipsy a light slap on the shoulder, and as she tossed her head and stepped sideways after the gray, he called cheerfully, "You scarcely know what you're doing and saying right now. What you need is a warm supper and some sleep."

He edged his horse over, turned into a narrow lane beside a

long row of cypress trees, and Gipsy turned too. A few steps down the lane and he said, "Here we are."

Blaze had no strength left. She felt herself lifted, set gently on her feet, and Stephen's arm holding her until she could stand. "You'll make it all right; only a few steps."

She was half aware of a white picket gate, the smell of sweet williams and a lighted lamp behind some stiff white lace curtains.

At Stephen's knock there were brisk footsteps and then the door opened and the lamplight shone out.

"Stephen?" asked a voice behind the upraised lamp. "And a young lady? And where is the mamma, Stephy?"

"Holding down the homestead," he said lightly, and went on, "This is Miss Allan, Selma. Mother's neighbor down in the Big Sur. Take care of her for the night, will you, and I'll see you both in the morning."

"But, of course! Your neighbor is my neighbor, Stephen." Happiness seemed to bubble through Mrs. Swen's voice, and when she led Blaze into the lighted room and pointed to a cushioned rocker Blaze sank into it.

Mrs. Swen put the lamp down on a small table behind Blaze and murmured, "Make yourself comfortable, please. I'll run see what time Stephen plans to be here in the morning."

Blaze scarcely noted that Mrs. Swen closed the door as she stepped out into the night. She heard a murmur of voices for a few moments and then her eyes closed, she leaned back and dropped off to sleep.

She thought she had merely closed her eyes, but when she opened them again she found Mrs. Swen smiling down at her and heard her say, "Now in the kitchen I've fixed a good bath. That makes as much rest as hours of sleep. You go have it and then some light supper and bed."

Blaze stood up reluctantly, sure that nothing could be as completely blissful as to rest in that deep rocker, but she laughed

[219]

as Mrs. Swen herded her toward the kitchen as though she were a little child.

"Everything is ready—warm towels, all. And I took the liberty to put you out a nightgown, a pair of too big slippers and the wrapper. You use them to please me, will you?"

"How kind you are," Blaze said, feeling that this little woman must be very happy, she was so thoughtful and so gay.

It wasn't a round tub, but a long one of light metal, and Blaze felt very impressed to see a tub that had been made just for bathing. She could stretch her legs right out straight, and she did, reveling in the softness of the warm water, the flower scent of an oval cake of hard white soap with foreign printing on it.

There were two tall pitchers of clear warm water standing beside the tub and so Blaze decided to wash the dust and burs out of her hair. At last she felt that if she lingered any more over her bath it would be rude, keeping Mrs. Swen up so late.

The warm towels were a luxury that Blaze was quite unused to, but the thing that really made her gasp was the gown. It was of thin soft stuff and trimmed with tucks so fine they were like a line on the goods. The tiny featherstitching, the frills of lace around the neck and yoke as well as at the wrists, made Blaze feel that such a gown should be worn to a dance rather than to bed.

She stepped into the wrapper, admiring the black dots on the white challis, the black ribbon that tied it at the waist. It would be wonderful to have things so pretty, and she wondered if town people wore such clothes every day.

She knocked on the door that led into the front room and then opened it, put her head in and asked timidly, "Would you tell me where I can empty the tub, please?"

Mrs. Swen put down some sewing and stood up. "You don't empty it any place, Miss Allan. What you do is have the supper now, and then I show you where you sleep."

"Oh, but I can't impose on you like that. Of course, I'll empty the tub and clean up after my bath." She drew a long breath. "The bath—I can't tell you how I enjoyed it. And to get into nice clean clothes. It seems as though I must be dreaming."

"You soon will be." Mrs. Swen laughed. "And don't you go worry about the few things I do."

She hurried off and came back with a bowl of hot milk toast, a dish of applesauce, and left Blaze to nod over her supper for a few moments and then reappeared to announce cheerfully, "And your bed is turned down and waiting, Miss Allan. Come. Right down this hall it is."

She picked up the lamp and Blaze followed her, stood waiting while Mrs. Swen raised the window and put the stick under it, placed some matches and a candle on the small table beside the bed. Then she took up her lamp and, smiling, wished Blaze a good night as she closed the door.

Blaze knelt down, whispered reverently, "Keep hold of my hand, God. You been so good to me."

She felt dizzily for the bed which she was leaning against, thinking she would fall asleep before she could even get into it. Tired as she was it made her laugh to think of sleeping on her knees when such a safe, warm bed was waiting for her.

She roused herself enough to pull the sheet up over her shoulders as her head found the pillow and she was instantly asleep.

A knock on the door was followed by the appearance of Mrs. Swen with a tray and a broad smile. Blaze sat up in bed, astonished to see the sun shining.

"Is it morning so soon? It must be, the sun is bright already."

"So it is, and lucky too." Mrs. Swen set the tray on the table by the head of the bed, saying, "Happy is the bride that the sun shines on, you know. And even if it was raining I'd still say you'll be happy. Stephy is very fine; you are lucky."

Blaze was so startled she could not speak. She had not said when, to Stephen, only "yes." He was high-handed and she loved it. This was a fine day for a wedding day. She blushed to think he had already told Mrs. Swen about the wedding.

Of course, they were old friends, but she had no intention of talking of her affairs with Mrs. Swen, so she merely said, "Do I drink my coffee while I'm still in bed? I never heard of anything so lazy, but it's certainly fun!"

"That is just what morning coffee is for." Mrs. Swen nodded. "But you won't be left dreaming over it long. You got to try on your dress."

"My dress?"

"That's right. You didn't know, did you? Well, Stephy he told me you left sudden from the Coast and he asked me could I fix you some clothes."

Blaze put down the coffeepot she had just picked off the tray. "I don't understand what you mean."

"Of course not," soothed Mrs. Swen. "One of my good customers she ordered a whole outfit for a trip to New York and the next thing I know she writes me from New York she made up her mind to get her things in New York. So I got the clothes on my hands and that was bad for me."

Blaze listened, said nothing.

"I couldn't ask her to pay, you know. If I did I'd lose her whole family, her friends—my whole business. Some of them are like that"—she shrugged—"but not all, or I'd have no business."

Blaze said thoughtfully, "That was very wrong for her to do. How could she be so unkind?"

Mrs. Swen shrugged, turned her hands up and pursed out her lips. "They don't think, that's all. They got everything; they don't know how it is to earn. It's all right, turns out good for you, being almost the size. I fixed the gray suit last night from measuring your dress. I think it fits good now, but you try on."

Blaze said timidly, "I'm sorry, but I don't know if it's right to have Mr. Janson buy me clothes."

Mrs. Swen put her hands on her hips, looked in amazement

at Blaze. "Don't tell me you're one of them Bloomer Girls, or New Women! That's not the way to manage men, I tell you that like your own mother would. We got too many of those funny young women in Norway already. No good comes of such un-womanly acting up."

Blaze had never heard of New Women, much less Bloomer Girls, and she sat quietly, unable to say a word to meet this strange argument, and Mrs. Swen evidently thought that Blaze was convinced by her words, for she urged, "Drink your coffee while it's hot and then we got to fly around. Stephy sends a carriage for us at ten and we go get the shoes and hat, the gloves and all."

Mrs. Swen bustled out calling, "I be right back with the suit and the other things."

Blaze felt her hand shaking as she poured out the coffee. She drank it, ate the breakfast roll, thinking that this breakfast was exactly like the one she had had on the ship. She caught herself wondering if Stephen had coffee and a sweet roll like this when he woke.

She got out of bed, put on the pretty wrapper, and slid her feet into the big slippers and opened the door.

"Mrs. Swen," she called.

There was no answer, so Blaze made her way to the room at the front of the house and found what she was looking for—her dress. It was a sorry-looking thing alongside the soft gray broad-cloth jacket that was beside it on the table, but Blaze hurried back to the bedroom with it and then it occurred to her that she must also find her shoes, her underclothes. She felt embarrassed at remembering that she had left them in the kitchen when she had her bath. Mrs. Swen would certainly think very poorly of her for doing anything so slovenly. No matter how tired and bewildered she had been last night, there wasn't any excuse for being so untidy.

Then it struck her that Mrs. Swen might have brought her things into the bedroom last night while she slept.

Blaze looked around the room, saw the corner cupboard with a curtain in front of it. Hopefully she pulled back the curtain and nodded her head as she saw her shoes, brushed and polished, side by side on the floor and on the shelves above all the rest of her things carefully folded.

She scrambled quickly into her clothes, recklessly picked up the clean comb that was on a narrow shelf below the small mirror.

Blaze peered at herself anxiously in the mirror, thinking that the soft feel of the nightgown and the wrapper she had worn so briefly had already made her vain. She was rather pleased with what she saw. Her hair had been damp when she went to sleep and had dried in soft, almost curly, tendrils around her face. There were no traces left of the welts from the deer-fly bites.

She danced away from the mirror thinking how bright her eyes looked since Stephen had said he loved her. Today was her day of days—her wedding day. With all her heart she wanted to look her very best for him. But she knew she would not feel right to be married in the lovely gray suit.

Mrs. Swen had said that it was all right for Stephen to buy her clothes. Thinking it over, Blaze felt sure Mrs. Swen was right. She caught her breath, her eyes soft with dreams as she thought that from this day on, for all her life, she would look to Stephen for everything she had.

But she was not Mrs. Janson until the wedding was over. She picked up the flounce of her calico dress, shook her head, but her will stood firm. She was Blaze Allan, her father's daughter, until she was married. She felt it would be a slight to her own family not to go through her wedding in what her father had bought and paid for.

She felt so excited over all these amazing things happening to her so unexpectedly, so quickly, that she started walking nervously around the small room, longing for Stephen to come, bashful at the thought of seeing him.

Mrs. Swen's cheerful chirp came down the hallway, her feet a quick patter, and Blaze opened the door on the words "—all this fitting."

As Blaze opened the door, Mrs. Swen bustled in, put a heap of clothes on the foot of the bed and said, "And you just got dressed and now you have to take off again so I can fit these, please."

Nervously, Blaze protested, "I don't think there is time. Stephen, Mr. Janson, he's coming any minute, and I know men hate to be kept waiting; my father does."

"Fiddlesticks," Mrs. Swen answered with a toss of her gray head. "A bridegroom acts nothing like a father. Waiting is good for them. But I let you off quick. I measured your dress last night, and your shoes, and my neighbor, she got them, right size too, already this morning. So you try the suit and if that fits right, I fix the others without more trying on."

While Mrs. Swen stood by, picking at seams, patting at folds and clucking like a benevolent hen, Blaze drew on the first black silk stockings she had ever seen, marveled as much at the silver buttonhook as at the soft lightness of high buttoned black kid shoes. There were white gloves and a small black purse, a white felt sailor hat with two sets of tiny black wings giving it a fly-away air.

Not until every detail was settled to Mrs. Swen's satisfaction, even to the black purse to be held at just such an angle, did she march Blaze up to the long mirror in her fitting room.

Blaze looked, then she blushed. She laughed nervously, trying to keep happy tears from filling her eyes. With awe and rapture on her face she turned from the mirror to the beaming Mrs. Swen.

"I can't believe that's me."

Mrs. Swen looked smug. "I guess even that Stephy be surprised what a good picker he is when he sees his bride. Fine feathers make the fine brides, like they say, huh?"

Laughter bobbed the giddy wings on the sailor hat as Blaze said, "I thought it was 'birds,' not 'brides.'"

Mrs. Swen shrugged. "Same thing. A bird without no feathers don't look so good either."

Mrs. Swen turned her around slowly, put in just one pin where the cuff fastened, said, "There, now with no more fitting I do the rest while you talk with your young man. Don't I hear him coming over from the hotel?"

Blaze could hear a light creak and clink, but it was a new sound to her. She looked out of the fitting room window and marveled at the matched sorrel team, the gay harness and the handsome rig. Stephen fastened the lines, jumped out and put the weight down and came leaping up the steps, whistling.

Mrs. Swen went to meet him and Blaze fled to the bedroom, scarcely daring to admit to her own self how handsome, how gay, how everything wonderful he looked.

As she slipped off the silk-lined gray coat, began to unfasten the intricate hooks of the high-collared and boned blouse, she was admiring the gray silk dress, the blue cloth dress and the heap of fine underclothes on the bed. She could not think of them as ever belonging to her; she could not think of clothes at all. She looked bright-eyed at the sun streaming in through the window and made her fingers fly over unfamiliar hooks to the tune: "Happy the bride that the sun shines on."

Her own dress was back on, she was fastening her moccasins, when she heard brisk steps spanking down the bare hallway and heard Stephen call, "Hello, the bride's dressing room! What's my chance to have company for a drive?"

Blaze swung open the door, laughing, and Stephen caught her hand. "This is luck. I was afraid you might be all pinned up in some dress-fitting snarl. But Mrs. Swen is a wonder; she says you can take time to go for a spin with me."

She answered, "I'm spinning already. I can't take it all in and I know I'm just useless here so I'd love to go for a ride."

"Fine! And we can make our plans as we go. I've got a few things left to do; the ring's—" he turned as he picked up her hand, kissed her ring finger lightly—"the ring's pretty important. We'll drive down into the town and you can try on the ring; that will be safer than my guessing the size."

Blaze walked close beside him out of the house, was helped into the carriage, and as he picked up the reins she said, "I wish you didn't feel that we had to go into the town." He looked at her questioningly and she knew she did not want to tell him what a horror she had of the pretty town right now. She said hurriedly, "I'd much rather drive some quiet pretty place and not even have a ring than try it on in town."

He put his big hand warmly over hers. "What you want, my sweet, is what I want."

Stephen slapped the lines on the sleek backs, and the carriage rolled off so smoothly and swiftly that it seemed like flying. It was enchanting to roll along behind those sleek sorrels, cushioned in comfort, shielded from the sun and seeing the fields, the hills, patches of flowers and the wide shade of oaks speed by.

Blaze made a little purring sound of contentment and Stephen asked, "You like this?"

She glanced up at him. "More than I could say. It's like another world—the sea so close, the sand so golden, the hills so smooth and soft."

He pulled the team off the road, stopped when the wheels were clear of it, and asked, "Would you like a week or two of living here? The hotel is very nice; a famous honeymoon hotel."

She shook her head, not realizing that her fright showed plainly on her face. The town was too small; that wicked old grocer might see her. The idea that he might spitefully tell

[227]

Stephen that he had the sheriff out looking for his wife threw her into a panic.

"Oh, no, Stephen, please. I want to go back to the country I know just as soon as I can."

It seemed to Blaze that he acted slightly withdrawn as he said, "There is nothing I know of that would keep us from starting back as soon as we are married." Then he brightened up, became the teasing Stephen again as he said, "That reminds me. I haven't asked you today if you'll marry me." He lifted her chin, his face close to hers, and asked, "You are going to marry me, and this very morning, aren't you, Blaze Allan?"

His mouth covered hers before she could answer and then she almost forgot what she had intended to say. But in a moment, she smoothed her ruffled hair, answered solemnly, "I was told by Mrs. Swen that I was getting married this morning. I didn't say 'no' to the idea when she told me, and I do say 'yes' again to you right now. Is that enough?"

His look thrilled her, but his voice was very casual as he answered, "No. But it's a good beginning." He turned the horses in the roadway and they drove off as he said cheerfully, "Well, we can't get married here, so—off we go."

It took will power to keep the quivering happiness out of her voice as she said, "I've never been to a marrying. But I know the words; they're in my mother's church book."

Stephen didn't smile when he told her, "I've been at a lot of weddings and they seem easy enough; just say 'I do' at the right time, and the rest is easy."

He started the horses back toward Mrs. Swen's house, asking, "Won't you come along and help choose the ring?"

She shook her head. "No. You'd ask me did I like this one better than that. What I'd like is what you choose."

She thought he sounded a trifle short as he said, "How could I pick out a ring that will fit? After all, you intend to wear your wedding ring, don't you?"

Blaze repressed a smile. So he could be sulky, could he? She was glad to find her idol was human enough to be like other men, want his way. She said lightly, "I'll measure with a string when you get me back to Mrs. Swen's place."

Stephen answered, "Would it be better if I waited until you change your dress? Mrs. Swen is fixing something for you to wear, and you'll be more comfortable wearing a suit."

"You want to spend the rest of your life in Mrs. Swen's front room?"

"Of course not. What are you talking about?"

Blaze said stubbornly, "I'm talking about getting married in my own dress. It's not grand, but my father bought it for me, and I'll stay Allan and like I am until—" She blushed, picked nervously at the thin calico, and asked shyly, "You can see I'd have to do that, can't you?"

He shrugged his shoulders. "You know more about how you feel than I do. But I thought girls always made a great fuss about their wedding clothes."

"I'm not getting married like other girls do. I can't look for things to be as they would if I was getting married at home." She looked at him shyly. "But I wouldn't change places with anyone."

He pulled up before Mrs. Swen's gate, sat holding in the team for a moment, and then said, "If you'd rather, Blaze, we can have the wedding at my house. Mother would like nothing better than cakes and dancing and a big fuss over a wedding."

She shook her head. "No, I'd rather it was this way."

He fastened the reins, put the weight down, and came back to give his hand to Blaze, who had hastily stopped herself from climbing out, remembering the captain's way of acting, as though no woman was able to walk by herself.

She gave him her hand and when her feet were on the ground very gravely took his offered arm and walked beside him to the door. He knocked and then said hurriedly, "I'll be back with the ring and the parson in about an hour. Will that give you enough time to get ready?"

She smiled impishly. "I'll be waiting in that much time."

He raised his hat, turned and strode off without looking back, and as Blaze went in through the door that Mrs. Swen held open she found herself wondering about Stephen. Something seemed to have made him very serious. She thought over everything that had been said, but she couldn't think of anything that could have changed things between them.

"Are men nervous about getting married?" she asked Mrs. Swen as she came in and the door shut behind her.

"Worse than a setting hen." Mrs. Swen chuckled. "But once it's over they settle down better than women."

Blaze drew a long breath. It was good to have the older woman's reassurance. She had been married; she must know what she was talking about.

She turned cheerfully to her struggle with the good-natured dressmaker, who was bound that Blaze should wear the beautiful gray suit, the gay new hat.

But it was Blaze Allan, Zande Allan's daughter of the Santa Lucia mountains, dressed in black and white calico, who bowed gravely to the beaming minister and his wife, who had come as a witness; took Stephen's hand when she was told to, said, "I do," with clear earnestness.

XI

But it was a white-faced and solemn girl with "Till death do ye part" ringing in her ears who listened to the minister's cheerful, "Well, I wish you great happiness, Mrs. Janson; and I offer you my congratulations, sir."

Stephen followed the minister out to his gig and Blaze heard the minister say, "Well, thank you, sir! That's very handsome of you, I'm sure."

Then Stephen was back in the parlor, smiling at her easily, saying, "Well, Mrs. Janson?"

She tried to hide her sudden panic, but knew she couldn't. She looked at him frankly, but her voice shook as she said, "I don't feel like 'Mrs. Janson.' I can't take it in. I'm still Blaze Allan and I want to go home."

She wanted to back away as he came over to her, but she stood her ground, found his arm very gentle about her shoulder as he said, "Nothing's changed, my dear. I'll think of you as Blaze Allan until you start thinking of yourself as Mrs. Janson. When would you like to start down the Coast? It's a long trip and it's getting late."

"We could start now. I'm ready."

"And I can have my affairs fixed up in less than fifteen minutes, so we'll go, if that's what you want." He picked up both her hands, touched his lips to the broad band of pale gold shining on her ring finger, and said lightly, "All I'm asking is the right to buy my wife a few comforts. I'll speak to Mrs. Swen for a minute, get the horses from the hotel, and be right back."

She knew she couldn't answer and she didn't try. Stephen let go of her hands, leaned toward her and kissed her on the forehead as lightly as though she were a small child. "You have nothing to worry about, my dear."

She blurted, "Please don't be kind to me, Stephen. I can't stand it."

He said very cheerfully, "All right. I'll beat you whenever you think life is getting monotonous."

He called over his shoulder, "I'll be back soon," and disappeared into the kitchen, from whence came the murmur of his and Mrs. Swen's voices—very matter-of-fact and comfortable voices.

Blaze dashed the tears from her eyes, telling herself she was a silly fool, but that cold feeling of bewilderment and uncertainty wouldn't leave her. She didn't want to ride off down the Coast with a man that she scarcely knew. She would like it if she was merely taking a trip with him—this charming gentleman who was as kind and gay as Captain Rudd. But she suddenly felt that she didn't know him any better than she knew the captain. How could she be Mrs. Stephen Janson when she felt exactly like Blaze Allan? And when she felt so uncertain about what being Mrs. Janson meant?

She circled the small center table, warily eyeing the legal paper that the minister had given into her hands and that she had hastily put down for Mrs. Swen's handshake, for the minister's good wishes, for Stephen's light, cool kiss. This was her marriage certificate, the minister had said. She looked at the fine lettering and shivered. This writing also she must keep until death gathered her.

Mrs. Swen bustled in, a light in her eye, caroling, "And now, Mrs. Janson, your husband got it all fixed. You pick what you need to take along with you from all the nice things, and we pack 'em so that they can go on the horse."

Blaze looked at her blankly, said, "I suppose so. Yes, I must take something—oh, dear, I seem to have lost any sense I ever might have had."

Mrs. Swen laughed. "I'm surprised at you. You sound like a bride."

Silently Blaze followed her into the sewing room, fighting a feeling that nothing was real. She tried to relate the elegant blue cloth dress to her life at home and could only feel dismay.

"They are not very practical."

Mrs. Swen looked at her sharply. "My God, girl, what's wrong with you? Practical? Of course not! What you want with a practical trousseau?"

Blaze looked at her doubtfully, saw that Mrs. Swen meant what she said. She shrugged her shoulders. "I've had a very practical life," she said. "I can't see myself as a changed person just because now I'll be called Janson instead of Allan."

Mrs. Swen said cheerfully, "Well, you got a practical husband as well as one that's well fixed. That nice Stephy, he ordered you six wash dresses to come down on the boat as soon as I get 'em done."

"Six?"

Mrs. Swen, folding undergarments in tissue paper, her mouth full of pins, nodded vigorously. Privately Blaze thought it was like having six dozen eggs in one August day when the heat made milk sour, eggs spoil, and the garden yielded too much of everything.

One new dress was wonderful. You could get acquainted with it, know every fold and pleat and button. All this stuff piling up bewildered her.

But Mrs. Swen's bewilderment as to how clothes could be packed to carry safely on a horse brought Blaze a sense of her own competence.

"They will go into a couple of big flour sacks, or sugar sacks, if you've got them. That's the way we pack our good dress when we ride to a dance."

[233]

Mrs. Swen produced the sacks, but washed her hands of any attempt to pack them safely, and so Blaze was busy on that job when Stephen drove up to the gate, fastened the team, and came in calling, "Mr. Janson is all set to travel. How's Mrs. Janson?"

Blaze flushed, but she felt enough confidence now to smile as she said, "Once all this plunder is tied onto the saddle I'm ready too."

Stephen shook hands with Mrs. Swen, murmured, "I owe you a lot that I'll never get paid, but you know how that is."

In a flurry of Mrs. Swen's good wishes and messages for his mother he picked up the two bags, and Blaze followed him out of the house.

There was no sign of Gipsy or the gray horse. Instead, the same gay buggy they had driven in before was waiting. Blaze wanted very much to know where the horses were, but she tightened her lips over the questions. She was married now. She must go with Stephen, trust his plans for them both.

Her head ached from the strain and emotion of the day, but she thought perhaps she was already learning to be a wife as she made herself lean out of the buggy, smile and wave gaily at Mrs. Swen as they drove off.

"I sent the horses out to the end of the road with a groom from the hotel," Stephen said as he wheeled the team into the hill road. "You won't get quite so tired, breaking the trip that way."

"Thank you," Blaze said woodenly.

She couldn't look at him. Everything she had thought enchanting about him—his worldly air, his elegance, the strong chin and broad shoulders—all seemed to become terrifying and alien as Blaze tried to realize that he was her husband.

She turned toward him, clutched his arm and stammered, "I do love you, Stephen. I wanted to marry you. I did want to, terribly. I was thinking about you all the time since I first saw you. But now I'm all mixed up and scared."

[234]

His hands were firm on the lines, his eye steady on the road ahead and his voice light and cheerful as he said, "I'm surprised at you, Mrs. Janson. You're acting as they say brides always do, and I expected you to act like Blaze Allan."

She gasped, then chuckled, and he flashed her a twinkling glance, but his voice was serious as he told her, "We'll learn to do a lot of laughing together, Blaze, and then learning to live together will follow along easily."

"I'm ashamed of feeling scared, but it's not such an easy feeling to laugh off and get rid of."

Having spoken frankly, Blaze found she could relax, feel gay and excited about riding in a shining buggy all trimmed with fringe. She even began to feel easy with Stephen and she told him the story of her job-hunting in Monterey. She told it all lightly, hastily deciding to leave out the old grocer, and was very glad she had when she saw how deeply he seemed to feel about the town reaction to an outsider.

She was beginning to think that though she had not found work she had gained a lot. Knowing that there was a world outside the fences of the Allan ranch was going to be a help in meeting the new ways of Stephen's life. And for immediate gain, the telling of the story had bridged the awkwardness between them, brought them almost to the end of the wagon road.

A few more bumps and ruts and the easy swing of the spring seat made Blaze laugh delightedly and call to Stephen, "It's a lazier way of traveling than riding a saddle. I'd get fond of a buggy very quickly if we had a road to drive over."

And she laughed even harder when he said, "Someday we will have a road and a carriage in the Big Sur."

She shook her head. "No man will ever gentle these Santa Lucia mountains down to where they'll carry a road. My mountains are wild colts, Stephen. They'd shake a road right off their backs and toss it into the sea."

He started to argue the question, but she grasped his arm,

[235]

whispered with awe in her voice, "Who's that gentleman with Gray and Gipsy?"

He raised his head, startled, and then he said, "Oh, that one. He's the groom, the man I told you brought the horses out this far for us."

Blaze looked puzzled. "He's certainly dressed up—more braid on his coat than even Captain Rudd wore. Overalls would come in a lot handier for him working with horses, I'd think."

Before Stephen could answer, the groom was standing beside the buggy, touching his cap with a brisk air as he said, "I found a nice sheltered spot for your picnic, Mr. Janson. If the place pleases your lady I'll spread the canvas and unpack the hamper." He reached up for the lines, held them while Stephen helped Blaze down, and then the groom stepped in, cramped the wheels and tied the lines to the hub.

Then he showed Stephen the sheltered place for lunch and asked, "Shall I come down with you, sir? The trail is rough and I could help you give the lady a hand."

Blaze spoke up. "No, thank you. I'll manage. And I can take care of getting the lunch ready."

Stephen said, as though she were doing him a favor, "Will you, Blaze? That will be fun." He turned to the gold-braided young man and said, "That'll be all for now, Bates. You can gather up things when we've finished lunch and then take the rig back."

Bates touched his cap again, bowed and said, "Thank you, sir."

Blaze went down what she considered a very good trail, Stephen following closely but not, she noticed with pleasure, acting as though she were helpless and would trip and fall down unless a couple of men were helping her.

The canvas and a thick plaid shawl were rolled together, fastened with leather straps. The big wicker hamper looked to Blaze as though it might hold any number of surprises.

[236]

Stephen spread the canvas, put the shawl on top of that, and asked Blaze if she would like to sit facing the sea or the mountain.

"I'll turn my back on Monterey," she said, her eyes bright with triumph. "With my back to the north I can look at the sea, the stream and the mountains."

Stephen shook his head. "Aren't you going to look at me at all?"

"Not very much," she laughed. "I'm plain hungry. I want to look at what's in that basket."

By the time a fringed tablecloth, bright silver, thin plates and glasses were lifted out Blaze thought she was prepared for anything. But when Stephen looked anxiously for a square box, found it, got it open and took from it a miniature wedding cake with a tiny bride and groom standing under a silver bell, Blaze was so touched that she had to turn her head, trying to take unnoticed dabs at the tears that would come.

"Just a moment," Stephen muttered, poking among the host of cardboard boxes. "Oh, yes, this one ought to be it." He drew out of this box a small white bouquet: a white rose for the center, white carnations around the rose and a close circle of white sweet william around that. It was set in a lace paper holder tied with white ribbon and the streamers had tiny silver bells fastened to them.

He handed the confection to Blaze as he told her, "I hoped you'd like it."

Blaze used it to hide her face as she murmured, "Oh, Stephen! I love it. I never saw anything so pretty, so perfect. My beautiful wedding. Oh, Stephen—"

"Happiness make you hungry?" He was handing her a plate of sandwiches, setting a glass for milk before her and grumbling, "A fine wife you're turning out to be, Mrs. Janson. You made me think you were going to fix all this lunch and here I am slaving away for you, not a bite for myself."

[237]

Blaze jumped guiltily, looked at him and then sank back comfortably. "You scared me. I'm not used to having men tease, not about food anyway. The Allan men are very serious about eating."

"So am I," he answered, picking up a sandwich and then forgetting to eat it. He reached for her hand, looked at it, turned the wide ring on her finger and asked, "Do you think you can be happy, Blaze? You'll find out about my shortcomings and I'll learn about yours. But—well, we can have good times together, can't we?"

She closed her eyes for a second, then looked at him, smiled and nodded, tightening her fingers around his hand for an instant before she took her hand away from its grasp.

In her heart was a riot of happiness and an incoherent prayer: Let me be good enough, long enough; let me earn this blessed kindness and faith I have found. Everyone else turned against me, but Stephen believes in me. I can love him and serve him, honor and obey him all my life and I'll still be in debt in my heart for his goodness.

Try as she might to contain her feelings, her inner happiness shone in the eager gestures of her hands.

"Stephen," she whispered, bending toward him. He turned his head so quickly that their two heads touched lightly and she jumped to her feet, laughing, poised as though to run as she called, "Let's go! I want to be back in the mountains. I feel as though I'd run and jump and shout, be giddy as a colt, once my feet are at home in the hills again."

"We're on our way." He took her hand, swung it, laughing as he made her take long steps to keep up with him in the few paces where they could walk side by side. But as they came to the short, steep climb to the road he let go her hand, stood looking down at her for a moment and then said earnestly, "Have patience with me, Blaze! I'm only a stumbling man, and women are so quick and sure of how they feel about everything."

[238]

She tossed her head. "That's what you think. I've taken a long step, Stephen, out of my world into yours. I'll stumble and try your patience plenty of times." She looked up at him, questioning, "Bates—with the gold on his coat—is he what you call a servant?"

"Yes. He's the groom from the hotel stable. Why?"

"I'd make a bad servant. I don't know what they do." She drew her eyebrows together, puzzling. "The Chinese man asked me to have food with him and his friends. Why didn't we ask Mr. Bates to share our lunch?"

"Bates would have been shocked out of his gold buttons, for one thing. I wanted to have lunch with you, just the two of us, for another. Last, but very important—it isn't done."

"Well," she said thoughtfully, "I'll learn my way about in your world as quickly as I can, but I'll stumble some. Maybe it seems wrong of me, Stephen, but I'm afraid I'll never want to pay much attention to whether things are 'done' or not done. Isn't it true that kindness is from the heart and manners are something laid on from the outside?"

He reached out quickly, gathered her in his arms and his lips touched her hair, the tip of her ear, as he murmured, "My little calico princess! Damn it, I love you too much." He drew a long breath, released her and said mysteriously, "Don't make me forget that, will you?"

"Why should I?" she asked dubiously. "What would make you forget—if you do?"

"Never mind," he said. "I won't put the burden on you." He shrugged his shoulders, quickened his steps, and Blaze, glowing and light-headed with joy, followed him nimbly.

She was handed into her saddle and sat holding her new hat in its gay box while the sacks were fastened on behind the saddles and Bates got directions to go retrieve the wedding cake and bouquet.

Stephen took great pains about getting the flowers properly

settled at her belt, pushed something into Bates's hand, which made him say, "Thank you, sir; thank you kindly!"

The wedding cake in its white box went into Stephen's saddle bag and they were off to the Big Sur country.

Stephen held his horse back and Blaze pulled over to the side of the trail motioning him to go ahead. He looked at her questioningly. "Don't you want to ride ahead, Blaze? You'll get all the dust if you're in back."

She laughed. "Women expect to eat dust in this country. Men go out in front so as to shoot the bears and kill the rattlesnakes."

"I've never seen a bear since I came here."

She chuckled. "And the snakes are still sleeping, but every man on the Coast would think I was the boss if I was out ahead. Right now I've had my fill of being different. I feel meek and like keeping a woman's proper place. And anyhow, there really are a few bears, great big grizzlies, back in the hills, so be a nice husband and protect me."

He made a funny nose, wrinkling up his face at her, but he rode out in front and she called after him, "This is fun! I can keep my eye on you and besides, I think you ride very well—for an outlander."

He called back, "Keep your left-handed compliments, young lady. I ride very well for anyone."

Blaze looked at the mountains, the sea, the flowers, as though she had never seen them, never really loved them before this day. This wonderful day, full of laughter and friendship, of strangeness and fear and delight.

Blaze looked at Stephen's straight back, his bright head, with a small twinge of envy. He looked so sure of himself. She blushed, wondering if secretly he too had his share of unease over the mysterious closeness of being a husband to his new wife. It was vaguely comforting that at times today he had seemed ill at ease.

To quiet the beating of her heart, not let her mind run ahead of the slow turning of time, she made herself think of yesterday when her tired feet were moving slowly over this same trail toward a shelter she could not picture. How different this day was from anything she could picture yesterday! Tomorrow would be like that—all the tomorrows. She could not stop planning. Would Stephen like to help her plant an orchard? Just a small one at first with little trees to grow as love grew. Would he think it was silly if she told him, maybe next year, that she would like to add a tree, a very special tree, for each child they had?

She could picture the growing orchard, the shared joy in small stumbling first steps, their quiet pride in little feet growing sure and swift on the darkening boards of those wide halls as the house grew older. She was riding toward lovely years full of good hearty laughter in a house with no fear in it anywhere.

Gipsy stopped and she looked up, startled.

Stephen had stopped, turned in his saddle and was looking back at her with an odd expression around his mouth. She looked around quickly and then blushed. This was where she had tried to hide from him a million years ago.

"Do you remember this place?" he asked.

Blaze looked at him wide-eyed. "No," she said slowly. "I can't say I do. Why?"

His eyes had an impish glint as he said, "This is Puzzle Hill, and I'm starting what's going to be spoken of, years from now, as my habit of always stopping and meditating here."

"Meditating?" she said innocently. "What's that?"

His face was very grave, his voice serious as he answered, "In this case it's wondering where my witch-wife hides her broom."

"Why, Stephen Janson! Do you mean me?"

"It could be. Anyhow, from now on I stop here and think about the queer ways of women." He turned aside from his teasing and asked, "What had I done to earn the rawhiding I got from you yesterday right on this spot?"

"I never said a word to you right on this spot."

"That's correct," he conceded, "if you're going to be fussy about a few feet." He pointed to the rock and the little bush. "Does that spot look more familiar?"

"I'm not feeling familiar with any of these spots. Let's go along, shall we?"

"I wasn't serious, Blaze; only curious." He coaxed, "Be nice and tell me what it was I did yesterday that got your claws all out."

She tipped her head down to hide the color she felt warming her face and said, "It was because I— Oh, well, you know, because I liked you."

He said flatly, "Well, I'll be damned!" He choked back a laugh and went on, "Is that the way you show affection?"

Her head came up haughtily and she said, "I had burs on my skirt."

"And so you wanted to put them under my shirt?"

She held her lips tightly over a chuckle that threatened to bubble out. "And I was streaked with dust and sweat and the flies were biting me like fury and I hadn't got a job and I had no place to go and I was hungry."

His face showed swift concern. "You poor little baby! I was the beast. I'd been making myself give you time to find out Monterey wasn't an easy place for you to solve your problem in. I must have been awkward and stupid about trying to help you, but I was trying. I still can't see why you turned on me so fiercely, though."

She looked at him frankly. "I was ashamed. I'd failed. I was tired and I was grubby-looking. You looked so clean and strong and sure of yourself. I'm sorry I did it, but—maybe I'll do it again sometime."

His voice was so kind that she couldn't even try to answer

[242]

him as he said, "If you do, I'll try to remember that what you want is to be left alone and I'll clear out until you get whatever hurt is bothering you picked off. You haven't failed, Blaze. You're only making a new start. So here we go."

He touched the gray lightly with his spur and Blaze let him get a little ahead on the trail before she started Gipsy. She stayed far enough behind so that talking was difficult, and as the redwoods waved their dark branches in a friendly way and the streams roiled over rocks and mountains faded behind them she forgot her shame. By the time they had crossed the last of the three big ridges and were riding under the dappled shade of the sycamores that bordered the Big Sur river, she was riding close behind Stephen.

He looked around and called back, "Don't you want to get down and rest for a little while?"

"I'd rather make all the time we can while it's still light. I'm not so very tired yet."

"I am," he answered cheerfully. "We'd better stop at the last ford. The horses can have their grain and get a drink while we get shut of the saddle kinks. Is that all right with you?"

"Of course."

She wondered if she would ever get used to having a man who asked what she would like instead of telling her what to do. Her father wouldn't think any better of Stephen for being so easy-going. She shuddered. If her father had had his way she would be married to Joe Williams. The thought was so horrible that she almost cried out, but she closed her mouth so that the sound was no bigger than a mouse squeak.

It was getting really dark by the time they had ridden past the cultivated fields and the little house where the river turned as it poured down from the mountain. There was no glimmer of light, no dog barked, and they rode silently by the fenced dooryard, splashed through the ford, and Stephen halted his horse.

[243]

Stephen swung down and limped toward her, groaning as he helped her down. "I'm getting old all right."

For a moment Blaze felt shocked and then she heard him chuckle. "No fooling, my right foot is sound asleep."

She said, "I'm not too wide awake myself," and walked about on the grassy riverbank as he gave the horses water and then divided the grain between them.

"Where are you, Blaze?"

"Right here." She was standing close beside him and he turned, slipped his arm under hers, and they walked silently beside the river in the first starlight, listening to the small song of the water, the busy crunch of the horses relishing their feed of oats.

Blaze stepped softly beside him, thinking that if she could she would choose to walk tiptoe at the edge of the swift river of life for a whole year.

She half whispered, "I like how the river turns more silver as the light goes. The stars look so big and white from the dark cup of this little valley. The Balm of Gilead smells good and I wonder how old you really are. Never mind," she said hastily. "That was a bold thing for me to say. It doesn't matter a bit— only I know so few things about you, don't I?"

For a moment she thought he pressed her arm a little closer to his side, but he said lightly, "We are even on that, I think. All I know about you is that I looked at you and liked you the moment I saw you. And, what's more, I still do. Let's see—how old am I? Well, I was twenty-seven last November. Does that seem very old to you?"

She took a quick breath. "Oh, yes, it does. Twenty-seven? It never seemed to me that you were as old as that."

She saw him tip his head to look down at her, his tone slightly nettled as he protested, "I'm not exactly senile yet, am I?"

She looked up at him. "I don't know what 'senile' is, but twenty-seven is getting close to thirty and that's quite old to me."

He gave her arm a little shake. "I'm going to get you mittens if you don't sheath those claws of yours. You're the first charming young lady who ever looked at me and told me I was an old man."

Blaze drew her arm from his, stepped in front of him and protested, "It wasn't that I thought you were old. I was thinking about my brothers; they aren't twenty, except Martin, and they act a lot older than you do. It's real hard for Martin to laugh, and my father gives in a lot if he gets as far as a smile."

She held out her hand to him with a timid, hesitating gesture, but as he saw the reaching hand, covered it with both of his, she said softly, "First I loved your looks. Then your kindness. Now it's your laughing so easy. I'm going to end up by being too deep in love."

He didn't let go of her hand, but he led her over to the horses, gave her a hand into the saddle and then took his time over giving the horses their bits, folding up the grain sack. Suddenly he turned and came over to her with long steps, standing by Gipsy's head as he said, "You make it hard for me to remember what I mustn't forget. Say those same words to me a year from now and you'll have to prove them."

He turned away abruptly, swung onto his horse and rode up the mountain without waiting for her to say a word.

Blaze felt a strangeness, a strain, in his voice and his quitting the rest camp without asking if she was ready to go. Her father would ride off like that; he never asked anyone if his plans matched theirs. Already she knew it was a queer thing for Stephen Janson to do.

Perhaps he was worried about how his mother would feel, having a daughter-in-law that was the talk of the Coast. She thought about it as she rode along the dark trail and felt certain that she had hit upon the thing that worried him, made him act strangely every now and again.

After they passed the tan bark camp and had less than two

miles still to ride, there was a bit of clear meadow where two could ride side by side. Blaze was watching for the wider sky which would tell her they had reached this open space.

As soon as she rode out of the dark tunnel of trees that had hid the stars, she touched Gipsy with her heel and the mare moved ahead swiftly and silently. Blaze was riding beside Stephen before he appeared to notice it, for as she leaned toward him and spoke his name, he turned as though startled.

"Stephen," she said again, "please stop a moment. I want to ask you something."

Gray, so close to his own barn, was restless, but Stephen held him in, waiting for her question.

She hesitated so long that he prompted her, "Yes, what is it you want to know?"

"It's nothing, I guess." She found it so hard to say, to know where to start. "Stephen, what will your mother think about this? I mean—you know—our being married."

He said frankly, "I don't think she'll like it. She was upset when I told her I was going to find you, ask you to marry me."

Blaze sat silently for a few moments, then she said slowly, "I find it hard to go where I'm not welcome, but I don't blame your mother for feeling that way. I don't know what to do. I know so well how she must feel about a woman who would so far forget herself as to slap a man—and at a funeral."

Stephen sounded quite cheerful as he told her, "He evidently had it coming."

Blaze choked, whispered, "You mean she never did like me?"

"She likes you fine," he protested. "She picked you out as a likely girl for me the time you came to the party. But from the way she talked, every woman at the funeral must have gone out of their way to tell her you were going to have Pete Garcia's child. That's what stirred her up."

Blaze felt a nerve shock from her scalp to her toes. She had a feeling of shrinking to nothing, falling through space. She

[246]

could still hear the sound of those words, "Pete Garcia's child," but she couldn't believe she had heard them.

She tried to say, "How could they say such a thing?" but she couldn't break through the nightmare feeling enough to speak. She sat like a dead woman, numb and cold, feeling the weight of the words, but not able to relate them to herself.

As though he knew how she felt Stephen pulled his horse over close to Gipsy, said, "Don't take it like that, Blaze! That's not like Blaze Allan. When a thing is—it is. You can face it. Get your chin up, Mrs. Janson, and let's go. The minute you come in through the door things will be all right."

"I can't," Blaze whispered. "It's terrible. I can't do it." She set her teeth and made herself ask, "What did you say to her when she told you that terrible thing?"

He took a deep breath. "I lied to her. There seemed to be only one thing to say that would be the best for all of us. I told Mother that any child you had would be mine."

Blaze gasped. "You didn't! You couldn't! We weren't married. How could you tell her that?"

"Because I love you. I wanted to protect you."

Blaze felt a passion of anger rising above her shock at what she had heard, only half comprehended, and her humiliation at the thought of going into the home of a mother-in-law who didn't like her, wouldn't want her. Dizzily she felt that this man she had so loved and admired must be a complete fool.

Scorn sharpened her voice as she said, "I can't understand what you say. Are you trying to tell me that you married me believing that I'd been lying about with Pete?"

He said hotly, "You took the one way to convince me and everyone else. You ran away."

She was too angry to try to explain. And deeper than her anger was the despair. He had not come for her because he believed in her. He stood with her father, her mother, the Garcias —everyone.

She must get away, get moving. If she spoke she would break down. But her will helped her to maintain dignity and she forced herself to say stolidly, "I'm done with you, Stephen. Good-by."

He reached out and caught Gipsy's bridle, held the two restless horses close together as he said, "I didn't go through hell over you to sit by and have you make a fool of yourself. And don't pretend with me, Blaze! I'd begun to think I had been wrong about how things were with you. But you told me yourself that you were in trouble."

It was Zande Allan's own daughter who thrust her face savagely toward him, crying out furiously, "That's true! I am. And it gets worse and worse till I'm half crazy. A lot of help you've been. I won't be married to you. I hate you."

He was as angry as she was. "Before this is over you'll be damned glad you've married someone who's willing to claim your bas—" he caught the word back—"your baby for his."

"Who said I was going to have a baby?"

"You did."

"That's a plain lie! I never said such a thing."

His elaborate patience was like a slap to her. "I wouldn't expect you to come out flat and admit it. What you said was, 'I'm in trouble.'"

Blaze stormed at him, "You turn loose of that bridle. I'm not going to listen to you talk riddles. I said trouble and I meant trouble. If I was having a baby I'd say I was having a baby. I never heard such stuff. I guess you'd call it trouble if you were a girl and your own father thought the same crazy thing you think."

Stephen said stiffly, "I'd like to believe you. I want to—but I can't. You did go down to that cave with Pete."

Blaze said slowly, "And I did ride into Monterey with you and through the dark of night. That's another of the things they're always saying a girl must never do. But I did it. Do you think any the worse of me for that?"

"Why should I?"

Blaze spoke bitterly. "That's what I'm trying to find out. Do you know that if any man or woman from the Coast saw me riding into Monterey with you, without my mother or father or your mother was along, there would be just as much talk as there was about me and Pete?"

"But we were on our way to get married," Stephen protested.

Blaze said grimly, "You might have been. I wasn't. All I meant to do was tell you I was sorry I was so rude when you had been kind to me. I didn't know you were thinking of marrying me when I set out."

He made no answer.

Stubbornly Blaze insisted, "I started out to ride along in the night alone with you. You tell me what is wrong about that."

He made an impatient gesture with his free hand. "It doesn't look well. There is nothing wrong in two people riding along the same road. You know that. It just doesn't look well. Men take advantage—" His voice trailed off and he looked at her apologetically.

Her body taut with anger but her voice bland, Blaze looked directly at him and asked, "Were you thinking about doing that to me?"

He stepped back, his face even in the dim light betraying astonishment as well as anger. "You know I wasn't. I respect you—"

She interrupted him, her eyes sad, her voice earnest. "And I respect myself. Surely I'm not the only person in the world that needs more than anything else to feel—" she struggled for the right words, went on—"I don't know how to say it. I mean that if I did things that were mean or underhanded, sneaky things, I'd know it; and I wouldn't like living with myself. That's not just my way of thinking—everyone must feel like that."

[249]

He said, rather sharply, "That is childish talk, Blaze. You're a woman, not a child. The rules that men and women live by have grown slowly and because there was need for them. The people who try to make rules of their own don't get much happiness out of it."

Blaze protested. "You fooled me. I took your good manners for a good heart. I'm beginning to think that Pete was the only good person in these mountains. He did ask me to stay with him in that cave—"

"There," Stephen said hotly. "I told you men took advantage of women who didn't keep a woman's place."

"He didn't do anything of the sort! He believed me. He's the only one that did." She bent her head, her face and voice shadowed with sorrow as she looked up at Stephen. "But Pete was like you. He believed the appearance of evil was worse than evil itself. He was so afraid of it that he died trying to get me safe out of that place so folks wouldn't turn against me. There wasn't any wrong except what's in the minds of my neighbors, my own parents, and—" she struggled—"and in the mind of my husband."

Stephen dropped the reins down in front of the gray horse, walked nervously back and forth for a few paces, and then stopped abruptly in front of Blaze. "We won't settle anything this way. You're tired and overwrought. We'd better go on home and after you've had some sleep and rest we'll talk."

Blaze shrugged her slim shoulders. "We've already talked too much."

Stephen said, "If all you say is true, I've done you a great wrong. You might sometime come to overlook my thinking you had been intimate with Pete Garcia. But I led my mother to believe that you had been making love with me. I made a fool of myself, but I was trying to make things easier for you. What do you mean to do about it?"

Blaze answered, "Nothing."

He protested, "Don't sound like that, Blaze! I'll tell my mother the truth about us—about Pete."

Blaze said dryly, "You needn't bother. I know whether you did or not. So do you."

He said angrily, "There's no reason to go out of your way to make things worse than they are. Certainly I owe it to you to apologize to you, explain to my mother."

Blaze said, "Let go of Gipsy's bridle, will you?"

He took his hand away and she gave the mare a nudge with her heel. She rode out ahead on the dim trail, her back straight, her head held stiffly. Stephen rode silently behind her and not a word was spoken between them until they had ridden into the Janson yard.

As Stephen helped his wife down, she felt his hand tremble and her heart softened. She looked at the top of his head as she slid down from her saddle, and for an instant she had a vision of a small boy in deep trouble. "Your mother loves you, Stephen. She's proud of you even if she's mad that you married a loose woman. But if she thought you lied to her against a girl— It's better to let things be. They'll work out."

He said sternly, "I'll have to do what I think best for both of us, Blaze."

There was a girl's indignation, a woman's anger in the answer, "And I'll have to bow my head and obey as I promised. Well, I promised to love and honor too. I don't. I don't even like you. But I'll make you the best wife I can. I'm an Allan and we keep our bargains."

"It looks like we're in for a hell of a honeymoon," Stephen exploded, jerking off saddles, slamming them on their racks and turning the horses in through the gate to the feeding corral.

He came back and took her arm, whispering, "There's a light on in the hall, but I think everyone's asleep. Maybe we'd better see them in the morning."

Blaze drew a long breath, sighed tiredly and nodded.

[251]

They went in the side door, through the kitchen and into the dimly lit hall. Stephen lighted a couple of candles, gave Blaze one and then he turned down the kerosene hanging lamp, blew out the flame, and the weary pair stole up the carpeted stair and down the hall toward the north end of the house.

Stephen said softly, "Here we are," and carefully felt for the doorknob, opened a door.

Blaze stepped in after him and stood at one side while he closed the door. He set his candle on a chest of drawers and Blaze looked around, amazed at the size of the room. It seemed to her to be almost as big as the whole Allan house.

Stephen spoke in a natural voice. "Mother sleeps downstairs and on the south end of the house. Tena has her room right off Mother's, so no one will hear us talking."

"No one will hear me talking," Blaze murmured. "I'm so dead tired I'm about to fall asleep standing up."

"Of course you are," Stephen said, his voice full of concern. He picked up his candle, crossed the room, opened a door opposite the one they had come in by, and held the candle high so that she could see.

"If you want a different room you can look them over and pick one out tomorrow. I'll light your fire and then I'll go get your things. I left them stacked out by the shed."

Blaze said, "I should have thought of them. I didn't think of anything."

There was a small fireplace built across the corner of the room with windows on each side of the fireplace and wide seats built beneath them. As the small pine branches and the foot-long pine cones began to give out their fragrant smoke, Blaze started over to sit on one of the cushioned ledges, but changed her mind and pulled a low footstool close to the fire and sat down, holding out her hands to the warmth.

The bright gleam of her new ring as it caught the glow of fire and candlelight fascinated her. With the finger and thumb of her other hand she turned the ring slowly. How warm it felt—warm clear through. But there was no warmth in her heart. Her shoulders slumped forward, her back bowed as her bright head bent forward to rest on her knees. The ring would wear forever; it had warmth and shine to it. Could she take the dull stuff her life had become and make it into something as glowing, as solid, as her ring?

She couldn't think. Her head felt so heavy, so heavy. Slowly it drooped down and down until the firelight faded from her gaze. She was not conscious of shifting her arms so that they rested on her knees, cradled her head.

At the sound of Stephen's voice she came instantly awake, as alert and wary as a wildcat. She jumped nervously to her feet, but in spite of her inner tumult she turned a quiet face toward him, held out a steady hand and said formally, "I'll take the things. Thank you for getting them and I'm sorry I put you to trouble."

He put the sack with her clothing into her hands, put the box with her new hat onto the foot of the bed, murmured, "Good night, Blaze. Sleep well."

He was closing the door after himself before she was able to grasp the fact that he was leaving her. Her face turned scarlet with shame and mortification as her feebly uttered, "The same to you," bounced back at her from a definitely closed door.

She stood holding the awkward floursack bundles, loathing herself for her feeling of shock that he had not attempted to stay. She told herself angrily that she wouldn't have let him if he had; all he had for her was pity, and she didn't want that. Because he was rich and strong and sure of himself he had stooped down to rescue her as though she were a drowning kitten. She didn't believe a word he said about loving her.

She dropped the sacks, stumbled over one as she ran across the carpet and noiselessly shot forward the little brass bolt that locked him out.

Then her anger ebbed, her knees gave way and she sank down, a small heap of fatigue and hurt pride, soundlessly weeping with her face pressed against the locked door.

The fire burned out, the candle dripped and melted, expired with a faint protest while Blaze Allan spent her wedding night sleeping against the door that she had locked. In the first faint light of dawn she woke, cramped and cold, and for a few seconds uncertain as to where she was. Then she remembered, felt for the sack that held the beautiful nightgown. She got into it and with her teeth chattering, knelt beside the bed and intending to pray, found herself thinking, over and over, Believe me, cherish me, love me, Stephen, and maybe everything will be all right.

She got up, felt her way back to the door, and without making a sound she drew the bolt on the door. Just as quietly she crept into the sanctuary of the high bed, smelled the lavender scent on the sheets and pillow cases, the lingering odor of cedar shavings in the feather puff, and with a comforting thought that life was not over and done in a day or a night, she put both arms around the fine fat pillow and slept.

XII

B UT in her sleep, Stephen Janson's new wife could not hold to her hope that somehow things would work out right. She fought her way to consciousness a dozen times, certain that in the darkness she could feel the cruel clasp of cold seaweed dragging her down into black ooze and slime. She was pursued by the curse Pete's uncle had put on her.

Her mouth was dry, her hands were cold and wet, and her eyes were hollow by the time daylight began seeping in through the window. She prayed for courage to face her first day of life in a house where no one wanted her.

Soon, in the next room, she heard Stephen stirring. Quickly she fluffed the pretty frill of her gown about her throat, shook out her hair and smoothed it, hoping she would not look half-drowned when he wished her good morning.

His door to the hall opened, closed softly after him. She could hear him feeling his way to the stairs, his feet whispering down the treads.

He was slipping out, not meaning to speak to her. He was running off, leaving her to face his angry mother by herself. Even as she told herself these things, Blaze knew that she didn't believe them. She was ashamed that her own fear made her mind strike out so savagely at Stephen.

She waited tensely for what seemed hours, certain that she could never sleep again, but the soft knocking on the door had been repeated three times before Blaze heard it. She straightened the cover, pulled the sheet over her shoulders and then asked timidly, "Yes? Who is it?"

The door opened slowly and Mrs. Janson's head and shoulders came in view as her soft voice announced, "Is only me. Could I come in, please?"

A mixture of dread and fright set Blaze's hands to trembling, but she answered naturally, "Of course. Do come in. Is it very late?"

"Lunch time soon," Mrs. Janson answered. She was walking briskly toward the bed as she spoke, and Blaze wondered if she would begin to scold about her lazing in bed half the day.

Mrs. Janson bent over, kissed Blaze on the forehead and said, "Velcome home, daughter! Now I got whole family, and that makes much happiness. Good years ahead for all us, I think."

Blaze let the breath go out of her, reached for her mother-in-law's fat little hands, bowed her head over them and whispered, "I was afraid you'd be mad at me."

"I vas," Mrs. Janson said calmly, "but I don't stay mad."

Blaze looked at her curiously, hesitating before she asked, "Did Stephen see you today?"

"For breakfast, yess; vouldn't talk. He told me you vas tired, might sleep long time. Then he vent down to the dock but he'll come back."

Blaze had her doubt of that, but she struggled to hide her confusion. Had Stephen told his mother anything more than that they were married? Should she try to tell his mother she was not bad?

Even as she thought it she knew that she was not going to do anything of the sort. Her husband's mother had made her welcome. She would accept that kindness, prove she was worth it.

She looked up at her, said frankly, "I feel bashful in a strange house, but I know you'll help me to get over it. My dress is wrinkled and not even clean, and the dress Stephen bought for me seems so grand I don't know if I should put it on."

[256]

Mrs. Janson trotted out of the room, opened the door that led from the outer room into the hall and called down the stair, "Tena, please? Make the irons hot. Blaze has clothes to press."

She came back smiling to ask, "You vant now to come down for coffee? I got wrapper you can slip over the nightgown. Is just me and Tena, and ve have a bite in the kitchen if you don't mind."

"I'd like it. And I've got a wrapper that Stephen got for me from Mrs. Swen; I can wear that." Blaze sat up in bed, pushed back her hair as she said, "Mrs. Swen was very kind; so friendly and helpful."

"Stephy's got good sense," his mother nodded complacently. "Vas just right place to bring you. Anything she makes, she makes good."

She started out of the room calling back, "I go make the coffee fresh. Don't hurry yourself, but Tena she's vanting to see a bride, so you come smiling, yes?"

She hurried back to the bed, put both arms around Blaze, murmured, "Everything turns out fine, isn't it?" and then, before Blaze could answer, she was out of the room and gone.

Every gentle word that Mrs. Janson spoke only deepened the conviction Blaze had that Stephen still believed the worst of her. But that was between herself and Stephen. No matter how her own heart ached she must keep up appearances in front of his loving and forgiving mother. But she would make seeing her parents an excuse for leaving quickly, and she need not be definite about coming back.

Blaze emptied the sack of her new things, shook out the wrapper and put it on. The gray suit was a bit wrinkled. She put it and the other things that needed pressing on the foot of the bed while she washed and made herself as neat as she could. Then she gathered up the clothes and started for the hall, hurrying through the room in which Stephen had slept, as though she were an intruder.

The silver-backed brushes on his dresser, the darkly shining desk with books standing on shelves above it, the soft carpet and wide carved bed made her conscious of her old scuffed moccasins hidden beneath the crisp new wrapper. She felt ashamed that all this elegance awed her, made her feel awkward and shy.

If things had been different, if only Stephen could have come courting her as he might have if her father had been anyone but Zande Allan. If only she could have been married from her own father's house with the blessing and good wishes of her family, with love and confidence in the future. But as things were she felt she scarcely had courage to keep on going down the long stairs to meet Tena and Mrs. Janson and play the part of a happy bride.

Blaze felt that her mouth was dry, but she walked into the kitchen, shook hands with Tena, who blushed violently when Mrs. Janson teased, "Tena would be a nice sister, isn't it?"

Blaze let the hint about Martin slide by, answering, "I hope we'll be very good friends, Tena. I've never had a girl friend who lived close enough to really get to know her."

"These hills, they're pretty lonesome place for young things," Mrs. Janson sighed.

"Not if you're married," Tena said sturdily. "I'm going to find me a husband, you watch now."

"You won't have to hunt," Blaze said. "I think you can take your pick of all the unmarried men between Piedras Light and Mal Paso."

Tena turned to the stove, pulled the irons back where they would not get too hot, and asked, "Shall I pour coffee now, Auntie?"

Mrs. Janson pursed her lips. "Oh, youst bring to the table," she said, "and the coffeecake out from the oven, and then ve can all sit cozy for second cup."

Blaze sat down, not tasting the coffee or the coffeecake, eating and drinking, listening to the comments of the other two women on the pretty style of her wrapper, the lovely color of the new suit, but thinking of home, of her father's face when she told him that she was married to Stephen.

"And I'll press everything while you have the bath," Tena was saying eagerly. "Then you can be all ready by the time she gets here."

Blaze looked up, said haltingly, "Who did you say was coming?"

Tena's china blue eyes opened wide. "Mrs. Allan, she's coming up."

"My mother? Is she coming here?"

Tena laughed. "No, no, Mrs. Zande Allan, your brother's wife."

Blaze felt her tenseness go. "Oh, Dulcie, you mean. I can't get used to the idea that she's Mrs. Allan as much as my mother is. Zande seems such a boy, I keep forgetting he's a family man now."

Tena blushed. "It's a nice name. I think so."

Mrs. Janson laughed indulgently, but said with some show of firmness, "You better keep the name you got for a few years yet. Sixteen is grown up for some, but you been kept pretty close. These mountain boys, they're too vild. Eighteen, or better tventy, plenty time to settle down for life."

Tena looked surprised. "How did you know? That's just what Martin said. He wants to get a good start in business before he marries. I'm going to wait for him though." She edged over to Blaze, put her arm around her and gave her a tight squeeze. "I wasn't going to tell a soul, anyway not for a couple of years— but I couldn't help it. I want you to start thinking of me as your sister."

Suddenly Blaze felt terribly old, realizing that her impulse was to shelter Tena, hold back time for her. But she made herself speak gaily. "Perhaps I can help Martin to know how to be a good husband." She smiled. "Did you know Martin has the Allan temper?"

Tena pursed her lips, shrugged her shoulders airily. "Not to me he doesn't show any temper."

She dragged the big ironing board in from behind the pantry door, set it from the table to the back of a chair and tested the irons.

"Irons are just right. I'll get a pressing cloth and do up your pretty things. You want you should have a bath?"

Blaze said she did, and in a small room off the kitchen she found the same sort of long, narrow zinc tub that Mrs. Swen had owned. Blaze carried pails of hot water from the copper boiler that was at the back of the kitchen stove. This tub emptied itself. Mrs. Janson proudly showed her the plug in the bottom of it, explained how the water drained out through a pipe and into the flower garden.

As she got into the pretty gray suit and settled the skirt smoothly over her hips with little pats, she thought how happy she could be here in this place where voices were gentle and everything was so new and beautiful. If Stephen could only believe the truth she had told him; if she could take out of her heart the dry ache that had come there when she learned what he had told his mother about her.

She looked at the slender figure in the gray suit and wondered if that could possibly be an image of Blaze Allan. When she bent closer, looked into her own weary eyes, she turned away sadly. Muttering, "I look older than Grandma," she picked up the folds of her skirt and made her way down to the sitting room where she could hear the excited voices of Tena and Dulcie.

Tena jumped to her feet when Blaze came into the room, calling triumphantly, "There, what did I tell you? Isn't she a pretty bride?"

Dulcie sat still, but she lifted her broad face to beam a welcome. "Sure, I'd trade faces and figures with her if I could—but for why? My husband likes me like I am."

Blaze came over to Dulcie, took her hand and looked down at her. "What more could you want, Dulcie?"

Dulcie stood up, a short stocky little figure in the ample folds of a dark blue calico Mother Hubbard as she walked excitedly around the big center table.

"I've not been married so long that I could talk like I knew everything," she said, "but I know what counts with my man—it's laughs. You'd never believe how crazy that fellow is for laughing."

Blaze drew a long breath. "Yes, I'd believe it. Zande didn't laugh much at home—but nobody did."

Dulcie sniffed. "Don't I know it! Work, that's what eats your pa and makes him grouchy. I bet he could laugh good as my Zande if he'd let hisself go."

The tall floor clock behind her boomed the hour and Blaze turned to study its strange foreign face.

"Is it one o'clock already?" she asked Tena, who nodded and reminded her, "It was after eleven before you got up."

Hearing this, Dulcie put her hands over her mouth and tried to stifle her giggle, but it got away. Tena found it contagious, and both girls shook with silent laughter while Blaze reddened.

Ignoring the sly eyes and giddy mirth, she said, "I wanted to ride over home this afternoon. Would you think I was rude if I started right away?"

"I'd think you was silly if you waited any later," Dulcie said. "You'll not get back before dark as it is."

Blaze went out of the room followed by Dulcie's "I'd rather pull taffy and laugh than to sew. But I guess I got to sew. I can't keep a baby warm by wrapping him in taffy, can I?"

She hurried off to find Mrs. Janson, and at last gave up and went upstairs to find her mother-in-law straightening the rooms

[261]

where she and Stephen had spent their respective wedding nights.

She said slowly, "I was brought up better than to go off and leave beds not made. I'm ashamed. I didn't even turn them back to air."

"Is a pleasure to do some little thing for you, Blaze," Mrs. Janson protested. "You got more to think of as beds-making on a day like this. I know how brides are."

She gave her comfortable little chuckle, but Blaze thought her eyes had a look of perplexity. She would have given a lot to be able to talk to her mother-in-law, tell her how uncertain, how unhappy she felt.

Instead, she said hesitatingly, "I want to ride home; see my parents. They will be worrying about me."

Mrs. Janson punched a pillow, her eyes avoiding Blaze. "There now, you go right and see them. I vas hoping Stephy vould take you, but he hurried right off so early." She looked out of the window, noted where the sun was, and urged, "Hurry off now. Else be dark when you come back."

Blaze bit her lip, said, "I'll not come back today, Mrs. Janson. Would you tell Stephen?"

Mrs. Janson's eyes gave no sign of her feelings. "I tell him; sure I vill."

Nervous and uncertain, Blaze stood hesitating for a moment and then she said, "I'll wear my old dress to ride in. This suit— it's so light I'll get it all marked up."

Mrs. Janson asked, "What's that make difference? You should ought to look like the nice bride so your mamma she'll be happy for you." She put all her charm into her coaxing. "You look so nice like you are now."

Blaze nodded. "I know. It does look lovely. But you see"—she reddened and stammered—"my father, he gets ideas. I don't want to look finer than he was able to do for me."

Mrs. Janson made a wry mouth. "I see how you mean. You

got it right, I guess, Blaze. Men can be hurt, get stubborn over foolishest things. You go fix yourself, but you think you better stay avay over all night?"

Blaze hurried into the small room beyond Stephen's, calling back, "I think it will be best to get things settled at home. It may take quite a while."

While she was changing her dress, saddling Gipsy, she felt a need to hurry, get out on the trail and well away from any chance meeting with Stephen.

But uncertain as everything seemed, she found herself watching the little striped snake that slid across the trail, the new bloom on the elderberries, the prickly chamise brush wearing the dazzling snow of their brief blooming season. The brushy hillsides looked just like big snowdrifts and the blue lilac surging strongly up out of the canyons made the chamise bloom seem like white clouds on a summer sky. Blaze noted the last few Johnny-jump-ups, the first larkspur blooming in the open pine glades, and pulled Gipsy to a rest when she spied the first tall white yucca bloom standing majestically on a rocky cliff.

Spring was hurrying on to meet summer; it was the promising part of the year, and the girl found herself humbled by bird song, flower scent and her feeling that she too was growing out of her springtime.

If only she could ride back to her childhood sureness that welcome and love were waiting for her in her home. It seemed almost certain that her father would tell her to get off the Allan ranch, stay off, just as he had told Young Zande when he learned that Zande had married someone he didn't like.

She pulled Gipsy to a halt, her heart faint as she thought of her father's feeling toward Stephen Janson. Her own sore heart had closed the door of her husband's house to her. How could she go back there, try to explain, beg for his faith in her?

She seemed to herself to be shrinking into a completely bewildered small girl, but one thing she did know. She had a duty

[263]

to her own family. She owed it to her parents to tell them where she had been, what she had done.

She started Gipsy off again on the hard trail home.

Although she rode more and more slowly, she came at last to the place where she reached down, unlatched the last gate and rode into the yard. Hannah Allan, her back turned, swung the noisy pump handle at the well house. Blaze dropped Gipsy's reins, dismounted and walked forward saying, "Let me do that, Mother."

Her mother straightened, turned swiftly and covered her face with her hands. Blaze heard her gasped breath and saw how limply her hands fell as she whispered, "Mercy, child, how you startled me!"

Blaze ran a few steps forward, halted uncertainly. "I didn't go to scare you; I didn't know what to say, or if you'd want to see me."

Hannah reached out her arms. "Just the sight of you—that's what I been praying for. I been worried sick."

Blaze ran to her, half laughing, half crying, and the two women were tight in each other's arms. Her mother's arms were so warm, so safe and loving that Blaze felt limp with relief until she heard her mother murmur, "What I been through, Blaze. I hope you never have to suffer so over a daughter of yours."

Blaze broke down completely, her troubles voiced through sobs muffled against her mother's shoulder. "I'll never have a daughter. I'll never have anything now. Oh, Mother, I'm so miserable. I'm married!"

Her mother shook her sharply. "Stop that, Blaze. Married? You can't be! Who to?"

Blaze tried to control her emotions but the crumpled, pitiful face she lifted to her mother's anxious look hid none of her sorrow. "Stephen," she said brokenly, "Stephen Janson. And he hates me and I hate him and I've left him. I wish I was dead."

Her mother looked at her for too long, with too searching a

[264]

look. Blaze hid her face in her hands before Hannah said, "You don't act much like it. Sounds to me like you'd been having a lover's spat. Fill the bucket, Blaze, and bring it in."

Blaze obeyed. Shaking the tears from her eyes, she bent to the pump handle, picked up the full bucket and walked with her mother into the kitchen. She set the pail down on the shelf beside the stove and dropped wearily down onto her old place beside the big table. She sat in an unhappy heap while her mother went into the pantry, brought out the coffee, ground it and started it brewing.

Then she asked timidly, "Father? Where is he?"

"With the boys. Over to King City. They took out some calves yesterday."

Blaze sighed. "I'm terribly scared to see Father. He was mad at me anyway, and now, when he finds out I'm married, he'll run me off like he did Zande."

Hannah answered grimly, "Well, he's not going to be pleased that you married Mr. Janson; you know that, well as I do. But if he runs you any place, it'll be back to your husband, and that's the right place for you."

Blaze said, "He can run me off the ranch and maybe I deserve it, but he can't make me go back to the Jansons. I won't go."

Hannah got the coffeepot, filled the cups. "Drink your coffee, dear; it'll settle you. You're all worked up and trembling. Soon as you feel quieter we'll see if we can't get things straightened out a bit."

Blaze blinked, shook her head, but she took the coffee cup and held it, warming her hands before she started tasting the strong fragrant drink. "Did you set my place at the table while I was gone? I worried about that. It hurt me, not being able to send you word."

"I put it out the first night. After that I couldn't. Where you been all this time, Blaze?"

"I went to Monterey to find work. I didn't find any." She slowly turned the broad gold circle shining on her finger. "Then I saw Stephen—" Blaze put both hands around the cup, held it tightly. "He asked me to marry him and—and he said he loved me." She hastily put the cup down, hid her face in her hands. After a moment she went on, "So I married, and then I found out he was only sorry for me."

She waited, but her mother said nothing. Blaze pushed back from the table, walked about the room for a moment as though it were not possible for her to be still, and then she went back to the table, put her hand on it to hide its shaking. "There's nothing you can say for him. He told me himself that he married me because I was going to have Pete Garcia's baby!"

Her mother's voice sounded strange and hollow even to the overtaut Blaze. Hannah asked, "Is that true?"

Blaze looked at her mother as though she were looking at a monster, said furiously, "Of course not! What's the matter with everyone? I'd of married Pete if I wanted to have his babies, wouldn't I?"

Her mother collapsed weakly against the table, caught her breath and laughed shakily. "Oh, you little goose. If you just talked sense you wouldn't get yourself into such trouble."

"Who's talking sense now?" Blaze asked her mother tartly. "You just now said I was in trouble. That's all I said to him—to Stephen, I mean—that I didn't want to marry him because I was in trouble, and he's so crazy he thought that meant a baby."

Hannah said dryly, "Well, it's a rather common way of putting something women won't come right out and say. And they always say it when an unmarried girl is in the family way."

Blaze looked exasperated. "There's a plain true word for anything that ever happens to anyone, men or women. Plain talk won't make a thing better or worse. And no fancy words are going to take anything away from a thing that's wrong."

Hannah held back a smile, thinking, "My, how you do take after your father."

Taking no notice of her mother, Blaze made her way around the table, sat down and picked up her cup. Hannah hastened to fill up both cups and as she put the pot back on the stove, she asked, "How did Mr. Janson's mother feel about this wedding?"

Defiance left Blaze and her eyes clouded. "She was against it. I don't blame her; she heard at the funeral all this stuff about me—having a baby, I mean."

"Isn't that one of the reasons you left your husband, Blaze? Did his mother ask you to leave?"

Blaze rushed to Mrs. Janson's defense. "Oh, no, Mother. She was so sweet to me; called me Daughter and was just as kind, and after Stephen told her that horrible lie about us too."

Hannah looked startled. "A lie about us? About the Allans?"

Impatiently Blaze protested, "No, no. About us; me and Stephen." She colored slowly, painfully, and forced out the words, "He told his mother that—that any baby I had—it would be his."

Hannah's cup tilted in her hand, coffee dripped unheeded on the table as she looked in wonder at her child. "And you're sitting there telling me that you left a man who not only told you he loved you, but proved it by giving you the protection of marriage and taking what he thought was another man's blame to himself?"

"Anyway, he told a straight-out lie to his mother against his own wife," Blaze angrily defended herself. "And you know very well what Father says about a bird that will dirty its own nest! And besides, we quarreled miserably and Stephen doesn't even speak to me."

"Not even when you told him you were leaving him?"

Blaze looked ashamed, answering faintly, "I didn't tell him or anyone. He went off this morning without a word. I couldn't

[267]

see any way out for us; he'd always believe wrong about me and Pete. I could see that, so I told his mother I wanted to see you and—and—I came home in my dirty old dress."

She put her head on her arms, leaned over the table and wept quietly.

There was no word, no move, from her mother, and after a time Blaze raised her head, dabbed at her tired eyes.

Very serenely her mother said, "Now you'll feel better. You had a good cry coming to you, honey. But, Blaze, I want you to trust me, believe me when I tell you that you have nothing to cry about."

"That's all right for you to say," Blaze sighed, "but you try to think how you'd have felt if Father thought such things about you, and there was no way for you to prove he was wrong."

There was a twinkle in Hannah's eye as she regarded her child. "Your husband already knows he was wrong. That's one of the things that bothers him right now. He knows it the same way that I know there's been nothing of real marriage yet between you two. If there had been you'd know too much to keep talking so foolishly."

"You mean if we ever were really together, he could tell, truly sure?"

Hannah nodded. "Truly sure. Women got a hard deal some ways, my girl, but nature looked out for a few things. Since you'd married him and still said you had nothing to do with Pete, your husband would know that what you said about a thing like that was true. I'm sure he'd think you know what he knows. Men always think women are a lot wiser about what goes on between man and woman than nice girls usually are."

For a long time Blaze sat with her hands quietly folded in her lap, her face thoughtful. As Hannah at last got up and started gathering together things for a simple supper, Blaze took a deep breath, let it out slowly, and relaxed her shoulders against the kitchen wall. "Stephen must feel dreadful that he told his mother such a thing about us."

"Oh, well," said Hannah comfortably, "humble pie is not too bad a dish for even handsome young men to eat now and again."

"I asked him not to say anything different about it to her; told him I didn't have any love for him or faith in him, but that his mother had, and it wasn't fair to her to take it away from her."

Her mother snorted. "You should of just picked up the kettle and scalded him; wouldn't of hurt him half as much." She walked close to Blaze, put her hand on her shoulder and turned her around to face her. "Pride's about the only thing menfolks really has of their own, Daughter. A woman that hurts her man's pride hurts him bad. You bear that in mind."

Blaze swallowed, nodded.

Her mother laughed, patted her shoulder. "You got lots to learn, honey, but love is a good teacher. And I'm not trying to tell you that good men can't be pesty as a bur under your belt. They are. But you'll learn to live together, and life well shared is a rich life, Blaze."

Doubtfully Blaze asked, "Do you think Stephen will come for me?"

"He'll ride in tomorrow," her mother called back from the pantry.

To herself Blaze murmured, "I wish I could feel that sure." But she turned to helping with the supper, only stopping now and again to listen hopefully for the sound of a knock that did not come.

XIII

TIME crawled along until midafternoon, and then it was Martin, Avery and their father who rode into the barnyard. Blaze whispered, "You go out and meet them, Mother. I'll stay here."

Her mother turned her head, raised her eyebrows and Blaze changed her mind, walked briskly to the door and was outdoors and moving down the slope to the barn ahead of her mother. "We're keeping dinner hot for you, Father," she called. "You hungry?"

As though nothing had ever happened Zande said briefly, "No. We carried grub and et over by Hidden Spring."

Martin stared for an instant, Avery grinned and winked. Then the men were on the ground, unloading packs, loosening cinches and getting the stock unsaddled and fed.

Hannah came up to the first packsack to be lifted off, poked in it with exploring fingers as she smiled at her men, and as Zande straightened up, put his hand on his back as though tired, she said, "It's good to have you home, and Blaze too."

Zande lifted his head quickly, looked at Blaze as though he had not seen her before. His face darkened and he turned to Martin. "You chaps get this stuff under cover. I'll call you when I want you up to the house."

Martin went stolidly at the business of caring for the saddles and packs, but Avery made for the shelter of the barn. Blaze realized that Tena was helping Martin grow up too.

Without waiting to see if his orders were obeyed, Zande Allan strode up the trail to the house, the two women following.

He opened the door, waited for them to go inside, and then stepped in, closed the door after him.

Hannah sat down at the table, picked up her knitting, but Blaze stood facing her father's angry frown, waiting for him to speak.

"Where the hell you been?"

Blaze said, "I came back to tell you exactly what happened the day Pete was drowned. You believed Joe Williams; you believed the neighbors. You wouldn't listen to me."

His face reddened with temper, he clenched his fists and took a threatening step toward her, raising his voice as he struck his fists together. "I've had enough of that. I'm not here to listen to you. I asked you where you been—answer me!"

Blaze was astonished to realize that for the first time in her life she felt no fear of her father's anger. She looked at his work-hardened hands, his bent back, and knew suddenly that this bluster was mostly to cover up the shame and sorrow he felt because he thought harm had come to her.

In the silence she could hear the agitated click of her mother's knitting needles and even as she noted the unsteadiness of the sound, it stopped. Hannah said, "Listen to Blaze, Zande. You owe her a hearing."

He turned to his wife. "So she's got around you, has she? Sneaking back to pull the wool over your eyes when I'm gone."

Blaze walked over to him, put her hand on his arm and said, "You don't really believe that, Father. How was I to know you were not here? I came home to talk to you. I was sure you'd listen before you started judging."

He turned away, sat down at the end of the table, and started pinching his chin between his thumb and bent forefinger.

"What you got to say for yourself?"

Blaze came over to the table, pulled out the end of the bench, sat down opposite him and said firmly, "Hear me through, Father. Please listen and don't shout at me, not even when I start by telling you I went down there with Pete because you've always been too hard on us."

He started to pull back from the table, his voice shaking as he said, "Why, you little ingrate—" but his words faltered and trailed off under his daughter's steady gaze.

Blaze folded her hands together on the table and kept her eyes on her father's face as step by step she led him with words down the trail to the cave, told him what Pete had said, what she had answered and how she felt, sparing nothing. He sat, taut as a strung bow, saying nothing until she told how she had stepped out of the sodden leather skirt. He had sat silent, his face betraying nothing of his feelings, but now he struck both hands on the thick board in front of him and his voice boomed like the far-off surf as he cried, "Shooting's too good for him. I'll break his neck with my own hands, the bastardly liar!"

"Joe Williams?" Blaze asked quietly. "No, you won't, Father. You'd hang for it and he's not worth it. He's just a dirty little man. Let him fry in his own fat. Forget him."

"Not by a damn sight. The dirty Peeping Tom. I'll shove his filthy talk down his throat; by God, I will."

Hannah sniffed as she said, "Far as I go he don't exist. I'll ride right by him and never see him at all."

Blaze nodded her head. "That's the one way to burn the hide right off him. The Allans are big people and it'll hurt him bad if we kill him off by never seeing that he's there."

"That's woman's stuff," Zande said contemptuously. "I'll crack my knuckles on his chin first time I catch up with him."

"And tell all this stuff to the sheriff?" Hannah asked.

Zande groaned. "Lord God, what's come over the world? It's getting so's a man can't even settle his own troubles without the law putting in. Makes me feel like picking up my stuff and lighting out for some open country where a fellow's his own boss."

Blaze got up, went around the table and climbed in beside her father, slid her arm through his, put her cheek against his shoulder. His eye caught the gleam on the finger of her hand covering his, and Blaze felt him go rigid. "What's that for?"

"My ring?" she stammered, her heart seeming to rise up, shut off her breath.

Hannah stabbed the needles through her wool, put the stocking on the table. "Blaze married young Mr. Janson yesterday."

"That's a lie!"

For a second Blaze felt a fury of anger rise in her and then she knew she'd heard a sound as cold and lonely as ice sliding off a gray rock in the fastness of the Ventanas.

She did not draw away from her father, but put one hand over the other, hiding the ring from his sight.

Hannah had picked up the knitting once more, slid the needles out of the wool and bent over the work as she started unraveling the rows of stitches she had just put in. There was much less of the sock when she finally said, "There—" as though she had arrived at what she wanted. Then she looked directly at her husband, said slowly and carefully, "Blaze is married, and a good thing for her. She was ready for marrying."

Zande said heavily, "I told the both of you what I thought of that fellow: no principles, no religion, a waster of the country, skinning the trees and letting 'em die."

He waited as though for any defense that either woman would offer, but neither of them said a word.

He sat brooding, apparently turning this new calamity over and over in his mind. Finally he put his hand on the table, pushed himself slowly to his feet and walked over to the door. As he opened it he turned and said, "No Janson will ever be welcome in this house. You can quit this damn foolishness and stay home, Blaze. You're not of age and I'll see it the law can't break it off, and that's a hell of a thing to come to an Allan."

As quietly as though she were talking of a plot of garden Blaze told her father, "You didn't marry Stephen. I did. It's my marriage, my life you're talking about breaking up. I am of age. Eighteen is legal for women. I found that out."

As though the words were torn from him Zande Allan said, "Then go back to him and stay away from here. You're same as dead to me if you do that. I'll take your name out of the Book."

Blaze walked over to him, stood close enough to touch him when she said, "That won't make you happy, Father. You can rub out my name, but I won't be dead. I'll be alive. And you'll miss me and try to hate me and the longer you try the harder it'll come to give in."

He said with a contemptuous lift of his shoulder, "You're half Janson already. In this house you wasn't brought up to answer your elders. Get your horse and get going."

Blaze put her hands behind her back, clasped them until they hurt, but she kept her voice steady. "You gave me Gipsy when I was eighteen because you loved me. I'm not going to use Gipsy to ride away from you." She stepped closer to him, took his sleeve between her fingers as she had when she toddled beside him long ago. "Do you think the world is so kind and good that I can do without my mother's counsel, without my father's love?"

"You can leave the horse here."

He slammed the door shut behind him and left.

Blaze turned a white face toward her mother, stared at the queer half-smile she surprised on her mother's face. Hannah stood up, said confidently, "He had to run out or he'd of give in. Don't worry, Blaze. Half what ails your father is having to admit to himself he was wrong about that Williams man. He

[274]

hates to eat crow worse than any living man, I guess. But he's fair; give him enough time to think it all out for himself."

"It seems to me I never did know Father to give in about anything."

Her mother smiled. "Do you think I could of lived with him for more'n twenty years if I didn't get my way at least half the time?" Her face took on a dreamy look and her voice was shyly tender as she said, "We had a hard time at first, but we've had a good life together—"

Hannah's voice broke off and she tipped her head to one side. She walked to the window, stood looking through the big gate and down the trail. "I think I hear someone coming."

Blaze tightened nervously, whispered, "Oh, dear!" She moved restlessly over to the window, stood beside her mother and said, "There's no one on the trail that I can see."

Hannah answered, "You know I got ears like a fox. There's someone riding up; he'll be in sight in a minute."

Blaze tried to stay calm, but her hands flew to her hair, she smoothed down her dress and felt of her collar to see that it was straight, annoyed with herself because her teeth seemed bound to chatter. She said jerkily, "Maybe it would be best if I went along now. Maybe it would be best—"

"Blaze, stop that!"

Her mother's voice was stern and Blaze blinked.

"If it is Stephen, nothing is going to happen any worse than a couple of men shouting at each other, and I don't think your man will shout; he's not that kind."

Then Hannah's voice softened and, giving Blaze a pat on the shoulder, said, "Go pack up your things, child, so you'll be ready to leave."

Blaze looked doubtful, but she went back to her old room, went over to her window and leaned her head against it for a moment of leave-taking. Then she picked up the grain sack she had packed the night before and walked out, closed the door.

"It's Stephen, Blaze," her mother called to her as she came into the kitchen. "He's riding in through the gate."

Blaze didn't look out of the window. Fearing she might lose her courage, she made straight for the door, was out of it and walking down the trail to the barn before she was aware that her mother was right behind her.

Stephen was riding in fast, had pulled up and swung off his horse before Hannah and Blaze were out of the dooryard.

Blaze stopped as she saw her father come out of the barn, walk over to Stephen.

Blaze fearfully watched as her husband dropped the reins, raised his hat, waved it gaily toward her, then clapped it back on his head and turned to her father, holding out his hand.

"I'd like to be friends with my wife's father," he said.

Zande growled, "You take a hell of a way to go about it, running off with my girl." He ignored the outheld hand.

Stephen took it back, put the hand inside his coat pocket, saying pleasantly, "I'm sorry you feel that way about it. It was my fault; I talked her into marrying me. I should have come here, talked it over with you first."

"I'd of told you to get out."

Stephen said frankly, "Then I'd have married her anyway, if she'd have me, so it's just as well I didn't ask you."

"Then take her and be off, the both of you. She doesn't belong here any more. I've told her so."

Blaze started forward again and Stephen heard her steps, turned and reached for the sack she was carrying. "I'm sorry, Blaze, to be the cause of trouble between you and your father."

Blaze said very clearly and slowly, "There is no trouble between me and my father. We understand each other, both of us being Allans."

She walked up to the towering Zande Allan, hooked her

thumb into the pocket on his overalls and said, "Why am I called Blaze, Papa?"

Her father set his lips stubbornly, said nothing.

Blaze smiled at him, said, "Then I'll tell *you.* You gave me that name so I could always find my way home. Blaze Allan can find her way. I'll be back."

Still silent, Zande turned away as though to go back into the barn, but Blaze had seen his eyes. She called after him, "Saddle Gipsy for me, will you, Father?"

Behind her Hannah whispered, "That's the way, speak up for yourself."

Stephen came over to Hannah, held out his hand to her rather hesitatingly, but she took it in both hers, saying, "Don't worry about her pa; he'll be all right; give him time."

Blaze felt a glow of pride in her new husband as he bowed over her mother's hands, saying, "How kind you are, Mrs. Allan. Thank you. I'll do my best to take good care of Blaze."

Blaze said, "I'll hold you to that. Tie the sack of my things behind your saddle, will you, please?"

He touched her hand lightly, smiled down at her and started tying the sack behind his saddle.

Martin came out of the milkshed with two buckets of milk, his head down bashfully until he was almost past, and then he muttered, "Hello, Mr. Janson," and hurried on to get out of sight before his father came out of the barn.

Avery was carrying grain to the chicken yard, whistling a tune very softly between shouts of "Here, chick, chick, chicken!" Blaze heard his whistling stop as his father appeared, leading the saddled Gipsy.

Blaze ran over to him and silently he offered his hand as a step to help her up. Blaze lifted her face and slowly shook her head. "I don't want to get on and go away without you wish me luck, Father."

Zande kept staring at his feet. He wouldn't look up.

other's hand.

Hannah said crisply, "If an old hen sits on a bunch of eggs she don't plan to sit on eggs forever. She'd be right ruffled up if they didn't peck their way out and grow up and start their own sitting. The same with children. Can't you have the sense of a hen, for heaven's sake?"

Zande's set face cracked in a sour grin and then he started to shake, let out a whoop of laughter and doubled up laughing.

"That's the comicalest thing I ever heard." He choked and spluttered until he had to wipe off his face on his sleeve. Then he straightened up, held his big calloused hand out again to his daughter, saying soberly, "All right, get along and start setting, chick."

Blaze reddened, but she said, "Wish me luck, Father, or I might hatch out a nest of buzzards."

He put his arm about her awkwardly, patted her shoulder and muttered, "You will. But you'll have to get used to it. I did."

Blaze made a wrinkled nose at him, pulled Gipsy around until she was right beside her mother, leaned down and kissed her as Hannah stood on tiptoe, her eyes overbright.

"Good luck to both of you," she whispered. "I'll come see you, Blaze."

"Soon, Mother. I'll be watching for you." Blaze whispered back as she reluctantly let go of her mother's hand.

Stephen said gravely, "I'll try to take good care of your daughter, Mr. Allan, and our door is always open to you."

Blaze longed to turn and wave, but she couldn't trust herself to look back and keep tears from her eyes. She and Stephen rode forward, side by side. Avery ran ahead and had the gate open when they got to it, and he climbed up on the top rail to give Blaze a bear hug as she stopped Gipsy to put an arm around him.

"You come home for Easter, Blaze, won't you, huh?"

She said hurriedly, "Yes, I will. And I'll bring Stephen and Dulcie and Zande too. You tell Mother, will you, Avery? I'd

Hannah said crisply, "If an old hen sits on a bunch of eggs she don't plan to sit on eggs forever. She'd be right ruffled up if they didn't peck their way out and grow up and start their own sitting. The same with children. Can't you have the sense of a hen, for heaven's sake?"

Zande's set face cracked in a sour grin and then he started to shake, let out a whoop of laughter and doubled up laughing.

"That's the comicalest thing I ever heard." He choked and spluttered until he had to wipe off his face on his sleeve. Then he straightened up, held his big calloused hand out again to his daughter, saying soberly, "All right, get along and start setting, chick."

Blaze reddened, but she said, "Wish me luck, Father, or I might hatch out a nest of buzzards."

He put his arm about her awkwardly, patted her shoulder and muttered, "You will. But you'll have to get used to it. I did."

Blaze made a wrinkled nose at him, pulled Gipsy around until she was right beside her mother, leaned down and kissed her as Hannah stood on tiptoe, her eyes overbright.

"Good luck to both of you," she whispered. "I'll come see you, Blaze."

"Soon, Mother. I'll be watching for you," Blaze whispered back as she reluctantly let go of her mother's hand.

Stephen said gravely, "I'll try to take good care of your daughter, Mr. Allan, and our door is always open to you."

Blaze longed to turn and wave, but she couldn't trust herself to look back and keep tears from her eyes. She and Stephen rode forward, side by side. Avery ran ahead and had the gate open when they got to it, and he climbed up on the top rail to give Blaze a bear hug as she stopped Gipsy to put an arm around him.

"You come home for Easter, Blaze, won't you, huh?"

She said hurriedly, "Yes, I will. And I'll bring Stephen and Dulcie and Zande too. You tell Mother, will you, Avery? I'd love to think of you living in my little room, playing your mouth harp. Wouldn't you like that?"

"Sure I would," he said gaily, "but Martin'll gom onto it." He grinned. "But I'll have the whole attic and that'll be great; only I won't have you."

Stephen called, "Yes, you will. We'll both have her, and a pretty nice girl, I guess."

Avery jumped off the fence, swung the gate in and latched it after them, shouting over his shoulder as he ran back to his egg-gathering, "She's red-headed and sulky, but she'll do."

Beyond the gate the trail narrowed and Blaze motioned Stephen ahead, warning him, "They'll be watching to see if you ride ahead."

As Stephen pulled out in front he teased, "Your father will be disappointed if I do anything he thinks is right, but I'll risk that if you want me to."

Blaze said stiffly, "Well, our ways are our ways, you know. And I'm bringing them into your house. Maybe they're not what you're used to but they're honest and they work."

"Red-head!"

He looked around at her teasingly and Blaze started to smile. Then her voice quivered and she said, "I'm scared, Stephen. Now I'm going to live your way, in your house, and we'll really be married and—I want to turn around, run home."

He stopped his horse, looked seriously at her, his voice very gentle as he asked, "Would you honestly rather go back, Blaze?"

She shook her head, motioned him forward.

"But I can't turn it off as if nothing had happened. Now I made my peace with my father, but I still feel I got it to make with you."

He answered, "Then peace it is, darling; only I don't feel peaceful. I'm boiling with love, my sweet, and I want to know that you are my wife."

Her eyes were shining, her lips soft as she looked at him, but

[279]

she said, "Please, Stephen, I want to tell you—" Her color deepened but she plunged boldly into what troubled her. "I wasn't just going home to see my folks. I was so mixed up over what you'd thought, what I said to you when I was angry, that I thought things were finished between us. But when I got home I wanted to be back with you, and I thought so much that I came to understand your having had doubts about me."

She thought his voice was almost edgy as he rode close to her, protesting, "I haven't a doubt, or the shadow of a doubt about you, left in me. Only I love you so very much, so *horribly* much. Let's go home, darling."

At that word "horribly" her heart again seemed to turn over, her bones melt. She motioned to him to ride ahead.

Stephen's horse swung over the trail in long steps that covered country as fast as a trot. Blaze knew every tree, every branch, every stone in the brawling narrow stream as the horses went down through the steep little canyon near the north edge of Zande Allan's holdings. This bit of country had its own special magic. She loved the mushroom smell that lingered under the piles of dry alder and sycamore leaves, but best of all she loved the gently rolling flat covered with incense cedars that was just beyond the canyon's rim.

When they rode into the first of the cedars she called, "Wait, Stephen."

He looked back, asking, "What is it, Blaze? Anything wrong?"

She shook her head, said nervously, "No. I want to show you a real fairy-ring of cedar trees. Right over there." She pointed off the trail toward the towering Ventana.

She pulled Gipsy off the trail and rode across deep pine needles and bracken that made a green and brown carpet patterned with sunlight. A hundred feet off the trail she stopped just outside a perfect circle of tall incense cedars and waited for Stephen to ride up beside her.

She slipped off her ring, held it out to him, saying, with

furious blushes, "I know you do love me, believe in me, Stephen, but doubt is such a strong thing, can come creeping back." Her eyes closed for a moment and then she looked full at him. "I know one way to make you sure of me for always."

He looked questioningly at her for a moment and then a twinkle came into his eyes followed by a look that left Blaze breathless. He swung off his horse, reached up his arms to her and she slid down into them.

THE END